"You asked Me to Kiss You."

"I asked you *not* to kiss me! I distinctly said that I had no wish to—"

"Oh, for God's sake," Samuel muttered, and to Veronica's shock he pulled her into his arms again, this time bending her over until her head lolled back, then kissing her with such raw abandon and desire that she went limp in the space of two seconds.

She clutched his shoulders frantically for support, and tiny frightened sounds like bird chirps squeaked past her lips. Yet her mouth softened willingly, and somehow her lips parted, and Samuel's kiss, born of frustration, turned to something else. She knew the moment of change, felt it in the pressure of his surrounding embrace, heard it in the break in his breathing. One hand slid down her back to the curve of her spine, drawing her closer; the other hand balanced her, holding her prisoner, making certain there was no escape . . .

Books by Nancy Bush

Lady Sundown
Danner's Lady
Jesse's Renegade
Scandal's Darling

Published by POCKET BOOKS

Scandal's Darling

NANCY BUSH

POCKET BOOKS

New York   London   Toronto   Sydney   Tokyo   Singapore

This book is a work of fiction. Names, characters, places, and
incidents are either products of the author's imagination or are used
fictitiously. Any resemblance to actual events or locales or persons,
living or dead, is entirely coincidental.

An *Original* Publication of POCKET BOOKS

POCKET BOOKS, a division of Simon & Schuster Inc.
1230 Avenue of the Americas, New York, NY 10020.

ISBN: 1-4165-0704-3

This Pocket Books paperback printing September 2004

10 9 8 7 6 5 4 3 2 1

POCKET and colophon are registered trademarks of
Simon & Schuster Inc.

Cover art by Donald Case

Printed in the U.S.A.

Scandal's Darling

Prologue

Portland, Oregon
September 1896

I have some bad news for you, sir. Sorrowful news. Perhaps you'd best come in and sit down by the fire. It's a wicked world we live in sometimes. Life just don't seem fair. Please, sir, hand me your coat and hat and follow me. . . ."

Samuel Danner stood motionless in the softly hissing gaslight of the hallway, aware of so many things at once: the hard beating of his heart; the steady, careful ticking of the grandfather's clock; the smell of roasting pheasant, Mary's favorite; the acrid taste of fear at McMurphy's trembling tone.

Without a word he followed the stooped butler, one of Mary's relatives who refused to take charity and insisted on working for his keep though Samuel and his wife would have preferred he simply live out his days in peace and luxury. In this moment of growing dread Samuel was glad for the distance their strange servant/master relationship offered.

He didn't take a chair. He stood by the fire, gazing into the flames as if their flickering mysteries would somehow save him from McMurphy's news. "What is it?"

His answer was a whisper. "Mary, sir."

A jolt of pain speared through him. He'd known from the

moment he'd entered the house. He'd *known*. "Is she . . . hurt?"

Choked sounds. Then silence.

"Is she dead?"

"Yes, sir."

Samuel's gaze lifted from the fire to the portrait minia-tures lined across the mantel. His wife's serious face stared back at him, humor evident in her gentle eyes. Mary McKechnie Danner. He loved her. Would probably always love her.

"It was an accident, sir," McMurphy said painfully when Samuel elicited no further information. "The horses got spooked and ran and Mary—Mrs. Danner—lost control of the carriage and it hit the trolley. A policeman came by with the terrible news. There were witnesses. Somebody thought there was someone with her on the seat, but nobody knows for certain."

"It doesn't really matter how it happened. The result's the same." His voice was strangely detached. Only vaguely did Samuel recognize it as his own.

"Yes, sir."

Silence. Horrible, yawning silence threatened to engulf him.

"But if'n you want to talk to someone about it," the older man struggled onward, "you can call on the officer who was first there. He'll talk to you."

"Thank you, McMurphy."

The dismissal in Samuel's tone couldn't be ignored and amidst snuffling sounds that would undoubtedly embarrass the old man later, McMurphy strode with fractured dignity from the room.

The pain inside was of a magnitude Samuel had never felt before. He stood by the fire, loath to move, for that meant this terrible moment would be over and he would have to cope with an even more horrible bleak and empty future.

Mary.

He closed his eyes, gripping his emotions with almost physical force. Someday he would learn all there was to know about her death. Someday he would care. For now there was only this wrenching loss. This despair. This total annihilation of his life.

Drawing a breath, Samuel opened his eyes, staring down at the miniatures. He collected the tiny framed pictures in his hands carefully, gazing at them for long, long moments, committing his wife's face to memory.

Then he swept them into the waste can.

Chapter

1

December 1897
London

The steamship, *Her Majesty,* rubbed squeakily against the harbor pilings. A steady, cold, foul-smelling breeze rose off the Thames and blended with the scents of oil and dirt and general decay. It was Samuel Danner's first impression of England and he didn't like it one bit.

Captain Shaughnessy sent him a sideways look. "All right, laddie. You're here now. So what's the game, eh?"

Samuel smiled faintly. For all the long days of their voyage from New York, the Irish captain had tried to engage Samuel in conversation, intrigued and interested in the quiet stranger who hailed from the wild, wild West.

But Samuel had no intention of revealing the true nature of this quest. For one thing: he couldn't. Whenever he thought of Victor Flynne and the bastard's indiscriminate destruction of anyone who happened to cross his path, Samuel's rage was so dark, deep, and intense that it took all his considerable will to keep from exploding into black fury.

Consequently, his rage imploded, creating a violent storm of emotion that Samuel had honed rapier-sharp and directed at the man responsible for his wife's death.

4

"Ya on a mission, laddie? Ya looks like you're on a mission."

"It's been a pleasure, Captain," Samuel answered, extending his hand to the red-bearded seaman.

"A *quiet* pleasure," Shaughnessy grumbled, shaking Samuel's hand. "Tell me one thing, eh? Ya ever killed an Injun? A red man out there in Orgun?"

"Oregon's a lot tamer than you might suspect. This is almost the twentieth century."

"Huh? Ya never killed no one?"

Samuel's answer was an oblique smile.

Shaughnessy swept off his cap and scratched his head, watching the tall stranger disappear in the direction of his cabin. The man was a mystery, sure enough. So still and silent, yet, by all the saints, he was a man to be reckoned with. Handsome as sin and deadly as hemlock—he'd bet his last farthing on it! But polite-like, too. The ladies on this voyage had all but ripped off their fur-lined gowns and laid themselves at his feet, but Mr. Cold-As-You-Please Danner had appeared mildly amused, nothing more.

Shaughnessy shook himself and hiked up his trousers. Hell, he'd have taken them one-by-one without a second thought. Why not? What did a man gain by denying his need for a little skirt? And Samuel Danner had been widowed quite a long while, over a year; he'd learned that much. So by rights the man must be as randy as a stallion chasing a mare in heat.

Except he wasn't.

"Goddamn Yank," he muttered with something akin to admiration.

He watched as Danner strode down the gangway, his long strides eating up the distance, his thick, russet-streaked blackish hair tossed by the frigid wind. He looked like a gentleman. Acted like one, too. But there wasn't a foppish thing about him. Captain Michael Shaughnessy had seen the likes of many a gentleman, and there were those that were good-looking enough to send ladies into a swoon but most didn't possess that certain something that Mr. Danner had. Shaughnessy prided himself on recognizing such things. He loved the sea, but when in port, he enjoyed himself with women, drink, and a preoccupation with human behavior. He considered himself an expert on these matters and now, stretching the limits of his mind and vocabulary, the good captain came up with the words he needed to describe the interesting Mr. Samuel Danner: ruthless, determined, arrogant, sexual.

Chortling to himself, he asked the saints to send him word on Mr. Danner from time to time. Because sure as Satan didn't rest, whatever—or whoever—had brought the remote Mr. Danner to England was about to meet his reckoning.

Lady Veronica Elizabeth Ashworth, eldest daughter of Lord Henry Ashworth, the earl of Charlwood, narrowed her mischievous amber eyes on the severely straight back of Northcroft, the family butler. The man fairly reeked of disapproval and disdain. Veronica, who could never abide his high-and-mighty attitude at the best of times, decided it was time to bring him down a notch or two—again.

Her fertile mind considered all her options: a frog from the pond at the south end of the grounds surreptitiously slipped down the back of his stiff neck; a pistol—unloaded, of course—leveled at his chest while she, Veronica, complained about not knowing quite which end to hold; a note pressed into his hand daring him to meet one of the downstairs maids for a clandestine rendezvous.

She grinned to herself. Poor Northcroft would probably take to his bed for a week and beg Cook, whom he loathed with a passion as deep as his dismal sense of propriety, to make him special tea and cakes.

Life at the Ashworth Manor would be spun into turmoil!

"Veronica!"

Her stepmother's voice brought Veronica up short and for a moment she stood on the upstairs landing as rigidly and poker-faced as Northcroft. Lady Madeline Ashworth, Veronica's father's second wife, lifted one ironic brow at the eldest of Henry's three daughters. It was a look of resigned disapproval. One Veronica knew well.

"Yes?"

"What are you plotting, my dear?"

"Plotting?" Veronica parroted innocently.

"Leave poor Northcroft alone and come upstairs and help me pick out my gown for this evening. You're too old for these games. You'll be nineteen next month, you've been through two seasons already, and you've managed to discourage every eligible husband—purposely, I'm sure—by behaving like an undisciplined hoyden."

"You're right," Veronica admitted without a shred of remorse.

"I would scarcely care except that you have two younger sisters who are *eager* to make a match but can't until you've made yours."

"I know." Veronica's father was *incredibly* old-fashioned about such things! He wouldn't hear of Chloe and Patrice even considering marriage while she, Veronica, remained a creaking old maid of nineteen. With a sigh, she followed Madeline up the blue-carpeted steps and along the upstairs gallery to her stepmother's private suite of rooms.

"Veronica, I'm completely aware that you're much more intelligent and much more mature than you care to let others see. But your intelligence seems to be the bane of your existence."

Veronica waited, a frown creasing her smooth brow. This was a new tack.

"I discovered yesterday's newspaper hidden between the mattresses of your bed this morning," Lady Ashworth went on as she strode into the blue and gold room. "And the sheaf of papers tucked inside it. Well, my dear, it was very illuminating reading."

Veronica went white. "Madeline, I—"

Madeline quickly lifted a graceful palm. "Take your time before you answer, Veronica, darling." Irony underscored every syllable. "I would hate for you to utter words in haste. Words you might later wish to retract."

Her heart in her throat, Veronica nevertheless remained silent. She was in serious trouble. More serious than last summer's ill-fated affair with Geoffrey Rowbury and *that* had been disastrous indeed! Nothing had happened between them, of course, but Rowbury's notorious desire to marry a wealthy, titled heiress, by using fair means or foul, had led others to believe Veronica had lost both her heart and her virginity in the rake's arms. In truth, she'd simply wanted to know what it was like to kiss a man—a man whose desires, though scarcely noble, she at least could understand. Rowbury wanted money and power, not sex. He'd seemed, to Veronica's innocent way of thinking, *safe*.

Unfortunately, he had been anything but safe, and only the rescue by one of the groomsmen had saved Veronica from a more serious fate. The fact that her bodice had been ripped open and Rowbury had managed somehow to slither out of his trousers had swept like a foul wind through the servants, the household, and half of London before Veronica's version of the story came to light.

By then it was too late. Her reputation, if not ruined, was sorely tainted. Her father's icy, cutting comment, "You'll have to settle for second best now. See that it isn't third," had left Veronica wounded and worried and convinced that she no more wanted a husband than she wanted Geoffrey Rowbury sticking his tongue down her throat again.

So she'd tried everything in her power to become as undesirable to the opposite sex as possible—with some success, she was proud to admit.

"You've been gambling," Lady Ashworth declared now in a dire tone. "You've let Lord Mathison place wagers for you, haven't you? How have you done, my daughter?" she added crossly before Veronica could hope to redeem herself. "Have you made money, or lost it?"

Madeline was seated at her vanity, her hands clasped in her lap, her blue eyes cold as the December wind howling around the eaves. Veronica knew she was walking a tightrope. She may have pushed her stepmother too far.

"I've won money," she admitted, opting for honesty. "Quite a lot, actually."

"And what do you have to do for Lord Mathison, so that he keeps your secret?"

"Nothing!"

Madeline heaved a huge sigh. "Veronica, you've shown a sudden and remarkable ability to tell the truth, please don't slip back into falsehoods now."

"But it's true. Wortham—er—Lord Mathison and I are just friends. It amuses him to front me. And I've made quite a lot of money for him as well," she added proudly.

Madeline made a choked sound. "I assume your arrogance is because he hasn't demanded payment from you, yet. Be assured, he will."

Veronica opened her mouth to argue but realized her stepmother wasn't speaking of payment in pounds sterling. She fought the blush that reddened her camelia white skin.

Madeline suddenly looked incredibly weary. "I'm afraid I'm going to have to take you in hand, Veronica. This Saturday evening the marquess of Wilshire is giving a party in honor of his youngest sister. The invitation list is extensive. Anyone who matters will be there. I've been instructed to find you a husband by midnight, and if you do not like my choice, I suggest you find one for yourself. You have four days and five hours until the deadline."

"You can't be serious!"

"I am completely serious. Your father, and his very influential friends, have told me for years that I haven't been strong enough with you. I've indulged you. They're right, you know, but because I was married before I was really ready, I wanted to give you time. That was a mistake. You've squandered your time and now you have none left."

Veronica laughed. "Oh, Madeline! You almost have me believing you."

"I am in deadly earnest, my dear."

Now Veronica saw the truth—in fact an entire vista of misery opened up before her widened eyes. Her heart lurched in panic. "I won't marry anyone I don't love!"

"I didn't love your father when we were first married," Madeline pointed out reasonably.

"And you don't love him now! I won't do it! I won't!"

Her answer was silence. An entombing silence that sent

the blood draining from Veronica's head. An implacable silence that nevertheless was a cacophony of doom.

Desperately, Veronica's gaze sought the clock on Madeline's sitting room mantel. She stood frozen for a full minute, then fled the room, nearly tripping on the long skirts of her gown as she ran for the sanctuary of her bedroom, her golden brown hair flying behind her like a banner.

Frost lay in patches on the ground as the cabbie pulled up in front of the home of the Honorable Anthony Ashworth, younger brother to the earl of Charlwood. "Here y'are, sir!" he declared. "Fifteen-twenty Berkshire Close."

"Thank you." Samuel paid the man as he stepped onto the cobblestone street in the elegant neighborhood. The horse's hoofbeats clip-clopped steadily away and fog—the renowned London fog from stories Samuel had read as a boy—settled against the houses like an ethereal second skin. At the street, two lamps, set in strong brick posts connected to a brick fence topped with wrought-iron spikes, sent out tentative aureoles of light.

Taking a deep breath, Samuel let the damp, frigid atmosphere soak into him. It was a strange, foreign city in which to be tracking down Flynne, but Samuel would have tracked the man to hell itself, if that's what it took to bring Mary's murderer to justice. Samuel had stumbled upon the truth of Victor's involvement in Mary's death quite by chance: One of Portland's waterfront whores had learned that Victor Flannigan, alias Victor Flynne, was the man behind the accident. Victor's henchman, a whoremonger named Pete, had been beside Mary on the driver's seat of the coach the day she died, and he'd purposely driven the vehicle into the trolley—all on Victor's orders. Mary Danner had died because of the age-old grudge Flynne held against the Danners, one and all.

Samuel had followed Pete's path to Seattle and learned the man had suffered an accident himself and was already cold in the ground. There were conflicting stories about that accident as well, convincing Samuel that Victor had tidied up behind himself once again, removing the man whose loose lips had put Samuel on Flynne's trail. But Pete had spread a few more clues before he left this world, confirming Victor was the true killer. With some careful questioning and bribing of Victor's associates, Samuel had learned Flynne had left for London and was mixing with the nobility.

The bastard. Samuel's hands curled into fists and his jaw tightened as he strode between the brick posts and up the set of stone steps of Anthony Ashworth's Georgian home. Lifting the brass knocker, he slammed it down hard, twice. He didn't care what it cost, he was going to find Flynne and avenge Mary's death even if it killed him as well.

Footsteps sounded and the door was opened by a maid in a starched black dress which rustled with even her tiniest movement. A funny, ruffled little white cap topped her head. When she spied him she frowned.

"Servants entrance to the back, guvnah."

Samuel managed to shove his knee inside the door before she could slam it shut. He pushed the door open steadily even while the ferocious little maid struggled to close it.

"Do I look like a servant?" Samuel asked, truly interested in her answer.

"You don't dress like a gent'lman should!" she declared, alarm flaring in her eyes at his presumptuous manner.

"How should I dress, then?"

"And you don't talk like a gent'lman, either. You talk like a Yank."

"Fanny!" a stern voice blasted from somewhere to Samuel's right. Glancing around, Samuel encountered the icy glare of a man in a black suit who was nearly as tall as he was.

"'E jes pushed 'is way in,'e did," Fanny complained. "I couldn't stop 'im!"

"What is your business, sir?" the man whom Samuel had decided was the butler asked in a glacial tone.

"I'm here to see Mr. Ashworth."

"The *Honorable* Anthony Ashworth."

"The *Honorable* Anthony Ashworth, then."

"Whom may I say is calling?"

"The slightly dishonorable Samuel Danner," Samuel replied ironically.

This bit of levity was sheer blasphemy if Samuel interpreted the horror-stricken looks that crossed both Fanny's and the butler's faces correctly. Americans must be completely out of their experience, he decided. But Samuel, who'd had more than enough of England's complicated social strata in the few weeks he'd been in London, was sick to the back teeth of all the rules he couldn't, and wouldn't, understand, and felt obliged to make his feelings known.

"Samuel Danner of Rock Springs," he clarified, looking down his nose every bit as aristocratically as the humorless butler.

"Rock Springs, sir?" the man questioned, flushing slightly, embarrassed that Samuel, with his uncouth manners and sarcasm, had put him in such an uncomfortable position.

"That's right. Why don't you let Tony know I'm here?" Samuel added for good measure, bringing a wince to the butler's stern face.

Samuel had never met Anthony Ashworth though he'd been given an extensive history on the man from Lady Agatha Chamberlain, a personal friend of Samuel's who'd moved lock, stock, and barrel from London to Portland, Oregon with her young granddaughter, Charlotte, in tow. The elderly noblewoman had been extremely closemouthed about the true nature of her heritage, but when she'd learned of Samuel's plight—or rather when she'd *divined* the situation for Samuel had kept the particulars of the matter to himself—she'd suddenly given him her nephew Anthony Ashworth's name and address and explained he was not only a man who could be trusted, but one on whom Samuel could depend.

Samuel, in turn, had divined that the Honorable Anthony Ashworth was the *only* relative Lady Chamberlain trusted.

Samuel had immense respect and liking for the stately

Lady Chamberlain and he'd accepted her handwritten introductory note—the one currently in his breast pocket—with the gratitude and respect it deserved. Entrance into the "Quality's" homes for a foreigner was almost socially impossible. Samuel had learned that, and learned it well, these past few weeks while he'd waited for Anthony Ashworth to return from his vacation on the Continent. Samuel had used the time to contact the local police and explain that he was searching for another American, one Mr. Victor Flynne, who was as wicked a criminal as any they had currently ensconced at the great prison at Coldbath Fields.

He hadn't been given the time of day. His clothes, his speech, his very manner put off even the authorities. Truthfully, the way they dropped *h*s made it almost impossible for him to understand them. His western drawl fascinated them; in fact they seemed to listen so hard to the syllables half the time they missed his meaning. Samuel had been one of the finest trial lawyers in Portland before he'd crossed paths with his renegade older brother, Jesse, and subsequently learned the truth about his beloved Mary. He then dropped his practice and set out on this quest, soon coming to the stunning realization that these Londoners considered him a country hick with about as much "Quality" as the lowest commoner.

His treatment at the hands of Ashworth's servants was proof once again that he was fighting an uphill battle.

"Either go get Tony or call the police," Samuel ordered flatly. "Because I'm not leaving unless you forceably evict me."

"Show him into the morning room," the butler told Fanny through his teeth. With that he marched stiffly up the sweeping black oak stairway, the hem of his jacket quivering with indignation.

Samuel followed the rustling maid down a darkly paneled hall to a room at the back of the house. The morning room was done in silver and white and was as cold as a remote star. The fireplace had been swept clean of ashes, and the place smelled of disuse. It was clearly a room saved for those of lesser importance.

With deceptive casualness Samuel lounged on the gray brocade couch and stretched his booted feet toward the beveled glass-topped coffee table. Fanny stifled a horrified shriek. Eyeing her blandly, Samuel let his feet fall to the floor, then crossed his arms behind his head and heaved a sigh, as if he were settling in for the next century.

She huffed away, sliding the double doors shut behind her with a sharp crack.

"Good God," Samuel muttered. The room was filled with dried flowers and porcelain miniatures and gilt-framed pictures all cluttered together on a myriad of tables which in turn were covered with layer upon layer of ruffled table-cloths. This, apparently, was the current trend in Victorian England, for every room of every house he'd been inside was stuffed to the gills with *things*.

He gazed past the clutter, through diamond-paned leaded glass windows which opened onto a small courtyard at the back of the house. Fog swirled in trailing fingers around the frost-dusted stems of bare rosebushes. Samuel suddenly longed for open spaces. Even Portland had been vast and wide and free compared to the confining blocks and dank streets of London. Lord, this city was filthy! He wasn't used to centuries of grime and humanity, and he wasn't entirely certain how he felt about England in general, and London, in particular.

But he wouldn't return to Oregon until he held Victor Flynne's life in his hands.

The doors slid open again on well-oiled tracks. Samuel climbed to his feet and looked across the room to the man in the doorway. "Good evening," Anthony Ashworth said in his precise British accent. "Mr. Danner, is it?"

"Samuel Danner."

The man's golden eyebrows lifted. Clearly he hadn't expected Samuel's cool tone. He was shorter than Samuel by several inches, but built more powerfully, although Samuel suspected any physical labor this man performed was strictly for athletic purposes or to keep his body from turning to fat. He had the well-tended look of all British gentlemen which Samuel had learned could be deceptive, because the British as a whole, were tough in their own way. They were well educated—the "Quality" British, that is—and could cut you to ribbons with razor wit and leave you bleeding if you underestimated them.

"What is your purpose here, Mr. Danner?"

Samuel reached in his breast pocket and withdrew Lady Chamberlain's introductory letter. He handed it to Ashworth who scanned it without the slightest flicker of emotion crossing his face.

"This could be a fake," he said after a moment.

"I suppose it could be," Samuel agreed.

"But I don't think it is." Ashworth gazed curiously into Samuel's eyes, a glint of humor in his own green-gold ones. "You are too self-assured and disrespectful to be anything but what you are. No one in London could imitate the way you speak, or know where to purchase a pair of boots like those."

Samuel glanced down at his worn leather cowboy boots. He'd changed into Rock Springs gear for this meeting with Ashworth; a truly perverse means of making a first impression. His lips twitched as did Ashworth's.

He held out his hand. "We don't see many Americans, Mr. Danner," he said, clasping Samuel's hand in a surprisingly strong grip. "Especially from the frontier."

"Until this trip I'd never been east of Colorado," Samuel admitted.

"You live in a vast country. Excuse me a moment." He turned back to the door, ducking his head into the hallway. "Rose, bring up some tea, please," he said to someone out of Samuel's range of sight, then he slid the doors closed once again and gestured for Samuel to resume his seat. "Tell me, how is Agatha? She disappeared in a cloud of fury without so much as a good-bye to any of us."

"She's fine. One hell of a personality."

His lips twitched again. "I want to hear all about her, but first explain why you're here and how you wish me to help you."

Samuel narrowed his eyes on his host and in that split second decided to trust in Agatha's judgment and confide in a man he hardly knew.

"I'm a fish out of water here, Mr. Ashworth. It's a hindrance."

"Ah, yes?" He inclined his head.

"I'm on a manhunt. I'm after the bastard who killed my wife. I'll either bring him to justice, kill him, or die trying. I won't quit, and no one will make me quit. I need someone of 'quality' to help me to find him." Samuel didn't even try to prevent the sarcasm that slipped into his tone. "Someone like you. But if you throw in with me, it won't do you a bit of good socially. My actions will undoubtedly embarrass you somewhere along the line. Someway."

"This is your means of arguing me to your side?"

Samuel laughed shortly, without humor. "I don't understand a thing about this country other than everybody talks with a different accent and judges you by whatever social level your accent places you in, no matter how infintesimally small that difference might be. I don't give a good goddamn. All I know is that somehow Flynne's got friends in high places, and if I'm going to flush him out, I need some, too."

"Flynne's the man you're seeking?"

Samuel nodded curtly.

"By saying he has friends in high places you mean he's mixing with the nobility?"

"Exactly."

Ashworth was clearly intrigued. "How did you come by this information?"

"I don't think you want to know," Samuel answered wryly, remembering with a twist of conscience how he'd practically seduced the information out of the daughter of one of Victor's most influential clients—a personal, favored friend who'd paid Victor to blackmail a competitor over some minor misdeed. Victor had managed to put that same competitor out of business. "Suffice it to say Flynne's got connections. Powerful connections. Someone's undoubtedly hiding him, or helping him in some way."

"No nobleman would aid a murderer." Ashworth was tersely positive.

"My information says otherwise. Flynne's a killer and a blackmailer, among other things, and one of your country's *noblemen* is hiding him. Furthermore, I suspect it's because the aforementioned nobleman has something to hide himself."

Ashworth inhaled a long, slow breath. The double doors slid open again and a maid—the Rose that Ashworth had spoken to earlier, Samuel presumed—brought in a silver platter laid with napkins, spoons, delicate china cups, and a steaming silver teapot. "Something to hide," Ashworth murmured as Rose prepared to serve them. "No, leave it. I can pour." He waved her aside and she hurriedly exited again. "I suppose this said *nobleman* could be me," he pointed out dryly.

Samuel inclined his head. "If it is, you've been forewarned. But that doesn't mean you're safe from me."

Anthony Ashworth met Samuel's determined eyes. "If this Flynne is anything like you, Mr. Danner, he's going to stick out like the proverbial sore thumb."

"He's an American. But that's as far as the similarity goes."

"I think I'm glad I cut my vacation short for I believe there's going to be a great deal of excitement right here at home," he said with humor.

"Does that mean you'll help me?"

"Consider me an ally, Mr. Danner," Ashworth agreed, then asked, "Are you always so direct?"

Samuel smiled. "I'm afraid it's a Danner trait—along with a stubborn streak that won't quit and probably too much pride. My brother, Jesse, calls it a curse—the Danner curse."

"And you've been afflicted with this curse?"

"What do you think?"

Ashworth poured them each a cup of tea, considering Samuel carefully. "I think I'm glad I'm not in this Flynne's shoes," he said deliberately. "Very, very glad."

Chapter

2

The ballroom was a dazzling sight: windows lavishly draped with emerald and silver brocade curtains and held back by twisted silver ropes; dark oak floors polished to an impossibly bright sheen; chandeliers dripping with crystal teardrops and gas candles; elegantly dressed men and women sparkling like rich jewels around the periphery of the room.

It was enough to impress even the most ardent skeptic.

Except that Lady Veronica Ashworth felt physically sick.

Her stomach was in knots and threatened to disgrace her completely if she didn't find some relief and quick. A balcony at the northeast end of the room looked to be her only chance of escaping the hot, cloying atmosphere of the ballroom, and so she beelined toward the gilt-edged doors with the same single-sightedness of a hound after a fox.

Halfway to safety, a silky feminine voice scraped along her nerves. "Hello, Veronica."

She turned and there was Amelia St. John, Society's current darling, whose sausage-curled blond hair was so pale her admiring suitors had jokingly termed her Snow White.

Veronica had innocently overheard her own description when she'd abruptly come upon a group of men at a party six months earlier: Drab Brown.

Snow White and Drab Brown. It shouldn't bother her, but it did. She didn't *want* to be Society's current darling, but she didn't want to be a laughingstock either.

Still, it was true that her golden brown hair was nothing special, unless you counted its weight for Veronica possessed the heaviest mane in her entire family. But nothing could be done to curl the recalcitrant locks. They hung thick and full to her shoulders, and though she'd once fretted that she would never be beautiful like her two younger sisters, now she considered it a bonus.

"Hello, Amelia," Veronica managed to greet her through slightly trembling lips. She glanced longingly toward the balcony doors.

Amelia had a flowered, lace-trimmed fan which she swung coquettishly in front of her lips, her blue eyes brimming with suppressed laughter. "Is it true your stepmother insists you find a husband by midnight or your father will *buy* you one?"

Veronica fought back a gasp. Horrid, horrid, rumors! "Of course not."

"How embarrassing, I dare say. I would faint dead away if anyone treated me so."

"No one, least of all my father, is buying me a husband," Veronica said evenly.

"Then how do you explain the fact that bets are being made over whether you'll go willingly to the altar, or whether someone will have to put a sleeping potion in your food when your father's offer of two thousand pounds is *finally* accepted?" Amelia fluttered her fan, her avid eyes glinting with evil intent.

"Two thousand pounds?" Veronica couldn't help repeating in a strangled whisper. "Someone's been having you on, Amelia."

"I think they'll have to use the potion," she declared, tilting her head assessingly. "James has placed a wager to that effect for the both of us."

James Fielding, Amelia's most persistent suitor, who was as handsome as he was coldhearted, chose that moment to curve his arm around Amelia's tiny frame, nearly swallowing her up against his superior height. Dramatically attractive, James had hair the color of afternoon sunshine—a dark, lush amber—and eyes nearly as blue and brilliant as Amelia's. For one season Veronica had been smitten with him, but that immature attraction had sputtered and died when she'd realized James was as empty and ugly inside as he was beautiful on the outside.

"Our Ronnie won't go willingly," he said, joining in Amelia's nasty pleasure at Veronica's expense. He had the unmitigated nerve to trail a finger down Veronica's pale cheek.

The balcony. With a lurch of her stomach and a renewed rush of panic, Veronica gathered up her pale rose satin skirts and tore past them to the balcony doors. Her hands shook as she rattled the levers open. Frigid air blasted the room. Ladies shrieked and everyone glared at Veronica.

She stepped outside, latched the doors behind her, and hung her head over the stone balustrade. Gulping air, she fought back a consuming dizziness while cold sweat beaded on her back and forehead.

It was a full five minutes before she realized she wasn't alone.

Hazily, Veronica lifted her head and saw the shadow of a man leaning against the opposite end of the balcony. He stood stone still, his face turned toward her but impossible to read in the evening light.

"Are you all right?" he asked.

Veronica involuntarily jumped. It was an American voice with a very attractive drawl. "Umm, yes. Thank you. I'm . . . sorry, I'm . . ." She couldn't think how to go on. "Are you a . . . guest here?" she finally stammered.

He nodded.

"How in heaven's name did you get an invitation to such a ridiculously exclusive affair?" she blurted out.

"God only knows."

That he didn't take offense made Veronica aware of how

truly offensive her remark had been. "I'm . . . I'm sorry. I didn't mean that. I'm not feeling well."

"So I gathered. I wasn't certain whether I should let you know I was here or not. Are you feeling better?"

She nodded jerkily. Her turning stomach had settled into an anxious flutter. Drawing a deep breath, she thanked the heavens above that she wasn't going to humiliate herself after all.

The man took several steps toward her and Veronica straightened sharply. She was alone on the balcony with a stranger, and given her already notorious reputation she didn't feel like adding grist to the gossip mill. Glancing his way, she saw he was much taller than she'd first thought. His hair looked midnight black, but a stream of light through the window revealed it was really a rich dark brown, streaked in places a few shades lighter and hued a deep red, like burnished mahogany. His nose was hawkish, his mouth faintly curving, almost mocking. She couldn't see the color of his eyes in this dim light.

"I am feeling better," she reiterated, her cheeks coloring slightly as she considered how he'd watched her hang over the balustrade.

"Good."

A wave of laughter reached their ears and both Veronica and her newfound companion turned toward the sound. Beneath her lashes, she shot him a sidelong glance and saw that his eyes were a deep, disturbing brown, nearly black, surrounded by thick, spiky lashes which enhanced their beauty and opaque remoteness.

He wasn't like any man she'd ever encountered.

"Would you—care to come inside with me?" she suddenly asked. "It's bound to be a truly *horrible* evening, and though I know you have no reason to care what happens to me, I could really use someone beside me tonight."

"You need protection?"

"Oh, no!" She laughed on a gulp of hysteria. "Oh, it's too embarrassing to even talk about! I'm sorry." Appalled by her own impulsiveness—a trait that continually got her into

22

trouble—Veronica reached for the balcony door handles. "Forget I said anything. Excuse me." She gasped when his warm palm covered her frozen fingers.

"I'll accompany you. What's your name?"

"Veronica." *Lady Veronica Elizabeth Ashworth,* she thought silently, knowing she should at least forewarn him of who she was and why people would probably snigger behind their hands when he escorted her inside.

"I'm Samuel Danner," he told her, twisting the gold lever while placing a firm hand in the small of her back and guiding her back inside the stifling ballroom. "Pleased to make your acquaintance, Veronica."

"Mr. Danner," she began, twisting around to look at him. "There's something you should—"

"Samuel," he corrected her, looking past her to the line of curious faces that seemed to have frozen in midsyllable when he and Veronica entered the room.

"—know. My stepmother and father have decreed that I become engaged by—"

"Well, well, well," a male voice boomed indulgently. "Veronica, love, you do surprise time and again, don't you?"

Groaning inside, Veronica instinctively shrank back against Samuel who placed his hands on her shoulders protectively. Malcolm Phipps, chief gossip and rumormonger among the "ton" had maliciously followed Veronica's exploits from the moment she was considered old enough to know better. The fact that in a fit of anger she'd called him an overstuffed peacock in front of "people who mattered," had put her name permanently in his file of "people to put in their place." Worse, the description had stuck because Malcolm, with his passion for bright colors, fastidious cut of clothes, immaculately groomed hair, and enormous girth, *was* an overstuffed peacock.

"Yes, well, why ever should I change now?" she asked, buoyed by Samuel Danner's silent support. "You'd be terribly disappointed if you didn't have something unkind to say about me."

Malcolm's combed gray brows shot upward before he could hide his surprise. For the last two seasons Veronica had avoided blackening her name with him any further and her sudden spirit took him aback.

"Who is your companion, my dear?" Malcolm asked, recovering himself, his gaze narrowing avidly on Samuel.

"Samuel Danner, this is Malcolm Phipps," Veronica introduced somewhat reluctantly. She would really have preferred Samuel's good opinion and support to last a trifle longer. Ah, well. One couldn't have everything. "Samuel, meet one of London's most celebrated bachelors."

"Good evening," Samuel said, extending his hand.

Veronica's mouth curved in delight as Malcolm started at the sound of Samuel's drawl. *Hah!* she thought. *Try to figure this one out, you noxious worm!*

He ignored Samuel's outstretched hand. "Veronica seems to have misplaced her manners. It's Lord Phipps."

"Malcolm's a viscount and he can't bear it if someone doesn't know that," Veronica inserted, helpfully. "Excuse us," she added, leading Samuel to the center of the room. "You can waltz, can't you?" she asked anxiously.

"Yes." Amusement filtered through that sweet drawl as his strong arm circled her back.

The crowd fell silent, only the strains of the string quartet sounding through the ballroom. Veronica's heart began to pound. She realized she'd made everything worse, as usual, by dragging this innocent stranger into her problems, making him the cynosure of all eyes.

There would be hell to pay, she thought, unable to prevent heaving a sigh.

"So, Veronica," he said, bending his head to whisper in her ear. "Are you going to tell me why we're being treated like pariahs? I can't believe it's just because I'm American."

"That's certainly a black mark," she admitted with faint humor. "American's are social impossibilities, especially if they have money. No one knows whether to be polite to them or cut them dead."

"I've experienced both."

She gazed at him curiously. It didn't seem to bother him in the least and she warmed to him. "Well, don't blame yourself for this. Our current ostracism is my fault, I'm afraid. I'm a dreadful embarrassment to my family. I need to find a husband, and I was told if I didn't select one—or rather, *one* didn't select *me*—my stepmother and father would pick one out for me. I must be betrothed by midnight tonight."

He seemed nonplussed. "Why?"

"Because my younger sisters are anxious to marry, and I must marry first."

"Why?" he repeated.

"*Because,* of course!"

"Oh, yes. *Because,*" he murmured, as if he understood implicitly.

"Not only that, but since Father's an earl it can't be just any man. It has to be someone with a title, preferably with money behind that title, and, given my history, someone who can take me in hand and make certain I stop acting like such a hoyden."

Beneath her hand she felt his shoulders shake with silent laughter.

"What's so amusing?" Veronica demanded.

"Just about everything," he answered. "So, you're to be engaged by midnight?"

"I'm afraid so."

"Is there anyone in particular you have in mind?"

Veronica peered over his shoulder at the men standing in groups around the periphery of the room or talking and flirting with the women. "I'm afraid not." She glanced up at him and saw dark eyes simmering with humor, not at her expense exactly, more as if they shared a joke together. Veronica's heart lifted. Here was someone who thought the whole idea as ridiculous as she did! "It's a matter of degree, really," she confided. "Worse choice to worst."

He grinned down at her, and she focused on his mouth a fraction too long, intrigued by his white teeth and the sensual curve to his lips. Glancing quickly away, her pulse started rollicking at the idea that she was making a spectacle of herself yet again.

"Why don't you start with 'worse'? Maybe there's someone marginally acceptable before you get to 'worst.'"

"You really want to know who's in the running?"

He shrugged. "Since I've walked in on the second or third act, sure."

Veronica absolutely adored the way he talked. She could have listened to him for hours. "Well, over there, by the alcove? That's the marquess of Wilshire. Or maybe you know that. It's his party. His name is Edward Durham. He's a true aristocrat and he's quite attractive." Her tone was so dubious that her partner gave her a long look.

"So why is he 'worse'?"

"Well, I understand his taste in women is . . . um . . ." Veronica faltered.

"Yes?"

"More *experienced* than I am." She shot him an anxious glance. "And anyway, he shows no interest in marriage whatsoever. He's rather . . . self-indulgent and likes it that way."

"So scratch the marquess. Next?"

"You see the man standing beside him? The even more handsome one? That's Jason Cromwell, fourth son of the duke of Thornborough. Penniless, I'm afraid. Gambled his way through quite a sizeable inheritance, I understand, but even though marrying me might help restore his funds, he won't even consider it."

"How do you know?"

"I know." Veronica grimaced. "It's my reputation, you see," she admitted as Samuel led her gracefully across the floor. Other couples had joined them, dancing close by as if eager to overhear their conversation and learn who Veronica's mystery man might be. "I'm too willful. And I've made some rather costly mistakes."

"You have a knack for stirring my curiosity," her partner said dryly. "What costly mistakes?"

Veronica wished she'd never embarked on this mission of

truth. "I kissed someone I shouldn't have and unfortunately he took it into his head that I was interested in something more. It created a bit of a scandal last summer."

"Dreadful," he murmured, and Veronica gave him a sharp look. He was having a difficult time not breaking out into laughter. "What about the blond man leaning against the wall? The one with a drink in his hand who's been frowning at us ever since we walked in here?"

Afraid he might be referring to James Fielding, Veronica reluctantly looked in the direction of his gaze. Then she laughed in relief and amusement. "Oh, no! That's Anthony Ashworth!"

"What's wrong with him?"

"Nothing. He's the best of the lot. But he's my *uncle!*"

Up until this moment Samuel had been thoroughly enjoying himself. Veronica was the first Englishwoman who seemed to say what was on her mind, and he found her innocence and lack of guile extremely refreshing. She reminded him a little of Lexie, and Kelsey, and his beloved Mary. But to learn she was Anthony Ashworth's niece threw him.

"What's wrong?" she asked with sudden perception.

"Nothing."

"You know something about Uncle Tony? Something bad?" she asked quickly.

"No."

"He isn't in trouble again, is he? Is that why you're here?"

Perplexed, Samuel gazed down into her lovely, anxious face. Her skin was creamy white, carefully cultivated and kept from the sun. Her eyes were a strange gold color: gorgeous, sparkling, and right now filled with growing dread. "I don't know what you're talking about."

"That's why you're here!" she concluded despite his assurances. "Oh, Lord! Of course! Tell me what he's done, and I'll fix it. Don't tell my father. Uncle Tony means well, he just does things to irritate my father."

"As far as I know, he hasn't done anything to displease your father," Samuel said with perfect honesty.

"You mean that?"

The beauty in his arms regarded him suspiciously. "Cross my heart and hope to die."

She frowned, as if she were taking his answer literally. "But you do know Uncle Tony?"

"I came to this party as Anthony's guest."

Veronica studied him closely, as if she were really looking at him for the first time. "How do you know him, then?"

"We have a mutual friend."

She tilted her head back to take an even better look. The movement revealed her decolletage as nothing else had, emphasizing the mounds of her breasts. Samuel wouldn't have been human if he hadn't noticed. Her rose-colored dress was snug and sleek and for a wild instant he wanted to slide his hands from the soft curve of her back over those rounded globes.

Shocked, he dragged his gaze from her chest, astounded by such a sexual thought. Since Mary's death he'd been all but impotent where women were concerned; he'd believed his own sexual desire had been buried beside her. To learn differently, on a dance floor in London, with an undoubtedly virginal member of the nobility in his arms—no matter that she claimed of possessing a reputation—as removed from all he knew as he could possibly be, was disconcerting to the extreme. He was suddenly aware of her small hand touching his shoulder, her breath whispering in and out of soft pink lips, the innocent, yet somehow seductive slant of those intriguing amber eyes, the fluidity of her movements, the soft crest of her cheekbones.

"A woman?" she suggested.

"Pardon?"

"Your mutual friend. I'll wager it's a woman."

A vision of white-haired, upright Lady Agatha Chamberlain entered his head, and he laughed aloud, drawing the attention of other guests. "Yes, a woman," he admitted, grinning.

"Is she beautiful?"

"Very beautiful."

"Oh."

"She's also in her eighties," he added with a soft chuckle.

Her puzzlement delighted him. It seemed every emotion crossed that lovely incandescent face. Samuel wondered how old she was. Young, he decided. Very young. Still in her teens.

What the *hell* was he doing here?

The music ended on a long, drawn-out, sweet-sounding note. Samuel released Veronica and escorted her to the side of the room. Instantly a crush of people surrounded them, and for reasons he didn't want to analyze too closely, he was glad that she pressed herself near him.

"You certainly don't waste any time, do you, Samuel?" Anthony's dry voice murmured behind his right shoulder.

He jerked around. "What do you mean?"

Inclining his head toward Veronica, Anthony eased back toward the south wall, his silent gaze inviting Samuel to join him.

Samuel looked down at the crown of Veronica's lovely head. He fought an impulse to touch that thick mane of hair. "Thank you for the dance," he told her, gently extricating himself from the crowd.

She glanced back, panicked. "You're leaving?"

"Just talking to good old Uncle Tony."

With birdlike quickness her manner changed. Lifting her chin, she said coolly, "It's been a pleasure, Mr. Danner." With that she gathered her skirts and strode in a truly unladylike fashion across the room to an isolated corner where she was immediately beseiged by a group of women who appeared to be firing questions at Veronica right and left.

The rest of the crowd glanced from Veronica to Samuel and back again. Sighing, for he knew she thought he'd abandoned her to whatever horrible fate she seemed to believe awaited her, Samuel joined Anthony by the fireplace.

"Do you know whom you were dancing with?"

"Your niece."

"My *favorite* niece," Anthony corrected in his deceptively easygoing style. "Harm one hair on Veronica's lovely head, and I'll have to call you out."

Samuel grinned and held up his hands. "I only danced with her."

"But I'm learning about you, my friend. The wheels are turning inside your head."

"I have no intention of even seeing your niece again," Samuel assured him. "You know who I want, and he's obviously not here."

"He wouldn't be. Social impossibility and all that."

"You brought me," Samuel reminded him.

"Yes, but you're—different."

Anthony would have liked to be more specific, but how did you tell an American, even one as perceptive as Samuel Danner, that though Society looked down on anyone outside its narrow confines, sometimes the exotic could be a welcomed exception?

And Danner was exotic. Even carefully dressed by Anthony's valet in one of Anthony's own suits—subtly altered to fit Samuel's taller, leaner frame—Samuel Danner was a man who stood apart from the usual crowd. It was his bearing, and his indifference. And maybe even his single-sightedness. Women, Anthony had learned the few times he had taken Samuel out socially, simply could not resist a man who had no interest in them. The challenge was thrown down as surely as a gauntlet. But none had had any success in catching his eye until Veronica.

Which worried Anthony immensely.

"Flynne would have to have some very influential friends indeed, to be invited to the marquess's party. Only someone as wealthy and impervious as the marquess would throw such a lavish party and then only for a special occasion."

"Meaning?"

"Meaning I had to practically blackmail someone myself to ensure your invitation. Trust me, Victor Flynne will not be here. However, the evening might not be a total waste for you . . ."

Samuel's interest quickened. "What do you know?"

"No one's talking about Victor Flynne. *Actively* not talking, if you know what I mean. Lord Jason went white as a sheet, for instance, when I casually mentioned the man's name."

Samuel's gaze centered on Jason Spencer-Cromwell. Fourth son of the duke of Thornborough, Veronica had said. Penniless. Gambled away a fortune. A perfect pigeon for Victor Flynne's trap if the man had been foolish enough to borrow money from Flynne's tarnished resources.

"I've been gone a long time," Anthony went on. "Too long, it appears. Ferreting out your man's going to take some doing."

"I can start with Lord Jason," Samuel said in a voice laced with irony.

"I have a better idea. You could speak to my brother, Veronica's father." Anthony sipped from his brandy. "Lord Henry Ashworth. The bastard who's currently trying to marry Veronica off to the first acceptable suitor. Since Veronica's made a few rather silly mistakes and caused Henry some trouble, it appears he's anxious to complete the transaction as soon as possible."

"By midnight tonight?" Samuel was amazed. He'd thought Veronica was speaking figuratively.

"So, I gather." Anthony's mouth tightened. "Look, Samuel, as far as Veronica's concerned, please do not make things worse. She's the only member of the family with any spirit and I know dozens of men who would do anything to have her, no matter what she thinks to the contrary. So give them a chance to dance with her. To begin courting her. Maybe her engagement won't quite begin at midnight tonight, but being with you will only delay the process and increase her misery.

"Do that for me," he continued, "and I'll introduce you to Henry." Seeing Samuel's look of disbelief, he added, "For her own good, stay away from her."

"Rest assured. I won't add to Lady Veronica's troubles," he answered dryly, thinking the English really worried a hell of a lot about nothing.

". . . a most interesting man," Amelia said, fanning herself lazily as she gazed over at Samuel and Uncle Tony.

"How deliciously mysterious the way you brought him in from the balcony! My goodness, Veronica. One would think you have gentlemen stashed everywhere from the ballroom to the carriage house."

Wilhelmina Stuart gasped at Amelia's bold reference to Veronica's indiscretion last summer. She was a simpering idiot with bow-shaped lips that were pretty now, but would look silly and insipid by the time Wilhelmina hit middle age, especially if she kept putting on weight at the same rate she had the last two seasons. The woman was an absolute glutton!

"Were you referring to Geoffrey Rowbury?" Veronica asked sweetly, showing her disregard for Society's rules once again for one never, but *never,* spoke of such things directly. It was all done obliquely; an insult slid in sideways was considered the height of sophistry and wit. Frankness was abhorred.

Amelia colored slightly, her eyes flashing. "Excuse me," she murmured, latching onto James Fielding's arm as she whispered something in his ear.

Veronica's eyes sought the room for escape. Would this unbearable evening never end?

"I must say," Wilhelmina began, then trailed off as she noticed an older gentleman heading Veronica's way with a look of determination in his eye. Lord Rathbone was homelier than a bulldog at the best of times and right now his face was red from too much rich food and drink.

Poor Veronica. Poor, poor Veronica!

Gathering her skirts Wilhelmina hustled away to make sure her friends were alerted to what could only be a jolly good show.

Samuel's brandy snifter stopped halfway to his lips as he watched the elegantly clad, older gentleman approach Veronica. Veronica herself looked quite dazed. She accepted his hand and was led to the center of the floor.

Conversation sputtered and died. The women who'd clustered around Veronica now stared in unabashed delight.

I must be betrothed by midnight . . .

As the man stared avidly down the front of Veronica's dress something inside Samuel rebelled. He stepped forward instinctively, but Anthony's iron grip stayed him.

"Don't," he commanded.

Samuel swore, shook off Anthony's grasp, and strode purposely across the floor.

Chapter

3

Veronica could feel the moisture from Neville Rathbone's sweating palm seeping through the silk back of her gown. She wanted to wriggle from his grasp, but was well and truly trapped. Rathbone whirled her around the floor with more finesse than she would have credited him, only stepping on her shoes occasionally, which was more than she could say for some of her partners this evening. But she was hot and felt completely done in and wrung out. Oh, to be home in the safety of her bed, away from this wretched mess!

"Have I told you how divine you look?"

Veronica darted him a quick glance. "Yes, thank you," she murmured, though the man's gaze was delving down the front of her gown. It was all she could do to keep from covering herself with her hands. Damn Madeline and her insistence that this was the *only* dress suitable for this *very special* occasion.

She drew an unsteady breath, wishing she'd worn the rope of natural pearls Madeline had suggested. But in a fit of pique Veronica had refused all jewelry, thinking—wrongly, as it turned out—that less adornment would mean less attention.

Now, Rathbone's eyes avidly absorbed every quiver of her breasts. Veronica wondered if it were possible to kick him without appearing to mean to.

The thought was rooting itself in her brain when she caught a glimpse of her father, standing at the side of the room, listening to something Edward Durham was saying. Catching her eye, Henry nodded approvingly at Veronica's choice of partner, the horridly ugly and lecherous Lord Rathbone.

Did that mean . . . ? He couldn't think she might consider Neville Rathbone as a suitable husband!

She left him in middance, her chest tight, scarcely able to breathe. Making a mental note to loosen her whalebone and laces, she sought some avenue of escape but before she had taken three steps, Samuel Danner clasped her arm.

"Veronica," he said, and she was so relieved she nearly collapsed against him.

"May I have this dance?" she asked with a wobbly smile.

"My pleasure," he said a trifle tightly and she looked up to see the dark look he sent Lord Rathbone.

Stifling a giggle, she allowed herself the pleasure of dancing with a man whose company she actually enjoyed. She loved the way he moved, the feel of strong hands leading her, the sound of his breathing. But they were scarcely around the floor once when Edward Durham, the marquess himself, asked for a dance.

Good manners dictated she must accept and though she longed to stay with Samuel, even he seemed to understand there was no graceful way to say no.

"You're looking quite lovely this evening," Durham complimented her, pulling Veronica tightly into his arms.

"Thank you." Her gaze searched for Samuel. His tall form was beside Uncle Tony; the two men were discussing something quite heatedly. Her?

"Your father says you're about to be betrothed." Amusement filtered through his cultured voice.

"I'm afraid so."

"And who is the lucky gentleman?"

Veronica slid him a look. Though Lord Durham was

exceedingly handsome, he was a man who indulged his appetites and Veronica had no desire to be rumored to be one of his conquests. Just dancing with him was dangerous. After all, there were scandals and there were scandals. "No one's been brave enough to step forward yet," she admitted, wondering if pleading a headache would end this intolerable evening sooner or if her father would see through the ruse.

The marquess laughed at her honesty, his grip tightening still further. Lord, she would swoon if the man didn't give her some breathing room! "Unfortunately, I can't offer assistance. My lovely Anne would never forgive me."

Anne Cromwell, Jason's sister, was the marquess's favorite paramour. It was well-known she planned to be his bride, but Edward wasn't in any rush to walk down the aisle. Even Anne's rumored pregnancy hadn't hurried him along, but since the lovely Lady Anne had never changed her elegant shape, maybe it was all a rumor anyway.

"I'm not terribly anxious for marriage," Veronica admitted. "It's being thrust upon me."

"Maybe you just need some—lessons at it."

"Lessons?"

He was so close his lips nearly touched her ear. Choked for air, Veronica nearly gasped when one of his hands slid daringly to the curve of her hip. Oh, God! she thought desperately.

Over Durham's shoulder, she searched the crowd for another glimpse of Samuel. He was still standing near Uncle Tony who was frowning into a brandy snifter. Silently Veronica sent the message that she needed help, but this time neither Samuel nor Uncle Tony seemed to notice. Her heart sank. She was stuck with the marquess.

"Where is Anne tonight?" Veronica ventured.

"She's visiting friends and unfortunately couldn't be here."

Veronica could read between the lines. Margaret, Edward's sister, the guest of honor, could not tolerate Anne. The two women loathed each other. But then Margaret hated everyone who looked twice at her brother. She was fraught with worry that Edward would marry and somehow leave her penniless. Veronica wouldn't be surprised if Margaret never married, content to feed off the marquess. It was silly, really, since everyone knew Margaret held ample funds in trust herself, but the woman—in Veronica's harsh opinion—was a born leech.

At that moment Margaret herself floated by in a tangerine-colored confection covered with ruffles which made her look exceedingly silly. She eyed Veronica haughtily, but even so, she seemed to be having an excrutiating time. The pained look she sent her dance partner, an egg-shaped man with tightly curled hair, spoke her true feelings.

Veronica hazarded a glance at the clock above the mantel at the far side of the room, just above Samuel's and Uncle Tony's heads. Ten o'clock. Two hours until her stepmother and father made good on their promise to pledge her to another man.

Her heart fluttered in her throat. Edward Durham's hands moved familiarly over her back. She shuddered. What a mess she'd made of things! How was she ever going to extricate herself from this latest folly?

Anthony glowered at Samuel. "I can't promise my brother's help if you persist in monopolizing Veronica's attention!"

"Monopolizing? I was trying to save her from that wretched old fool who was slobbering all over himself, attempting to look down the front of her dress."

"That wretched old fool is Lord Neville Rathbone," Anthony retorted icily.

Samuel had to bite his tongue from pointing out that he didn't care if the man was the next king of England, he was a perverted relic. But he'd offended Anthony by being *kind* to Veronica. He had to tread more carefully.

"Why do you think Henry will be able to help me find Flynne?"

Anthony hesitated. He couldn't decide whether to

completely trust Samuel Danner. "I asked questions of everyone I know. I tried the name Victor Flynne, and Victor Flannigan, as you suggested. The reaction has always been the same: silence. Maybe a moment of panic. I'd about given up learning anything else until I encountered a very, very drunken Thomas Houghton."

"Who's Thomas Houghton?" Samuel asked when Anthony paused.

"A rather weak individual whom I'm acquainted with."

Samuel smiled faintly. "And Houghton said?"

"He said, and I quote, 'Talk to your brother. Henry'd know about Flynne. Be careful.' "

Samuel digested this information in silence then sent Anthony a sidelong look that caused Ashworth to lift one elegant brow. "Is your relationship with Henry close enough for you to ask him about Flynne directly?"

"You're a perceptive devil, aren't you?" Anthony remarked dryly.

"It was something Veronica said."

"Indeed?"

"She seemed concerned that you might be in trouble again and begged me not to tell her father."

"Oh, Veronica!" Anthony muttered beneath his breath, shaking his head.

"She'd said she'd fix what was wrong and that you really meant well, but that you just liked to irritate Henry."

"Wretched child," he murmured in exasperation.

Samuel's gaze settled on Veronica once more, watching her deep pink skirts swirl, her lush mane swing slowly behind her. He'd met women more beautiful, but he doubted he'd ever met one more guileless, more ravishingly attractive in a simple, individual way. She was nothing like Mary. His Mary, who was the most sane, sincere, completely trustworthy woman he'd ever run across. Veronica seemed flighty, wild, and impulsive in comparison.

Yet, there were similarities. Similarities between Mary and Veronica that he sensed but couldn't name. Except for one similarity—the way he felt while watching another male stake claim to her: cold hostility and black anger.

Why in God's name he should care about Veronica he couldn't fathom. Good grief, he barely knew the child. But in an absurd way she was an outsider like himself, and for that he felt compelled to help her.

At that very moment she shot him a look of pure distress and, forgetting his vow to appease Anthony and before he'd truly considered the rashness of his actions, he was striding across the polished dance floor once more, tapping Edward Durham on the shoulder of his well-cut suit.

"Excuse me, but Lady Veronica promised to dance this dance with me."

"My good man . . ." the marquess sputtered, positively enraged. Veronica practically jumped into Samuel's arms, her relief evident.

Edward's lips tightened, but then he turned to Veronica. "It was a pleasure, my dear."

"What was he saying that made you look so stricken?" Samuel asked as soon as he'd whisked her to the center of the floor.

"He suggested I needed lessons on marriage."

Samuel's brows drew together. "Meaning?"

"I'm not completely sure, but I didn't like his tone."

Samuel's fingers tightened on her arm and back. Veronica felt comforted rather than threatened and was marveling over this strange reaction when Samuel muttered through tight lips, "My God, what a group of degenerates!"

"Are you referring to the marquess's honored guests?" Veronica asked in delight.

"You don't really have to be engaged by midnight, do you?"

"I told you. It's my stepmother and father's decree."

"Nobody can force you into making such a momentous decision in such a short period of time."

His black eyes were full of determination. His jaw hard. She liked his face, the absolute conviction he felt about things so evident in every line. She wanted to rest her palm on his smooth shaven cheek, but propriety forced her to quell the urge. Still, her heart beat unnaturally fast, and she felt strange stirrings inside her. Stirrings she was bound and determined to examine more closely.

"I have no voice in this decision."

"The hell you don't."

Veronica's mouth dropped in amazement. She'd never had a *gentleman* swear at her. "I should be grateful that the decision's being made before I end up a dreadful, pitiable old spinster."

"You'll hardly end up that."

Warmed by his possessive tone, Veronica smiled to herself. In his arms, her other problems seemed to melt away.

As if mocking her, the clock chimed eleven. Veronica drew a sharp breath, her eyes darting to her father who was still entertaining the conversation of Neville Rathbone. One hour. *One hour!* Surely Father couldn't mean it.

"Do you want to be engaged?" Samuel asked, looking down at her.

"I don't think so." She laughed shakily.

"Then can't you just refuse?"

Veronica imagined herself turning down all offers. Any offers, she reminded herself with a wince. Her suitors weren't exactly standing in line.

Samuel saw the wince, but misinterpreted it. "What would your father do, if you refused? Beat you? Starve you? Send you away?" He turned his handsome head to regard Henry. "He doesn't look so terrible."

"He prides himself on his looks," she heard herself say, shocked that the thought sprang so easily to her lips. "I mean, he's handsome, don't you think? My mother fell for him instantly. Love at first sight." Sadness crept into her tone.

Samuel knew that Madeline Ashworth was Henry's second wife, that Veronica's mother had died when Veronica was very young. But he didn't know the circumstances of Cordelia Ashworth's death.

And Veronica didn't tell him. "You waltz rather well," she said, changing the subject.

"I was forced to learn by an expert."

Veronica's beautiful lashes lifted and her amber eyes

stared expectantly into his. She was waiting for an explanation but Samuel was as reluctant to talk about Mary as Veronica was about her mother.

"When midnight arrives, I predict nothing will happen," Samuel said. "Your father can't force you into anything."

"If I don't accede to his wishes, it will only be worse."

"Worse than marrying someone you don't know, don't care about? Someone who may repulse you?"

"What are you so angry about?"

He drew himself up short. "I don't know," he said in surprise.

She smiled up at him, a glorious, mischievous curving of luscious pink lips. Samuel had been desperately trying to put her out of his mind all evening in order to ensure Anthony's continued allegiance but hadn't succeeded. From disbelief that her father would really expect his eldest daughter to discover a husband by midnight, to total outrage that such a thing could possibly exist, Samuel's temper simmered, then boiled over. He was now coldly furious and he couldn't begin to understand why it mattered so much.

Veronica looked over his shoulder and he felt her body shudder. "What is it?"

"It's almost midnight," she whispered.

Her already smooth, milky skin turned even whiter. Resisting the urge to run a finger down her sculptured cheek, he said, "It won't happen."

"There are men—gathering around my father." Her fear was palpable.

"He can't force you," he repeated fiercely.

She drew closer as if needing his protection. "Is that how it is in the States? Women get to choose their husbands?"

"Mostly."

"What is your job, Mr. Danner?"

"I was a lawyer. And it's Samuel," he said again.

"Was?" Veronica questioned.

"Excuse me, Lady Veronica," a smooth masculine voice cut in. "I'd like the honor of a dance with you."

Mockery was evident in the man's tone and demeanor and even before Samuel turned to meet the blond man whose eyes had lasciviously dissected Veronica's body parts everytime she was whirled by, he took an instant dislike to him. Irrational behavior for a man who prided himself on rationality, Samuel reminded himself, reluctantly shaking the usurper's smooth palm.

"Um . . . Samuel Danner, this is James Fielding. Lord Fielding, may I present Samuel Danner." Veronica had flushed to the roots of her lush brown mane.

"Where do you hail from, Mr. Danner?"

The slight stress on the *Mr.* wasn't wasted on Samuel. He gazed into the man's sky blue eyes, noticing the thick careful wave of his hair, the sharp cut of his clothes. A dandy. "From Oregon," Samuel responded in his slowest drawl.

"The States?" Fielding's gaze raked him from head to toe.

"One of them."

"The marquess must have friends in faraway places. I never would have suspected," he murmured. "Come, Ronnie."

With a last glance for Samuel, Veronica was scooped into Fielding's arms. Irked, Samuel stalked back to Anthony, his expression grim.

Anthony's expression was even grimmer. "Well?" he demanded when Samuel made no move to explain his ridiculously chivalrous actions.

"Veronica's terrified of what happens at midnight."

"Maybe Henry will come to his senses and drop this ridiculous and humiliating plan." Ashworth sipped on his brandy, waving away one of the servants who offered him a glass of champagne from a linen-covered tray.

Samuel narrowed his attention on Lord Henry Ashworth, the earl of Charlwood. Veronica was right. The man was handsome as sin. And cold as money. At least that was Samuel's immediate impression, colored as it was by the man's decision to rid himself of his eldest daughter. Silver hair, black tuxedo, mirror-polished shoes, and an indifferent manner to those surrounding him: Henry was as warm as an ice floe.

Samuel hailed a servant. "A brandy," he ordered. "At least three fingers."

The man's nostrils flared in disapproval but he did as he was bidden and soon Samuel was taking a healthy gulp of some of the finest brandy he'd ever tasted. The marquess might be a lecherous Sybarite, but he didn't skimp on the extras.

"You're watching Henry rather closely," Anthony observed, leaning an elbow against the mantel next to Samuel's. "Or is it Veronica who holds your attention?"

"How does Henry know Victor Flynne?"

"You'll have to ask him yourself."

"Will you make an introduction for me?"

Anthony snorted. "Yes. But don't expect Henry to treat you any differently than one of the servants. He's an inveterate snob."

"Mr. Danner, isn't it?"

The voice was to his left: trilling, feminine, and as correct and precise as everyone else's. Samuel glanced at the woman. Blond, blue eyed, pretty—she clearly thought she was the most gorgeous creature at the party.

"Samuel Danner." He took her extended hand, realizing he was supposed to kiss it. *If only Jesse could see me now!* he thought, bending over to place his lips on the back of her cool hand. He could barely stifle laughter.

"I'm Amelia St. John. You're here with Veronica?" She fanned herself languidly with a ridiculous ruffled fan.

"Actually I'm here with Mr. Ashworth," Samuel told her, including Anthony as part of the conversation.

"Hello, Amelia," Anthony said, smiling faintly.

She looked down her nose at him. "Anthony."

Samuel was curious what new drama he'd uncovered between Anthony and Amelia. But he realized Amelia's attention was distracted by Veronica and James Fielding. Still, there were undercurrents between these two that could be felt by even the most insensitive.

The clock on the mantel purred slightly, winding up for its hourly chimes. Samuel turned to stare at it, unreasonably depressed. A collection of voices murmured in anticipation at the first droning bell. By the twelfth chime a hush had settled over the room and all eyes fell on Veronica who turned as pale as death.

Chapter

4

Ronnie, darling," James whispered in her ear. "You're the center of attention." His voice was filled with malicious enjoyment.

Veronica couldn't catch her breath. The colors of the room swirled together, the faces of the guests a blur, the expectant hush pounded in her brain like a cacophony of noise.

"You're not going to swoon, are you?"

"No, James," Veronica squeaked out.

"Has anyone offered for you, do you suppose?" he asked, turning glittering eyes to Henry who looked annoyed by the crowd's expectancy.

"Excuse me." Veronica swept off the floor, her skirts rustling around her trembling legs. She headed straight for Uncle Tony and Samuel; either one would do. But it was Samuel who caught her by the arm, whose darkly handsome face stared down at her with concern. "I . . . feel . . ."

"Come with me," he ordered, his strong hands guiding her back to the balcony. Before they'd reached the French doors the string quartet began playing a quick waltz, clearly as a means to break the charged mood.

"Oh, my God!" Veronica moaned behind her palm as soon as the cold air hit her flushed face.

"Are you all right?" Samuel lifted her chin, frowning at the tears gathered in the corners of her luminous eyes.

"I feel sick," she quavered.

Without further ado, he forcedly leaned her over the balustrade once more. Veronica's humiliation was complete and she closed her eyes and let the tears stream down her cheeks. Her stomach twisted and quivered, but she was saved from being sick by an effort of sheer willpower. Samuel's hand was on her shoulder, comforting her, which made her only feel a thousand times worse.

Moments passed. The world stopped spiraling. Veronica struggled upward and swiped at her eyes, embarrassed beyond bearing. "They're all waiting for my father, or me, or someone to make some kind of announcement."

"Let them wait."

"I am really sorry . . . please forgive me for being such a disaster! Normally, I have much better control."

"Would you introduce me to your father?"

Veronica blinked rapidly. "Didn't Uncle Tony?"

"I've come to the conclusion an introduction from Anthony would not endear me to your father. I think I'd be better off with you."

She laughed without humor. Better off with her. If only he truly felt that way then *he* could offer for her! Once the idea took root she couldn't shake it, and she stood silent for long moments, thinking hard. "Mr. Danner, I would be happy to make the introduction. But I need something in return."

He frowned. "What?"

"Would you—offer for my hand?"

"What?"

Veronica pressed her advantage. "We wouldn't have to go through with the marriage, but it would give me some time to come up with an alternative plan. Please. I'm begging you!"

She counted her heartbeats in the silence that followed. Samuel ran one hand through his hair, a thoughtful gesture that belied the emotional stress he was feeling. Had Veronica known him better, she would have recognized that she'd affected him deeply. But because he was a stranger, she didn't see the change in his expression, the moment where he half wished he could say yes.

Instead, she heard only his answer. "I'm sorry, Lady Veronica. I'd like to help you, but I'm not willing to play such silly games."

"Please meet me upstairs in my rooms, Veronica," Madeline's disapproving voice commanded as soon as they were home for the evening.

From the back of the hall the grandfather's clock tolled the hour: two o'clock.

Veronica removed her cloak and muff and handed them to the parlor maid. She was cold and shivering but knew Madeline would not allow her to stand in the room looking as if she were ready and eager to escape. Nothing but sheer and complete capitulation would satisfy her parents now.

From the moment Samuel Danner had refused her offer of marriage, the evening had deteriorated into a living hell. Her father was waiting for her as soon as she and Samuel reentered the ballroom, grabbing her arm with a proprietorial gesture, leading her back to Neville Rathbone whose mustache quivered with ill-concealed glee, his tongue rimming thick lips in anticipation.

Neville had asked for her hand. Henry was seriously considering his offer. The guests at the party already believed she and Neville were engaged.

Now Madeline flung her wrap onto the chintz sofa. "Veronica, I'm at my wit's end!"

"Madeline, I—"

"Don't speak, Veronica." She lifted one palm, her expression resigned. "Please."

Veronica hunched her shoulders. This was much worse than last week's little talk. She waited while her stepmother sank onto the vanity stool and removed her earrings and necklace. Light bounced off the diamonds. Madeline flung her gloves down and made the row of perfume vials shiver and tinkle.

Veronica's gaze dropped to the flower-patterned carpet. She was unable to defend herself now. Oh, if only Samuel Danner had asked her father for her hand! It didn't have to be a real engagement. Just something to keep her from being forced into marriage and at the same time allowing her father to save face. Lord, what a mess! And at every turn it only got worse!

Neville Rathbone. She broke into a cold sweat.

"You have put your father and myself in an impossible position." Madeline sighed. "Your actions have forced us to demand you marry and now . . . now . . ."

She couldn't go on. She merely stared at her reflection in the vanity mirror before lifting worried eyes to meet Veronica's.

"I know that Father is very angry with me."

Madeline gave a decidedly unladylike snort.

"But I don't believe he wants me to marry Neville Rathbone any more than I want to marry him."

"Lord Rathbone is not the issue."

"Oh, yes, he is!" Veronica burst out. "He's three times my age and all he talks about is illness and death. He wants a nurse. He doesn't want me."

Madeline didn't respond immediately and Veronica took hope.

"He's only offered for me because he knows I'm desperate and there's a chance I'll say yes."

"He doesn't want a nurse," Madeline said softly.

"Pardon?"

She sighed. "He's taken with you, Veronica. As a man is taken with a woman."

Fear settled deep in Veronica's bones. She didn't want to hear this. "Do you think Father will agree to the match?"

Madeline drew a deep breath and her jaw tightened. "Not if I can help it, but, Veronica, you would try the patience of a saint."

Veronica rushed to her, clasping her arms around the woman who'd been more a mother to her than the dim recollection she carried of her true mother. "Oh, I knew you wouldn't let me down!" she cried in relief.

"Now, don't think it will be easy. Your father is set on having you married by summer."

"I'll find someone else." Veronica's head bobbed enthusiastically. "It won't be hard, I'm sure. Just not Lord Rathbone. Someone . . . younger."

"You'll have to attend a lot of parties," Madeline went on thoughtfully as she unclasped her necklace. "And you'll have to be more attentive. Young men want to be listened to. Look rapt when they're speaking. But don't engage in conversation about current topics like you're prone to do. No man wants a woman who discourses on politics and world events."

"I never—"

"Yes, you do! You're constantly showing up your father and he resents it. Darling, why do you think he's so stubbornly insistent on having you married? As someone's wife, he can act as if your failings are someone else's doing. But as his daughter, living in his house, under *his* care . . . you're a terrible reflection upon him." Madeline shook her head. "And then your little tricks on Northcroft and Lady Eveline . . ."

"It wasn't a trick! Eveline fancies Father and I was sick of the way she tries to rub up against him every chance—"

"Veronica!"

"—she has just like the fat feline she is. You know it's true. Why just last week she made an excuse to stop by just because Father had taken the afternoon off. She was waiting by the door—"

"Stop it!" Madeline clapped her hand to her mouth, fighting back laughter.

Veronica thrust her fists on her hips. "She was wearing all those feathers," she went on determinedly. "As soon as Father walked in, she pressed up against him. I'm surprised she didn't smother him. All I did was set Tomcat on her. You know how he likes feathers."

Madeline's blue eyes danced, partly in horror, partly in amusement.

"You have to admit, she deserved it."

"I admit nothing of the kind. This is exactly the type of behavior you've got to stop!"

"She only fancies him because he's an earl."

"We're not discussing Lady Eveline!" Two high spots of color had entered Madeline's cheeks. Sensing she'd gone too far once again, Veronica heaved a sigh and lapsed into dutiful silence. "If you want my help, you must listen to me."

"I do want your help," Veronica inserted quickly.

"Then behave yourself. No more tricks."

"No more tricks," she repeated reluctantly.

"No more reading the newspaper and absolutely no more betting with Lord Mathison or anyone else."

Veronica nodded.

Madeline narrowed her gaze on the contrite head of her favorite stepdaughter, troublesome problem that she was. "No more anything that could cause discomfort, embarrassment, or disgrace for your father. Use your head, Veronica, or I can't be called upon to save you from Lord Rathbone."

The faintest of nods was seen. Madeline smiled to herself, knowing Veronica's spirit wasn't crushed in the least. But if the child would just restrain herself for the next few weeks, this whole silly engagement scheme would be pushed from Henry's mind. Madeline would certainly do her part to keep her husband occupied.

Chapter

5

I declare, Anthony has truly taken leave of his senses this time." Jennifer Armstrong declared, puffing out her chest haughtily. "He's allowed that Mr. Danner into his house as if the man were a personal friend." She clucked her tongue. "Anthony had better lock up the silver and his best brandy. The man looks half-wild."

Veronica's hands were folded tightly in her lap. She slid a glance at Madeline who'd merely lifted her brows in inquiry over the rim of her teacup. Veronica's two younger sisters, Chloe and Patrice, both looked appropriately shocked.

Jennifer settled farther into her chair, warming to her theme. "You don't suppose Anthony's got himself into some kind of trouble, do you?" she asked delicately. "Trouble with this man, I mean."

Madeline frowned faintly. Veronica was boiling. How dare Jennifer! The hypocrite! Jennifer had been married to an elderly, wealthy gentleman who'd had the great courtesy to die within six months of the wedding and leave Jennifer independently wealthy. Her husband had expired gratefully in his sleep, released from this demon of self-righteousness and iron will, and Jennifer had happily moved on to handsome, desperate younger men to keep her entertained. She'd reputedly left a string of lovers in her wake. She did as she pleased, and though that should have endeared her to Veronica, the fact that she still saw fit to demean everyone else was infuriating to the extreme.

Angry words bubbled on her tongue. It was impossible to sit here and listen to this!

Madeline shot her a stern glance and Veronica silently beseeched her to lift this terrible restraint and allow her to speak freely.

"I'm sure Anthony knows what he's doing," Madeline said quietly.

Jennifer's hand hovered over the tray of tarts Madeline passed to her, swooping down to snatch a luscious apple cream confection. She delicately nibbled away as more narrow-minded opinions spilled from her lips. Veronica could scarcely watch without laughing. The woman was built like a trunk and managed to eat that tart and three more in record time, all the while taking tiny little bites as if she couldn't possibly manage an entire sweet.

What a phoney! What a disgusting charade! And to think, because of Madeline's new plan for her to act like a seemly young woman, Veronica would have to entertain dozens of women like Jennifer Armstrong who were connected to eligible, *marriageable*, young men.

"Are you staying in the city all winter?" Madeline asked politely.

"Ah, yes. Although Byron so loves the country."

Byron was Jennifer's nephew, her deceased husband's brother's son. Byron Hartwell was purportedly a decent, by all rights handsome, available prospect whose lack of a title and money might encourage him to marry someone of nobility even though her character was slightly soiled.

Madeline was counting on it. Veronica was sick with fear of it.

But it's got to be better than Neville Rathbone, Veronica reminded herself sternly, settling her temper to a low simmer.

"Anthony does not have a history of 'knowing what he's

doing,'" Jennifer declared. "He won't take a bride, nor will he make the slightest effort in finding one. He rarely goes to parties. Spends all his time at his clubs in the company of men."

"Are you implying something, Jennifer?" Veronica couldn't help breaking in.

"Anthony knows how to increase his wealth," Madeline said quickly. "He's very much interested in his own businesses and spends a lot of time and effort in keeping them running smoothly."

Jennifer's sharp gaze cut into Veronica whose face reflected angelic innocence. "I only meant, he's not been the same since Catherine threw him over. Though he's not an earl, he does know how to make money. I'd be the first one to say so."

You lying old harpy!

"Veronica, would you ask Bessie to bring more refreshments please?" Madeline said with forced politeness.

Veronica didn't hesitate. Anything to escape the cloying withdrawing room! It was much better when they called on others rather than being at the mercy of whoever should choose to call on them. Jennifer was the worst. How long would it take before the subject of Veronica's needy state would be broached? How could Madeline delicately suggest that Jennifer's nephew might be interested in her?

God save me, Veronica thought, depressed, as she went in search of the maid.

Bessie was in the pantry as was the day's newspaper, the latter lying about in plain sight. "Lady Ashworth would like more refreshments," Veronica told the scullery maid, unable to prevent herself from adding, "Mrs. Armstrong is hoping to put on more weight."

Bessie flushed, scandalized, as she scurried to the kitchen. Veronica picked up the paper, scouring the headlines, her heart pounding as she read as fast as she could, tarrying as long as she dared.

She ignored the society page, more interested in today's news, but a headline caught her eye nonetheless: BETROTHAL IMMINENT. Before she realized the full content of the article, her own name leapt out at her. ". . . Lady Veronica Elizabeth Ashworth, eldest daughter of Lord Henry Ashworth, the earl of Charlwood, is about to become betrothed to Lord Neville Rathbone, who asked for her hand last Saturday night at the marquess of Wilshire's birthday party for his sister, Lady Margaret. The viscount is delighted in his choice of wife and remarked that he couldn't wait for the wedding day. No comment from Lady Veronica, but sources say she is happy with the decision. . . ."

Veronica sat down hard on the pantry stool. Happy? *Happy?* She was still staring into space, her teeth clenched, when the front bell rang. Hearing Northcroft's distinctive strides she vanished from the pantry and the incriminating newspaper and fled toward the sitting room. Her face was flushed and hot. Would the net of destruction tighten ever further until there was no hope of extricating herself?

She heard voices in the hallway, then the sitting room door abruptly opened. Gasping, she straightened, her pulse pounding as if she were caught in some embarrassing act.

"If it isn't Lady Veronica," Samuel Danner drawled.

Well, hell, Samuel thought, coming face-to-face with Veronica. He'd thought his memory of her was overrated, but she was as lively and beautiful as spring's first blossom. Her hair was bound by a dark net but its weight kept it resting against her shoulders. Her eyes were clear and gold and direct; her dress fawn brown with dark stitchery and though the effect was somewhat subdued, it couldn't hide Veronica's natural ebullience and spirit.

"Mr. Danner," she greeted him coolly. He acknowledged the cut with a slight nod. After all, he'd thrown her marriage proposal back into her face. She wouldn't thank him for that.

Spying the man coming into the room behind him, Veronica burst out, "Uncle Tony!" then practically threw herself into Anthony's arms, taking him somewhat by surprise.

"Veronica," Anthony greeted her, returning the hug.

"I'm so glad you're here," she said with feeling. "It's been a positively horrid week! You can't imagine what it's like listening to"—her voice lowered and she peeked over Anthony's shoulder toward the door—"Jennifer Armstrong and others. She's in the drawing room with Madeline, Chloe, and Patrice."

"How fortunate for us all," Anthony murmured dryly. "Is Henry here?"

"He's at Charlwood, but he's supposed to be home tonight."

"The family estate," Anthony explained for Samuel's benefit. "I thought he was due back yesterday."

"I did, too, but apparently he was delayed." Veronica's gaze landed on Samuel briefly, but slid away before he could meet her eyes.

He was irritated. Both because of the rush of pleasure he felt at seeing her again, and the fact that she'd even entertained the idea that he would let himself become embroiled in her romantic affairs. He felt sorry for her, yes. Disbelief that such antiquated marriage arrangements were still in effect, definitely. But he was unwilling to involve himself in these ridiculous society games.

So, why then, did she make him feel that *he* was somehow the guilty party!

"Samuel would like to meet Henry," Anthony explained just as the sitting room door slid open still farther.

Madeline peeked inside. "I thought you were looking for Bessie," she accused Veronica.

"I was. I told Bessie you needed more refreshments."

"Good evening, Anthony."

"Good evening, Madeline. I'd like you to meet Samuel Danner," he added when her expectant gaze landed on his guest. "I was hoping to catch Henry at home, but Veronica says he's at Charlwood."

To Samuel's amusement Madeline looked him up and down, as if uncertain what to make of him. "Henry should be back later today. If you would care to come into the drawing room, you can wait for his return."

Anthony hesitated. It was late for making calls and he had

no desire to be in the same room with Jennifer Armstrong. Still, he knew how anxious Samuel was to learn anything about Victor Flynne and they were at a stalemate unless Henry could provide some illuminating information.

"Thank you, Madeline," he accepted and he, Samuel, and Veronica followed her back to the withdrawing room.

Samuel felt that same overpowering sense of claustrophobia he experienced every time he was invited into another English home. The room was richly beautiful, but it was stuffed full of *things*. Dark paneled walls were relieved by peach and green brocade couches and love seats. A rich, velvety carpet covered a glossy oak floor, and a huge fireplace sent shafts of orange light and radiant heat into the shadowy corners of the room. But pressed flowers under glass and dried arrangements covered the tables. Miniatures of the family, spread here and there across the tables and mantel, fought for space beside figurines and silver-framed portraits. Miniatures. Portraits. For a moment Samuel's chest constricted. *Mary,* he thought. *Everything comes back to Mary.*

"Well, there you are, Lady Ashworth! I was beginning to wonder if I'd been forgotten." a booming, feminine voice rang out, bringing Samuel back to the present with a bang. "I will speak to my nephew, but I must warn you, he prefers to be treated like a guest. He wouldn't stand for being left like a beggar in the drawing room."

She was the fiercest-looking woman Samuel had ever encountered. Sharp eyes scoured him from head to toe, her massive bosom heaving with outrage. If this was Jennifer Armstrong, he sympathized completely with Veronica.

"I'm so sorry, Jennifer," Madeline rushed in. "This is Samuel Danner, and of course, you know my brother-in-law, Anthony Ashworth."

"Always a pleasure, Anthony." She held out a plump hand, still eyeing Samuel.

Anthony cleared his throat. "Truly," he said, lightly kissing her hand.

"Mr. Danner." She moved her hand toward him and he was forced to gather it in his fingers. This hand-kissing custom never failed to make Samuel feel ridiculous, but he nevertheless obliged.

He caught sight of Veronica in his peripheral vision. Her lips were twitching but she was careful to keep her eyes focused on a spot somewhere above Jennifer's head.

"The dishonorable Samuel Danner of Rock Springs," Anthony added dryly, wringing a gasp from Jennifer, a warning look from Madeline, and a sparkle in Veronica's clear eyes. The two younger girls giggled nervously.

"Patrice, Chloe, you left your embroidery upstairs," Madeline said meaningfully.

"Oh, Madeline. Don't make us leave!" Chloe protested.

"We would much prefer to stay." Patrice bobbed her head enthusiastically.

"The vicar has requested a jar of Cook's special preserves. Someone needs to drop it by. Which errand would you prefer to do first?"

Chloe managed to hide her feelings fairly well; Veronica's next younger sister was quickly mastering the art of deception. But Patrice stared at Madeline in horror. The vicar was known to sermonize long and loudly with the least provocation.

"We'll do our embroidery," Chloe murmured and she and Patrice left the room.

Veronica swallowed a smile, but her moment of amusement ended when Jennifer declared, "I understand your engagement to Lord Rathbone is a frivolous rumor. Much like the rumors abounding last summer."

"Quite," Veronica said through a false smile.

"How unfortunate for you, my dear, that Geoffrey Rowbury is such a scoundrel. Dreadful accusations. Now my nephew, Byron, would never allow such scandalous accusations to be spread. He absolutely abhors gossip."

"He sounds like a paragon of virtue," Veronica remarked.

Movement off to her side caught her eye; Samuel Danner was fighting back laughter.

Unaware, Jennifer fixed her sharp gaze on Veronica. "He is a man, therefore he sees things differently from us. Wouldn't you say so, Anthony?"

"Pardon me?" Uncle Tony looked uncomfortable.

"I believe she means men and women don't think alike. I would have to agree," said Samuel.

The sound of his drawl caused Jennifer's head to snap around in shock. She stared at Samuel, for once completely at a loss.

"More tea?" Madeline suggested a bit desperately, reaching for the bellpull. Apparently she'd given up finding excuses for Veronica to leave the room.

Jennifer fussed with her dress, a yellowish silk that emphasized her sausage shape and turned her skin sallow and greenish. To Veronica's amusement and horror, she was sending sideways glances Samuel's way. Sizing him up for her next *affaire?*

Dear God! Should she warn him? Veronica turned to find Samuel's dark eyes assessing her with something like bafflement, or maybe exasperation. She tried to work up some indignation against him. After all, he'd shattered all her fantasies and embarrassed and humiliated her at the marquess's party. But feeling his heavy gaze, her heart skipped a beat then pounded uncomfortably hard inside her chest.

"Are you staying in London long, Mr. Danner?" Jennifer asked silkily.

"It depends on whether I conclude my business here very soon."

"What business are you in?"

"Mr. Danner was a lawyer," Veronica inserted before he could answer. "A barrister," she added when Jennifer remained silent.

"I understand the term," she retorted icily. "Are you no longer in the legal profession?" Her gaze skated to his boots and back to his face.

"I'm conducting some personal business."

"Personal business?" Veronica asked lightly.

Madeline scowled at her and Uncle Tony heaved a quiet sigh.

"I'm paying back . . . an old debt," Samuel answered after a deliberate moment.

Outside the window the afternoon had worn into evening and rain was falling, steaming the windows and shining wet on the leaves of the laurel hedge. Samuel frowned. He and Anthony were planning to eat at one of Anthony's clubs; they were meeting Thomas Houghton, hoping he could shed more light on Flynne.

Still, just for a moment, in the close warmth of the room, with the gaslight faintly hissing, turning the crown of Veronica's head a lovely gold, Samuel wished he could make it all stop for a while. An evening with a woman as intriguing as Veronica would be a welcome relief from his dark thoughts.

"It looks as if Henry will be later than I anticipated," Madeline said as the conversation lagged.

"We should probably come back another time," Anthony concurred.

"Thank you for tea," Samuel told Madeline. "It was a pleasure meeting you, Mrs. Armstrong," he added.

At the front door, while Anthony was retrieving their coats from the butler, Samuel was surprised to discover Veronica beside him. She was close, close enough for him to smell the fragrance of her hair. It was sweet and light and utterly captivating.

"I should never speak to you again," she said with a faint smile. "You've humiliated me beyond bearing."

"You didn't really expect me to offer for you, did you?"

She tilted her head. "It would have made the situation much simpler."

"No, it wouldn't have. Your father would have learned the truth and then what? Prison? A beheading? Clearly you would have earned stiffer punishment than a mere arranged marriage."

Her laughter burst out, beautiful and infectious, surprising him. "Lord Danner," she mocked gently. "You underestimate my talents. He would have never found out." Then, as if hearing how devious she sounded, she faltered. "I must apologize for my behavior at the marquess of Wilshire's party. I wasn't . . . feeling well."

"I know."

"It was a bit of a strain . . . that evening. But it's over now."

He could have let the subject drop. Indeed, if he'd learned anything these past weeks in London, it was what the proper thing to do was for nearly every occasion. But he didn't feel like being proper where Victor was concerned. And he didn't feel like being proper where Veronica was concerned, either.

"Did you see this evening's paper? The society column?" she asked lightly.

"The society doings in London are hardly of interest to a westerner like myself," Samuel said slowly.

"Then you missed the headline. The one that practically announced my betrothal to Neville Rathbone."

"Rathbone?" he repeated blankly.

"Yes, Lord Rathbone. The devil who had my father cornered all evening at the marquess's party!" Her lips flattened defiantly. "But I shan't marry him. I'll do something drastic first."

"Like marry Mrs. Armstrong's nephew," Samuel suggested ironically.

"Unless I want to alienate myself from my family, I'm doomed to accede to my father's wishes." She was perfectly honest and a little sad.

"There must be another way," he said, but Anthony was standing silently behind them, listening, looking a bit worried. He kissed his niece and he and Samuel had turned to the door as one when footsteps sounded on the outside steps. Bare moments later the door swung inward and Henry Ashworth, the current earl of Charlwood, strode inside.

"Father!" Veronica greeted him.

"Hello, Veronica." His look raked Samuel as he asked her, "What are you doing hovering by the door? Where's Northcroft?"

The butler made quick time, hearing Henry's voice. Ignoring Northcroft's greeting, Henry tossed the man his coat and hat. Then he turned abruptly to Anthony. "Did you wish to see me about something?"

"I was hoping to catch you at home. I wanted to introduce you to a friend of mine"—he indicated Samuel—"Samuel Danner."

Henry's brows lifted ever so slightly. "You're that American from the marquess's party."

"Yes." Samuel offered his hand which Henry stared at for a moment before giving a perfunctory shake. "It's a pleasure to meet you, Lord Ashworth," he said dryly.

"I'm afraid it will be a rather quick introduction. I've just returned from the country and I'm very tired. Veronica, was there something else?" he asked pointedly.

For a moment Samuel thought Veronica might rebel; for a moment he hoped she would. But then with a stiff curtsey that belied the fire in her eyes, she picked up her skirts and retired to the drawing room.

"Samuel and I have some urgent business we need to discuss with you," Anthony said.

Henry frowned, his irritation plain. "Perhaps next week."

"Would Tuesday be convenient?"

His brother's mild tone caught Henry's attention. "Fine. There are some things I need to discuss with you in private, as well. Is that convenient for you, Mr. Danner?"

Samuel found he disliked Henry immediately— immediately and intensely. He could scarcely believe this man had sired a woman as warm and lovely as Veronica but there was an unmistakable look about his face that made the resemblance clear. Samuel wished now he'd paid more attention to the miniatures. There was bound to be a picture of Veronica's real mother and Samuel found his interest in her growing.

"I'll look forward to it," Samuel answered.

"We'll meet you here," Anthony agreed, hustling Samuel out to the coach.

"What the hell is going on between you and your brother?" Samuel asked when they were underway.

"What do you mean?"

"You act as if you loath one another."

"Oh." Anthony smiled faintly. "We do. Someday, if you get to know me better, I'll tell you why."

"Tell me now," Samuel suggested. "Because I need your brother to help me catch a murderer and if there's a problem between the two of you, I want to be aware of it."

"It's nothing to do with Flynne. Don't worry. It won't inhibit your search."

His flat, cold tone warned Samuel the conversation was at an end. Normally, Samuel would demand answers but he'd had enough of games and social mysteries for a lifetime. With a sigh, he settled back into the coach's fine leather cushions and closed his eyes.

Expecting a momentary respite from his problems, he was annoyed to discover Veronica was in the forefront of his mind. No one, not even Henry Ashworth, could really resign his firstborn into a loveless, empty marriage with someone like Neville Rathbone. It was all a drama designed to fill the cold, empty hours of winter while Londoners waited for better weather. It had to be. In a week, two or three at the most, Henry's pique at Veronica would be over and the whole episode forgotten.

At least he fervently hoped so. Otherwise he might feel compelled to consider her offer.

Chapter
6

Morning sunlight streamed through the crack in the heavy drapes that covered Veronica's bedroom window. Reluctantly, she dragged herself out of bed and crossed to the small alcove, pulling back the curtains. A cool, wintery morning met her, barely warmed by a pale sun. The branches of the oaks were shorn of all leaves. Everything outside looked damp and bare and frigid.

A coach stood at the front doors, the horses stamping restlessly, plumes of steam shooting from their nostrils. Her father's coach. Henry never rested. He worked dawn to dusk, though apart from his estate management Veronica had no clear idea what he did.

Awake now, she hurriedly dressed and rushed downstairs. "Madeline?" she called from the foyer, then, after receiving no answer, she slid open the withdrawing room doors. No one. Deciding her stepmother must be in the morning room, she strode down the hall and through the partially opened doorway. "Is there some new torture awaiting me in my quest for a suitor this morning?" she asked, the words shriveling in her throat as she spied her father standing behind Madeline and looking sorely put out.

"Sit down, Veronica," he greeted her coolly.

She'd expected him to be gone. At least half an hour had passed since she'd witnessed the coach outside her window. Something must be wrong, she thought with genuine dread.

"Father, I—"

"Sit down."

She sat.

Madeline was looking down at her lap. This must be very serious indeed.

"Neville Rathbone has asked for your hand."

This was hardly shattering news but Veronica's heart thumped with fear. She clasped her hands together and waited, a scream already forming behind trembling lips.

"I've agreed to the match."

"No!" Veronica gasped.

"It will be a short engagement. Long enough to be seemly; short enough to have the deed accomplished by late spring or early summer. Neville's as anxious as I to complete the transaction."

"Complete the transaction!" Veronica stared at him helplessly. "Am I another business dealing, Father?"

"Don't be difficult," he answered sharply.

"I won't do it! I will not marry that old toad!"

"Veronica . . ." Madeline moaned wearily, dropping her forehead into her palm.

"You most certainly will marry Lord Rathbone!" Henry bit back. "Furthermore, if there is any way to hurry this marriage along without causing more scandal, I shall do it!"

Veronica's eyes burned. She'd never been close to her father. He was too austere, too strict, too much like his own father, Veronica's grandfather, William Ashworth, who'd ruled his home as a dictator and driven his wife to an early grave. Just as Henry had driven her mother to her death when Veronica was but five.

"Father, he's only marrying me because he needs a nursemaid. He doesn't love me. I'm not certain he even likes me!"

"It is immaterial to me what Lord Rathbone's motives might be."

"She has a point, Henry," Madeline broke in tentatively. "The man is old enough to be her grandfather. Surely, there must be someone more suitable. Jennifer Armstrong's nephew, Byron, would make an excellent match and he's only five years older than—"

"I have given Lord Rathbone my word!" Henry shot his wife a contemptuous glance and Madeline fell silent. "You will help make the announcements and handle all the details," he told her, checking his pocket watch. "Now, I'm late for an appointment. Don't make a fool of me, Veronica. Accept this with good grace."

In shock, Veronica watched as he brushed Madeline's cheek with his lips, then strode from the room. The click of the front door latch was like the final curtain after his exit.

Without a word Veronica whirled out of the room, rebellion in her heart.

If Samuel had expected Lord Henry Ashworth's chilly demeanor to thaw, he was cured of that hope the instant he was shown into the earl's den late Tuesday afternoon. Ashworth was busy with his accounts man who was scribbling furiously while the earl looked down on him from across his desk. Henry was clearly a man who insisted on being involved in the business of his estate and for that Samuel almost respected him.

Almost.

"Anthony . . . Mr. Danner." Ashworth indicated the two oxblood chairs in front of his massive mahogany desk. The accounts man discreetly gathered some papers and left.

Steepling his fingers, Henry regarded Anthony and Samuel with cool disinterest. The shape of his eyes and the color of his hair reminded Samuel of Veronica; the rest of the man was truly alien.

"Samuel's looking for someone," Anthony said without preamble. Narrowing his gaze on Henry, Samuel scrutinized the man's stonelike face for even the barest change.

Henry's expression didn't alter by the flicker of an eyelash.

"He's a blackmailer. An American. Samuel has known

him by two names, but that doesn't limit the man's use of an alias, by any means."

"You've known a blackmailer?" Henry turned to Samuel.

"We've crossed paths," Samuel acknowledged with a faint smile. Intimidation had never worked on a Danner, but the vaunted Lord Ashworth could hardly know that.

Anthony continued, "He calls himself Victor Flynne, or Victor Flannigan. He's responsible for crimes ranging from blackmail to murder."

"Indeed." Henry gave Anthony an ironic look.

"And he's here in London. Samuel's come here specifically to find him."

Ashworth favored Samuel with a cold stare. Samuel stared right back. Though less hot-blooded than his brother, Jesse, Samuel had to fight the urge to reach across the desk, grab the man by his shirt, and shake some sense into him.

"How, pray tell, can I help you?"

"You know him, too," Samuel said bluntly.

Henry tensed, but then relaxed. "I certainly do not."

"According to an associate of your brother's, you're the person to ask about Flynne. I think—"

"That's preposterous! I know no blackmailers or murderers. I demand to know where you heard this pack of lies." Henry burst out.

"Wait a minute," Anthony cut in, shooting Samuel a warning look. "No one's making accusations. You may not know who Flynne is directly. But he's here in London, desperately trying to make the acquaintance of every nobleman he can find."

"I resent the insinuation that I have 'befriended' the man," Henry rapped out, not appeased.

Samuel found Henry's denials a tad too adamant. Almost before an accusation was made, he was slashing down all efforts to connect himself with Flynne. Automatic self-protection? Maybe. But Henry's overzealous attempt to exonerate himself convinced Samuel that Thomas Houghton had been right: Henry *was* the man to talk to about Flynne.

"Let Samuel describe Mr. Flynne," Anthony suggested. "If you've seen him, maybe you can help us."

"He's rather nondescript." Samuel didn't wait for Henry to launch into more excuses. "Five foot nine or ten, mid to late thirties, unremarkable apart from his occupation. Brown hair and eyes, I believe. Average build. Victor deals in subtle blackmail. Nothing overt. He gains confidences, then uses them to his advantage. Anyone who's brushed his acquaintance should be warned: The man's a parasite."

"I'm sure if Mr. Flynne were in London, attempting to break into Society—that is what you're suggesting, isn't it?—that the news would have reached my ears." Henry's voice was glacial. "His accent would be remarkable even if nothing else would be. I'm sorry, Mr. Danner. I've never heard of the man, nor of anyone fitting that less than specific description, nor of *blackmail* in any form. And I would have, I assure you. That is probably what your 'associate' meant when he named me," Henry added coldly for Anthony's benefit.

Anthony nodded. Samuel couldn't tell whether he truly believed this malarkey or not, but it didn't matter. He would have bet his last cent that Lord Henry Ashworth, current earl of Charlwood, was a tremendous liar.

"Good day, gentlemen," Henry said succinctly, and Anthony and Samuel were summarily shown the door. As the butler waited for their exit, Samuel couldn't help hoping for a glimpse of Veronica but to his intense disappointment she was nowhere in sight. Next time, he thought, grimacing a bit as he wondered why it appeared to matter to him so much.

Saturday evening the house was decorated as if for a ball. Silver satin streamers were looped over the stairway rail, pinioned by pink chiffon bows. The chandelier had been taken down and cleaned until each polished teardrop glistened like sparkles on water. All the servants bustled through the house, with excitement or tension it was impossible to tell. Veronica guessed it was tension: Her father was impossible to please. Woe to the inexperienced maid who dropped a dish. Expulsion without references would be imminent.

Now, sitting in her room, hands clenched, her jaw set, Veronica stared dismally at her reflection. A small dinner party—for forty guests—in her honor. She lived in dread that her father would announce her betrothal tonight and she'd positively begged—got down on her knees and *begged* Madeline for a stay of execution. Luckily Madeline was as intent as Veronica to stop this travesty before it became public record. Rumors were rampant, but until her father formally announced the engagement, there was still time to save face.

The white and frosted pink gown draped across the bed mocked her. Veronica glared at it through the mirror. The wretched dress would turn yellow with age before she willingly donned it. She would never marry Neville Rathbone. She would die first. For one awful moment she envisioned herself in Neville's arms, his wrinkled face and yellow teeth leering down at her. She felt physically sick.

"Here m'lady." Lily, the upstairs maid who'd been urging Veronica to get dressed, picked up the gown and gave it a sharp snap. Her hands anxiously smoothed the fabric, as if the dress weren't already immaculately pressed. "It's time."

"I'm not putting it on."

"M'lady!"

"Lily, hang that awful gown in the closet. I've no interest in appearing in that dress—or any other—so my father can show me off like his prize mare!"

"M'lady!" Lily practically shrieked on a gasp. She stared at Veronica through huge, fearful eyes, then obediently hung the dress on a hanger. Unable to help her mistress, she stood in a corner of the room, wringing her hands.

"Stop worrying, Lily." Veronica couldn't hide her impatience. "I'm simply making a point to my father."

"But I don't . . . I wouldn't . . . the master'll be so angry!" She rolled her eyes in the direction of the door, as if fearing Henry would suddenly fling open the door and demand they both be beheaded for their disobedience.

"Please, m'lady," she moaned. "T'will be my termination for certain!"

"It is hardly your fault if I refuse to get dressed," Veronica pointed out reasonably.

"*'Tis* my fault!" She bobbed her head with such force, her white mobcap slipped down over one eye.

"No, Lily."

The maid shook her head and bit down on one knuckle, paralyzed by fear. Veronica's impatience turned to frustration.

"I would rather be drawn and quartered than face that beastly crowd downstairs!"

"Please, please, m'lady . . ." She held out her hands beseechingly.

"Oh, all right!" The maid's distress was so visceral Veronica could bear it no longer. Grumbling to herself, she grabbed the gown off the hanger and slipped it over her head. Lily instantly jumped to help her. With trembling fingers she closed the little pearl buttons through their loops down Veronica's back.

"The curling iron's hot," she added, rushing to bring it to the room as Veronica seated herself at her vanity.

She made a face at her own reflection. "I won't do it," she whispered fervently, determination stamped across her piquant face.

Lily returned with the iron and attempted to curl Veronica's thick mane, finally settling for a thick smooth wave which swung against her shoulders like a mink mantle. Seconds later a knock sounded at the door and Lily nearly dropped the iron.

Madeline swept inside.

She looked lovely in a deep dusky blue which highlighted her dark hair. But her expression was tense and unhappy. "The guests are all downstairs waiting."

"Good." Veronica deliberately brushed her hair.

"Lily, leave us," Madeline ordered, perching herself on the edge of the bed and meeting Veronica's eyes in the mirror as Lily quietly left the room.

"Is my intended here?" Veronica asked through brittle lips.

"I'm afraid so."

They shared a faint smile. Veronica was half-tempted to confide in Madeline that she would move heaven and earth to stop this marriage but decided that Madeline already knew; and Madeline didn't want to know.

"Is there any chance Father might change his mind?"

"I don't think so."

"Did you talk to him? Later. After he had time to reconsider?"

"Veronica, he's set on this marriage."

"I can't go through with it! I can't!"

"I know, darling."

"No, you don't!" She slammed the brush down on the vanity. The vials of perfume rattled and tilted precariously. "Why does it have to be this way? Why can't I make my own decisions."

"Come on, Veronica. Hiding up here won't stop the inevitable."

Madeline clasped Veronica's hand, pulling her from the vanity stool. Smoothing her hair away from her face, Madeline tried to hide her own troubled thoughts. But she was bound by Henry's wishes and without further ado she guided her recalcitrant stepdaughter into the gallery.

Music greeted Veronica as soon as she stepped outside her room. A string quartet filled the house with sweet song. Sweet song for a bitter day, Veronica thought sickly.

In the hall below, several groups of people stopped chatting to look up and smile. Amelia St. John's smile was sly. Veronica groaned inwardly. How had she ended up on the guest list?

"I would not have invited Amelia!" Veronica whispered through tight lips.

"Your sisters were trying to help," Madeline whispered back. "They asked that we invite some of your friends as well as our own."

Veronica nearly choked. Chloe and Patrice were so witless!

She descended the stairs on trembling legs. Wortham Mathison's face swam into view. He reached for her gloved hand and she clutched him with the desperation of a drowning woman.

"You look lovely, my dear," he greeted her, adding for her ears alone, "If I were a betting man, I'd have to place against you, I'm afraid."

She swallowed a hysterical giggle. "If I were a betting woman, I'd have to place against me, too."

"I'm so sorry," he said with real feeling, totally unlike his normally light, slightly caustic manner.

"Thank you, Wortham."

"Veronica!" Amelia detached herself from James Fielding, her hand lingering on his arm a moment longer than necessary. The last sucking of a leech. "What a marvelous gown! You look so fetching. Your fiancé won't be able to take his eyes from you."

"I am not spoken for yet, Amelia."

"Don't let Neville hear that," James remarked. "Ronnie, darling, may I have the honor of escorting you to dinner?" He held his arm for her to take. Veronica would have much preferred Wortham Mathison's, but she accepted James's offer with good grace. This wasn't the battle to fight. That one still lay ahead of her.

The dining room was filled with guests, most already seated, but they rose to their feet when Veronica entered, clapping politely. Veronica's heart froze. This was totally uncalled for, unless . . . ?

Her anxious gaze lit on Neville Rathbone. He grinned his ghastly rigor smile at her. The seat next to him was vacant and while Veronica's pulse pounded in her ears, James Fielding deposited her at the empty chair.

"Don't you look lovely, my dear," Neville greeted her, pulling back her chair. She felt the light brush of his fingers against her hair as she sank down. An icy shiver slid down her back.

Henry, looking elegant and commanding, stood at the

head of the table. He tipped his silvered head in Veronica's direction and without the slightest hesitation, announced in a booming voice, "It is with the greatest pleasure that I present Lord Neville Rathbone and his future wife, my eldest daughter, Lady Veronica Elizabeth Ashworth!"

Chapter

7

Samuel paced the confines of Anthony's study in frustration. He'd been in London how long now? Five weeks? Six? What had he to show for it? A dubious relationship with the earl of Charlwood and his more approachable younger brother, Anthony. Hardly the kind of newsbreaking events conducive to bringing Flynne to justice.

He smacked his fist into his palm, stopping in front of the fire, one hand pressed against the mantel as he stared into the smoldering red lumps of coal.

Tonight Anthony was at Veronica's engagement party. A private dinner at the Ashworth Manor. White-faced, Anthony had given him the news earlier that afternoon, when Madeline had appeared on the doorstep, begging him to convince Henry to put off the engagement announcement until she could convince some young fop named Byron to ask for Veronica's hand. Madeline and Anthony had then made quick time to Ashworth Manor but to no avail. Henry was bound and determined to marry off Veronica and he was planning to surprise both Veronica and his guests with the announcement later this evening.

"Bastard," Samuel bit out softly.

Anthony had dressed for the party with all the enthusiasm of a man facing the guillotine. Samuel had been left to count the hours, wondering how Veronica would react to the news that she was bound to that ugly lecher who'd undressed her with his eyes at the marquess of Wilshire's party.

He straightened and crossed the drawing room to the piano, stared out at the persistent January rain sliding off the dark leaves of the laurel outside the window, then gazed down at the keyboard. Lightly he ran his hand over the ivory keys. Mary used to play. She was terrible. No sense of rhythm or timing and the only songs she knew were bawdy tavern ballads. Her father, Cedric McKechnie, was a Portland merchant and manufacturer of buggies and carriages whose wife had died in childbirth. A good, loving father, Cedric's weakness was liquor and Mary learned at an early age which Portland drinking establishments were her father's favorites. Even during the brief six magic months of her marriage to Samuel she still dragged him out of a place or two, sometimes with her husband's help, sometimes all on her own.

Samuel smiled in reflection. She'd been a hell of a woman.

Veronica Ashworth's face swam into vision: her thick hair, bright eyes, and sideways smile. Marriage to Lord Rathbone . . .

He exhaled sharply. Veronica wasn't his problem, for god's sake. She was just a silly noblewoman with more looks than sense and what she did, or didn't do, was nothing to him.

"Mary would have never gotten herself into such a ridiculous mess," Samuel said aloud to the empty room, the words echoing hollowly.

He glanced at the clock. Almost midnight. How long did these damn dinners last? Anthony had sworn he'd only be gone a short time. He had no more wish to witness Veronica's sentencing than Samuel had.

Muttering to himself, he picked up his forgotten brandy, irritated that he seemed obsessed with thoughts of Veronica this evening. Sinking into one of the side chairs, he closed his eyes and listened to the rain beat against the leaded glass panes.

Control, he thought, sipping the brandy. Control was his middle name. He'd practiced it all his life, had even mastered the illusion.

Samuel shifted uneasily. The truth was he did pride himself on his ability to mask his feelings. It was habit, mostly. A learned behavior from his youth which had hardened into rock solid resolve after Mary's death.

Opening his eyes, Samuel narrowed his gaze on the glossy sheen of the black piano. Learning Flynne was instrumental in the loss of his wife had created a fissure in Samuel's dearly won control. He'd accepted her death the way a man accepts the inevitable. Part of God's unfathomable plan. Nothing to be done. So sorry, old sport. Bad luck. A terrible tragedy.

But now he knew her death had been orchestrated by Flynne and Samuel's control had dangerously slipped. He raged inside, his need for vengeance as hot and liquid as lava. He didn't care what it took, or whom it hurt. He wanted Flynne and he was going to have him, even if it cost him his own life in the bargain.

". . . May is such a wonderful month for a wedding. June weddings are all the rage, but May is such a wonderful month. When I was young, we all wanted to be married in May. There were a group of us girls. We all said, 'May is *such* a wonderful month.' I remember . . ."

The elderly friend of Madeline's droned on and on, but Veronica scarcely heard her. Her ears buzzed. Her whole head throbbed. She felt as if she'd been transported to another planet. She was *not* in this room and her father had *not* consigned her to a fate worse than death.

Through glazed eyes, she looked around the drawing room. Reality intruded and she was here, at this dreadful dinner party, trying hard to keep down the three bites of food she'd ingested from the seven course meal and look somewhat attentive to Harriet Rowe who was still rambling on about May weddings. Listening to Harriet's reminiscences was a trial, but still infinitely better than attempting to carry on a conversation with Amelia, or James, or even her friend, Wortham, who was so full of pity for her that Veronica felt like bursting into tears everytime he looked her way.

She caught a glance at her reflection in the beveled mirror above the fireplace. Her pallor was chalk-white but even so she looked remarkably calm. Neville, after trying to engage her in conversation at the dinner table—to no avail—had hovered around her like a cloying odor. Finally, however, the men had retired into the study for brandies; the women to the withdrawing room for socializing. Veronica was standing apart from most of the women, silently willing the evening to end. Her *intended,* was undoubtedly being slapped on the back by all his well-wishers.

Oh, my God! she thought painfully, imagining the scene in the study.

". . . and that's when the jonquils were in bloom. And roses were just starting to blossom . . ."

Veronica's lips trembled. They were probably drinking brandy and exchanging winks and raising glasses.

". . . I wore periwinkle blue that spring and my friend Edna always said I looked best in pink. But I wouldn't listen. I liked blue and blue really is my color, no matter what Edna says. However, Edna was right about yellow. I look absolutely jaundiced in yellow, any shade . . ."

Her father was probably waiting to hammer out the details of the arrangement. Maybe they would shake hands on it. Or maybe they would actually sign a document, sealing her fate legally.

It was enough to make one violently ill.

". . . Edna wouldn't dance. Even though she was very light on her feet for such a large woman, she was terrified of being in a man's arms. I told her, 'Edna, they're just as afraid of you as you are of them.' My mother told me that. So, then . . ."

"Excuse me, Harriet," Veronica murmured, clutching her skirts as she escaped to the hallway. Northcroft was just handing Uncle Tony his coat and hat. "Take me with you," she begged in her uncle's ear. "Please! I can't bear another moment in this house!"

"Veronica," he said, turning to her just as the den door opened on a cloud of cigar smoke and Neville stepped into the hall, a strange smile on his lips.

"Leaving, Ashworth?" Neville asked in a gravelly voice that shook with age.

Tony nodded. "It's getting late."

Neville drew a disdainful breath through his nostrils. "Yes, well, young people never learn proper manners these days. Don't know when to leave." He threw a dark look at the door of the withdrawing room where women's gentle laughter rose in small waves.

"Please, Uncle Tony," Veronica begged under her breath.

He clasped her icy hands in his warm ones. "Tomorrow is Sunday. I'll take you riding in the park."

"Might have to wait on that, Ashworth. I'm planning to take my prospective bride on a drive with my new team." Neville coughed loudly. "Good for the lungs. Doctor prescribed it. Makes me feel like a young colt myself!"

"I'd rather go riding." Veronica's rude retort sent Anthony's brows sky-high.

"I'm afraid that's impossible, my dear. I don't enjoy riding."

Veronica had scarcely looked at Neville all evening, unable to bear even a glimpse of his skull-like face. But now she turned her furious gaze on him full force. Anger simmered in her amber eyes like a gold flame. Neville was clearly taken aback. "I plan to go riding tomorrow," Veronica stated evenly. "With my uncle. I'm afraid our drive will have to wait."

Neville scowled, just as Harriet Rowe tottered out of the drawing room. "My dear," Neville began, but Veronica effectively cut him off by giving Anthony a kiss on the cheek.

"I'll be ready around one," she said with false brightness. "Good night."

"Good night," Anthony murmured.

"It will be a lovely spring this year!" Harriet declared as

Veronica gathered her skirts and hastily scurried toward the stairs.

Anthony's last glimpse of his spirited niece was a vision of rustling skirts, clambering high-button shoes, and a look of relief as she escaped to the first floor. Neville was left to an illuminating conversation with Harriet Rowe which Anthony was only too glad to miss.

The last guest was gone. The last coach rattled away over the cobblestone street. Chloe and Patrice were in their rooms and Madeline and her father had turned down the gaslights although Veronica suspected they weren't quite asleep yet.

Henry had ordered her downstairs when he'd realized she'd left for bed while they still had guests. Complaining of a very real headache had been no salvation for Veronica; she'd been blasted by Henry's ire in the comparative privacy of the pantry, her father shaking her arm hard several times as if he would prefer to shake her until her teeth rattled.

She hadn't loved her father for many years. Maybe she'd never loved him. But she'd respected him, wanted to please him even when her actions seemed to speak the opposite.

But those bonds were broken now. He'd never struck her; he hadn't struck her tonight. But the desire for violence had flamed briefly in his cold eyes and for reasons buried somewhere in her own subconscious she'd been sick with fear.

Veronica shook herself. Her father capable of violence? Impossible. Yet, she would hate to test his patience to the limits all the same. Even so, she hated the thought of marriage to Neville Rathbone still more, and it was time to change the course of her life.

Dressing in a dark dress and black cloak, Veronica tiptoed down the back stairs like a wraith, hurried along the narrow passage to the kitchen, removed the key from its hook beside the door and let herself into a rain-drenched night where the stars were just beginning to appear in an inky sky.

The grooms were asleep above the carriage house. Moving silently, Veronica patted several horses, choosing her favorite, a pure black mare named Tinsel for reasons which she'd never understood.

Tinsel wickered when she saw Veronica. "Shhh," Veronica whispered, rubbing the horse's nose, her heart hammering in her throat, her ears straining for the tiniest sound. Carefully she led the mare outside and mounted her bareback, legs astride.

This was something Veronica had learned on the estate when she was a young girl. She'd received a tongue-lashing to end all tongue-lashings when she'd been caught by her father. But it hadn't quelled her secret rides, nor convinced her a sidesaddle was a necessity; she'd just become more careful. Now, feeling like an alien in her own home, she rode the horse through London streets to Uncle Tony's house.

It was foolish. She was a woman alone at night. She had no weapon—not that she would know in the least how to use one if she did. But it wasn't *right* for a woman to be alone on the streets; Society would crucify her if word ever got out. The thought brought a smile to her lips. A brisk wind whipped at her hood, and the sudden exhilaration of freedom brightened her mood in spite of the repercussions that were bound to land on her head when this midnight journey was discovered.

What can they do to you now? she asked herself reasonably. *Marry you off to someone more repugnant than Neville?*

The gaslit streets were full of coaches, carriages, and wagons. London never slept. Huddling inside her cloak, Veronica kept her eyes on Tinsel's bobbing neck. No one paid her much mind. Her sex wasn't even readily apparent beneath the dark cloak and astride the mare. Still, it was a relief to see Uncle Tony's wrought-iron gates loom beside her and she slid off Tinsel with a last anxious glance around.

The gates were locked, of course, but there was a bell which she yanked on anxiously several times, filling the night with persistent ringing.

"Who's there?" Anthony's butler peeked around the front door and glared irritably toward the gate.

"Hodgson, it's me!" Veronica waved and pulled off her hood.

He stepped outside and peered through the misty night.

"Lady Veronica!" The man nearly choked as he hurried to the gate. "Is anything wrong?"

"No, no. Everything's fine. I just—I must see my uncle. Will you take care of Tinsel?"

Hodgson blinked at the horse in horror. "I'll call Gaines," he said, referring to one of the groomsmen.

Veronica didn't wait. She ran up the path to the house, breathing in the smell of wood oil as if it were fabulously exotic and expensive perfume as she entered the foyer. Sometimes it felt as if Uncle Tony's home were *her* home. It should be. If only it were . . .

She left her wish unformed. She was who she was and there was no changing that. But she could certainly try to alter her unsavory future. Acting like the perfect daughter these past few weeks hadn't worked; it was time for desperate measures.

Men's voices murmured from the den. Her heart lifted. Uncle Tony was awake! He must be talking to Samuel Danner, she thought with pleasure.

Knowing she was risking her uncle's ire, she crept to the den doors, thankful for the small crack which allowed her a limited view and the ability to hear every word.

". . . can't sit on my hands any longer," Samuel was saying. His voice, as ever, was unmistakable even though he wasn't currently in Veronica's wedge of sight. "I'm offering money for information. Every cent I own, if I have to."

"You'll have every cur in London selling you false information. Save your money. It won't help you."

"Flynne's as eager for a bribe as anyone." Samuel strode across the room, framed in the crack of the doorway momentarily. He wore no waistcoat and his sleeves were rolled up his arms, his forearms lean, dark, and muscular. His shirt was unbuttoned and she glimpsed a tantalizing patch of dark hair at the base of his throat. "If I could rig it so he didn't know I was behind the money."

"The bounder must know you're in London. If the man's half as smart as I suspect, he'll stay clear of any nefarious dealings until he knows whom he's dealing with."

Samuel was terse. "Victor Flynne's Achilles' heel is money. Cold, hard, cash—stolen, not earned. He's a ruthless extortionist and a murderer. There's no man he wouldn't cheat. No one he wouldn't use."

Veronica frowned, surprised to realize the name Victor Flynne seemed enticingly familiar. Where had she heard it? From Samuel? No . . . Uncle Tony? Someone had been discussing Victor Flynne recently. She was sure of it.

"What are your plans, once you find Mr. Flynne?" Anthony asked.

"My plans?"

Veronica strained to listen.

"I'll go back to Portland," Samuel said after a moment. "Your aunt Agatha—Lady Chamberlain, that is," he corrected himself, his tone lightening slightly, "will want to hear all about you and your family."

"Just because she sent you to me doesn't mean she'll recognize the Ashworths as relatives," Anthony said ironically.

"Flynne's my main objective now." Samuel brought the subject back to hand, cutting off his intriguing comments about Lady Chamberlain.

The front door opened behind Veronica and she jumped guiltily. Hodgson stamped his feet, glancing from Veronica to the den door. "Would you like me to announce you, my lady?" he said with gentle irony.

"No, no, thank you." Flustered, Veronica gently rapped on the door panels before sliding them open.

She didn't know who looked the more surprised: Uncle Tony or Samuel Danner.

"Veronica!" Uncle Tony exclaimed. "What on earth are you doing here at this time of night?" He looked past her, expecting Henry, or some other chaperon, to appear.

Samuel regarded her with thinly veiled suspicion. Veronica's heart sank. Was he no longer her friend at all?

"I had to get away," she blurted out. "It was simply awful. My father is a beast!"

"Are you saying he doesn't know you left the house?" Anthony stared at her. "You must go home."

"I would rather be burned at the stake than spend one more second in my father's house! He sold me, Uncle Tony! To the first buyer. I won't stand for it!"

"Don't overdramatize, Veronica."

"Do you think I'm overdramatizing?" she challenged quietly, angry tears sparkling in her eyes.

Anthony grimaced. "Does Madeline, perhaps, know you're here?"

"No one does."

Groaning, Anthony closed his eyes. Samuel Danner looked faintly amused.

"How did you get here?" Samuel asked curiously.

"I . . . rode one of the horses."

"Alone?" Anthony was aghast. "My God, you're as foolhardy as everyone says!"

"Maybe I am," Veronica declared defiantly. "I don't care anymore. If they're going to treat me as if I have no will, I'll prove them wrong. I have a strong will."

"I don't believe anyone will contest that," Samuel remarked dryly.

Veronica sent him a speaking look. "I will not marry that despicable old goat. All he really wants is a nursemaid. I have money of my own. I'll buy him a nursemaid!"

"Neville Rathbone can buy his own nursemaid, if he wants one," Anthony remarked tersely. "You know that. And you know exactly why he wants you!"

"No, I don't. Perhaps you should explain it to me." Her lips were a line of rebellion.

Anthony's mouth was just as stubbornly set. Samuel, voicing thoughts he hadn't realized were so vivid in his mind, bit out angrily, "He wants to make you his wife so he can have a young and lovely bedmate, as you know perfectly well if you'd use half the brain God gave you!"

She made a choked sound.

"Danner!" Anthony looked stricken.

"What?" he demanded furiously.

The magnitude of his blunder grew clear as he watched the blood drain from Veronica's face. Damn this infernal Victorian society! he thought with an inward groan. Didn't

Veronica even understand what happened between a husband and wife?

Swearing beneath his breath, he reached for his brandy. But Veronica's pallid face pricked his conscience and when she swayed unsteadily, he strode to her side, reluctantly wrapping an arm around her delicate waist as he mentally chastised himself for forgetting what useless, hothouse flowers these English ladies were.

She didn't swoon, thank God. Instead, she drew a long, unsteady breath and glanced up at him, her golden eyes mirroring both distress and stubborn determination. Samuel's heart lurched uncomfortably.

"I will marry the devil himself before I marry that man!" she said through her teeth.

"There's nothing you can do about it," Anthony retorted in exasperation. "I don't like it, either, but have the good grace to accept your fate without creating a new scandal."

"You're a fine one to talk about scandal. You delight in torturing my father. The more pompous and dictatorial he becomes, the more wild and frivolous you become."

"This is not about me."

"If I were a man, someone would at least ask me if I wanted to be married. No! *I* would do the asking!" Veronica pulled away from Samuel, her body shaking with emotion, her attention directed at her uncle.

"You are not a man," he snapped out. "This is a pointless argument!"

"You just can't bear to be reminded of the truth." Veronica was past caring about seemly behavior. "You can do as you like while I have to bend to my father's wishes. Mark my words, Uncle Tony. He'll be sorry!"

"Veronica, Veronica . . ." Anthony dropped his head to his hands.

"How do you plan to avoid this marriage?" Samuel stepped into the fray.

She shot him a fierce look from beneath her lashes. "Don't worry. I won't beg you to intercede for me again."

"I'm not worried." Samuel was annoyed at Veronica's tone.

"You asked Samuel to help you?" Tony demanded incredulously. "What in God's name did you ask him to do?"

"I asked him to offer for me."

Suddenly, at the height of this flaming argument, Veronica remembered where she'd heard the name Victor Flynne. She recalled the exact moment, nearly the entire conversation where the name Victor Flynne had been mentioned.

At her father's house. Less than four weeks earlier.

Coldness prickled her skin. She bit down on her bottom lip.

"What is it?" Samuel asked quickly, too astute by far to miss the change.

"Nothing."

Something, Samuel silently argued, interested in spite of himself by Lady Veronica's mercurial mood swings. Following instinct rather than reason, he turned to Anthony. "Would you mind leaving Veronica and me alone for a moment?"

"I don't think—" Anthony began, ever the proper Englishman.

"I promise not to soil her reputation," Samuel interrupted dryly.

"My reputation is my own affair, soiled or otherwise," Veronica retorted with an edge.

Samuel couldn't help smiling at her spunk. She was watching him with those huge, expressive eyes of hers, clearly as uncertain as Anthony was about what he had in mind. *He* didn't even know what he wanted, but it seemed damned important for him to have a few moments of private conversation with this wretched minx all the same.

"Veronica?" Anthony asked.

"I'll speak to Mr. Dan—Samuel alone."

With a look that warned him to behave himself or dire consequences would follow, Anthony shook his head and left the room, sliding the den doors closed behind him.

Veronica still had that distracted air. Busy thoughts were circling her fertile mind. Samuel waited, half expecting her to confide whatever was weighing on her mind.

Her skirts rustled seductively as she crossed to the globe beside Tony's desk, absently spinning the orb ever so slowly, her gaze faraway, through the darkened windows. "The other evening I asked you to offer for me," she said at last.

Samuel stiffened. Though he sympathized with her plight, the silly foolishness of all this matchmaking irritated him. He was disappointed. For God knew what reason he'd expected more from her.

"I remember."

"You refused me. I can't say that I blame you. The situation is all so ridiculous." She smiled at him somewhat sadly. It was a smile guaranteed to melt his heart but Samuel steeled himself against it.

"It is ridiculous," he agreed cautiously.

"You're looking for a Mr. Victor Flynne. Is that correct?"

Only years of hiding his feelings kept Samuel from dropping his jaw in surprise. He stared at her.

"I overheard you before I came in," she enlightened him. "You were discussing a blackmailer with my uncle. Mr. Flynne."

"Eavesdropping?"

Instead of being abashed, she grinned charmingly. "It's a dreadful habit of mine. One among many. I think I can help you, Mr. Danner."

"You?"

"Would you be willing to help me, if I help you?"

He laughed aloud. "A bit of blackmail of your own, Miss Ashworth? If I do this, you'll do that . . . ?" He shook his head, crossing the length of the deep red oriental carpet to where she stood by the globe. "Play your games with someone else. I'm sorry you're betrothed to the odious Lord Rathbone, but it's not my concern. If you—"

"Victor Flynne has visited my father," Veronica cut him off.

Samuel bit back the rest of his words. His chest constricted. "You're a beautiful liar," he muttered harshly.

"I overheard them talking. I didn't see him. They were closeted together in my father's study. They were discussing money." She threw him a glance, half-triumph, half-disgust. "I am not a liar."

"Except when it suits you," he reminded her and she blushed to recall how much she'd confided to him on the several occasions they'd met. He knew her too well.

"Mr. Flynne *was* at my father's house. But he can't be as evil as you seem to think. My father would never consort with a blackmailer. Never."

"Desperate men take desperate measures."

"My father is hardly a desperate man. He and your Mr. Flynne must have been discussing business."

"Business!" Samuel snorted in disgust.

"I'm not making this up!" Veronica glared at him. "Victor Flynne visited my father several weeks ago. They were engaged in a very involved discussion for approximately an hour. I went riding and when I returned, Mr. Flynne had gone."

"What were they discussing?"

"I have no idea."

"Oh, come on, Veronica. You were eavesdropping. You know it was Victor Flynne. Tell me what they talked about."

His tone was a gentle drawl, but Veronica knew sarcasm when she heard it. With an effort, she cast her mind back to that day. She hadn't seen Flynne. She had scarcely been able to hear him, he spoke so quietly. But there was an intensity that had crackled inside the room, nevertheless, and her father, who rarely raised his voice above conversation level, had bellowed something at Flynne.

"My father said, 'My reputation endorses my business,'" Veronica recounted slowly, thinking hard. "'Who I am is as much a part of my income as the profits from my estate. If you don't realize that, Mr. Flynne, you're a fool.'"

"And what was Flynne's response."

Her brow puckered. "I don't recall."

"Do you know what you are, Miss Ashworth? You're an opportunist. If you'd heard I was looking for the finest piece of horseflesh in the country, you'd produce pedigrees on your own stallions and mares to boggle the most jaded buyer. You haven't given me enough, not even to whet my appetite."

He didn't believe her! Veronica was astonished and incensed. "Your Mr. Flynne was at my father's house!" she insisted. She struggled to remember. "Flynne made some comment about being perfectly aware of my father's reputation. How he counted on it. No! How he *banked* on it."

Samuel was listening now. Listening hard.

Veronica regarded him squarely. "You told Uncle Tony you were willing to pay every cent you owned for information on Flynne."

"And . . . ?" His dark eyes assessed her.

She gulped down her own misgivings. "If you offer for me, I'll let you know if your Mr. Flynne has any more dealings with my father. I'll spy for you. I'll spy on my own father for you."

"No."

Frustrated, Veronica sought hard to convince him of the truth. She struggled to remember more of Flynne and her father's conversation. She could almost hear the words. Something about them had rubbed her skin like sandpaper. Her father had been furious. Their conversation was hard as diamonds. The tone of their voices had arrested her, interested her enough to make her want to eavesdrop even though she knew she'd face harsh punishment if her father discovered her lurking outside his door.

"My father made some negative comment on Flynne's own reputation," she remembered, "and then Flynne spoke up clearly. He said, 'I'm thriving, Henry.' I thought that was odd, that an American would call my father by his Christian name. Then he added kind of smugly, 'Just like Portland. Just like always. Are we in agreement?'" Veronica gazed at Samuel. "That's nearly word for word."

Samuel's breath was tight in his lungs. She wasn't making it up. She meant this. He didn't trust Veronica's game playing, but he believed she wouldn't reach to such extreme lengths just because she hoped he might be able to stave off her engagement to Rathbone. There were other methods she could use; other men she could cajole. She'd overheard something. Something damning. He believed that much. And she said she'd heard Flynne's name spoken aloud.

"You're already engaged," he pointed out again.

She brightened. "Unhappily. My father would certainly entertain another offer if he felt it might make me happy."

"But if you break your engagement to Rathbone, won't that be another scandal?"

"Absolutely!" A smile broke across her lovely face. "But I'll make a perfectly horrid scene and ruin any chance for saving face with this proposed marriage to Rathbone anyway. My father knows this. But if he thinks I might accept another man's proposal quietly, even eagerly"—she blushed and cleared her throat—"he might be persuaded to change his mind. As I said before," she rushed on, "it's just a ruse. A way to let my father think he's solved the problem. You can break the engagement later. I'll act inconsolable and the issue will be put to rest."

Silence settled between them. Samuel thought about his brother Jesse's unusual reasons for marrying Kelsey. He'd needed a wife to become accepted into social circles out of his range. He'd needed to be socially accepted because he'd been after revenge on one of Portland's most influential businessmen. He'd needed Kelsey to legitimize him.

Not so different from my situation, Samuel realized. He could use Veronica, and she could use him.

Not so different at all.

But it was trickery. And trickery was Flynne's calling card, not Samuel's.

"Well?" Veronica plumped one fist on her hip and lifted an expectant eyebrow.

Trickery. At war with himself, Samuel dispassionately regarded Lady Veronica Ashworth: a young, vivacious, beautiful, passionate, joyous creature desperate to save herself from a loveless marriage. And was that so wrong? She needed someone younger, a man whom she could love. The one and only time he'd been engaged was to a woman he'd loved: Mary.

But Veronica didn't love *him* and he couldn't possibly

pretend to be in love with her. It was ridiculous. The height of folly. Unthinkable.

"Would you like to help pick out the ring?" he asked her sardonically.

She fought the grin that lightened her sweet mouth and managed demurely, "I'll defer to your superior judgment."

"Like hell," Samuel snorted.

Mirthful amber eyes sparkled up at him.

A match made in heaven. Or a silk-lined hell . . .

Chapter

8

Neville Rathbone had desired Veronica Ashworth since that day in April when he'd noticed she'd begun blossoming into a young woman. Slim and lovely with high, softly mounded breasts, lush, sun-streaked, fawn-colored hair, sculpted cheekbones, and eyes like dark, smoldering topaz —Neville had felt stirrings of lust he'd thought were long dead.

Love at first sight, but a love in vain. There was no way someone as winsome and beautiful as the eldest Ashworth daughter would even look his way. Neville had accepted the truth because there was no alternative. He was too old for her. He was too ugly. She would never have him. He'd hidden his jealousy when other, younger men had shown her attention. He'd died a little each time she rained her smile on some unworthy fop who would only break her heart.

But then, oh, glory, a miracle occurred: Veronica earned the wrath and displeasure of her autocratic, powerful, and miserably upright father, Henry Ashworth, the earl of Charlwood. Neville's fantasies blended with the prospect of reality. He saw himself bedding the lovely Veronica, holding her down against the bedsheets, thrusting into her—her sleek, young legs clasped around him in ecstacy, her thick hair flung wild against the pillows, her face contorted with pure pleasure.

Just the thought of it now brought Neville's mostly flaccid member to attention. He smiled, delighted. He'd been having some trouble in that area just recently, but thoughts of Veronica Ashworth made him feel like a randy stallion.

He had to have her.

Had to have her. . . .

Frowning down at the vellum envelope brought to him by his valet, Neville drew a long breath. It was a summons from the earl himself. A bad omen, this.

"Tell Giles to bring round the coach," he snapped to the valet.

"Yes, m'lord," he murmured with a click of his heels.

Neville ground his teeth. Damn Ashworth. If this was some kind of delay in his plan to marry Veronica . . .

With a growl of frustration, he headed downstairs, waiting impatiently for his groomsmen to bring the coach to the front door. In the drawing room, his gaze wandered toward the collection of firearms mounted on the wall. He was good with a gun. Excellent, in his time. How many years did he have left? It wasn't that he was so old, really, but the passing years had not been kind. Half the time he worried his body would disintegrate before he had his chance with Veronica. The vials of pills his doctor prescribed were growing with each passing season.

Pulling a pistol from the wall, he weighed it in his blue-veined hands. If Ashworth's summons proved to be a negation of his betrothal, would he, Neville Rathbone, have the courage to do something about it?

Would imprisonment be worth the risk of having Veronica?

Envisioning her laughing eyes and luscious body, Neville shuddered.

Maybe it would.

The Ashworth's drawing room wasn't as stifling as some and Samuel stretched his long legs toward the beveled glass table situated in the center of the grouping of couches and chairs. Gold candles and greenery brightened the table; however, nothing could brighten the shocked white faces all staring at him.

"You have audacity," Henry Ashworth clipped out with loathing.

"I'm sorry, Father," Veronica intervened brightly. "I should have told you sooner. Samuel and I . . ." she glanced at him, her eyes shining. Only her trembling lower lip gave away an otherwise marvelous performance. ". . . we didn't realize how much in love we were. We can't bear to be apart." She slipped a shaking palm into Samuel's warm hand.

"You are engaged to Lord Rathbone," Henry reminded her icily, tearing his furious gaze from Samuel's impassive face to glower at his daughter.

"I know. I'm sorry. But I never really wanted that engagement. You know that."

"I don't give a damn whether you want it or not! You're betrothed to Rathbone, and you'll marry him. He's your own class, Veronica!" he hissed.

"He's old and ugly and vile!"

"You've hatched this plan between you. You want to escape and Mr. Danner," he said nastily, "wants your money."

Samuel had taken about all he could take. "If I wanted your money, I certainly would have found an easier way to have it than marrying your daughter."

"There is no easier way."

"There's blackmail."

Dead silence reigned. Madeline and Veronica looked confused. Anthony looked both pained and resigned. Henry was coldly furious. "I don't know what you mean by that remark, Mr. Danner, but if that's some kind of threat, may I remind you that you're a guest here."

"I know exactly what I am," Samuel answered with deceptive softness.

This conversation wasn't proceeding the way Veronica

wanted it to at all. "Please, Father," she said, holding Samuel's hand in a death grip as if she half expected him to bolt from her grasp. "Please respect my feelings. I love Samuel."

He slid her an amused glance, watching the hard swallow she made after that bald lie.

"You are incapable of any deep emotion," Henry said damningly. "You will marry Rathbone. That is all."

"Henry," Madeline interrupted softly. Her husband's already flushed face darkened to brick red. "Perhaps this is an alternative solution. After all, Neville is over twice Veronica's age and she is bound to be widowed very young. You remember the terrible situation Penelope Farrington found herself in. She was miserable after the death of her husband."

Veronica's startled gaze landed on Madeline's face, but Madeline refused to look at her. A bubble of laughter filled Veronica's throat; one she tried desperately to quell. Penelope Farrington had been jubilant upon her husband's death and become the worst scandal in town. She'd taken lovers and spent money wildly and thrown off years of careful breeding to live like a Sybarite. She'd been the name on everyone's tongue; Veronica had heard stories that had made even her blush.

Henry's lips were a white line. Samuel sent her a questioning look, but like Madeline, Veronica didn't trust herself to return his gaze without bursting into laughter.

"The matter is settled," Henry bit out just as Northcroft rapped lightly on the door and announced the arrival of Lord Rathbone.

"I'll see him in the den." Henry turned sharply on his heel.

"I'm planning to marry Veronica with or without your consent," Samuel heard himself say. Henry stiffened in midstride. Samuel had to fight back his own surprise. He hadn't wanted this battle, didn't believe in it. But by God, he wasn't going to let Veronica's bastard of a father dictate her life for her.

"Show Mr. Danner out!" Henry bellowed to Northcroft who looked positively sick at the prospect as Samuel rose to his full height.

"I'm going with him," Veronica declared.

"No, you're not! You're going to your room. Stay there until I order otherwise."

"I've been a prisoner in my room ever since my visit to Uncle Tony's," Veronica responded with spirit. "It hasn't changed how I feel about Samuel, nor will it in the future."

Samuel had to admire her performance. If he didn't know better, he'd half believe her himself.

"Take me with you," she suddenly said, clasping his hand. Automatically Samuel pulled her protectively to his side.

Henry hissed scathingly, "Veronica, if you walk out that door, you are disowned. You will never be allowed inside this house again. You will forsake your family and friends. Think carefully before you make this irrevocable decision."

She quivered beside Samuel, her whole body shaking with emotion. But in a controlled voice, she answered, "This is not my decision, it's yours. You're the one forcing me away. Please, *please,* don't do this. I will never marry Neville. Never! I can't bear the sight of him!"

A cold draft blew into the room. Samuel looked over his right shoulder to see the estimable Lord Rathbone's face turn ashen, then an ugly, contorted purple. Henry was speechless with rage. Veronica stared at Neville, embarrassed but resolved.

But it was Neville who spoke first.

"Lord Ashworth, I regret to inform you that the engagement is off!" he boomed in fury. "Your daughter is unsuitable as a wife."

"Neville, Veronica's angry at me, not you," Henry tried to appease.

"Nevertheless, I withdraw my offer. Good day."

He left in impotent fury. Something niggled at the back of Samuel's mind. An uneasy warning. But his attention was snapped back to the situation at hand as Henry snarled, "Scandalous bitch! You've won your engagement. Go marry your American and get out of my sight!"

He slammed out of the room with Northcroft scuttling after him.

Stormy silence followed. Veronica collapsed onto the settee. "My God," she said cradling her head in her hands.

"It will be all right," Madeline assured her, though her eyes were clouded with worry. "He's given you permission to marry Mr. Danner." With grace and a natural ability to smooth over the most awkward moment, Lady Madeline Ashworth extended her delicate hand to Samuel Danner. "Welcome to the family . . ."

"You should have never agreed to Veronica's harebrained plan!" Anthony raged, wearing a path in the carpet of his den. His blond hair nearly stuck on end, an unusual state for the normally elegant younger Ashworth brother. Samuel was silent. Anthony wasn't telling him anything he didn't already know. "Now look at the mess we're in!"

"We're in?" Samuel asked, swirling his brandy.

"Yes, my friend. *We're* in. I, too, have been added to Henry's enemy list because of my association with you. And though my brother and I rarely see eye-to-eye on anything, we are forced into this association by virtue of our birthright."

Samuel looked up from the amber depths of his drink. "According to Veronica, you've chosen your own methods to infuriate Henry."

"But this is different! This is *Veronica!* Do you have any idea what will happen to her when you throw her over? She'll be a laughingstock, a pariah. No suitable man will offer for her. Ever!"

"And Neville Rathbone was suitable?" Samuel shot back.

"Of course not. But she could have found a way out of that ridiculous engagement if you hadn't interfered. Excuse me," he added sarcastically, to Samuel's darkening expression, "it's all Veronica's fault she's in this horrid predicament, I know. Don't you give a damn what happens to her, man?"

"Yes," Samuel hissed.

"Then what do you propose to do?"

"I'm going to play out this charade until I find Flynne."

"You bastard."

Samuel glared at Anthony and deliberately set down his drink. "If you think Veronica's any happier living under her father's roof, abiding by his self-motivated dictates, being a lovely, useless ornament meant for sale than by being engaged to me, go change her mind. Tell her what a bastard I am. Then see if you can talk her into marrying Rathbone after all. You can smooth things over with good old Neville. He was just saving his dignity today. He *wants* Veronica. In the worst way. I felt it while he was there. He'll hurt her. Really hurt her, if he gets the chance."

"And what does that make you?" Anthony asked scathingly. "Her savior?"

"She chose me as her way out. I don't like it either. But I'd walk through the depths of hell to get Flynne. So, don't tell me what to do."

Samuel was on his feet. A tall, glowering, dark man who radiated purpose and determination. Anthony Ashworth couldn't help feeling that same power and trust he'd encountered when Samuel had first shown up in London. Deciding it was time for diplomacy, he said, "Veronica's my favorite niece. She reminds me of—" He cut himself off, remembering a pair of blue eyes in place of Veronica's gold ones. But the impish smile was the same, as was the irrepressible impulsiveness and basic joy for life.

"It's time to do something besides waste time," Samuel said, standing by the window. "Now that my betrothal has been accepted by Henry," he added sardonically, "I'm going to be spending some of my time with Veronica. Hopefully, she'll remember more about Flynne's association with Henry."

"They can't know each other. It's impossible."

"Improbable. Not impossible. As soon as Flynne's mine, Veronica's free of me. She can break the engagement. I'm not good enough for her anyway," Samuel said without rancor. "All she has to do is point out what a dreadful mistake it was getting involved with an American and she'll be right back in the arms of Society."

Anthony stared at him. "You're going to break her heart," he predicted.

The newspapers had a field day with Lady Veronica Ashworth's latest exploits. Veronica stole a look at one of the evening editions and felt a shiver of apprehension when she read the headline: EARL OF CHARLWOOD'S ELDEST TRADES ONE BETROTHAL FOR ANOTHER.

The story went on to detail how the wealthy Lord Rathbone had been tossed aside for the younger, more handsome, nameless rogue from the Oregon frontier. Though it was written carefully, the article had a vaguely sexual slant that Veronica only glimmered. But even she could see it was painfully obvious the gist of the story was how she'd preferred the more physically desirable Mr. Danner no matter how lowly his origins.

The article made her feel soiled and dirty.

"Your father is furious," Northcroft declared haughtily, sneaking up behind Veronica. Malicious joy brightened his beady eyes for he was glad this naughty child was finally getting the punishment she deserved.

Veronica leveled him with one look. "Yes, I believe he is."

Northcroft strode away, spine stiff.

"I certainly shan't miss *him* when I leave," she muttered to herself. *When I leave.* The thought hit her with an almost physical blow. When I leave where? she wondered half-hysterically. Since her betrothal to Samuel, she was expected to be making some sort of preparations but it was all such a grand farce that she scarcely knew what to do. She was not looking forward to her father's fury when he learned she had no intention of marrying Samuel and that Samuel had no intention of marrying her.

But that was in the future. For now, she'd bought herself some time—as long as her father continued to believe she and Samuel were truly serious about each other. To that end, she was going to have to make a very convincing display of love and yes, passion.

In her room, Veronica changed for bed, then hesitated,

staring through the window. The sky was dead black and clouds covered what little moon there might have been. The scene did little to brighten her mood. Tomorrow was Saturday. If Samuel didn't come to see her, she was going to have to call on him. The society column would only convince her father so far; Samuel had to appear extremely interested. Since that terrible scene in the withdrawing room, Samuel hadn't been to see her once.

Flopping onto the bed, Veronica's fertile mind developed plan after plan, only to discard each and every one. Frustrated and afraid this charade would never work, she finally hit on a solution, but one so daring that her mind shied away several times before she allowed herself to truly consider it.

Samuel would never be able to play this game. It was impossible for him. He was only helping her because he needed help in return. And yes, she would help him if she could. But it still wouldn't be enough to convince her enraged father that theirs was a love match. Not if Samuel didn't respond correctly.

He needed to truly court her. Lavish her with attention. Take her riding, to the opera, send her flowers . . .

What would he be like if he were truly courting her?

Veronica concentrated hard on that vision. She could see his handsome face, the lurking, sensual smile, hear the dry tone of his voice deepen with passion, feel his hard fingers grasping her arms as he pulled her against his strong, masculine body.

Suddenly her skin was aflame, a wave of some unnamed emotion sliding over her from head to toe. Veronica jumped up, shocked by her reaction. "You goose," she said, aloud, annoyed.

Clasping her hands, she paced off the dimensions of her room. Thoughts of Samuel had given her another idea. What if she could make him want her? Really *want* her? The way everyone seemed to think Neville Rathbone wanted her. What if she could make him fall in love with her? Just a little. Just enough to convince her blasted father that he truly desired her for a wife.

Would it be so hard? Impossible?

SCANDAL'S DARLING

She wasn't unattractive; not beautiful, she knew, but not quite the Drab Brown she'd been accused of either. Perhaps, if she used some feminine wiles—she could pick Amelia St. John's shallow little brain for some ideas along those lines—maybe she could win a piece of Samuel Danner's heart.

Chapter
9

Veronica fisted one gloved hand inside her cloak. In the cold light of day her plan seemed extremely daunting, to say the least. As the carriage rattled across the cobblestone streets she lifted her shoulders inside her fawn-colored jacket, attempting to ease the tension, then plucked anxiously at the bow tight against her throat. *Damn and glory,* she thought angrily. Subterfuge was not her way, but there wasn't any other choice. She couldn't announce to Samuel that she planned to make him fall in love with her.

"Oh, it's all too silly for words," she muttered as the carriage pulled to a stop in front of Uncle Tony's gate.

"You can return to my father's," Veronica told the driver with forced gaiety. "My fiancé will bring me home."

"As you wish, Lady Veronica."

She waved him away, then passed through the well-oiled wrought-iron gate and hurried up the steps to the front door. Hodgson swept open the door before Veronica could even knock. Her hand was still raised when Samuel himself stood on the stoop, his dark brows lifting in surprise.

"Well, hullo, Veronica," he drawled, the sound shooting feather light fingers of delight up her arms.

"Hello . . . Samuel. Are you going out? I . . . wanted to see you."

"I've got an appointment I can't miss."

"With whom?" she blurted out.

Hodgson attempted to hide his dismay and at a look from Veronica, disappeared into the house leaving Veronica and Samuel alone on the steps on this bright, breath-freezing February morning.

"I'm meeting Anthony at his club for lunch."

"But it's too early," she protested. "Couldn't you spare me a few moments?"

Samuel, who was about to make the acquaintance of Anthony's "friend," Thomas Houghton, who'd first delivered information about Flynne, frowned at his lovely "bride-to-be." "How about this afternoon? I'll be back about—"

"No. No, I sent my driver home." Her mind whirled rapidly. She didn't dare ask to be included; a woman was never allowed inside the men's clubs. "We need to spend some time together," she explained. "If we're going to be engaged, we have to at least try to act like we're happy about it. Otherwise my father will know it's a farce!"

"He's granted his consent and all of London knows about it." Samuel was brusque.

"It's not enough. Please . . ." She laid one delicate, gloved hand on his forearm and gazed into his eyes with what she hoped was a melting glance.

Samuel's eyes met hers but in their liquid brown depths was no hint to his true feelings. Could he see she was a fraud? Oh, Lord, she shriveled at the thought! Unable to hold his gaze a moment longer, she pulled back her hand, embarrassed.

"Veronica, I've got an important meeting before lunch that I'm unwilling to miss. Could we talk about this later?"

She nodded. "All right. But wait . . ." He'd brushed past her and stood on the brick pathway that led through the gate to the street, staring at her with barely concealed impatience. "Three days from now, there's another party. A friend of my father's. We need to attend together."

"Veronica . . ." he sighed.

"You need to take me out. Show me off. It's what my father expects after our unconventional engagement."

"I'm afraid I'm not that much of an actor. Leave it be. Enough damage has been done and I'm no closer to Flynne!"

She seized on his frustration. "Yes, you are! Father's got a business meeting next week. I don't know what it's about, but I'm almost positive he said one of the men's names was 'Victor.'"

Despite Veronica's assurances that Flynne was a regular visitor to her father, Samuel had his doubts. Anthony had assured him morning, noon, and night that Lord Henry Ashworth would never associate with the likes of a blackmailer. If Anthony were right, and Samuel tended to believe him over his undeniably beautiful but self-serving niece, then his "engagement" to Veronica was a waste of time and any moment spent with her was a diversion from his goal: Victor.

"Someone named Victor is visiting your father next week." He didn't bother hiding his skepticism.

She nodded eagerly.

"You are lying," he said softly.

"I'm telling the truth," she argued.

He strode back to her in ground-devouring strides, the black suit Tony had lent him making him seem more alien and dangerous somehow.

"Do you seriously expect me to believe that just because you've wrangled me into this messy engagement, that fortune has smiled on me and suddenly Victor Flynne is delivered to my door?" He towered over her. "I'm not gullible, Veronica. I'm just desperate."

She swallowed. "I did hear the name Victor. But . . . it could be Victor Reardon. He's a banker friend of my father's."

"My God." He shook his head. She couldn't tell whether he was amused or furious.

"But that doesn't mean your Victor won't show up. I *know* he's been at the house. I know he has. I just want you to . . . take me to the party . . . and spend some time with me," she finished lamely, blushing a deep red. She was no good at this. She was downright inept.

Samuel stared down at her and the moment spun out endlessly. She couldn't breathe. The bow was choking her. When he finally spoke she visibly jumped.

"All right, I'll take you to the party."

Veronica smiled in relief. Never one to back away from a challenge, she asked in a small voice, "And could I see you this afternoon? We could go riding . . . or something else . . ."

"I'll pick you up around three," he said by way of acknowlegment. "Now, can I drop you at your father's?"

She nodded, hurrying after him as Gaines brought a carriage around from the back. "I promise I won't embarrass you. I do know how to ride."

"Fine." Samuel was short. "And Veronica . . ." He clasped her hand and helped her up the carriage step.

She smiled at him eagerly.

"He's not *my* Victor Flynne. The man I'm after is a ruthless, avaricious blackmailer. In the future, please bear that in mind."

"Damn Samuel Danner to hell," Victor Flynne muttered quietly, crumpling the morning edition into a thick ball and throwing it onto the fire where it burst into violent red flames that instantly withered to a black lump whose ends pulsed like a heartbeat.

Victor watched in contemplative silence, his face set, only the shadow of a smile touching his lips. He'd struck blows at all the Danners—puny, impotent attempts that had done little damage and instead sent Victor scurrying across the Atlantic, his tail firmly tucked between his legs.

But now he had an opportunity—a *golden* opportunity— to reverse that terrible history by eliminating the youngest Danner and salvaging what was left of his tattered self-respect.

The glory of it. Victor sank back into the chair of his modest but respectable London home. It was no grand manor; it wasn't even a single residence. These rooms were let to the top echelon of the working class, and that's all he was. The working class.

But Victor had plans. Big plans. He loathed London with a consuming passion, hating the smokestacks and filthy water and cold, gray streets. It was the one thing he had in common with Samuel, had he but known it, this dislike for the glorious city they'd both ended up in. But if Victor's plans came to fruition, he would be on the first boat back home. All he needed was money. Lots and lots of money. Dirty money was fine. *Any* money.

And Samuel Danner's head.

How unbelievably rich it was: The two were happening together. The fates were certainly smiling upon him. With the aid of one unwitting accomplice—the tempting and impossibly naive Lady Veronica Elizabeth Ashworth—both wealth and Samuel Danner's miserable life were within Victor's reach.

Glorious, glorious day.

Chuckling, Victor poured himself a brandy, enjoying the liquid in small, throat-burning gulps as he savored the victory soon to be. This very evening Samuel would be meeting an "associate" of Victor's, one who would set the wheels in motion.

For weeks Victor had been hearing tales of the handsome Yank who'd been questioning all and sundry about one blackmailer and murder. He'd been worried at first. Afraid Samuel would unravel his carefully woven tapestry of blackmail amongst London's exalted aristocracy.

But then—incredible luck—Samuel had crossed paths with Lady Veronica—Lord Ashworth's scandalous firstborn—and somehow got himself betrothed to the lovely decoy.

What sweet, delicious irony! Lord *Henry* Ashworth's daughter. Lord Henry Ashworth, whose soul was as worm-riddled as the blackest, most rotten apple.

Smiling to himself, Victor's restless stare followed the flickering ashes of the dying fire. Lord Ashworth was

Victor's latest marionette. Pulling Ashworth's strings was almost too easy. The man was a born pigeon: rich, consumed with his reputation and good name, blindly dictatorial, weak. And possessed of a very dirty past.

The perfect man to drag Victor out of the depths of his own private Danner-imposed hell. The perfect man, albeit unwittingly, to help destroy the youngest Danner.

The Danners. Victor's lips curled. That family's combined efforts had toppled him from his own lofty tower. Because of those devil-spawned Danners, Victor knew more about desperation and poverty than any decent man should.

And God knew he was a decent man.

A roar of laughter filled the room. Victor rocked in his chair with wicked mirth.

Yes, the wheels were in motion.

The Honorable Anthony Ashworth's club was richly paneled, heavily carpeted and draped, filled with leather chairs studded in brass. Samuel was allowed entry only because Anthony had given him his card and had informed the management that he was expecting an American guest.

Even so, as he climbed the steps to the upper landing, Samuel felt the interested, calculating stares of other members, men who knew each other well, who'd known each other's families for generations, who judged a man by his wealth and place in society.

Samuel shook his head. He'd thought Portland society was closed and narrow. This was something else again.

In the dining room Anthony was seated at a table near the back, away from the gorgeous view of the small park in the rear, tucked in an alcove where small brass-shaded lamps threw spots of light on a polished tabletop. The man beside him sported a round girth, but if he was worried about his weight it wasn't readily apparent. He drank claret as if it were water, or possibly a life-giving balm; he poured it down his gullet.

Anthony was seated against the leather cushions, looking slightly bored and amused. Houghton wasn't a close friend of his; Houghton wasn't a close friend of anyone's, if Samuel had read correctly between the lines. He was merely tolerated because his bloodlines were outrageously pure.

Which probably accounted for his raging stupidity, Samuel decided.

For Houghton was stupid. According to Anthony, he continually spurted delicate information. If Houghton learned of an indiscretion or shady business dealing, it was front page news within the hour.

"Samuel Danner, Thomas Houghton," Anthony introduced. "Tom, this is the man I was telling you about."

"From the States, eh?" Houghton poured another claret and offered Samuel some snuff. Samuel declined and Houghton stuck some inside his gums, sucking on it and regarding Samuel uneasily. "Looking for a man, what? A Mr. Flynne?"

"Yes."

"It's purely a money problem," Anthony inserted. "You know how these things develop. Mr. Danner would like to meet with Mr. Flynne and straighten the situation out equitably for all parties concerned."

A load of lies and blarney. Samuel was impressed at Anthony's attempt to keep things "civilized." But all he wanted to do was choke the life from Flynne.

Houghton sucked on his lip. "Why would you think I could help you?"

"Because the last time we spoke, you told me if I wanted to know about Flynne, I should ask my brother," Anthony reminded him.

"I don't remember." Houghton scowled.

"It was that night at Harrentons."

And you were drunk as a toad, Samuel thought to himself silently. Houghton apparently remembered because his expression changed. He left to spit out his snuff in the spitoon by the door, then returned just as luncheon was served, a richly stuffed roasted goose, surrounded by vegetables, fruit, and draped with a sweet-smelling sauce. Houghton tucked into the food with all the delicacy of a stevedore.

"I remember now," he said around a mouthful. "Put the

bite on old Danley, amongst others. Thought he'd done the same to your brother, but I was wrong."

"Who's Danley?" Samuel asked.

Anthony's breath hissed between his teeth. "A silly fool," he said in a strange tone. "Can you remember any other names of Flynne's victims?"

"Sorry," Houghton mumbled.

"Where can we find Danley?" Samuel asked.

There was silence at the table, then Anthony enlightened him. "Danley's dead. Died in his sleep from an overdose of sleeping tablets about three weeks ago. The poor fellow was wallowing in debt. Some think he killed himself."

"Why was he wallowing in debt?"

"Unofficially? There were half a dozen huge bank withdrawals. Cleaned out his account."

"Blackmail," Samuel said tersely.

Houghton made a strangled sound, as if he couldn't even hear the word. "There's a man you could see. Mr. Dirkson. He'll help you."

The information seemed torn from him. Staring into Houghton's alcohol-bleared eyes Samuel wondered if Victor were perhaps putting the bite on him, too.

Time would tell.

"Good afternoon, Lady Ashworth," a voice from a lavish carriage said as Veronica sat atop Tinsel. The voice was familiar. Neville Rathbone.

Veronica glanced behind her where Samuel, in denim and cowboy boots, sat astride one of Uncle Tony's geldings. No English saddle for him. After swearing succinctly, he'd rid himself of the offending article and now sat on the horse bareback.

"Er, good afternoon," she murmured, wishing Samuel would end his conversation with Uncle Tony and join her. The two men had been involved in a heated debate from the moment they'd returned from the club. Veronica could have been wallpaper for all they noticed her and when she'd tried to involve herself in the topic, they'd made it clear she wasn't welcome.

"You look lovely, my dear. Lovelier than anyone here."

Ladies' Mile was where all the fashionably dressed, elegant women rode when the weather was nice. However, being that it was February, only the avid enthusiasts were out and Veronica was amongst real horse people, not the ton. She wasn't afraid of looking a fool, however; she could ride with the best of them.

But what was Neville doing here? The curtains across his carriage windows were nearly drawn. She could barely make out his face within, the bright sunlight was so blinding.

"I'm sorry things turned out the way they did between us," he went on. "I understand you're engaged to Mr. Danner."

"That's correct." And she fervently wished her intended would pay her some more attention.

"Would it be inappropriate for me to ask that we take that carriage ride sometime soon. The one I suggested last week?"

"You still want to?" Veronica asked, amazed.

"It would certainly stifle the rumors about you and your new fiancé," Neville pointed out. "An amicable parting to what could have only been a mistake for both of us. Wouldn't you like that?"

"Um . . . yes. I suppose so."

"Then I'll call for you soon." The carriage began moving away. "That color becomes you, my dear."

Veronica's heart beat fast. She couldn't contain her relief to see Neville's carriage pull away and out of sight just as Samuel and Uncle Tony joined her. She wanted to throw herself in Samuel's arms and draw from his strength and protection. Silly goose, she thought in surprise. Whatever's the matter with you?

"Care for a race?" Samuel asked, his dark gaze skating over her deep gold and blue habit and high-crowned riding hat, sidesaddle, and general air of gentility.

Veronica swallowed a smile. She could read his mind. He thought she was no horsewoman at all.

Well . . .

A touch of the riding crop and Tinsel was galloping down

the path, bit in her teeth. Veronica's hat snapped at the chin strap, her shining hair billowing in a cloud behind her. She laughed aloud, but Samuel streaked by. She cried out in surprise. The gelding wasn't fast. How could he burst past her that way?

When she reached him Tinsel was blowing heavily. Samuel suddenly threw back his head and laughed.

Veronica wanted to kill him.

"You look furious." He chuckled.

"I am. You had no right to be so reckless."

"Me?" His jaw dropped, then he spied the lurking dimples as she fought to hide a smile.

To Veronica's delight and surprise, he slid off his horse and pulled her down from Tinsel. For a split second she was in his arms before he stepped back, grinning like a devil. "You can ride," he said with admiration. "Even on that infernal thing."

"Don't you have sidesaddles in America?"

"Only if we have to. Don't mention them to my sister."

"You have a sister?" Veronica seized on this personal information. "Any brothers?"

"Three of them."

"And they all live in . . . Portland?"

"Well, Jesse lives in Portland. The other two are in Rock Springs, my hometown, which is about thirty miles from there. You lost your hat," he added, amused.

"And I've retrieved it," Uncle Tony said in a quelling voice as he trotted up. Sliding to the ground, he handed Veronica the dirt-stained article. "You are both certifiably mad. This isn't a racetrack. Let's rejoin civilization for tea at my house."

Veronica would have liked the moments alone with Samuel to continue but she had no choice since Uncle Tony seemed to consider himself their only suitable chaperon. She couldn't understand it. Uncle Tony, who had always been on her side, seemed to disapprove mightily of Samuel, yet it was clear he admired, respected, and even liked him.

It was a mystery, one Samuel seemed to understand, however. As they returned to Anthony's, she shot sideways glances in Samuel's direction, adoring the hard lines of his face, the lines of humor beside his eyes, the aura of strength, determination, and control he emitted without being aware of it.

Adoring?

She caught herself up short. Good heavens. She didn't adore anyone.

At that moment a round matron who was precariously plopped upon a sway-backed pony glared at Samuel in alarm. "Howdy, ma'am," he said in greeting, nearly toppling her from her perch. Veronica laughed aloud. He grinned at her and her heart soared.

Unfortunately, the afternoon deteriorated from that point. Once back at Uncle Tony's, it was as if Samuel had forgotten her existence. He grew more and more distracted as the evening wore on. Veronica was depressed. What was it going to take to get him to notice her? She would never gain his attention if this were to go on.

"How was your meeting this morning?" she asked.

"Victor's definitely here in London," Samuel answered.

She thought about her strange conversation with Neville, but seeing the tight slant of Samuel's mouth, she knew he wouldn't be interested in any of her own problems.

"Are you certain you don't want me with you?" Uncle Tony said to him.

"I'm going alone."

"Where are you going?" Veronica inquired. When neither man answered, she asked, "Is it dangerous?"

"Veronica, keep your lovely nose in your own business," Uncle Tony said with a smile.

"It *is* my business. Samuel's my fiancé."

Samuel made a strangled sound. Uncle Tony heaved a sigh.

"Well, he is," she stated firmly. "At least for now. He's promised to help me. You've both promised to help me."

"And we shall," Uncle Tony soothed, but his patronizing tone was too much.

"Maybe it would have been better if I'd let myself marry

Lord Rathbone. I wouldn't have had to beg him to spend time in my company."

"Why don't I take you home?" Samuel suggested. "Is your father in town?" At her curt nod, he added, "If he sees us together, will that please you?"

Blast the man. Couldn't he care enough to *want* to be in her company? Couldn't he gaze at her fondly, maybe even passionately, like he wanted to kiss her so badly that it took every ounce of willpower to keep from dragging her into his arms?

"Well?"

"I realize it is a great deal of trouble for you, Mr. Danner, but I'd like this charade to continue a few more weeks, if you wouldn't mind. I understand that being a man, you have much more important things to do—" her sarcasm was heavy—"that I, being a mere woman, couldn't possibly comprehend. However, we have a common goal, at least for the moment. Try very hard to keep that in mind while you plan your very important mission against Mr. Victor Flynne."

"I'll take that as a yes," Samuel said dryly, following Veronica's stiff spine outside.

She spoke not a word on the way home and at the gate to her own home, swept out of the carriage in a glorious fury. Her cloak snagged on the door, however, slightly ruining the effect, but the icy glare she sent Samuel kept the smile that threatened the corners of his mouth from becoming an out-and-out grin.

At the door he touched her arm. "What do you want me to do? To keep your father believing we're desperately in love?"

"Pay more attention to me. Try to act as if you want to be with me," she said immediately.

"We're here together now."

"That's true. But it's not enough."

He waited, and Veronica screwed up her courage to tell him what she really wanted to say. After all, it wasn't like she loved him. "Earlier today, I would have suggested you kiss me when one of the servants or my sisters was watching so that my father would be sure to hear the gossip whether he wanted to or not."

Samuel couldn't contain his grin now. All day he'd been uneasy and tense. He wasn't sure yet whether tonight's meeting was a setup or not. Veronica had been both an annoyance and a respite from the hours of waiting.

Looking down at the pout of her lips and gold fire in her eyes, he concentrated on something beside Flynne for the first time in hours. "And now?"

"Now I wouldn't kiss you even if Father offered me my freedom!"

"Wouldn't you?"

His arrogance astounded her. "No, I wouldn't."

"Why, Lady Veronica, that sounds a lot like a challenge."

In dawning horror, she froze as Samuel slid his hands around her upper arms, yanked her against his hard chest, and kissed her full on the mouth.

Veronica muffled a shriek. She tried to pull back but his hands were iron manacles. She stiffened in shock. His lips, hot against hers, curved into that infuriating grin she was beginning to both love and hate. She struggled impotently, torn between the desire to slap his handsome face and the very real danger of coming to enjoy the sensation of his mouth pressed against hers. Oh, she'd been kissed before. Once by a boy scarcely older than herself who'd missed her lips and sloppily smacked the side of her cheek, leaving a disgusting wet trail on her cheek. Then there was that infamous time with Geoffrey Rowbury, though she'd scarcely felt his lips because she'd been battling some very determined hands.

The last time she'd been kissed was when a sophisticated older gentleman had backed her into a corner alcove and pressed his lips to hers in what she could only describe as a snarl. Her mouth had been mashed against his teeth and she'd been so disgusted she'd felt like retching. Luckily, she'd managed to keep that embarrassing reaction back, but the bubble of laughter that had emerged instead had infuriated him to the point of his sending out another scandalous rumor about her: She was so inept she hiccuped when kissed.

But this . . .

She stopped struggling, instinctively sensing that her efforts to extricate herself, after practically demanding he kiss her, would only prolong the moment. Samuel, for his own perverse reasons, seemed to now be giving her all the attention she'd ordered and then some. Despite a need to remain cool and furious, her heart began to flutter like some anxious caged bird, and she found herself concentrating on the incredible combination of softened lips and hardened kiss and the taste and texture of a man.

So, this was what kissing was all about. This was why women swooned and why men enjoyed it equally as well. Veronica's own mouth softened, parted, half-amazement, half-pleasure. She loved the way he smelled, the taste of his mouth devouring hers, the convulsive grip of his hands as he crushed her to his chest.

Her head reeled. Instinctively, she clutched his shirt. Her heart thumped wildly. This was nothing like Geoffrey Rowbury or any of her other fumbling swains. Her senses quickened, turned to fire. She suddenly wanted to feel his weight pressing her to the wall, wanted to feel his body hungry and demanding for hers.

These thoughts circled her head in dizzy succession, but almost as soon as she relaxed and gave herself up to the moment, Samuel slowly pulled back. She stared at him, dazed. His dark, almost black eyes, regarded her with friendly amusement and something else. Something she desperately wanted to explore further.

Looking down, she saw her hands were still clutched in the fabric of his shirt. With a choked moan, she unclenched them, amazed and horror-struck.

"Think anyone was looking?" he asked, glancing at the ground floor windows.

"Looking? I . . . I hope not." Her voice was thin and shaky. She cleared her throat.

"You hope not?"

"I . . . well, this wasn't what I wanted."

"You asked me to kiss you."

"I asked you *not* to kiss me! I distinctly said that I had no wish to—"

"Oh, for god's sakes," he muttered and to Veronica's shock he pulled her into his arms again, this time bending her over his arm until her head lolled back, then kissing her with such raw abandon and desire that she went limp in the space of two seconds.

She clutched his shoulders frantically for support, tiny frightened sounds like bird chirps squeaked past her lips. Yet her mouth softened willingly and somehow her lips parted and Samuel's kiss, born of frustration, turned to something else. She knew the moment of change, felt it in the pressure of his surrounding embrace, heard it in the break in his breathing. One hand slid down her back to the curve of her spine, drawing her closer; the other hand balanced her, holding her prisoner, making certain there was no escape.

Veronica was too overwhelmed to want anything but his searing kiss. She moaned in wanton surrender. For an intense moment she forgot everything: where she was, whom she was with, what she was really doing. She wanted the kiss to go on and on. Then suddenly his mouth wasn't punishing hers, it was plundering her throat, kissing the line of her jaw, the fluttering pulse at the base of her throat. Her senses reeled. Her hand drifted over his chest, feeling the hard thump of his heart.

Just as suddenly she was swaying on her feet, planted upright, his hands holding her at arm's length. Veronica blinked and Samuel gazed down at her through dark, knowing eyes that seemed to mirror her own growing alarm.

"Good night, Veronica," he said, turning on his heel.

"Saturday . . . the party . . ." she blurted after him.

"I promise I'll behave."

He left without another good-bye and Veronica, shaken, pondered that remark as she entered the house. Her lips trembled and she searchingly touched her mouth where the heat of his possession still lingered.

Giggles erupted from the stairway. Patrice's hands were

pressed against her cheeks, her eyes filled with scandal and excitement.

"Breathe a word of this to Father and I'll slip a leech in your bathwater," Veronica direly informed her youngest sister.

"I thought he was going to ravage you right there!"

"Shows what you know about men."

Her youngest sister arched one brow and not for the first time Veronica wondered if both her siblings might know something about the opposite sex that she seemed to have missed.

But what Patrice didn't know was that she'd witnessed a carefully orchestrated scene designed to unlock the jaws of the most reluctant gossip. And Patrice wasn't reluctant with her tongue. She would spread the word as quickly and thoroughly as any town crier and by nightfall Henry Ashworth would realize Veronica's was a love match.

Love match . . .

Once more she touched her finger to her lips, wincing a little as she remembered her own culpability. Kissing Samuel had felt *good!*

"Damn and glory," she muttered, hitching up her skirt and climbing the stairs.

Chapter

10

Hullo, guvnah. How 'bout some suds, then?"

Samuel sized up the hunkering soul seated opposite him from the top of his dirty silver hair, down the front of his soiled shirt and trousers—which looked to be ten years old and at least that long since they'd been washed—to the toes of his hole-worn boots.

"Mr. Dirkson?" Samuel inquired evenly, silently lifting two fingers to the barmaid in response to the man's request.

The man belched out a laugh and slid into the booth opposite him. Even for the Swan's dubious clientele, Mr. Dirkson was a rung down the ladder. Rubbing a hand over his beard, the man wiped away a bit of food tucked inside the bristles. He then fixed Samuel with keen eyes.

"You been lookin' for Mr. Flynne some time now, eh? And y'come to ol'Dirk."

"I was given your name and this address."

"My, my, y'sound like a cowboy, don'cha?" He chortled as the barmaid, virulently blond and wide as a battleship at the hips, thumped two pints on the table. She snapped a towel at the grimy top, as if she were swatting a fly, then grunted in satisfaction at her cleanup attempt.

The Swan was a first-class dining establishment.

Samuel waited as Dirkson slurped and burped through the pint. He slid his own untouched glass across the table to the man who snagged it with one beefy hand, delighted by Samuel's generosity.

"Flynne knows yer lookin' fer 'im."

"I'm not surprised. I haven't made a secret of it."

"'E'd pay plenty to know you're 'ere at the Swan alone with me."

"But you're betting I'll pay more," Samuel finished dryly.

"I like them boots y'got, guvnah."

Samuel glanced down at his dusty, beaten leather cowboy boots. It hadn't taken much deduction on his part to realize his best "Society" clothes wouldn't be needed at the Swan. He'd dropped them in favor of breeches, boots, and a return to farmwear. "They're yours for Victor's address," he said evenly.

"Oh, whoa there, cowboy! I don't like 'em that much! That information's gonna cost plenty more."

"I don't believe you know where Victor is."

Dirkson laughed. "Oh, I know. And I'm gonna tell ya, too. But we gotta settle on a price first."

"What is it you want?"

"Five hundred pounds."

Samuel leaned across the table until his face was mere inches from Dirkson's. "If I had that kind of money, I'd pay a more respectable source."

Dirkson licked his lips, slightly put off by Samuel's unwavering, intense expression. "Yer bargainin' me, ain't ya, guv?"

"Good day, Mr. Dirkson."

Dirkson's mouth dropped open as Samuel strolled out of the Swan. He hadn't been able to bribe the blighter at all.

Samuel's departure drew interested looks from the customers who weren't used to seeing denim and boots or hearing a western accent, especially one wrapped around such proper English. But Dirk, who'd already met Victor Flynne, wasn't as distracted by Samuel's personna.

Dirk shuddered. Gawd, if the man didn't frighten him

more than even Flynne, and that were saying a lot! Flynne was a scoundrel, that were sure. The bleedin' crook knew how to weasel information, all right. Hadn't he read ol' Dirk a list of misdeeds upon their first meeting? And hadn't he, Dirk, then had to promise this meeting with one Samuel Danner, a Yank with a grudge as big as the Americas, just to stay out of the rozzer's hands?

Dirk snorted, dolefully eyeing his empty mug. It sure had seemed easy—meeting Danner. And if it made Victor bleedin' Flynne happy, so much the better. The man was as slimy as the banks of the Thames and just as slippery, and Dirk was willing to do about anything to get the leech off him.

But now . . .

With a shrug, Dirk grabbed his hat and plopped it on his head. With a glance at the change Samuel had left, he quickly pocketed the shilling meant for a tip. The blonde glared as he passed but he winked at her and slapped her sumptuous behind. He knew how to treat women.

But he didn't know how to treat Flynne. Uneasiness filled his rather unimaginative mind. Flynne wasn't going to like how the interview with Danner had gone.

Saturday night Veronica spent extra care with her appearance, suffering through Lily's efforts to curl her hair and help dress her with only a few minor moments of irritation. What a fuss! And now she was nearly late.

"Thank you, Lily," Veronica dismissed the maid. She walked to the center of the room, adjusted the cheval mirror and gazed critically at her reflection. A nice figure but a rather unremarkable face.

She grimaced at herself. "Ugh."

There was a quick knock, then Chloe entered the room, looking fresh and bright in a spring green gown. Veronica sent another dubious look at her reflection. She wore pale lilac. Did she look too washed-out? Against Chloe's brilliance, she felt like a shadow.

"You look marvelous!" Chloe enthused. "I can't wait to

go! Do you know who's on the guest list? The duke of Westbourne!"

"Isn't he married?"

"Yes, but his eldest son is very much available!"

"And a rake and a womanizer of the worst kind, if you can believe all the rumors."

"Well, men have different needs than women," Chloe professed wisely. "Especially gentlemen. A good wife knows these things."

Veronica frowned at her sister. "What do you mean?"

"Oh, Veronica, don't play ignorant with me!"

"Are you saying you would be willing to overlook your husband's indiscretions because *men* have different needs than women?"

Chloe fluffed at her skirts. "Do you know any gentleman who doesn't have his . . . secrets?"

Veronica was shocked. "I wouldn't condone it! Not from my husband. I'd leave him if he exercised his *needs* with some other woman!"

"Do you think American men are so different from English?"

"No . . . yes . . ." Veronica was irritated to be drawn into this conversation. "If Samuel wanted another woman, he would have asked her to marry him, not me."

Please God, don't strike me down for this blasphemy, she prayed silently.

"Patrice told me about what happened on the front stoop." Chloe clucked her tongue like an old hen. "And Madeline told Father."

"And?"

"Everyone's thinking of moving up the wedding date. Madeline's going to talk to you about it this evening." Misinterpreting Veronica's stricken look, Chloe added smugly, "You're not the only one who can eavesdrop. I've heard a few things about your Mr. Danner, too."

"Move up the wedding?" Veronica repeated faintly. Then, "What things?" as Chloe's last comment penetrated.

"Oh . . . well . . . Father said, 'Better join them in matrimony before Veronica gives him what he wants and he changes his mind altogether.' "

She was stunned. Utterly speechless that her father would voice such a condemning opinion of her.

"There was talk of moving the wedding to March," Chloe added. With a sweep of skirts she sailed from the room, leaving Veronica with a hopeless, empty feeling.

Samuel had suffered with Anthony's wardrobe long enough to convince both him and Anthony that he needed his own suits. Henceforth a tailor had been commissioned and tonight Samuel found himself deciding between a gray and a black suit.

Of course the evening was formal; everything here seemed to be. Choosing black was only appropriate and required one brief flicker of thought before he slipped the jacket off the hanger. Anthony's valet, Maddock, who was ever-vigilant, ever-anxious to do his duty, tried to take the jacket away. Samuel held on for dear life. No one was going to help him dress.

"May I draw your bath, sir?" Maddock asked, hand clenched on the hanger, his face as expressionless as a sphinx.

"No, thank you." Samuel extracted the suit from Maddock's grip.

"Might you prefer the gray suit, sir?"

Samuel thought of McMurphy, Mary's distant relative who'd insisted on acting the part of butler. McMurphy was a joyous jester compared to this dour character.

"I'm happy with the black."

Maddock nodded, waiting for Samuel to undress. Samuel shook his head and opened his mouth to just bluntly tell the valet he preferred doing it himself when Maddock, misinterpreting, came over and began helping Samuel unbutton his shirt and trousers.

"Thank you, Maddock," Samuel said, suppressing laughter and exasperation as he took a step backward. "I think I can handle this myself."

"May I be of any other assistance?"

"Let's hope not."

Stiff-spined, Maddock departed. Good Lord, the British were strange. Yet, as unapproachable as Maddock was, he was better than Hodgson, who seemed to regard Samuel as a member of some aberrant race, and Fanny and Rose, Anthony's downstairs maid and tweeny, both acted as if he might drag them to the basement and rape them if they so much as met his eyes.

Lord, what a household. What he wouldn't give to be back in Portland.

Fifteen minutes later he was in the downstairs hall, waiting for Anthony to join him. Anthony was only attending this affair to keep an eye on Samuel and Veronica. He detested parties and everyone who attended them, but he didn't trust Samuel with Veronica. A waste of time. Anthony should spend more time on his own love life, Samuel thought. There was nothing between him and Veronica.

Nothing.

In fact he suspected Anthony's affairs were more colorful. Clearly there had been something between him and Amelia St. John. Also, Veronica had once asked him if he'd talked to Catherine, clearly a woman from Anthony's colorful past.

Would either woman be at this evening's event? Samuel smiled as he thought about relating the news to Lady Chamberlain when he returned to Portland. It might make for an entertaining afternoon.

What would Agatha think of Veronica, her grandniece? What could he tell the autocratic Lady Chamberlain that would define Veronica? She was young, lovely, impulsive, interesting, absolutely desirable . . .

"Jesus," he muttered, infuriated with himself.

He doubted Agatha even knew of Veronica's existence, such was the self-imposed ostracism from her own family. Picturing how he might explain his own relationship to Veronica made him grimace.

What the *hell* was the matter with him? One teasing kiss had turned into a few moments of raging lust, a feeling he'd been totally unprepared for. Veronica's innocence and capitulation had only added to his own desire. When he thought of those moments outside her home he writhed inside with self-reproach.

Worse than that, the feel of her in his arms, her skin, her mouth, her fresh scent—he was unable to get her out of his mind.

"Damn it," he muttered, pacing the hall. Now he had to escort the beautiful little troublemaker to this party. Hell. She was his fiancé.

Hodgson appeared from the back of the house. He gathered Samuel's hat and coat. Ignoring the hat, Samuel took the coat.

"It's a most unpleasant evening, sir. The fog."

This was more than Samuel had elicited from Hodgson during his entire stay. "The notorious London fog?" Samuel asked.

Hodgson looked unsure what he meant.

Anthony came downstairs, collected his hat and coat with barely a nod of acknowledgment to the butler, then preceded Samuel outside to the waiting carriage. "I've been to more pointless affairs since you arrived in my country than I've had to attend the last five years."

"You don't have to go," Samuel said mildly.

"And leave you alone with Veronica?"

"I am not going to hurt Veronica," Samuel replied, exasperated. "This engagement was her idea," he reminded him once again.

"And you are playing your part extremely well."

"What does that mean?"

"It means you practically seduced my niece in full view of the street and Henry's so eager to have Veronica married, he's considering moving up the date!"

"Where did you hear that?" Samuel demanded.

"From Madeline." He glared at Samuel like an outraged father.

"Oh, for god's sake!" Samuel exploded. "I am sick to death of all of this! Help me find Flynne, Anthony. Stop pussyfooting around and get your teeth into this. You want Veronica safe from me? Then call in the police, Parliament, the goddamned Queen of England, if you have to. As soon as

I have Victor I'm leaving England and you, and Veronica, and this entire nation will never see me again."

"All right," Anthony snapped back. "I'll light a fire under the chief inspector and make certain the police are at your command." His mouth curved slightly. "But it would be best to leave our beloved Victoria out of this."

Samuel snorted in disbelief. "Well, God save the queen," he muttered sardonically and Anthony stifled a smile.

"Veronica, love," Malcolm Phipps's cultured voice greeted Veronica the moment she entered the ballroom. Oh, blast. She didn't ever want to see Malcolm and especially not tonight when she was worried sick over what Samuel would do when he discovered Father was trying to move up the wedding. Glancing behind her, she assured herself that her erstwhile fiancé was still at her elbow though his dark, inscrutable expression did not bode well for a light, fun evening.

"It's good to see you, Malcolm," she said stiffly. *And may God not strike me dead for another lie.*

Samuel, who'd been polite but as distant as the North Star since the moment he and Uncle Tony had collected her, coughed behind his hand. Out of the corner of her eye she caught his slow smile and her spirits lifted. At least she could still amuse him. Apparently their disastrous last encounter hadn't soured him to her completely.

"That color certainly becomes you," Malcolm gushed, his cold eyes belying the compliment.

"Your suit is lovely as well," she replied sweetly. Malcolm was in full bloom tonight: blue jacket and trousers, green and blue brocade waistcoat, iridescent bracelet. Samuel's polite cough turned into a series of strangled choking gasps. Uncle Tony clapped Samuel on the back, hard, several times.

Phipps was outraged. He hid his anger behind a polished veneer of maliciousness. "Congratulations, Mr. Danner." Extending one smooth palm, he shook Samuel's strong brown hand. "You have certainly plucked the crown jewel from our midst."

Veronica blushed. Did Samuel hear his meanness, his need to put her in her place?

Samuel stared at the man a moment. Veronica held her breath, afraid of what he might say. "Lady Veronica is indeed the most beautiful woman in the room." She swung around in surprise to stare at him. "Your admiration is well-founded," he added, blandly meeting Phipps's angry gaze.

"It's lucky you're a man who can disbelieve those terrible rumors surrounding her. I'm sure they were all false, no matter what Geoff says."

Veronica's throat hurt.

"I'm glad you feel that way, Phipps." Samuel gritted out a smile. "It's nice to know you're a man who can be depended upon to play fair with a woman's reputation. Excuse us."

Veronica's eyes widened. Malcolm turned three shades of purple as Samuel pushed her onto the dance floor. Society's reigning gossipmonger had been outfoxed, outmaneuvered, and outshone!

"Oh, no," she whispered, as Samuel drew her into his arms with rather more force than necessary.

"What?"

"I'm afraid Malcolm's skin color clashes with his clothes."

Samuel's attention jerked to her bright face and dancing eyes. Then he shot a glance toward Phipps. "I believe you're right."

"You're quite good at this, you know."

"At what?"

"Verbal lancing."

Samuel's lashes lowered briefly. "Malcolm Phipps is a first-class bastard."

"Mmmm. As long as he's first-class, he won't mind."

He gave a short bark of laughter and whirled her away from Malcolm's side of the room. The party was at the home of the Langston's; distant relatives of the duke of Westbourne. Veronica's father had mainly accepted the invitation for Chloe and Patrice who were anxious to embark upon romances of their own. He himself could not attend and so Madeline had chaperoned Henry's younger daughters.

Even though she'd coerced Samuel into escorting her to this event, Veronica had not looked forward to the evening. Parties were not her favorite social event by any means. Most of the time she was humiliated or teased or ignored, and even though she'd known she would be with Samuel tonight, she still hadn't eagerly anticipated being in this hot room with these beautiful, vicious people.

However, it was nice to be in Samuel's arms. She'd almost forgotten how he'd rescued her at the marquess of Wilshire's party, but she remembered now. She also remembered what it was like to kiss those masculine lips and be crushed within those steel arms.

"What is it?" Samuel asked, when Veronica jerked involuntarily.

"I'm hot, aren't you? Could we walk outside, to the terrace?"

"And have your uncle believe I'm stealing you away for some sordid lovemaking? You really know how to tempt fate."

"Uncle Tony?" Veronica asked, perplexed.

"I've been getting an earful of advice from 'Uncle Tony' about you. He doesn't trust me with you."

"I trust you," she said sincerely.

Her answer seemed to take him aback. "I think our kiss was an ill-conceived idea," he admitted frankly. "Madeline told Anthony that your father wants to move up the date of the wedding."

"Oh, you know?"

"Yes, I know." He narrowed his gaze at her thoughtfully. "I thought hurrying the wedding would be too scandalous for you English bluebloods."

"It is, normally, but then the situation isn't normal, is it? After all, I'm scandalous."

"Hmmmm."

Veronica wasn't certain what that meant but it didn't sound good. "I'm sorry for involving you in my problems, Samuel," she said truthfully. "I have a knack for making a bad situation worse. I didn't realize Patrice would relate our kiss so—vividly. It certainly stirred up my father. Of course, it might just be another excuse for him to finalize this marriage," she added with heartbreaking honesty.

"Your father's a fool," Samuel said flatly.

Encouraged by his loyalty, Veronica let herself relax in his arms. She felt safe and protected. With a pinprick of shock, she thought how nice it would be if their proposed marriage was in earnest.

They danced several more slow waltzes before Samuel handed her over to Anthony who'd requested a dance. Veronica was loathe to let Samuel go, but he was more than anxious to put some space between them. It wasn't that he didn't want her in his arms. Lord, no. The truth was, he wanted her in his bed, and Samuel couldn't reconcile himself to wanting any woman other than his beloved Mary.

Mary's image wavered in front of his eyes and he desperately tried to hold onto it. Mary was sanity; Veronica insane indulgence. But Mary was becoming harder and harder to remember while Veronica was warm flesh and blood, wit and wonder, and a good deal of trouble.

She'd distracted him from his goal too much already. This engagement was fast getting out of hand, he determined, ordering another drink.

Glancing around the draped and festooned ballroom, he noticed Chloe. She was batting her eyes and waving her fan—all for the attention of a rather dull-looking fellow who appeared perennially bored.

"The duke's eldest son," a feminine voice said at his elbow. Samuel turned around to regard Amelia St. John. "He's the one Chloe's making a fool of herself over. She's much too young and unimportant for him to notice."

"Is he in the market for a wife?"

"A lot of girls have set their cap for him, to no avail," she said with a certain amount of smugness.

"And you?"

Her eyes darted to James Fielding, then slid to where Anthony was waltzing with Veronica. "I'm considering Lord Fielding's proposal."

But you would prefer one from Anthony Ashworth, Samuel read between the lines.

She arched a delicate brow. "I hear you and Veronica are moving up the wedding. How exciting! Should one assume you and Ronnie plan to live in London, then?"

"One should never assume anything," Samuel remarked, excusing himself. Lord Jason Cromwell had just arrived. Samuel hadn't forgotten Anthony's remark at the marquess of Wilshire's party that the man had turned white at the mention of Victor Flynne's name. But for the past few weeks Jason had been impossible to run down. Now, here he was—more than a little inebriated and swaying on his feet as he ordered another drink.

Fourth son of the duke of Thornborough. Gambled away a fortune.

"Good evening, m'lord," Samuel greeted him with a trace of irony. The man was drunk as a skunk.

"Evenin'." He frowned at Samuel's western drawl. "Do I know you?"

"I'm a friend of Anthony Ashworth's."

"Ah, yes. Lady Veronica's fiancé."

Everytime he heard himself so labeled it made him squirm. He was going to have to do something drastic to get out of this engagement. It may have bought Veronica some time, but it hadn't panned out so well for him. So far she'd learned nothing new about Victor Flynne from her father or anyone residing at Ashworth Manor, and he'd wasted valuable time doting on her.

And enjoying every moment, a grim, honest voice inside his head reminded him.

"Anthony said you're acquainted with a Mr. Victor Flynne," Samuel said aloud.

Jason choked and choked on his drink, until tears flowed freely from his eyes. "Don't know what you mean," he muttered. "Never heard that name before."

"You borrowed money from him," Samuel guessed. "And are paying it back at an exorbitant rate." Cromwell gazed at him through hollow, glazed eyes. "It's just the start, you know," Samuel added, realizing he'd hit upon the truth.

"He'll find another way to keep you paying. And you'll pay and pay until he's sucked the lifeblood from you."

"'Scuse me." He stumbled for the door, sick-white.

"You certainly know how to clear a room!" a feminine voice giggled. Samuel turned his attention to a moderately overweight, somewhat pretty, giddy woman. "Did you threaten him with sobriety!"

"Something like that," Samuel admitted.

"I'm Wilhelmina Stuart," she simpered, holding out a gloved hand to be kissed. "I've been dying to meet you. The man who rescued Veronica from Neville Rathbone! Everyone's so jealous."

"Jealous?" Samuel sought about for escape, but Wilhelmina attached herself to him as if he were a long lost friend.

"No one had the courage to ask for her hand, don't you know, until Lord Rathbone stopped talking about his ails long enough to step forward. We were *all* aghast! Poor Veronica. Lord Rathbone is hardly anyone's romantic fantasy."

Anthony and Veronica swept past. Sizing up Samuel's situation, Anthony smothered a smile. No rescue there. Then Veronica's piquant face appeared over Anthony's shoulder. Seeing Wilhelmina, her eyes sparkled with mirth.

Blast! They were going to leave him to this fate.

". . . but then you came forward," she was babbling on. "Veronica's own white knight! Now her other suitors are green with envy!"

"Her other suitors?"

"Oh, James Fielding professes to love Amelia, but he longs for Veronica. You can see it in his face. Her unfortunate liaison with Geoff ruined her chance with him, though. James can't abide a soiled reputation. But it's different now."

Samuel gave her his full attention. "Why?"

"Because it's clear that *she's* chosen *you*. Someone entirely wrong for her. Oh, it's so deliciously romantic. Only Veronica could pull it off without completely destroying herself."

Samuel wasn't certain he understood, but he was sure he

didn't want to ask her to elaborate. As it turned out, he didn't need to.

"And look at Byron Hartwell. Jennifer Armstrong's nephew," she added to a bewildered Samuel. "Jennifer was approached by Madeline on Veronica's behalf, but before Byron had a chance—*poof!*—there you were. And then there's Wortham. He's her close friend, you know, but he's half in love with her himself. A woman knows these things."

"I'm sure." Though her narrative was drivel, it was giving him an idea.

"Of course, Malcolm professes to hate her. Veronica's certainly felt the sharp side of his wicked tongue more than once. But Malcolm hates everyone and I don't really think he hates her as much as he wants us all to believe," she finished sagely.

"What would happen to Veronica if our engagement were broken?" Samuel inquired.

Her eyes widened and she gasped. "Oh, heavens, you're not going to throw her over, are you?" Clearly, the idea enchanted her.

"No, of course not," he answered hurriedly. He didn't want to add to Veronica's troubles needlessly. "Of course, Veronica may feel differently."

"Are you saying Veronica may throw *you* over?" She nearly fainted with delight at this juicy bit of gossip.

"Sometimes one can't help what fate has in store," Samuel managed with a straight face.

Wilhelmina clasped a hand to her ample bosom. "Oh, my. Veronica does live dangerously, doesn't she? If your engagement should end, why, my heavens! Veronica could become the latest rage! She would be as zealously sought after as the most fabulous treasure!"

"Thank you, Miss Stuart." A hollow emptiness invaded Samuel's stomach, but he ignored it as he bent over Wilhelmina's hand once again.

"What could Samuel possibly be discussing with Wilhelmina?" Veronica asked Anthony.

"The latest fashions?"

"Be serious!"

"How many courses she hopes her next meal will be?" he suggested.

"Don't be mean!" She laughed.

"Sorry," he said without the slightest bit of remorse. They danced in companionable silence but Anthony noticed how closely Veronica followed Samuel's movements. "You aren't in love with him, are you, darling?"

She stiffened. "In love? Don't be ridiculous!"

"I'm a lot of things, Veronica. But I'm seldom ridiculous."

Veronica searched for some rebuttal, but he knew her too well. Better than she did herself sometimes. "I'm not in love with him," she assured him. But even to herself the words sounded forced and overly bright. "I'm not," she added defiantly.

"It would never work out. The man's on a quest and once that quest's over, he'll be returning to his own country."

"I am aware of Mr. Danner's situation," Veronica answered a bit testily.

"I just don't want your tender heart to be broken," he said gently.

Veronica was still pondering her uncle's well-meant, but unneeded, advice when she was returned to Samuel's side once more.

"You haven't been completely honest with me," Samuel greeted her and Veronica was instantly on alert.

"What do you mean?"

"You said you were so scandalous that you couldn't buy a husband, but I've learned there are any number of gentlemen who would be eager to make you their wife."

"Oh, yes?" She didn't believe him. "And who are these purported suitors?"

"Look around you." He gestured to the groups of men scattered around the periphery of the room. Remembering how often she'd felt those same men sizing her up and finding her lacking, Veronica sighed.

"Not a man in this room would consider me eligible wife material," she said, her voice shaded with a degree of bitterness she couldn't quite disguise.

"I think you're wrong." Samuel gazed down at her, his dark eyes unfathomable.

"Well, what does it matter now?" Veronica shrugged delicately. "You're my fiancé. No one else will offer for me."

"I'm aware of that," Samuel said, his eyes following the curve of her lips, lingering there, his voice distracted. "Come on. I'll take you home."

Veronica was disappointed by the abrupt ending to their evening and though her mind tripped ahead to their parting and the memory of the other day's searing kisses, Samuel merely said good-bye by pressing his lips to her hand.

With the dreary sense that Samuel was planning to rid himself of her somehow, she slowly climbed the stairs to her room. She couldn't let Samuel throw her over. She couldn't! Her father would sell her hand to the highest bidder so fast she would be married to a wealthy lecher equally as awful as Neville Rathbone by summer at the latest.

She had to devise a counterattack. This was war. A war she desperately needed to win.

But how could she keep Samuel from leaving her to a fate worse than death?

Flynne! She'd promised to procure him information on Flynne. She could double her efforts. Grow bolder in her quest. She could search her father's desk or follow him about. Surely, sooner or later she would have something worthwhile to tell Samuel. And then he would feel beholden enough to keep up the engagement pretense awhile longer.

It was worth a try, at least. But she would have to begin immediately. Elsewise, Samuel Danner would throw her to the proverbial wolves, and Veronica would rather "die a horrible death" than be betrothed to another man. Any other man, in fact, except Samuel himself.

Chapter

11

Cool late morning sunshine brightened the corners of the drawing room. Veronica's head was bent over her needlepoint, but her mind was racing. She glanced upward. Madeline was arranging flowers in a vase atop the piano—the first courageous blossoms of tulips and crocuses making a splash of red, yellow, and purple against the darker corners of the room. Chloe was seated on the bench, absently picking out a tune, and Patrice, a book of poems in hand, was curled into an armchair, her restless gaze wandering around the room.

They were all bored out of their minds.

Veronica could hear the tick of the clock in her head. Her nerves were taut. She wanted to scream. When could she escape to her father's study? How? The house was full of people and if Northcroft caught her he would be sure to report her.

"The duke's son didn't even look at me!" Chloe suddenly cried, slamming her hands on the piano keys in a resounding, discordant crash.

"You didn't seriously expect him to, did you?" Patrice asked mildly.

"Yes, I did! I'm pretty. Prettier than you! Prettier than Veronica."

"Chloe!" Madeline said sharply.

"Well, it's true," Chloe retorted stubbornly. "Why do all the men stare at Veronica? It's not fair! She's not even a beauty like Amelia St. John."

Veronica sighed, wondering what in the world Chloe was ranting about. "The men don't stare at me and even if they did, it wouldn't be for the reason you imply. I've got a terrible reputation."

"They look at you with lust," Chloe said softly, tears shining in her eyes.

"Hush!" Madeline snapped.

Veronica jabbed her finger with the needle. "Blast!" she muttered, throwing the work aside. "If they look at me with lust, it's because they think I'm a . . ." She paused, biting her tongue. Her sisters waited, breaths bated. Madeline's blue eyes warned her fiercely to quit while she was ahead.

"Never mind. You are the prettiest, Chloe. No one would dispute that."

"For all the good it does me!"

"Oh, for goodness sake." Veronica lost patience. "You wouldn't want the attention I receive, believe me."

"Wouldn't I?" she sniffed.

Veronica appealed to her stepmother, annoyed beyond measure. "Could you talk some sense to her?" she asked Madeline.

"Men do stare at you, Veronica." Madeline's answer shocked Veronica to silence. "Maybe it's because they believed you've behaved outrageously. Maybe it's because you've chosen an American and they're intrigued. Maybe it's because they sense you possess an attraction that's more than skin-deep."

Chloe gasped in hurt and outrage. "Thank you so much," she murmured bitterly.

"Oh, Chloe."

Madeline stabbed a red tulip next to a group of yellow ones before turning impatiently from Henry's self-centered middle daughter to his disbelieving eldest. "Whatever it is,

Veronica, it's powerful. Perhaps it's just as well Mr. Danner has offered for you."

Veronica's heart kicked over. Fooling her father was one thing; deceiving Madeline quite another. She felt a complete fraud. She hated not telling her the truth about her engagement.

"The duke's son couldn't take his eyes off you," Chloe said miserably.

"Neither could your fiancé," Patrice remarked. "He followed you with his eyes."

Veronica had to stop this now. "Samuel? He talked the whole time to other women."

"You really love him, don't you?" Patrice murmured dreamily. "You're lucky Lord Rathbone offered for you first. It forced you and Samuel to acknowledge your love."

Veronica emitted a strangled sound. She nearly set Patrice straight in a hurry before she realized everyone was staring at her. Collecting herself, she said, "You're right. I'm so lucky. Samuel might have delayed our engagement if it hadn't become imperative to act now."

"Maybe I should have a flagrant love affair. Then men will start noticing me, too."

"Chloe, go to your room." Madeline had had enough.

"I'm not the one who was caught in the carriage house with Geoffrey Rowbury!" she protested on a screech of injustice. "Why is Veronica never in trouble? She's the one who does everything wrong!" With that she ran from the room, nearly knocking Northcroft down as she burst into a flood of tears and slammed the sliding doors behind her.

"Madame, there's a gentleman caller to see Lady Veronica," Northcroft announced stiffly.

Samuel! Veronica jumped to her feet and rushed into the hall, sliding to a stop in front of a man she didn't recognize. He was big and slow and his clothes didn't seem to fit. She was sure she'd seen him somewhere before but she couldn't quite place him.

"Th' masder's in th' coach," he said with great difficulty.

Memory kicked in. It was Giles. Neville Rathbone's

coachman. Belatedly she recalled Rathbone's invitation. "Oh. Excuse me. I'm not really prepared . . ."

"I'll tell Lady Ashworth that you'll be going out," Northcroft said smoothly from behind her.

"Thank you, Northcroft. I can speak for myself." She gritted on a smile.

"As you wish." He disappeared down the hall just as Madeline appeared in the drawing room doorway.

"Lord Rathbone has invited me for a drive." Veronica searched her mind for a reasonable excuse to decline, but for once her fertile mind was blank. "I accepted his invitation," she finished lamely.

"Where is Lord Rathbone?" Madeline asked the hulking Giles.

"In th' coach," he struggled.

Madeline looked worried. "Do you think you should go?"

Veronica hesitated. She'd already told Neville she would take a drive with him and this would give her an opportunity to apologize for the terribly rude remarks she'd made about him. "I'll be fine."

"Be . . . careful," Madeline advised as Veronica collected her cloak.

"I'll be back by three," Veronica said, kissing Madeline on the cheek.

She didn't want to go. She had plans of her own. But staying in the house discussing how lustfully men looked at her was hardly an afternoon's entertainment and anyway, she wasn't going to be able to search Father's study with her sisters and stepmother about. Maybe she could find a way to get them out of the house tomorrow.

But now she fervently wished she'd told Samuel of the obligation to Neville. Giles was hardly warm company, and Lord Rathbone himself wasn't much better.

Neville was reclining against plush black squabs as Veronica was helped inside the coach by Giles. He looked particularly aged and withdrawn. "I'm afraid I've been unwell," he lamented as Veronica settled herself beside him, as far away as she could possibly scoot. The carriage was not designed with opposing seats. "I thank you for honoring my invitation."

Veronica was having second, third, fourth, and fifth thoughts about it, but she kept them to herself. Giles must have flicked his whip on the horses because they started forward with a jolt. The coach itself was luxurious, if rather musty and old, but Veronica suspected that was more from disuse than lack of luxury.

They drove toward the park and Veronica relaxed slightly. Her mind was distracted. It might be possible to sneak down and examine her father's desk tonight. The drawers were locked, she knew; but she also knew where the key was kept. Years of misbehaving and rebelling had their rewards: She'd unrepentedly searched her father's books and personal items for years—the price of boredom.

Neville coughed, then reached for her hand. Veronica's skin crawled. She let him hold it for several moments before gently pulling free.

"Where are we going?" she asked, when she didn't recognize the streets outside the window.

"To my town house."

"Excuse me?" she asked.

"Don't be worried, my dear. We won't be alone. The house is full of servants."

Alarm bells rang in her head. No gentleman with pure intentions compromised a young lady's reputation by bringing her to his house, no matter how many servants he employed. Besides, servants weren't considered acceptable chaperons. The best servants were extremely loyal to their masters and therefore Society, for better or worse, didn't give credence to their accounts of seemly behavior.

She was in serious trouble.

"I'm afraid your illness must be catching," she said, pressing fingers to her left temple. "I feel a raging headache coming on. Do you think this is wise? Perhaps it would be better if I just went home."

"Oh, I'm perfectly fine now, my dear. It's just rather close in the coach." He didn't move a muscle to aid her.

Veronica's pulse beat fast. What did he really have in mind?

The carriage pulled to the rear of the house, another bad sign. Neville led the way through the back door, leaning heavily on Giles as he negotiated the steps. Veronica was torn between running for her life and keeping some semblance of propriety. She could imagine the headlines when it was learned she'd run in terror from her ex-fiancé's home—a man in his eighties!

That thought consoled her until she stole a look at Neville. He wasn't in his eighties at all. Sixties, maybe, possibly younger. But he was frail and weak. Frail and weak.

Reluctantly, she followed him inside to the darkest drawing room she'd ever entered. It could have been draped for mourning—the curtains were deep brown, almost black, the furniture heavy, no white lacy antimacassars or dried flower arrangements to alleviate the cold austerity.

And where were the servants? Apart from Giles, she hadn't seen one.

"What an interesting room," she remarked as Neville seated himself heavily beside her on the love seat. Uneasily, she noted that his skin was flushed. Not illness, excitement.

Silly goose! You're letting your imagination run away with you!

"Would you like a cordial?" Neville asked.

"No, thank you."

He rang for the maid but it was Giles who appeared, balancing a silver tray atop his beefy hands which bore a crystal decanter and two glasses as he shuffled into the room. Neville dismissed him with a wave. Veronica tore her gaze from Giles's retreating form to the vile-looking liquid Neville poured into both glasses.

"Here," he urged, ignoring her dissension and pressing one of the drinks into her hands. Veronica gripped it as if it were an iron rod, something she could smash down on his head if necessary.

She suddenly thought of Samuel—of his touch, his drawl, the quirk of his smile, the thickness of his eyelashes and amusement in the black depths of his irises. Her pulse pounded so hard it hurt. Her throat was dry as sandpaper. *Oh, Samuel,* she thought with sudden clarity. *I want you. I love you. Please, please come rescue me!*

The realization jolted her. She wanted Samuel more than a pretend suitor. She wanted him to love, even to marry. She wanted him for her.

"You have the loveliest skin," Neville said softly, his eyes traveling over the crests of her cheekbone, to the purity of her gold eyes and the shining splendor of her hair.

"Thank you." Veronica could scarcely speak.

"Have a drink. It's made by some friends of mine in the country. Very sweet, but delicate. Please. Take a sip."

"What time is it?"

"A little after one, I believe."

Perspiration beaded on her chest and she felt cold and clammy. She rose to her feet. When Neville remained seated, merely eyeing her in askance, she felt immeasurably better. She even sipped the cordial which, as he'd described, was light and fruity.

There was no need to panic. He was, after all, merely an elderly gentleman who wanted company. Calling herself names for her lively imagination, Veronica strolled to the hearth where a fire was slowly dying. The room was stuffy. There was no need for further heat.

"How is your . . . fiancé?" he asked.

She threw him an embarrassed look. "I'm sorry about how this all happened. Samuel and I—"

"It's perfectly all right, my dear," he cut in with a smile. "I want you to know that. It's the real reason for this meeting."

Veronica should have been convinced but she couldn't help feeling uncomfortable. Her gaze traveled around the room, lighting on the swords, pistols, rifles, and other weaponry displayed on the wall. This was a man's home. No woman had been in attendance here for many years, if ever.

"You're being very gracious about it," she said lightly.

"Please sit down." He patted the seat beside him. "It makes me feel like a terrible host that I can't stand beside you."

Once more Veronica perched on the edge of the couch. Good heavens, what was she afraid of? She was far younger than he, undoubtedly stronger. He was just a pathetic man whose dreams of recapturing his youth had briefly revolved around her.

Still . . .

"Would you care for another?" he asked, lifting the decanter.

"No, thank you." She felt slightly dizzy already. Having only tasted alcohol once before, when Wortham had invited her to share a bottle of champagne which had subsequently made her violently sick, to the despair of Madeline who'd sneaked her to bed without her father knowing, Veronica was loathe to repeat that fateful mistake.

"The first time I saw you, I couldn't get you out of my mind. You were so full of life." Neville lifted his empty glass, turning it around in his hand, smiling.

Veronica was uncertain how to respond.

"It was at that moment I knew I had to have you."

Veronica blinked. "Pardon me?"

"I had to have you. As many have before." He rang the bell once again and Giles reappeared. "Please show Lady Veronica to the front bedroom," Neville said conversationally. To Veronica, he added, "I offered marriage. Remember that."

Samuel's impatience knew no bounds. He wanted to kick in the door, grab Henry Ashworth's smirking butler by the throat, aim a rifle and blast out every damn window in Ashworth Manor. Damn, but these people were deliberate! Manners were everything. Nobody knew how to deliver a straight, honest answer.

"Where is Veronica?" Samuel asked Northcroft again, slowly, as if he believed the man were dense.

"Lady Veronica has gone out," he intoned through his nose for the third time.

Sensing Northcroft was enjoying himself, Samuel turned a page from his brother, Jesse's, book and lifted the man by his starched collar, dragging his alarmed face within inches of Samuel's own. *"Out* is not the answer I'm looking for. Either tell me where she is, or direct me to someone who will."

Northcroft turned white, then purple with outrage. His lips moved but no sound issued. Samuel thrust him aside and rapped on the drawing room doors twice before sliding them open with such force that they slammed into the wall.

Madeline gasped, her hand to her throat. The youngest daughter, Patrice, stared wide-eyed.

"Mr. Danner!" Madeline recovered herself, flushing at his rudeness.

"Where is she?" he demanded bluntly. He'd made a start last night in engaging other suitors for Veronica's hand, but now he wanted to make certain she understood what must be done. There were no other alternatives. Unfortunately, Northcroft's attitude had made him impatient and angry and if Madeline forced him through the rigamarole of artful conversation he was certain his temper would blow.

Samuel's anger was also a shield for a more unpalatable truth, had he but known it. He didn't want to give Veronica up. He didn't want some other man to have her.

But more than that, he didn't want to face his feelings.

Madeline opened her mouth, closed it, then opened it again. "Veronica's with Lord Rathbone. An obligation she felt needed to be kept."

"Lord Rathbone?"

She shook her head in confusion. "I think Veronica felt a bit badly for the way things turned out. She wanted to make amends."

"When did they leave? Do you know when they'll return?"

"Veronica said . . . around three."

Samuel stared at her. "It's three-forty-five."

"I realize that, Mr. Danner." Madeline's spine stiffened, but there was a shadow across her smooth face.

"And you're scared to death. My God." Samuel, who'd been intent on forcing Veronica to see that other men wanted her—more *worthy* men—and that she should throw in her lot with them, not him, felt as if he'd been punched in the stomach. He had a clear idea of Neville Rathbone's true intentions—aged, infirm or not.

"Give me his address," Samuel bit out, and Madeline instantly complied.

Veronica was torn between true terror and amusement. Neville was stronger than he looked, and definitely far younger than she'd first imagined. Fifty-eight, he was. She'd elicited that information while trying to escape his latest chest-crushing advance. The whole situation would be a farce: him grabbing at her skirts, her deftly eluding his grasp, if it weren't for the viscerally frightening fact that he'd arranged to have them locked inside this bedroom and that Giles was in full agreement with his master's demented wishes. The hulking servant was planted just outside the door. When, and if, Neville should tire of the game, he was there to ensure victory.

"Lord Rathbone," Veronica gasped, fighting for breath. She was near the fireplace, damning the fact that Neville had apparently secreted the poker elsewhere. "If you think I won't report this—this ungentlemanly behavior—you're sadly mistaken."

"No one will believe you." He wiped sweat from his brow, grinning like a Bedlam inmate. He seemed to enjoy the chase as much as his expected victory.

Veronica shuddered. She should be more frightened, she supposed. She'd nearly swooned when Giles had swung her over his shoulder when she'd balked at going upstairs. She'd fought like a wildcat but he'd merely thrown her across the bed and walked out, locking the door behind them once Neville was safely inside.

Most of the past hour had been spent in conversation: Neville on one side of the enormous bed; she on the other. Anytime he reached for her she scrambled across the coverlet. A silly, relentless game. They were both out of breath.

"When do the servants return?" she asked, gasping a little.

"I never expected this to last so long," he admitted, "but luckily, I had foresight. We'll be alone until tomorrow."

"Someone will come looking for me!"

"Who? Your father?" Neville's tone was almost sympathetic. "If he believes you've brought more scandal on his name, he'll hope you never return."

"If *I've* brought more scandal on *his* name?"

"No account of what transpired here today will wash away the stain of your past offenses," Neville pointed out with chauvinistic logic.

"You sicken me," Veronica whispered.

With that he lunged for her arm, fingers tangling in the lace trim at the end of her sleeve. He jerked hard and she stumbled forward, into his arms briefly, long enough for her to crack him hard on the side of the face with an open-sided slap and for him to snatch wildly at the front of her gown, ripping the bodice to the waist until it peeled forward, revealing her corset.

She felt hard fingers clutch at her breasts. Furious, she slammed her gloved fist into his yellow teeth. Blood stained his lips. She scrambled backward, hoping she'd finally shown him she meant business. He touched a finger to his mouth. When he looked at her, his eyes were hot with desire.

Oh, God, she thought, losing faith. He'd never been in the least bit ill. It had been a ruse. The only sickness which consumed him was lust. And he'd succumbed to it.

He meant to rape her.

Why, then, wasn't she screaming with pure fear?

Because that's what he wants.

She knew it without being told. Only her wits, and the passing time, were her allies. Eventually someone would come looking for her. All she had to do was fend off his advances until then.

But how long would it be?

"The police will believe me if I prove I've been violated," she declared, dodging to the left as he grabbed at her. No vases cluttered the bedside tables. Nothing to hurl at him.

"How do you plan to prove that? Everyone knows Geoffrey Rowbury bedded you. The fellow's bragged about it more than once."

"That's a lie!"

"And that uncouth westerner's already had you as well. You're spoiled goods. A gentlewoman who wants any man who has the courage to take her is nothing but a whore."

"You're disgusting." Veronica was furious.

"If I like you, I'll still marry you."

"I'm marrying Samuel Danner because I love him and he'll kill you when he finds out."

"He'll thank me."

She couldn't believe it. Her hair had torn loose from its pins and hung in strands before her eyes. She shoved it away, breathing hard, unknowingly drawing his attention to the soft mounds of her breasts which swelled above her corset. There was a picture on the wall above Neville's left shoulder. If she could maneuver to that side, there might be time to grab it and slam it over his thick skull.

She feinted to the right. Neville snatched at her arm, grabbing her gown. Veronica jerked back. Fabric ripped with a wrench. A stretch of smooth forearm appeared. Neville lunged once more and Veronica tore across the bed, reversing their positions. "I will crucify you!" she hissed. "You will be scorned by Society. A laughingstock amongst men who matter!"

"My power is limitless compared to yours, Veronica, my dear. It is you who is already scorned. You, whose reputation is already crucified."

"You are too pathetic to hate!" she cried. "But I'm succeeding at it, nonetheless."

"Come here."

Now! She twisted for the picture, her fingers yanking the frame. But it was bolted on. A mistake! He grabbed her from behind, slamming her against the wall. A small cry of pain escaped her lips.

Then a thunderous pounding sounded below, at the front door, and Veronica heard Samuel bellow, "Goddamn it, open this door or so help me I'll break it down!"

The most awkward-looking man he'd ever seen answered Samuel's demands by cracking open one-half of the double doors. "Th' masder ain't 'ere."

"The hell he's not." Samuel was cool with rage. Back in control.

"Go 'way."

A split second before the door slammed in his face, Samuel kicked forward, surprising the burly servant so that he stumbled backward. Slipping into the hall, Samuel stood on the balls of his feet. He could have been back in Rock Springs. Years of Portland society shed away. Months of British propriety evaporated. He didn't care what he had to do and whom he offended in the process—he was going to find Veronica. Now.

"Where is—"

A faint feminine cry sounded upstairs. The heavy giant heard it, too, and he charged Samuel with a fierce growl. Samuel ducked out of the way, toward the stairs. The giant grabbed his arm, spinning him around. Samuel sent two lightening jabs to the man's midsection. Nothing. He was made of stone.

"Christ." Samuel muttered, his mind imagining the scene upstairs. He had no doubt that Neville was intent on raping Veronica.

How the *hell* did he get involved in these things?

"Go 'way!" the man roared, rushing him. Samuel clasped the stairway rail with both hands and jumped upward, smashing one boot beneath the man's chin in a cracking blow. The giant stopped dead but didn't fall. The force had sent shock waves through Samuel's whole body. Jesus. The man was bloody granite.

"Go . . . 'way . . ." he slurred. He took two steps to the right, swayed to the left, then went straight back and landed with a thundering crash that sent the overhead chandelier into a circular sway.

Samuel was up the stairs in a heartbeat. The key was in the door and he turned it, throwing open the doors in one fluid movement.

The scene that met his eyes stopped him in his tracks. Neville had Veronica by the hair, a heavy swath of it wrapped around one hand. Her head was bent back in a painful arc. In his other hand he held a small knife, a wicked-looking thing poised under her left breast. Her dress was ripped to the waist, her skin shining in the soft gaslight hissing from a bedside lamp.

"Let her go," Samuel said softly. "If you don't, I'll kill you."

"But you'll lose your lady fair, first. And you won't risk that."

"If you let her go, I'll let you live," he answered reasonably.

"You're a liar, Mr. Danner."

"Bastard!" Veronica hissed through her teeth. Neville gave her hair another yank and tears formed in her eyes.

That was all Samuel could stand. He made a flying leap at the both of them. Surprised, Neville didn't have time to react. Veronica kicked backward just as Samuel's body hit them like a freight train. Neville choked.

"Damn you . . . son of a . . . bastard . . . rapist," Samuel muttered, slamming his fist into Neville's face again and again. Blood spurted from his nose.

Veronica stumbled away, spent, furious, and half choked. "Don't kill him," she begged. "Don't kill him."

Samuel hauled Neville to his feet, dangling the man on legs that had lost their support. Murder was in his eyes. His hand clasped the older man's throat.

"Don't . . ." Veronica yanked at his arm. "Please . . . please . . . don't! You'll go to prison."

"For saving you? I don't think so," he said through gritted teeth.

"The court won't see it that way. Lord Rathbone has friends."

"Damn them all to hell."

"Samuel. Please."

Samuel's rage slowly diminished. A pulse beat at his temple. Neville was a wet rag, limp and useless. Reluctantly, he released his death grip, one hand propping the near unconscious lord against the wall.

Chapter

12

"Sit," Samuel ordered, ten minutes later as he helped Veronica into Anthony's carriage. Tucking her cloak around her, he pretended all was well for the benefit of the footman who'd driven him here. Climbing in beside her, he slapped the ceiling with his hand, instructing the man to drive. As soon as the coach jerked forward, he seated himself beside her.

She was hugging herself tightly. "Will he live?"

"Unfortunately."

"He tried to . . . he tried to . . ."

"I know." He cut her off. Veronica, who'd always shown strength and independence, looked near collapse. Samuel ached for her. He slipped a protective arm around her shoulders.

Veronica wasn't certain how she felt. Part of her wanted to bury her face in his chest and cry. Another part wanted to laugh hysterically. Who would believe such a story? A third part wanted to race back to Neville's house and murder the man with her own hands, much as she'd prevented Samuel from doing.

Instead she drew a heavy breath and said tremulously, "I'm glad you arrived when you did."

"Yes."

His tone was cool and it penetrated Veronica's fogged brain. She looked at him in confusion.

"Do you think it's my fault?" she asked in disbelief.

"No."

"Yes, you do. You're furious. I can tell."

"I'm not furious," he corrected tautly. She glared at him mutinously and he demanded, "Why in God's name did you go with that lecherous bastard in the first place? You knew what he wanted. I *told* you what he wanted. Why didn't you listen to me?"

Veronica was too upset herself to sense his anger was a reaction to fear. His cold words hurt. Neville had been right. Even Samuel blamed her for what had happened. She was so angry and humiliated she couldn't speak.

His grip around her shoulders tightened. She shrugged against his arm. "Don't touch me."

Instantly he pulled away. Conversely, Veronica wished he was still holding her. She'd just discovered she loved him. Now she wanted to kill him.

"I'm so very sorry that I nearly got myself raped. How terribly careless of me. I must have asked for it."

His dark eyes met hers. Gold sparks of pure fury flew at him and he belatedly realized how wrong he'd been in venting his frustration with Neville at her. "I'm sorry," he managed.

"Don't be," she snapped. "I'm a loose woman with a scandalous reputation. I let Geoffrey Rowbury have his way with me, and now I let Neville Rathbone. My self-control is virtually nonexistent, but then I'm merely a woman, and women can't be trusted with their emotions, can they? That's what chastity belts were designed for. Maybe you should invest in one for me, since we're engaged. Goodness knows which man I'll take to my bed next."

He swore softly through his teeth.

"In fact, now that I've discovered how wonderful lust is,

I'll practice it daily," she said on a wavering voice. "I truly enjoyed having my clothes ripped off."

"Stop it," he said in a quiet voice, torn apart with self-recrimination.

"You men are so good at deciding what's best for us women. If you want to stop me, you'll have to use force . . . like Neville."

There was steel beneath Veronica's exterior he'd never guessed at. Sick with self-reproach, Samuel was boiling inside with emotions better left untouched.

"I've got a better idea: Why don't you kiss me?" Veronica taunted, shaking inside. "That'll not only shut me up, it'll remind me of the only thing I'm good for." In her own fury, she didn't wait for him to react, she simply took the initiative and pressed her mouth against his.

It was meant as a douse of cold reality; it came on like a hot gush of desire so intense Samuel closed his eyes and wrestled against wants, needs, and emotions that were so out of place now as to be sick and perverse.

But Veronica's scent enveloped him, her small, delicate hands held his face, her mouth crushed his, not in passion but fury. His body reacted as if she'd given him an aphrodisiac, and maybe an aphrodisiac was what it was to a man who'd buried his feelings along with his wife.

Now he wanted to kiss her back, drag her into his arms, pull her yielding body atop his hard one, indulge the raging tide of desire. "Goddamn it," he muttered against her sweet lips, his eyes squeezed shut, his back pressed against the cushions.

Veronica slowly drew back. Samuel's handsome face was drawn and haggard; his body taut as a bowstring. She was innocent enough to be confused by the pain he seemed to be experiencing; savvy enough to understand it had everything to do with her.

With dawning surprise, she realized he wanted her. Like Neville had. Like Geoffrey Rowbury. For some reason she'd expected him to be different and though she'd planned and plotted to have him fall wildly in love with her, she'd never truly believed she could make him desire her.

But he was different, she realized a beat later. For he was determined not to give in to his wants. That was the reason for his anger, she thought with a rush of relief.

But it didn't excuse him.

Fifteen minutes later they arrived at Uncle Tony's town house. Samuel practically leapt from the carriage, reluctantly helping Veronica down. One look at Veronica and Uncle Tony turned on Samuel, but Samuel's clipped, "It was Rathbone," stopped him cold.

"Rathbone. He couldn't possibly."

"Couldn't he just," Samuel drawled furiously. "Get a hold of Madeline. Bring Veronica some new clothes. Unless you want a hue and cry the likes you've never seen before, you'd better protect her."

Uncle Tony looked dazed. "Veronica . . . ?"

"I'm all right." She smiled shakily.

"I'll take care of everything," Anthony said, the shock wearing off as anger took its place.

Ten minutes later she was alone with Samuel. "Go on upstairs," he suggested, pouring himself a drink. He lifted a brow in question, silently asking if she wanted the same. She shook her head. The cordial still lay heavy on her stomach. "I'll call the maid," he added. "What's her name?"

"Um . . . Fanny's the parlor maid. The tweeny's name is . . ." She drew a breath. "I can't remember."

"Fanny?" Samuel called loudly into the quiet hallway. "Blasted servants. They're never around when you need them."

They stared at each other across the length of the room. Setting his glass on the table, Samuel strode toward her, staring down at her ashen face, feeling like a complete and utter heel. "Come here," he said, taking her hand and leading her upstairs. Veronica, who knew more about scandal than anyone should, felt another bubble of hysterical laughter fill her throat. If Malcolm Phipps could see her now, being led to another bedroom by another man in the space of a few hours. Why his tongue would wag so furiously, it might flap right out of his head.

"I'll find someone to draw you a bath. Relax. It's over now."

She sat down on the edge of the eggshell white brocade comforter that covered one of Uncle Tony's guest beds. Silky drapes framed the ornate mahogany bedposts and looped around the canopy. The sight of it made her feel safe and clean. She wanted to curl up beneath the blankets.

"I was trying to do the right thing by accepting Neville's invitation," she felt the need to defend herself.

"The right thing would have been to refuse him."

"I did not know he planned to attack me."

Samuel rubbed a hand around the back of his neck, his mouth pulling down at the corners as if he were in pain. "Well, you should have known. You publicly humiliated him. No man's likely to forgive that and Rathbone decided to take matters into his own hands."

"I never dreamed he would go so far. We were supposed to be going for a drive. I was trying to be polite. And I thought he was old and weak."

"I know." Samuel swore softly.

"You *do* blame me!" she declared, leaping to her feet, so infuriated she could scarcely see straight.

"I blame myself for not expecting this."

Veronica didn't know whether to be upset or happy that he seemed to feel she was his responsibility. She chose to be upset.

"I don't need to listen to this. I can take care of myself."

"That's the biggest lie, yet. Women always lie to themselves. Even Mary used little tricks to fool herself into believing something was the truth when it wasn't and she was the most rational, intelligent woman I've ever known."

"Who's Mary?" Veronica asked instantly.

"No one," he clipped out. "The issue is you and how you use that featherbrain inside your head."

Veronica's mouth dropped open. Love, or no love, the man was downright insulting. "I didn't ask you to come save me. In fact, I wish you hadn't. I would have extricated myself without your help."

"You were doing such a capable job of it this afternoon," he pointed out ironically.

The scene suddenly filled her head: Neville grasping and grunting, his cold hands and filthy desire, the weight of his body pinning her against the wall. All the starch went out of her and she sank onto the bed once more.

"Veronica . . . ?"

She shook her head, blotting out the image. Then she remembered the way she'd felt when she'd kissed Samuel in the carriage. That's what she wanted. Something wonderful to take the place of Neville's ugliness. If only Samuel would comfort her and caress her and make her forget. She wanted to kill him for being so insensitive.

"Go away," she said miserably when she felt the bed depress beneath his weight as he sat down beside her.

"What am I going to do with you?" he murmured, his own anger melting beneath true compassion.

"Do you think you could just hold me?" The plea slipped out before she could stop herself. Embarrassed, she quickly added, "I know our engagement is a fraud. I'm just feeling kind of—numb—right now."

"I wish I'd killed him."

She gazed at him, into his dark, liquid brown eyes.

"He hurt you, and for that alone, he deserves far worse than he's going to get."

She smiled, loving the protective growl in his voice. Maybe he did care a little. "You didn't want to kiss me in the carriage, did you?"

"No."

"You were afraid I might think you were just like him."

Samuel's jaw tightened. Her perception could cut as deeply as a knife.

"Don't worry. I know you're not."

"You've got to stop being so trusting or you will get yourself in serious trouble," Samuel warned. "I've had my moments, too."

"What do you mean?" When he didn't immediately answer, she guessed, "Oh, you've used women, too? Used their bodies?"

Samuel was taken aback. "No! Any—relationship—I've had with a woman has been consensual."

"But you have had relationships," Veronica pressed, not wanting to really know, but dying for information all the same.

"A few."

"Who's Mary?" she asked again.

"Mary was . . . my wife."

She was shocked to learn he'd been married. "What happened?" she asked in a small voice.

Samuel didn't want to talk about Mary ever, especially her death, but he owed Veronica something for inadvertently making her feel as if he blamed her for Rathbone's attack.

"She was killed in a carriage accident a little over a year ago."

Veronica's innocent eyes searched his face, her expression so tender and sympathetic that Samuel had to turn away.

"I'm sorry," she murmured.

"It's been a long time. It doesn't matter now." *Liar.*

"I think it matters very much."

"When you feel better, we've got to find a solution to this engagement or your father will end up making us follow through with the wedding."

Would that be so terrible? she wanted to ask but knew already that, to him, it would be. "What would you like to do?"

"I've already taken action," he admitted. "Last night I let it be known that you might throw me over. I'm devastated, of course."

"Of course." She hid her pain behind a smile.

Samuel stared down into her face, conscious of her bravery and pluck, feeling like he was betraying her somehow by extricating them from a situation neither of them wanted. Her skin was ivory, smooth as polished silk and just as soft. "I know it wasn't your fault," he said softly.

"Then why didn't you want to kiss me?"

"Because, apart from everything else, the timing couldn't have been worse. Rathbone's a filthy bastard," he said softly, with a smile, "but he has good taste."

"Then why are you trying to get rid of me so desperately?"

"I'm trying to help you find someone you can really love," he explained gently. "Someone to build a life with."

Veronica searched his face. He was completely sincere. "Don't try so hard," she suggested.

"Veronica . . ."

"I want"—she hesitated, willing him to understand something she didn't entirely understand herself—"to feel like I matter to someone. Could you make me feel that way?"

Samuel's breath caught. "You matter to a lot of people: Anthony, Madeline, your friends."

"I want to matter to you."

"You do matter to me."

"Show me," she said softly.

Samuel froze, staring down at her soft, lovely face. Dimly, he realized she'd made him a substitute for the horror she'd suffered at Neville's hands. More clearly, he saw the treacherous path this emotional reasoning was taking. But her eyes were soft and anxious, her lips pink and quivering. Reacting on instinct rather than sense, he kissed her lightly on the mouth, drawing in the sweetness of her scent and taste as if it were nectar from the gods.

Desire swirled behind the dam of his control: dangerous, dark, and powerful. It roared in his ears, deafened his common sense. He shouldn't be here alone with her. He shouldn't be toying with emotions ripped raw by trauma. It was dangerous for him; pure devastation for her.

He jerked back. They stared at each other. Veronica's eyes were glazed, her mouth deep pink, lips parted. Groaning, Samuel kissed her again. He'd be damned for this. He knew it. But desire had no conscience. Of their own will, his hands swept off the barrier of her cloak, sliding around the arch of her back. Of their own will, his lips crushed hers, his tongue thrusting into her mouth.

Veronica responded with innocent provocation, clinging to him, softly whimpering. His hand slid beneath the torn fabric of her bodice to her corset, feeling the heat of her skin, gently touching the swell of her breasts.

He groaned with passion and desire he hadn't felt for so long. Maybe never. The forbidden fruit had never interested him, but now, *now,* he wanted to push her soft body down on the bed and kiss her senseless, push himself into her, fulfill them both with wild, reckless lovemaking.

He broke away as if she burned him, turning her back to him.

"What's wrong?" Veronica asked.

"You know damn well what's wrong!"

"I want you to kiss me."

"It's not just kissing!" he ground out in exasperation, groaning at the feel of her hands stealing over his shoulders, her breasts pressing against his taut shoulder blades.

"You kissed me like you never wanted to let me go. Do it again," she begged breathlessly.

"Don't you have any clue where this will lead?"

She hesitated. "Yes . . . I'm not completely without experience."

Now, what does that mean? Samuel twisted to stare at her, but it was a mistake. Her hair was tousled and thick, her eyes luminous, the swell of her breasts an enticement no mortal man could resist. "If Anthony saw us now, he'd call me out."

"Uncle Tony doesn't run my life. Neither does my father," she said with bitter rebellion.

He opened his mouth to argue with her, to convince her she was flirting with danger beyond her ken. But she pressed her lips gently to his before pulling back, her eyes full of innocent desire. He stared at her for a long, long moment. Thoughts of Mary had always intruded when any female showed an interest in him. He'd had no trouble fending women off on the trip to England—women who were interested in a night of pleasure and no more.

But Mary wasn't in this room. Veronica: lithe, young, sweet, composed of flesh and blood and spirit—Veronica was here and he wanted her.

Regrets died without remorse as Samuel gathered her close once again. But instead of her lips, his mouth found the vulnerable arch of her neck, the quivering pulse at her throat, the sensitive, shell-like pinkness of her ear.

She trembled at his sweet assault. Her head lolled back, eyes closed, shocks of pleasure sweeping over her. When he lay her back on the brocade bedspread it was the most natural feeling in the world. She felt his hands at her rib cage, his fingers release the ties of her corset, the spill of her breasts into his palms. His groan of pleasure was a triumph to her. She'd known it would be this way with him. She kissed him with abandon, shocked and thrilled at the sight of his dark head bent to her breasts, the heat and shooting thrills of his mouth sucking hard on her nipple.

It was wrong, wrong, wrong! The physical enactment of everything she'd been accused of. But it was sweet and heady and she couldn't prevent a moan of pure ecstacy. She ran a hand over his hard shoulders, fingers coiling in the thick hair at his nape.

He lay half-atop her. His control seemed to snap and suddenly she felt the aching thrust of his hips against hers. She was shocked by the hardness, completely undone by the intimacy of the act. Fear penetrated her desire-drugged brain.

She struggled desperately. "Samuel! Don't!"

He froze as if she'd doused him with a bucket of ice, rolling away from her in one fluid movement. He was across the room so quickly she scarcely had time to draw a breath.

At the door he hesitated, turning to look at her. Veronica was suddenly conscious of her bared breasts. She covered them with shaking hands.

He looked at her as if she were a loathsome tease, or that he was a monster abasing a vulnerable child, or *something* entirely wrong and hurtful.

Before she could put her thoughts in words he opened the door and slipped through, calling for the maid in a hoarse voice that made her feel infinitely worse, infinitely at fault.

With a cry of pure misery she flung herself facedown on the coverlet.

Chapter

13

Samuel leveled the rifle at a distant oak. A block of wood, painted white with concentric circles of red, was nailed to the trunk of the tree. He closed his ears to the warble of the birds and the soft soughing of a distinctly chilly breeze through the limbs of the surrounding oaks. The country. England's idea of the country, at any rate, was a relief from the smelly, overcrowded city.

Boom! The rifle blasted, kicking his shoulder with enough force to jerk him half a step backward.

Anthony moved up beside him, his incredulous gaze on the target. "You hit the center," he said in wonder.

"I started shooting at a young age," he answered.

What would Anthony think if he knew Samuel, at the tender age of thirteen, had tried his damnedest to take a man's life? The man had been fleeing from a crime and Samuel had taken aim several times, only missing his target by inches. Of course, Samuel's murderous aim had been in self-defense; the man had threatened his mother, brothers, and entire family. But it was still a rather remarkable tale to someone as steeped in manners and tradition as Anthony Ashworth.

"If I were Flynne, I'd take the next ship out of England," Anthony remarked.

Samuel merely grunted as he reloaded. It wasn't Flynne he was thinking about. Veronica was foremost on his mind. Veronica was the reason he'd jumped at the chance to head for the country and fire away with a rifle. Frustration was eating him up alive.

But he couldn't let Anthony know that.

As if reading his thoughts, Anthony said, "When I think of Rathbone and what he attempted . . ." He leveled his own rifle at the target, teeth gritted. *Boom!* The acrid smell of cordite filled the air but the shot was several rings away from center. "I see his face instead of the target."

Samuel sighted down the barrel. He didn't see Rathbone's face though he completely agreed with Anthony's sentiment. He didn't see Flynne. He saw himself, lying atop a lovely innocent with more courage than brains, more passion than sense.

Boom!

"You missed!" Anthony was shocked.

"No."

Staring hard, Anthony saw that the bullet has passed so close to the first that the wood was literally blown away between the two marks.

"God help England if there's another war with the States!" he muttered.

Samuel grinned for the first time in days.

Veronica sat glumly in the drawing room. Neville Rathbone's sexual attack had been hushed up as if the man himself had been gagged. Part of her was relieved, part of her was appalled. After all, the man had intended to commit a crime of the vilest nature. Shouldn't he be punished?

She'd said the same to Madeline who had agreed completely. It was Veronica's father, who, if he learned the truth, would blame Veronica and forbid them to ever speak of the issue again. This newest scandal would reflect poorly on his good name.

Add to that the fact that the police were loathe to act

against a member of the nobility, no matter what the crime—the decision was made not to press charges.

Of course Samuel and Uncle Tony had been outraged. It was all Madeline could do to keep them from taking matters into their own hands. Begging for some time while she assured them she would handle Lord Rathbone in her own way, Madeline had smuggled Veronica out of Uncle Tony's house and into their own.

That was why Veronica was now entertaining two of the most odious women of her acquaintance, Jennifer Armstrong and Lady Eveline Spencer, to ensure the proper gossip found its way through Society. Gossip that would blacken Neville's name, yet be ambiguous enough to keep Henry from blaming his daughter.

Glancing at her stepmother, Veronica couldn't help but smile. Madeline was amazing, so artful and clever that one never knew when she was working her magic.

If only she, Veronica, could work that same magic on Samuel.

With a sigh, Veronica replayed those moments in his arms. Just recalling the feel of his body sent tingles of excitement shooting through her limbs. Lord, what was wrong with her? He probably despised her now. Her seesawing emotions had sent her careening to a new disaster. She'd wanted him and would have let him take her, she realized with devastating self-honesty. She loved him and wanted to be his wife.

Had she hoped to wring a real commitment out of him by playing on his sexual desire?

The idea made her cringe. A few more moments of painful self-evaluation relieved her, however. No. She wasn't entirely certain of her motives those passionate moments, but they hadn't been so calculating. She'd wanted him in the most primal, simple, natural way. That was all. A reaction to Neville's attack? Undoubtedly.

But she still wanted him, even though he clearly didn't want her.

"Ladies, I have something dreadful to discuss," Madeline said solemnly.

Both Jennifer's and Eveline's ears pricked up eagerly.

"I hate to speak badly of someone when they're suffering," she continued, passing a cup of tea to Veronica and another to the maliciously horrible Lady Eveline. Today Eveline wore rings of white feathers around her throat, forcing her to stretch her neck above the ruffled layers. She looked rather like an overstuffed swan.

Wouldn't Tomcat have a field day with Eveline now? Veronica thought with an inward smile as she primly sipped her tea.

"Oh, I know." Eveline talked through her nose. "But sometimes it's a disservice to others if certain facts aren't brought to light."

Jennifer Armstrong's lips pursed. "Is this about Mr. Danner?" she asked in a knowing voice.

Veronica sent her an icy look.

"No, Mr. Danner has been the soul of discretion and propriety," Madeline was quick to interject. "I'm afraid it's about Lord Rathbone. Would you care for some cakes?"

"Lord Rathbone?" Jennifer repeated, staring raptly at Madeline. She took two cakes without dropping her eyes, nearly toppling a puffy white confection onto the carpet.

"Veronica," Madeline said softly, turning to her stepdaughter. "Will this be too painful for you to relive?"

There was a twinkle in the depths of Madeline's blue eyes. Veronica sighed heavily and stared at the toes of her shoes. "It is difficult . . ."

"What happened?" Jennifer demanded, agog.

Lady Eveline snorted, appalled at the other woman's lack of manners. Veronica had to admire Madeline's subtle tactics.

"Lord Rathbone made an inappropriate advance to Veronica," Madeline announced. This disappointed both women but Madeline had expected this. "Veronica would be the first to admit to her naivete where Geoffrey Rowbury was concerned and we all know how *that* turned out."

"Disgraceful," Lady Eveline murmured condemningly.

"Scandalous," Jennifer added with less interest.

Madeline sighed. "I'm afraid Henry never understood."

"A father should worry about his daughter's reputation," Lady Eveline pointed out with a cold glare at Veronica. She was always quick to defend Henry. Of course, she was always quick to drape herself over the earl each and every available opportunity.

Veronica tried hard to look contrite.

"Henry may have inadvertently sent the wrong message to Neville." Madeline's brow furrowed. "For that's when Neville's weakness asserted itself."

"What weakness?" Jennifer paused, a cake halfway to her lips.

"I can't see how you can blame Henry for Neville's indiscreet behavior!" Eveline glared down her nose.

Indiscreet? Veronica choked on her tea.

"I'm not blaming Henry," Madeline answered smoothly. "It's just that he didn't understand how much Veronica was victimized by Mr. Rowbury. Henry felt she could have discouraged Geoffrey more and therefore he didn't show as much empathy as he normally would have."

A bald-faced lie. Her father never showed her any empathy regardless of the situation.

"Neville believed the sordid lies about Veronica's reputation. He believed the scandal. Darling, if this is too painful . . . ?" She threw another look Veronica's way.

Veronica shook her head. With her best attempt at shamed misery, she cried in a thin voice, "Neville attacked me. With far more vigor than Geoffrey Rowbury!"

"My dear," Lady Eveline gasped.

"Darling . . ." Madeline handed her a violet-scented handkerchief which Veronica pressed to her lips. She wondered if she could squeeze out a few tears but the effort escaped her. She didn't feel victimized anymore because Madeline was helping her fight back. She managed several miserable sniffs, however, and with murmurs of sympathy, Madeline draped a protective arm across her shoulders.

"Lord Rathbone is so strong?" Jennifer inquired skeptically.

"He's disguised his true nature for years," Madeline inserted quickly. "The man is obsessed! Veronica was saved in the nick of time by her fiancé who recognized Neville's sickness for what it was. Neville has feigned illness and infirmity to win our sympathy and lull us into believing him a harmless old man. In truth, he's a monstrosity. He's lucky to be alive after Samuel Danner discovered the truth!"

"I told you that man was wild!" Jennifer declared, her eyes shining. "Veronica, dear, tell us exactly what happened! What did Mr. Danner do when he discovered Neville's intentions?"

"Well . . ." Veronica dabbed at her dry eyes. "Samuel's from the States, you know. The West," she stressed. "He sometimes loses control a bit."

"Did he hit him?" Lady Eveline leaned forward on her chair.

"He lifted him off his feet by his collar. I have never seen a man so deadly furious." That, at least, was the unvarnished truth.

Jennifer was in a state of ecstasy. "Oh, my dear, how frightening! You were—unscathed—though?" At Veronica's nod, she murmured with less interest, "How lucky! Did you think Mr. Danner might kill Neville?"

Veronica hesitated, wondering how far she could go. Madeline nodded almost imperceptibly. "If Neville had resisted, Samuel would undoubtedly have done him serious injury, but I think Neville knew that. Neville went white and Samuel . . ." She coughed, as much to hide her own laughter as add to the effect. "His language was blistering! I daresay, I nearly swooned."

"What a terrible ordeal!" Lady Eveline murmured, her gaze sharp. She was smart enough to wonder if she'd been set up. But Madeline's face was all innocence and concern. Jennifer had swallowed the bait whole. She looked suitably shocked by the story. Her eyes bright with avaricious desire as she thought about Samuel's heroism.

Veronica felt a sharp stab of jealousy. If the woman made one move toward Samuel, she was in for a fight.

"We must keep this to ourselves," Madeline added laughably, for there was no doubt both women would spread the news quicker than the evening papers.

Madeline showed Lady Eveline and Jennifer out and when she returned, she was all business. "This could backfire," she said, worried. "It could make Lord Rathbone a romantic figure and increase the scandal surrounding you."

"It will make Samuel the romantic figure," Veronica replied. "Jennifer's already setting her sites on him!"

"You really want Mr. Danner?"

"Yes."

"I thought the engagement was merely for your father's benefit," Madeline murmured in surprise.

Her stepmother's savvy never ceased to amaze her. "It started out that way," Veronica admitted candidly. "But it's not the way I feel now."

"And Mr. Danner?"

Veronica smiled faintly. "Actually, I don't think he likes me very much right now."

Madeline looked unhappy. "I don't know what's worse: marrying for the sake of marriage, or marrying for love, when the love's one-sided. Veronica, you must be very careful with your emotions. Your father . . ." She cleared her throat. "It would just be better if he didn't know how you feel."

Veronica understood. Henry Ashworth discounted women as thinking, feeling beings of equal importance to men. Women had certain functions: running a household, being an object of amusement, providing a title, or money, or conferring social status upon the man. But if she was to put her wants first, then she would have to be reminded of her place.

No, Henry could never know how badly she desired Samuel because then he would make certain she could never have him.

"Thank you, Madeline," Veronica said sincerely.

Her stepmother merely smiled.

In denim trousers and a cotton work shirt, Samuel strode up the steps to Veronica's house, slapping dust from a Stetson that he settled on his head in direct disregard to

London fashion. Northcroft, stiff as a board and cold as the North Atlantic, reluctantly allowed him entry.

"Lady Veronica's in her room," Northcroft informed him in chill tones. He eyed Samuel from head to toe, then showed him into the morning room.

But it was Madeline who joined him ten minutes later, her face clouded with worry.

"I didn't tell Veronica you were here. I wanted to speak to you first myself."

All Samuel wanted to do was apologize. He couldn't get the vision of Veronica draped across the bed out of his mind. He couldn't get the feel or scent or taste of her out of his soul. He wanted to end this engagement *now!*

Madeline folded her hands together, looking for all the world like she was praying. Samuel waited.

"She's very much in love with you," Madeline said.

Of all the reactions he'd expected—recriminations, anger, righteous indignation—this was the furthest from his mind. And the furthest from the truth. "Veronica wants her freedom and I'm the vessel she chose to achieve it," he answered levelly.

"No. She wants you, and I'm worried that you'll hurt her terribly."

"You and Anthony," Samuel muttered in exasperation.

"If you're careful with her emotions, I'll help you in any way I can."

"Help me what? Arrest Flynne? Lady Ashworth, I appreciate the gesture, but association with your family hasn't helped yet. I don't see it helping in the future. Tell Veronica I'd like to talk to her."

Madeline sighed. She left the room with a heavy heart. She'd so hoped she could aid Veronica, but unless Samuel changed his mind it didn't appear that her stepdaughter would fare any better with men than she had.

Madeline had suffered at the hands of men all her life. Her father had been an overbearing tyrant who'd wanted sons and been blessed with five daughters. When Madeline, who was the picture of propriety, was but fourteen he began introducing her to wealthy and/or titled gentlemen. Her beauty was instantly appreciated and when Lord Henry Ashworth, the earl of Charlwood, recently widowed and handsome as sin, began taking an interest in her, Madeline's father approved of the match without his daughter's consent.

Madeline, however, would have given her consent gladly. She'd sensed Henry was somewhat autocratic; most men were. But she would be mistress of her own home and if that meant raising three headstrong daughters by Henry's first marriage, so be it.

She hadn't counted on Henry's history, however.

For years she'd ignored the undercurrents within the household. Henry's three daughters were oblivious; so would she be. So when she discovered proof of her husband's infidelity—an article of his clothing left in one of the servant girl's bedrooms—she kept the information to herself.

A lady understood that men were different from women in regards to physical needs. Madeline went about rigidly enforcing the rules of propriety, and when Veronica's high spirits began causing problems, she did as Henry would have wanted: blaming Veronica and forcing her to Society's ways.

But now she knew that had been a mistake. Men like Neville Rathbone . . . and Henry . . . had had their way too long. Madeline was determined to tip the scales in her own sex's favor. She wanted someone she knew to marry for love, marry a man of substance who would give her all the emotional rewards she so desired.

"Veronica?" She tapped on her stepdaughter's bedroom door. "Samuel's downstairs waiting to see you."

Veronica flew out of the bedroom, eyes shining. Madeline's weighted heart sank yet further as Veronica grabbed her skirts and hurried downstairs to meet the man she loved.

Madeline followed slowly, in time to hear, through the crack in the door, Samuel say quietly but firmly, ". . . the other night was my mistake. I promise it won't happen again. But you need to be the one to dissolve this engagement, otherwise your beloved Society"—his voice deepened with irony—"will once again tear your reputation to ribbons. Neville Rathbone should be hung by his . . ." He laughed shortly. "Well, anyway, I'm sure you feel the way I do. At our next, and last, social engagement, will you do the honors?"

There was a long beat of hesitation, then Veronica said in a surprisingly controlled voice, "Consider the matter resolved."

There was no account of Neville's attack in the papers but the word was a rocket of gossip through the Quality. Veronica's reputation was indeed discussed in depth, but the overall opinion was Neville had lost his head over an unorthodox, interesting young woman whose spicy history, rather than condemning her this time, only added to her intrigue, helping her fast become Society's latest darling despite her somewhat scandalous past.

Madeline's counterattack against Neville couldn't have been more successful. One moment Veronica was scorned by all; the next she was the most sought after woman in the city.

But Veronica was equally aware that Madeline, who seemed to have taken her desire to marry Samuel as a personal quest, was waging a losing battle. Samuel couldn't wait for her to accept the next invitation and pronounce their engagement over and done with. He would be her escort, if she so desired, but he was firm about wanting to be through "doing his duty."

It was such a dreadful coil.

Now, Veronica gazed with little interest around the room of people who'd attended Harriet Rowe's soiree. Samuel was beside her, a perfect escort, but he was clearly waiting for her to make her announcement. Veronica was torn between the desire to throw herself on his mercy and proclaim her love and to stamp her well-shod foot down on his toes. Instead she smiled at all and sundry, her arm draped through Samuel's and wished with religious fervency that he would be struck senseless by Cupid's arrow.

Failing that, she hoped the ceiling would crash down upon his stubborn head.

To add to her woes, Samuel's casual words to Wilhelmina Stuart had set off another circle of gossip. It was already commonly believed that Veronica was on the verge of throwing him over even though she hadn't breathed a word to anyone to that effect.

Veronica sipped a glass of pale, peach-colored punch, sensing Samuel by her side as if he were part of her. It was so annoying. How could he kiss her like he was dying for her one moment, then shut her out as if she were a leper the next?

"Blast," she muttered beneath her breath.

"Did you want something?" he asked.

You. "No, thank you."

"Are you having a good time?"

I'm dying inside. "Marvelous."

Neville was notably absent. Society had closed ranks against him and sided with Veronica. Rumor had it his doctor had advised an extended trip on the Continent. Good riddance to the coward, Veronica thought.

"Would you care for another drink?" Samuel asked.

I would rather taste your lips. "Please."

He returned with a glass of punch and a crystal plate with several small sandwiches. A group of well-dressed nobles was arranging itself around the piano where a talented young man began to sing a haunting, romantic ballad.

Samuel cocked one brow, as if he couldn't bear the sentiment. Veronica wanted to scream with frustration. Did he have to be so clear that he found being her fiancé so intolerable? Was she supposed to feel relieved that nothing had happened between them that night in Uncle Tony's bedroom? That, unlike Neville, he held complete dominion over his own desires? That he'd heard her cry of "Don't," and now refused to even touch her?

"Your friend, Wortham, can't take his eyes off you," Samuel noted.

"Wortham is merely a *friend.*"

"I believe he'd like something more."

Veronica gritted her teeth in irritation. Wortham was indeed watching her. She smiled at him and he immediately crowded to her side. Samuel tried to drift away but luckily was prevented by a group of chattering women.

"The pianist is something special, isn't he?" Wortham said, eyeing both Veronica and Samuel with a thoughtful expression.

"Very talented," Veronica agreed.

Samuel didn't respond, but at that moment James Fielding spied their little group, released Amelia's hand, and sauntered over next to Samuel. His assessing eyes skated over Veronica's pink gown. "Wretched luck with Neville, Ronnie, darling," he said.

She sensed Samuel's muscles tighten beside her. "I would rather not talk about it."

"Of course." James looked slightly contemptuous. "It's dreadful how these incidents keep happening to you."

"Maybe you ought to close your mouth before someone else does it for you?" Samuel suggested in a deceptive drawl.

Veronica's heart jumped in delight. Wortham choked on a cucumber sandwich, coughing so hard he had to bend over.

James didn't see anything humorous in the remark, however. "Excuse me," he said icily, returning to Amelia's side.

Another guest entered the room and a stir of excitement electrified the crowd. Veronica strained to see who it was, then drew a startled breath.

"It's Catherine!" she murmured when Samuel turned to her for elucidation.

"Who's Catherine?"

"Catherine was the woman I'd hoped to make my wife," Anthony said dryly, coming up behind them.

She was a small woman with blond hair and laughing blue eyes. She bore, in fact, a marked resemblance to Amelia St. John, except that Catherine was older and possessed a bright, sweet temperament evident in the humor in her face that Amelia could never hope to achieve.

Anthony strode directly up to her, said something in greeting that brought a smile to her lips, then led her to the group surrounding the pianist. It was artful, correct, and polite and only Veronica knew how much it cost him. He'd loved her so desperately.

Moments later he returned to Veronica and Samuel. "Care to take a walk in the garden?" he asked his niece. Seeing Amelia St. John's avid eyes following Uncle Tony, Veronica agreed, reluctantly leaving Samuel's side.

"I promise I'll stay until the end," Samuel said, arching one brow.

"Don't worry, I'll handle everything," she assured him, annoyed.

"You've fallen in love with him, haven't you?" Uncle Tony remarked, as soon as they were alone.

Veronica would have been overjoyed to deny the obvious, especially with Samuel so eager to turn her over to someone else. Watching his tall, handsome form move toward a corner near the door, she drew a painful breath. "For all the good it does me. He expects me to end our engagement tonight."

"Ah . . ."

They walked through the French doors and beneath a trellis twisted with the thorny vines of roses. Water dripped gently through the branches, the reminder of the latest torrent of early March rain. Laughter and music flowed outward in waves.

"Does he know?"

Veronica hesitated. "I believe he thinks I'm so desperate for a husband that I'd pretend to be in love with him."

"He won't let himself see the truth. That's good. If he knew, it would be a lot more difficult for you."

She thought of Catherine and understood. "What happened between you two?" she asked, and he didn't pretend to misunderstand. Instead he pulled out a cigar, lit the end of it, inhaled deeply, then watched the smoke dissipate into the dripping rain.

"I think I was too much in love. I would have done

anything for Catherine. Climbed Mount Everest, walked across Africa. I've made a lot of mistakes in my life." He shrugged. "Not taken enough responsibility. Mocked Henry and his title. Gambled some, even been a bit of a rogue. But with Catherine it was different."

"What happened?" Veronica asked gently.

"She didn't love me enough. And then I gave her a reason, an opportunity to leave me." He grimaced. "I spent an evening with Amelia. All on the up-and-up, but Amelia made it sound like more than it was and Catherine wrote me a letter saying how much she wanted to stay friends. Anything more than that was impossible."

"I'm sorry," Veronica murmured.

He was philosophical. "It would never have worked anyway."

"Amelia is a poisonous witch!"

"It wasn't Amelia's fault."

Veronica sighed. "I have this terrible feeling there's a lesson in here somewhere."

He chuckled. "I just don't want you to expect more than Samuel Danner can give you. He was married once, did you know that?"

"To Mary."

"He told you about her?"

"A bit."

Anthony nodded. "That's all he's told me, as well: a bit. But anytime he speaks of her it's with reverence. I'm afraid she's reached sainthood in his mind."

Veronica didn't want to hear this.

"You can't fight a dead woman, Veronica," he added gently. "Even if you could, Samuel will be moving back to Oregon eventually. Do as he suggests and end this crazy engagement before Henry pushes you to the altar. You'll fall in love with someone else."

Veronica managed a faint smile, but she kept her thoughts to herself. She knew the odds were stacked against her. She knew Uncle Tony was giving her wonderful advice.

But she had no intention of taking it.

An hour later the soiree was breaking up and Veronica hadn't uttered a single word about her engagement to Samuel. She couldn't bring herself to.

His dark expression said he knew she'd failed him, and on the carriage ride home he scarcely spoke to her.

She was afraid he wouldn't walk her to the door, but he did, hesitating on the top step. He was cold with anger, however, and she wasn't certain how to react when he said, "It's not going to work, Lady Veronica."

"Pardon me?"

"You know exactly what I'm talking about. I have no intention of taking a wife. If you want to embark upon an affair, I might be persuaded, but marriage is out of the question."

"Did I ask to marry you?" she demanded.

"The longer you take in keeping up this pretense, the closer you come."

His arrogance was incredible!

"Do something by next week or I'll take matters into my own hands," he added in a dire tone.

"Don't worry," she snapped. "I won't be a burden a moment longer than I have to." With that she slammed the door in his face, her heart sinking as she wondered how long it would take her father to sell her off to someone else.

Chapter

14

The door to her father's study was locked. Veronica peeked through the keyhole, her ears tuned to every creak and squeak in the house. If someone caught her, there would be hell to pay, but it couldn't be any worse than the fate that awaited her now that she'd told Madeline Samuel wanted to break their engagement.

Madeline would be forced to give the news to her father fairly soon and how he chose to act upon it, Veronica could only shudder and guess.

From the pocket of her skirt she withdrew a heavy key, pilfered that morning from Henry's bureau. She'd known where to find it. She hadn't misspent her youth without learning a few things along the way.

Though she was certain she hated Samuel with a passion, she hadn't quite given up the idea of helping him. In the back of her mind was the faint hope it would somehow change his mind about her.

Slipping the key in the lock, she winced at the grating *click* it made when she turned it. Heart pounding, she slipped inside, noiselessly closing the door behind her.

The room was cool and dark, every inch of wall space

taken up with elaborately carved mahogany bookcases. A massive desk sat in front of the paned windows that overlooked a private hedged garden—a garden which could only be accessed from this one room.

Veronica worked fast, systematically checking every drawer, cranny, and crevice, reading every file, paper, and note she could get her hands on. Nothing.

Next she examined the books. There were hundreds of them. With painstaking care, counting the minutes inside her head, she checked each bound volume. She was only a third of the way through when she heard someone at the front door.

She froze.

Northcroft answered the knock.

"Is Henry in this afternoon?" Lady Eveline asked in her throaty voice.

"I'm sorry, madame. The master of the house is at his office. Lady Ashworth is shopping with her daughters."

Veronica's lips parted in delight. Northcroft didn't know she was still at the house.

"I'll just leave my card, then," Eveline said, disappointment sharpening her voice.

Moments later the door closed and Northcroft's footsteps retreated. Breathing a sigh of relief, Veronica continued her search. Opening a small volume of love poems—an odd book for her father to possess—a lavender-colored paper fluttered to the floor.

She picked it up. Inside was a rudimentary love note signed in an uneven scrawl by the parlor maid her father had fired the summer before.

The parlor maid everyone had assumed the footman had got with child.

An hour later, Veronica paced back and forth across the drawing room carpet, anxiously awaiting Madeline's return. Now she knew why her father, who'd shown a distinct affection for the parlor maid, had summarily fired the poor girl. The note had discussed their cherished moments together; proof enough that Henry had indulged in an illicit affair.

Yet he had the audacity to be infuriated by *her* behavior!

Shaking her head, she hugged herself, feeling suddenly cold. She wasn't naive enough to believe the parlor maid was Henry's first conquest. Unfolding the love note from her pocket, she considered discussing it with Madeline. But maybe Madeline didn't know. Maybe all she would do was hurt her with proof of her father's infidelity.

Maybe she, Veronica, had a half brother or sister.

Oh, God.

If only she could talk to someone who could advise her. Samuel . . .

Veronica grabbed her cloak, repressing the nagging thought that she was just using this as an excuse to see him. Damn and glory. What did it matter now? She was so shocked and befuddled she could scarcely think straight. How could her father demand perfection from her when his feet were made of clay?

If only she could help Samuel. If only she could get out of this house, out from beneath her father's thumb.

If only . . .

An idea entered her whirling brain as the footman brought round the carriage, a daring plan that could help Samuel find Victor Flynne. It was outrageous and foolhardy but could be effective.

Veronica clutched her reticule so tightly her hands hurt. Her heart pounded. No! Even she couldn't embark on such a risky plan. It was destined to fail, destined to blow up in her face.

But it was the perfect way to flush out a blackmailer, and what did she have to lose anyway? Her father's love and respect?

With sudden decision, she ordered the waiting coachman, "Please take me to Lady Amelia St. John's."

And Samuel, I hope I'm not making another terrible blunder!

* * *

The Swan hadn't improved with a month's time, Samuel decided, smelling indefinable sour odors that would turn the stoutest stomach. He turned his pint around on the tabletop, frustrated beyond measure. Mr. Dirkson, Flynne's emissary, hadn't shown. Damn the man! Flynne was dangling Samuel at the end of a string and there wasn't a single thing he could do about it.

But that wasn't the worst of it. Oh, no! His fury was self-directed for a very different reason.

He couldn't get Veronica off his mind.

"'Nother pint?" the blond barmaid asked, grinning.

"Not yet. Thank you." He'd barely touched the one in front of him.

"Y'waitin fer Dirk, ain't cha? 'E's a dirty one, make no mistake." She regarded him with a mixture of curiosity and pity. "Wha'cha buyin' from 'im?"

Samuel gave her a long look. His mind flashed on that memorable meeting he'd once had with a whore named Patricia Lee. She'd come to him with information about a murder. Mary's murder.

"I'm trying to buy information."

"'Bout what?"

"A Mr. Victor Flynne. Sometimes goes by Victor Flannigan."

She screwed up her face in powerful thought. Clearly she wanted to be the one to impart good news. She didn't lie; he had to credit her that. She just shook her head and sighed in disappointment.

"You looks like a gen'leman, ta me. Wish ah could 'elp ya." She was clearly sorry. "Don't trust Dirk none. That wot 'angs with the rats, are one, I always say. Bad sort, Dirk. Keep yer money in yer pocket, else Dirk's dirty 'and'll grab it when yer not lookin'."

"Thanks for the advice."

He left her an outrageous tip which elicited a chortle of delight and many thanks and good wishes on him and his. Outside, in the thick misty rain, he thought about Mr. Dirkson and a feeling of depression enveloped him. Another useless foray. A diversion? Was this Victor's way of getting him away from the heart of London so he could go about his murdering, blackmailing ways without a Danner on his tail?

Turning up his collar, Samuel hailed a passing hansom cab back to Anthony's town house.

Veronica's heart hammered in her chest as the carriage pulled into the curved drive of St. John Manor. Calling on Amelia was either divine inspiration or supreme folly, but she couldn't think of a woman with a more spiteful tongue, and that was saying a lot.

Spying another carriage parked in the drive ahead of her, Veronica groaned. James Fielding was visiting. Dreadful luck.

"Lady Veronica Ashworth," the footman announced after reading her calling card. A few minutes later she was shown into the drawing room where James stood in front of the fire, one arm resting on the mantel, as if he were deliberately posed. Amelia was also standing, her curiosity apparently so great that she couldn't bear to remain seated while Veronica was shown in.

"Ronnie, darling," James said smoothly as she entered. She was forced to reach a hand to him in greeting which he kissed with hard lips. A shiver of revulsion raced up her spine.

"I must say, I'm surprised to see you." Amelia's brows lifted. Her hair was bound in pink ribbons, too girlish for someone with her acquired sophistication.

"When one is desperate, one takes desperate measures," Veronica answered ambiguously.

"Desperate?" James sauntered over to the couch as Veronica perched on one of its cushions.

"Not I. A friend of mine is suffering a terrible fate." She tried to imagine how Madeline would handle this. She must tread carefully indeed. She couldn't afford to overplay her part. "She has found herself in serious, serious trouble, I'm afraid. The result of poor judgment and infatuation."

"Trouble with a man?" Amelia asked with interest.

It would be impolite for them to question exactly whom she was speaking of; the art of conversation was steeped in rules. Veronica shot a look of concern in James's direction.

"Oh, don't mind James," Amelia assured her. "He's the soul of discretion."

"I'm sure," Veronica murmured with a sardonic edge. "But this is a very delicate matter. My friend has been indiscreet and now the very worst has happened."

Amelia gasped. "Her husband has found out!"

"No, she is not married. Yet."

"She is with child," James said bluntly, eliciting a squeak of half protest, half delight from Amelia. Veronica, who'd been leading up to this tale, was surprised he'd caught on so quickly. But then James generally thought with other parts of his body before his brain, she reminded herself grimly.

"Please. I require your utmost confidence in this matter," Veronica appealed. "It is not possible for her to—continue —with this situation."

"Why have you come to Amelia?" James asked.

An excellent question, Veronica conceded, but one she was prepared for. "The woman in question is a member of Society. She will be ruined if this situation should come to light. Amelia is a woman of sophistication and influence." She turned to Amelia, swallowing down the bile of deceit. "I'm not suggesting you personally know of someone who can help my friend, but within the realm of your acquaintance, perhaps there's a doctor who could advise her?"

Oh, Madeline! You'd be proud of me if you ever approved of this foolish undertaking!

"As you say, I know of no one personally." Amelia's eyes assessed Veronica's slim figure as if she were sure it was Veronica herself who was pregnant. Veronica had expected this reaction, but since nothing could be farther from the truth, she didn't mind the speculation.

"Time is of the essence," Veronica pressed.

"It always is in these cases," James remarked.

Amelia attempted to squeeze out the identity of the woman in question but Veronica cagily avoided a direct answer. Her mission accomplished, she quickly took her leave. As she gathered her cloak, however, she found James at her elbow. On the steps outside, when she would have turned to her carriage, he suddenly remarked, "An abortionist costs a lot of money, Ronnie, darling. Is your American lover so poor he can't help you? Or are you keeping this secret from him as well?"

"I came to Amelia on behalf of my friend," Veronica retorted icily. "I can see speaking in front of you was a mistake."

"Speaking in front of me is the only way you'll get what you want," he corrected her. "Amelia doesn't know up from down about the issue you tossed at her feet. I'll send you the man you need. But don't pretend we don't know whom this abortion is for."

"You know nothing about me, James. And you never will."

He wrenched up her chin with one hard palm. "I know everything I need to know, you wretched whore."

She slapped him hard, then turned to her carriage. Divine inspiration? she thought shakily.

Supreme folly . . .

It was with a considerable amount of willpower that Samuel kept himself from checking on Veronica as soon as he got back to city center. His fear for her safety bordered on the paranoid, and he reminded himself that the less he saw of her, the better for both of them.

His first call, therefore, was on Lord Jason Cromwell. He found, as he'd found every other time he'd tried to meet with the elusive Lord Cromwell, that the man was unavailable. But today luck was with him in that Jason's sister, Anne, was willing to receive him.

He couldn't imagine what he would discuss with Anne but it was at least a foot in the door. A dour butler led the way to the morning room where Anne was seated stiffly in an uncomfortable-looking high-backed chair, her reddish blond hair coiffed to perfection upon a delicately boned head. Her eyes were blue, her nose tiny. Only her mouth was a disappointment, pinched and petulant and spoiled.

"Mr. Danner," she greeted him coolly. "Your eagerness to see my brother seems almost obsessive."

"It is obsessive," Samuel admitted with a smile.

She jerked in surprise at his directness. "Could I help you in some manner?"

Samuel's gaze narrowed on her face. He'd had all he could take with the Quality's parlor games. "Only if you're willing to dig up family skeletons and expose them to a complete stranger."

"I'm sure I don't know what you mean."

"I believe your brother is being blackmailed or coerced or harassed in some way by a man named Victor Flynne. Flynne uses several aliases; Flannigan for one. I would like very much to find Mr. Flynne." He glanced at the polished silver plate on the table. "I don't have a card, but you can reach me at Anthony Ashworth's town house. If Lord Jason would like Flynne brought to justice, have him contact me."

Anne stared at him in shocked wonder.

"Good day, Lady Anne."

The love note was completely knocked from Veronica's head until dinnertime when she was forced to see both Henry and Madeline across the same table. It burned in her pocket. Oh, how she wished she could talk to Samuel about it.

"The wedding date has been set," Henry announced, folding his napkin carefully across his lap. "April twenty-second."

"What?" Veronica stared at him, mouth agape. She looked to Madeline for help, but Madeline was just as shocked as she was. Chloe and Patrice looked at them all in awe.

Henry dipped into his soup. "My understanding is that Mr. Danner's very anxious to marry you. That is what you said, isn't it?" His tone was sardonic.

Veronica was speechless. Clearly Madeline hadn't had time to give him the news about her broken engagement.

"Could the date be postponed until May?" Madeline suggested, unable to meet Veronica's panicked eyes.

May is such a lovely month for a wedding, Veronica thought a bit hysterically, thinking of Harriet Rowe. *Oh, Lord! If this rumor gets out, Samuel will murder me with his bare hands!*

Henry shook his head. "I've asked Mr. Danner to stop by this evening to finalize the details. We'll judge his reaction to my suggestion."

"Did you tell him why you wanted to see him?" Veronica asked desperately.

"What is the matter with you?" he demanded, annoyed. "Mr. Danner will learn the subject of my interest when he arrives."

"But, Father . . ."

"Enough, Veronica! For once in your life, try to behave respectfully."

Respectfully? When she now knew he was incapable of respect himself?

Without a word she laid down her napkin, scraped back her chair, and left the table. Henry caught up with her at the bottom of the stairway, his grip tight on her arm.

"You may go to your room, but you will come down when Mr. Danner arrives," he ordered in a steely voice.

She met his gaze wrathfully, staring him down until he released his grip. Her mind was on the expelled parlor maid. As soon as he let her go, she dashed upstairs, a new problem consuming her.

Samuel will think I'm the one who pushed up the wedding!

Veronica groaned and dropped her head in her hands. She hated Samuel knowing how much she wanted and needed him. She hated feeling like mere chattel. She wanted worth as a person, worth as a thinking, feeling human being.

For the first time in her young life she seriously questioned the values she lived by. What purpose did she have, hoping for a husband, arranging flowers, painstakingly creating antimacassars and needlepoint cushions, playing the piano or harp, being an object of admiration for her father, or husband, to show off to other men? Surely there must be something more for a woman than to just pray for a kind, successful husband?

Veronica considered. Over the years she'd created small stirs and scandals as a means to fight the barriers of femininity. But now time was running out. She was desperate for freedom.

Was that all her love was for Samuel? A chance for a new, adventurous life?

Veronica badly wanted to believe it, but it wasn't true. She did love him, and loving him was a worse trap than the one she'd just described.

"Damn and glory," she muttered crossly, changing her dress for something more suitable to entertain a gentleman. Gentleman? Hah. Samuel Danner wouldn't hesitate to defy convention for the sake of his quest, even if it meant throwing her to the wolves.

She moved the crumpled love note to the pocket of her spring green gown, wondering what to do about it. Descending the stairway, she was about to search for Madeline when the front bell rang and Northcroft admitted Samuel.

He wore a dark suit and looked so incredibly handsome it almost took her breath away. Fighting her silly attraction, she greeted him a trifle coolly.

"My father's about to test your mettle," she whispered fiercely in his ear when Northcroft was out of earshot.

"Really? Swords or pistols?"

"Words. Dates. April twenty-second, to be exact. He wants to move up the wedding."

"You haven't told him—"

"I told Madeline the engagement's off," she cut off his furious words. "Apparently she hasn't had a chance to give him the news."

"Bloody damn! This has got to end."

"I am taking care of it," she said through her teeth.

Samuel's gaze dropped from her angry face, to the fists propped on her hips. Though he suspected she would bite off his head if he said so, he found her adorable when she was angry. Against his will, his eyes slid to the swell of her breasts and the nip of her waist. God, but he had to stay away from her.

"I'll have to press Dirkson," he said, thinking aloud. "And Cromwell and Houghton. One of those *gentlemen* is sure to crack given the right amount of pressure. Tell your father I couldn't stay. That'll give you time to let him know the true nature of our relationship."

"Mr. Danner . . ." she said when he turned away.

He glanced back, surprised at the formality.

"I think you should know that I would rather marry a scorpion than spend a moment longer engaged to you."

His grin of amusement made her want to stomp her foot in frustration.

Veronica couldn't have been angrier if her father had told her he was reconsidering Neville Rathbone's offer of marriage. She was through hoping Samuel would save her. She had to make her own choices. Her own plans.

"I would like to see you in my study," her father's voice suddenly penetrated her thoughts. He threw open the doors and bade her enter.

With resentment simmering in every vein, she seated herself across from him at his desk. Henry attempted to stare her down, his eyes cold, one hand reaching for the humidor that held his imported Cuban cigars.

"What are you hiding, Veronica?"

"Hiding?" He caught her by surprise. She'd been certain he was going to berate her for letting Samuel "get away."

"What happened to Mr. Danner?"

She relaxed. This was more what she'd expected. "He had business to take care of."

Henry glowered at her. "If he opposes this marriage—"

"He won't. Samuel's just as anxious for the wedding as I am," she said, crossing her fingers. This was not the time to be truthful.

"Were you in my study earlier?"

Veronica blinked. "In your study?"

"Someone has rifled through my papers. Whoever they were, they were very clever. But a few items were out of place. Madeline says you were here alone today."

One lie per argument was enough, Veronica determined. Besides, she was interested in his reaction. "I was looking for some information for a friend of mine who's in trouble."

"In *my* study?" He was furiously indignant. "What sort of information?"

"Something to help her out of a difficult situation. I didn't find it."

"My study is personal. My desk is personal," he said through his teeth. "This may be your home, but this room is strictly off-limits. My business is private." A weighty pause ensued. "You cannot possibly understand my private papers. Should you discuss anything you've seen or read with your simpleminded friends, I'll disown you."

A familiar refrain. "Yes, Father."

He dismissed her with a sharp wave of his hand, his brow deeply furrowed. Veronica suspected he was worried about what she might have discovered. With good reason, she thought bitterly. He possessed no morals and no kindness.

Why had Madeline ever agreed to marry him? Possibly she'd had no choice.

For the first time in a long time Veronica thought of her own mother. What had happened to her? She wanted the truth. All of it.

Hunching her shoulders, she realized she needed some new means of escape now that her engagement was ending. She wished she had relatives who would come to her aid, but Henry had no family that she knew of other than Uncle Tony. Her mother's family had cut all ties to the Ashworths when Cordelia died, and Veronica had seldom seen any of them. But Samuel had been introduced to Uncle Tony by some distant relative in Oregon, she remembered with a start. What was her name? Chamberlain. Lady Agatha Chamberlain.

Maybe that was the answer, she thought with renewed hope. A life in Oregon. Way out west with some long-distant relative.

And a chance to be near Samuel? a wicked inner voice asked.

"I would rather marry Northcroft," she said aloud.

Chapter

15

Victor Flynne tallied the neat entries in his ledger book. He'd nearly run out of time in London, thank the Lord. Danner had alerted the authorities and cut such a swath through the Quality that Victor could no longer trust his pigeons to keep their mouths shut.

Except Dirk, that is. Dirk wouldn't talk because Victor could threaten him with intense, killing labor at Coldbath Fields for his myriad of crimes of theft and assault should Victor's own indiscretions come to light.

Which reminded him of Lord Henry Ashworth . . .

Victor had a little unfinished business with the pompous earl and his lovely daughter, Veronica.

Clucking his tongue, he leaned back in his chair, clasping his hands at the base of his neck as he envisioned the intriguing eldest Ashworth offspring. The poor little fool was looking for an abortionist. Apparently Danner had got her with child and thrown her over. Unlikely Danner behavior, as Victor well knew, but there was no doubt Samuel was still pining away over his dead wife and it was possible he'd bedded and impregnated Veronica in a weak moment.

His brow puckered. A shame about Mary, really.

A diffident knock sounded on his door. Victor glanced about, to the stacked boxes here and there. An unfortunate aspect of his profession was the need to move rather more frequently than he wanted to.

"Who is it?" he asked, knowing full well, but it never hurt to be careful.

"Dirk."

Victor opened the door and bade the smelly Dirkson inside. "You know what I want?" he asked the dirty idiot.

"Yessir."

"I'll let you know when. Willoughby's been contacted."

"'Ow ya gonna git 'er outta th' 'ouse?" he asked.

"Leave that to me. You just do your part. Good day, Mr. Dirkson."

Victor closed the door, shaking his head in disbelief at the quality of people he had to work with. And Dirkson—that imbecile—wanted partial payment in the form of a pair of cowboy boots!

Clearly the world needed more people like himself to clean up the flotsam and jetsam of humanity.

The following day Veronica was up with the birds. She had plans to make. But late in the morning, as she was pulling on her gloves, a telegram arrived addressed to her.

> Lady Veronica,
> Your request has been forwarded to a mutual
> friend. He will call on you this afternoon. His
> calling card will bear a familiar name.
>
> > Good luck,
> > James

James Fielding? Icy fingers of dread crept up Veronica's spine. She changed her mind about going out. She didn't want to miss this mysterious caller. Who could he be? Could he have any connection to Victor Flynne, or had this chance for blackmail eluded the elusive Mr. Flynne? Oh, Lord! Could the man in question be an *abortionist?*

Veronica panicked. She had to get everyone else out of the house. She wished her family possessed a telephone. How dearly she would love to merely pick up an instrument and call someone to please—*please*—invite her stepmother and sisters over! She desperately needed to be alone when this man appeared at the door.

She was racking her brain for an answer when, for once, fate smiled upon her.

"Chloe and Patrice have a dress fitting," Madeline informed Veronica after lunch. "Would you care to come with us?"

"Oh, Madeline, I'm so sorry. I'm feeling kind of tired this afternoon. I think I'll just take a nap."

Madeline shot her a disbelieving look but she let it go. By two o'clock Veronica was alone in the house with just the servants. Her only real problem was Northcroft, but he could easily be distracted should it prove necessary.

With great anticipation—and a certain amount of trepidation—she settled in to wait.

"Hear the wedding's been moved up, don't you know," an acquaintance of Anthony's said, winking as he passed by the table where Samuel and Anthony were dining. Samuel threw the man a cold look, frustration eating him alive.

"Veronica doesn't know the meaning of keeping her word," he muttered irritably. "That's the fourth comment today. The next time someone makes a remark, I'm going to set him straight."

"Seems to be an inordinate amount of speculation," Anthony agreed. "For an intelligent woman, Veronica's acted less than brilliant over you, I must say. Put an end to this engagement, Danner, by all means, but be kind. I think she's got some harebrained idea that the longer it lasts, the more it will mean."

"You don't know what you're talking about," Samuel growled.

"Try to remember what it feels like to be in love so you can let her down easy. She does care, Samuel. And Veronica's feelings run deep."

It irked him that Anthony felt he had to be coached. He didn't believe for a moment that Veronica's feelings for him were anything more than gratitude that he'd helped her out of a tight spot.

"Hello, Anthony," a smooth voice broke in. Samuel glanced up to find James Fielding giving him a smug, assessing look. "Mr. Danner."

There was something positively revolting about the man. They shook hands and Samuel eyed him closely. He seemed to want to say something, but didn't know how to go about it.

"Something on your mind, Lord Fielding?" Samuel drawled.

"Veronica, naturally, considering her delicate situation."

Fielding's gaze intensified. His eyes were as cold and unrelenting as a cobra's.

Samuel had had enough. "The wedding is not going to be moved up. What Henry wants isn't necessarily what Veronica and I want. In fact, I doubt there will be a wedding at all."

"Really?" Fielding's eyes narrowed thoughtfully.

"Veronica seems to be losing interest in me," Samuel added for good measure.

"Are you saying what I think you're saying?" Fielding asked quickly.

"I'm saying there won't be a wedding."

"You bastard." Admiration tinged his voice. "You'd leave her to face social ruin! Unless the brat isn't yours," he suddenly remarked, his expression changed. "How delicious! Our Ronnie's reputation was well earned after all. Too bad she got caught in her own web of deceit."

"What are you implying?" Anthony demanded.

"Only what everyone already knows." Fielding's lips curled in a cruel smile. "One bloody engagement . . . You never meant to take her to the altar at all, did you, Danner? Got what you want without it."

"Better shut your lying mouth," Samuel said, his blood beginning to boil. He detested Fielding. His remarks about Veronica were wicked and damning and untrue.

"Are you saying the child isn't yours?"

"What rot!" Anthony sputtered furiously.

"Veronica isn't pregnant," Samuel bit out, half rising from his chair.

Fielding stepped back. "So, the father's the last to know. She came to Amelia and me with the news herself," he went on quickly when Samuel's expression grew threatening. "Asked to be recommended to a less than scrupulous physician."

"Rubbish." Anthony jumped to his feet, as furious as Samuel.

"A pack of lies," Samuel spit through his teeth.

"So, it's really the first you heard of it. Interesting."

Samuel grabbed the man by his starched collar. Fielding's eyes popped open in shock. Anthony's breath hissed through his teeth. This was his club. Rules of propriety must be observed.

But Samuel didn't give a damn.

Pulling James's now ashen face down to his determined one, Samuel said with quiet force, "Lady Veronica is not pregnant and if she gave you that impression, it's for some other reason. Spread any more lies about her and I'll break your filthy neck."

"Don't blame me for your mistakes."

Samuel's fist jabbed him in the nose. Quick. Sharp. Blood gushed. Fielding howled in outrage, clutching his bleeding nose with both hands as Samuel strode from the club. He could still hear Fielding's cries of pain as he pushed through the front doors and called for a hansom.

Victor had thought long and hard upon his plan. It had to be subtle. It had to be sweet. It had to remove Samuel Danner from his trail once and for all.

And it had to involve the delectable Lady Veronica.

He sighed with regret. He'd made a promise to himself long ago not to involve Danner women in his plans. The Danners were a bloodthirsty lot and when it came to protecting their women they were out-and-out crazy.

Mary McKechnie Danner's death had been an accident. Kelsey Danner's injuries a diversion. And Lexie, well . . .

But that was all the past. This was the present and though he'd learned the hard way to leave Danner women alone, this opportunity was heaven-sent.

Besides, the luscious Lady Veronica wasn't truly a Danner woman. She was merely a pawn, for use by both him and Samuel. He knew the way Samuel's mind worked too well to believe the youngest Danner had actually fallen for such a silly—though mighty pretty—featherbrain as Henry's first-born. He would be doing Lady Veronica a favor, really, by taking care of her problems in one fell swoop. Briefly, his conscience tweaked him. He hated hurting women, he truly did.

Ah, well . . .

With a sigh of acceptance, he glanced down at the bouquet of flowers in his right hand, then brushed imaginary dirt from his lapels and adjusted his silk top hat with careful precision as he paid off the cabbie and mounted the stairs of Ashworth Manor. Later, the Ashworth servants would recall a well-dressed man had called on Veronica, but they wouldn't quite remember his features. Victor's Damocles sword was his unremarkable looks. No one paid him a second glance. He melted into the scenery, as unobtrusive as dust motes—there, but never really acknowledged.

"Good afternoon," Victor said to the butler, a sour-looking man who stood stiff as a post. "Lord Ashworth requested that I drop these papers by his home." He held up a sheaf of legal briefs which would have no meaning to Henry Ashworth at all.

"I'll see that he gets them, sir."

"And these flowers were left on the porch for a . . ." Victor pretended to examine the card. "Lady Veronica?"

Distaste crossed the butler's features. Victor was amused. So, the lovely Veronica hadn't won this fellow's shrunken heart.

At that very moment a door on the north side of the hall burst open and Veronica herself rushed out.

"Who's there?" she asked the butler, her gaze turning to Victor.

He had to catch his breath. My God, she was something!

They'd never been this close before. He hadn't recognized her true beauty. It wasn't an obvious, head-turning quality. It was deeper, richer, as remarkable and interesting as his own looks were bland and dull. Her hair was thick and rich and faintly streaked with gold. Her eyes two glittering topaz gems. And her figure—petite, feminine, lush . . .

Victor brought himself up short. This was no time for distractions.

She was regarding him with a raging curiosity that twirked something inside his stomach. She was memorizing his looks. In surprise, Victor realized he was flattered and for a moment he responded to her attractive femininity as a man responds to a woman. He must be careful.

He handed her the flowers. "There's no name, I'm afraid. It appears you have a secret admirer."

She looked at the card, then back at him. "Thank you, Northcroft," she dismissed the butler who took the papers Victor had brought and stiffly retreated.

Victor chuckled to himself. Later, Henry would undoubtedly realize who'd abducted his daughter, but there wasn't a damn thing the inflated earl could do about it. Victor had him in the palm of his hand.

"And you are?" she asked, gazing at him through intelligent eyes. She was hardly a featherbrain, he thought belatedly.

"A business associate of your father's."

"Really."

Something in her tone sent alarm bells flashing. She knows, Victor realized, ridiculously pleased by her perception.

"You sent me a telegram this morning," she accused.

"I'm sorry, ma'am. I don't know what you're talking about."

"My father has very few business associates from the States, and that's the worst British accent I've heard in a long while, Mr. Flynne. What is your real purpose in coming here today? I'd like to know."

So, she'd found him out, for all the good it would do her.

Victor was saddened that their acquaintance should have to end so abruptly. She truly was a diamond amongst glass.

"Blackmail," he admitted, giving her the answer she expected, then watched her lovely eyes widen in horror.

She couldn't believe her ears. Not only had she rooted out Samuel's enemy, the slimy bastard admitted it with a certain degree of pride.

She couldn't speak. She just stood there in total, unrelenting shock.

"I'll be in touch," he added, acknowledging her with a brief finger to his top hat as he let himself out the door.

It could have been a dream. Veronica blinked, then dashed after him. "Wait!" she called, but Victor was already slipping into the cab that had been waiting for him at the curb. She ran forward but the hansom pulled away and wheeled up the street.

She ran to the carriage house. "I need a carriage!" she yelled. "Now! Hurry!"

A stable boy gaped, wide-eyed, a bucket in his hands.

"Oh, for god sakes!" Veronica grabbed Tinsel and fought to bridle her, her hands shaking. "Help me!"

The stable boy struggled with the sidesaddle which Veronica swept from his hands in disdain. She threw a blanket over the back of the animal and a regular saddle. Wrapping up her skirt in one hand, she tossed one shapely leg over Tinsel's broad back. The stable boy's eyes widened farther till they seemed to pop from his head. Veronica's pantaloons were visible to above her knees.

"Tell Samuel Danner where I've gone," she barked out. "Remember this! It's important!"

"Ye . . . ye . . . yes, ma'am," he stammered.

"Victor Flynne was here. He just left. I'm following him. Do you understand?"

"Ye . . . ye . . ." He gave up and nodded.

"I'll be back as soon as I can."

She wheeled Tinsel into the roadway and urged the eager animal forward and after the slippery Mr. Flynne.

Chapter

16

If only she'd brought a gun . . .

Night was less than two hours away and she was alone on horseback once again. She'd escaped injury the first time because she'd been cautious and had worn a concealing cloak. This time she'd rushed headlong into danger.

But she was on Victor's trail. Leading Samuel to Victor would have to change Samuel's opinion of her. Maybe he would even let himself like her a little. More than just chattel. Maybe he could even think of her as a woman.

Remembering his kisses, she knew her logic was kind of faulty. He *had* responded to her the right way. He just hadn't wanted to. She was banking that helping capture Flynne would make him want to.

She refused to recall that she hated Samuel Danner and that she had no interest in marrying someone so dead set against being involved with her. There was no time for second thoughts anyway. She was committed. The rest could be sorted out later.

Tinsel moved at a fast trot; galloping would attract unwelcome attention and wear the poor mare out much too quickly. She'd thought she could catch up to the hansom with little trouble. The streets were busy. Victor couldn't go far.

But she hadn't counted on the enormous amount of carriages and coaches and hansom cabs combing the streets, or the children hawking their pies or begging, or the street cleaners' slow, deliberate progress as they scooped manure and dirt to the curbs.

Anxiety chased butterflies around in her stomach. She couldn't have lost him. He had to be somewhere close by.

Then suddenly there he was! Straight before her. She recognized the notch in the cab's right back wheel and settled a very grateful Tinsel into a walk about thirty yards behind it.

Drat, she thought. Her hair. She hadn't bound it, or hidden it. Now it flew behind her like a cape, directing attention to the lone woman riding astride. Not only was she a spectacle to those around her, she was a flaming beacon to Flynne.

But there was nothing to do now but hope he didn't look back.

The cab turned a corner and zigzagged down several narrow, mean streets. Indefinable, stomach-lurching smells drifted from piles of forgotten garbage. Tinsel snorted and shook her head, as if she too were disgusted by the odors. The walls of the buildings leaned inward, blocking out the sun, a dreadful, evil canopy that made Veronica shiver.

At the end of one of the worst of the back streets she spied a shaft of bright light. Eagerly, she kicked Tinsel's sides. The horse stepped quickly, ears pricked forward.

"'Ey, thur, missy. Get outta th' way!" a driver yelled when Tinsel half bolted out of the alleyway. "Cor! Ya blind?" He blinked at the sight of a well-dressed lady riding astride. Veronica was forced to rein in as the man's carriage was angled half-across the end of the alley.

"Excuse me. I'm sorry." She glanced anxiously around for Victor's cab. The rear end was just sneaking around another corner. Veronica clicked her tongue to Tinsel, guiding her in the right direction, circling around the back wheels of the carriage blocking the alley.

Suddenly the man with the carriage leapt forward, yanking on Tinsel's bridle. Veronica gasped. Tinsel squealed and reared, but he held on tightly.

"What do you think you're doing?" Veronica demanded, clutching Tinsel's mane. "Stop it! You're scaring her!"

For an answer the man grabbed her leg and jerked hard. Veronica shrieked, sliding sideways, scrabbling for a hold. "Are you mad?" she cried, frightened. He yanked again and she tumbled to the ground.

"Let go of me!" she declared furiously, then cried out in surprise when he jerked her to her feet, pinning his arm around her waist so tightly she could scarcely breathe. She hit at him with her fists. "Get your grubby hands off me!"

Her pleas fell on deaf ears. He tossed her inside the waiting carriage. Catching a good look at his face, she was not encouraged by his evil grin. She was being abducted!

Lunging for the opposite door, she nearly freed herself, but he pulled her back, smiling like an imbecile as he pinned her to her seat. She glared at him with imperious fury.

"Sorry, m'lady," he said without a trace of remorse. "But ya gots ta come wif me. The doc's waitin'. It ain't pretty, but it's life, wot?"

"Pardon me?" Veronica asked in a strangled voice.

He winked at her and had the gall to pat her flat stomach as she pressed herself against the cushions, her skin crawling at his touch. "The rich can afford wot the poor man can't, wot?" The carriage jerked forward and Veronica grabbed for the door handle again. He pulled her hands away with frightening ease. "My horse!" she cried, too afraid to face the truth of this bizarre situation.

"We got 'er, m'lady. Doncha worry yer pretty 'ead. It'll be over soon."

"What will be over?" she dared ask.

His eyes drifted tellingly to her stomach once more. *Oh, God!* she realized. *I'm being taken to the abortionist!* On the heels of that thought was another, more terrifying conclusion. *Flynne set this trap! He showed himself in order to capture me!*

Oh, Samuel, she thought with both fear and hysterical

amusement. *You warned me about Flynne and I didn't listen. Again.*

"Where is she?" Samuel demanded, brushing past Northcroft and striding into the house.

"Excuse me, sir." The butler was affronted.

"Where's Veronica?"

"I'll inform Lady Ashworth that you're here," was his stiff answer.

But it was Madeline who was called, not Veronica.

"I want to see Veronica," he said tightly.

Her expression was distinctly frigid. "Mr. Danner," she greeted him in a voice like an arctic blast.

He read her mind. "Whatever trouble Veronica's in, it's not because of me. I'd like to speak to her."

"As would I, but Veronica's not here."

"Where is she?"

"I'm sure I don't know."

Samuel swore silently and pungently to himself. They stared each other down. "If you've heard the same rumor I have, then Veronica's in serious trouble. I need to speak to her."

Madeline seemed about to retort, then remembering the servants' eager ears, led him instead into the drawing room. Before she could speak, however, Samuel said flatly, "I don't believe she's pregnant, and even if she is, I'm not the father. I think this is some new, outrageous lie being spread by James Fielding and Amelia St. John."

Madeline hesitated, frowning. "I believe you."

Her sudden about-face surprised him. "Then why . . . ?"

"Because if she was pregnant, it had to be because of you!" she explained, coloring slightly. "Oh, Lord! What's the child got herself into now? Henry will be livid!"

"Where is she?" he asked for the third time.

"I don't know. She was gone when I returned. Perhaps the servants could tell you more."

That was all he needed to hear. Samuel tore through the house, terrorizing the shyer servants with demanding questions, losing his patience with those who talked too much about nothing important. Finally, at the carriage house he found the information he sought: Veronica had taken Tinsel and chased after someone named Flynne.

"Damn it," he muttered in true fear as he jumped up to the driver's seat beside Anthony's coachman. "Go on. Get a move on," he ordered through his teeth and the man snapped the reins at the team.

A feeling of intensifying dread enveloped him as he followed Veronica's trail. Where had she gone? What new trouble had she stirred up? He was torn between total frustration and aching fear. If something had happened to her . . .

He shuddered, unable to complete the thought.

The route she'd traveled was easy to trace; she was remembered by her outrageous dress. One woman went so far as to pretend to swoon over the sight of a woman riding *astride* and showing a shocking amount of undergarments in the process.

Samuel had no patience with anyone. As he followed Veronica's movements, his temper rose into the red. He didn't question why he was so furious with her, he just was. When he found her—and after he thanked God that she was safe and unharmed—please, let that be true—then he was going to wring her lovely, troublesome neck.

The place was in Seven Dials—a wretched hovel with poor ventilation and a dark backroom where "Doctor" Willoughby performed his secret surgeries. It smelled of hopelessness and human despair and desolation. If there was any place closer to hell on earth, Veronica couldn't imagine what it would be.

Gooseflesh rose on her skin. Dr. Willoughby himself was enough to curdle milk. He eyed her with the lascivious interest of a lover, all the while assuring her in a soothing voice that "all will soon be well" and this "little inconvenience will be taken care of."

"Would you like help unbuttoning your dress?" he asked eagerly.

Veronica sent a speaking look to her abductor whom she'd

subsequently learned was named Dirkson. He, too, appeared more than anxious to help.

"I do not need help," she informed them both, "for I am not getting undressed."

"Oh, yes, yes," Dr. Willoughby hustled toward her and grabbed her hands between his pudgy soft ones. "We must hurry or it will be too late."

"I am not pregnant!"

"There's no need for that now." He clucked his tongue and tried to shoo Dirkson from the room. Dirkson just grinned his abominable grin and leaned against the wall, enjoying the show.

"I am not pregnant, have never been pregnant, and if, and when, I become pregnant, I will never have an abortion!" she declared in ringing tones. "Now let me go before you face a prison term for kidnapping and God knows what else!"

"I'm very sorry, my dear, but the decision's out of my hands. If you're going to stand there, Dirk, lend a hand. Throw her on the table. Let's get this over with."

He spent precious, wasted minutes circling the area where Veronica was highjacked until a rather crafty street urchin divested him of several pounds and pointed him in the right direction.

Now, as night was falling he came to an area of London no sane person would visit even in the light of day. "Seven Dials," Anthony's coachman rasped in a frightened voice.

"A goddamned slum," Samuel bit out.

Veronica, blast your hide!

Why couldn't she act like all the other Society ladies? Amelia St. John might be a pain in the ass, but she was undoubtedly at home safe and sound while Veronica was in God knew what trouble.

He took a deep breath as he swung himself back onto the driver's seat once again, conscious of a thousand unseen eyes following their progress through the garbage-strewn streets. His chest was tight.

If she wasn't all right . . .

Clenching his fists, he blocked the image of her limp and mortally wounded body from his mind. With firm control, he locked up his emotions, then swung himself back to the ground and pounded on the warped door of a tenement at the end of the street, shouting to be let in.

Veronica was beside herself. Was the man daft? "I have no need of an abortionist, no matter what rumors you've heard." She struggled against his determined, demented grip as he pushed her toward the surgical table. "Release me this instant!"

Dirkson chuckled, a dirty, amused gurgle. "Give up them airs, missy."

"Lie down," Dr. Willoughby advised.

"Why are you so insistent?" Veronica demanded. "What does it take to make you hear me? I am *not* pregnant!"

"Stop being difficult." Dr. Willoughby lost his patience.

"This is madness!"

"Mr. Flynne demanded this service and he's going to get it," Willoughby shook his head, as if he were dealing with a recalcitrant child.

"Victor Flynne?" Her heart sank at confirmation that Victor's meeting with her had been a setup to this abduction. "He must believe the rumor, but I'm telling you it isn't true. If you persist with this, you'll cause a lot of needless pain and suffering."

Dirkson picked at his grimy teeth with a toothpick. "When Victor asks fer somethin', yer better givit."

Victor asked for *this?*

Fear crawled icy fingers up her spine. She was in true peril. Somehow she'd become a pawn in Victor and Samuel's deadly duel, and Dr. Willoughby was on direct orders to give her an abortion whether she needed one or not! *He's using me to get at Samuel,* she realized with a flash of insight. *He thinks I'm more precious to Samuel than I am!*

"There's been a terrible misunderstanding," she said in a tremor-shaken voice.

Dr. Willoughby stared into her ashen face. "We'll give her ether. Won't hurt so much," he said with cold compassion.

Veronica struggled. Dirkson came back with a damp rag soaked in ether. She gagged at the smell.

She fought against the rag, twisting her head back and forth, her chest heaving. One hand jerked free. She slammed one small fist into Dirkson's eye, then scrabbled backward, flailing wildly with her feet, sending a tin pan flying across the room which had been resting on a surgical tray next to the table where she lay. "Get your filthy hands off me, you bastard!"

Her frantic fingers closed around a pair of scissors.

"Mebbe over there?" the slatternly woman suggested, wiping greasy gray hair out of her eyes and pointing to a listing stone building whose shutters were wedged tightly closed.

"Thank you."

Samuel slapped dirt from his black trousers. He'd tossed off his coat long ago. Signaling the driver to follow, he strode across the street to the building in question.

Lifting his hand to knock, he froze in midmotion. To one side of the building stood a horse, its hide wet with sweat. From the way the stable boy had described Tinsel, Samuel was certain this neglected creature was one and the same.

He quietly tried the door. It was securely locked but the timbers surrounding it were rotted. A prickle of apprehension slid up his back. Veronica was inside. He knew it. God help the man who harmed one hair on her shining head.

Samuel smashed his booted heel into the door. It sagged inward slightly, the jamb splintering at the lock. Two more swift kicks and he was inside.

The sound of a tin pan banging drew his attention to the side door near the back of the room.

"Get your filthy hands off me, you bastard!" Veronica's furious, terror-stricken voice choked out.

Samuel slammed his shoulder against the door and broke through it in a flying leap.

The sight that met his eyes was horrifically comical. Veronica, her hair swirling wildly around her head, her dress half-unbuttoned down the back, her feet kicking at Dirkson who was vainly attempting to pin them down, was holding another man at bay with a wicked-looking blade.

"Touch me and I'll cut off a finger!" she spat. She slashed at Dirkson. "Or maybe something else!"

Samuel didn't ask questions. He threw himself at Dirkson, slamming the bigger man to the wall.

"Ooof," Dirkson grunted. Two quick jabs to the nose and one to the throat and Dirk buckled at the knees. Samuel whipped around, so angry that he'd already grabbed the other man before he realized that Veronica had the scissors pressed between the man's thighs.

"Don't! Don't!" he was begging, his eyes fixed on the scissors, his Adam's apple leaping up and down.

"Who is this man?" Samuel asked.

"A butcher," she declared fiercely.

"I was only doing what I was told! He said she wanted an abortion. I was trying to help."

"Who's he?"

"Victor Flynne," Veronica answered, flicking Samuel a look. In her eyes he saw all the terrors her anger had masked, terrors she was desperately trying to suppress.

Samuel carefully took the scissors from her hand. The man stifled a cry, which turned into a sigh of relief as Samuel leveled the point at his bobbing Adam's apple instead of his more intimate parts. "You're working for Flynne?"

"I owe the man a favor. He . . . he threatened to tell the police about . . . about . . ."

"About?" Samuel urged in a quietly deadly voice.

"My practice!" he blurted out.

Dirkson groaned. Samuel threw the man in Dirk's direction. "Flynne ordered you to pick up Veronica?" he asked Dirk who was gazing around blearily.

Dirkson dazedly wiped blood from his nose. "She needed to get rid o'the babe."

"The hell with that. Victor hired you for far worse." Samuel was livid. "Where is he?"

"'E moves around," Dirk mumbled.

"You show me where he is, or I'll kill you myself, so help me God."

"I'll try, Guvnah . . ."

Touching Veronica's arm, Samuel led her away from the two men and outside into the clearer air. Her pallor was grayish white.

"Keep an eye on the two men in the back room," he ordered Anthony's coachman. "Have you got a pistol?" At the driver's nod, Samuel said, "Good. I'll send the police here as soon as I can."

With that he bundled Veronica inside the carriage but when she realized he was driving, she climbed up beside him on the driver's seat, trembling uncontrollably.

Samuel's anger abated slightly. Without being asked, he buttoned up the back of her dress. She made a choking sound, then drew a long breath.

"Thank you."

"It's a good thing you're all right," he growled.

Veronica, who'd managed fairly well up until this point, felt her composure disintegrate as she tried to smile.

"Because if you weren't, I don't know what I'd do," Samuel added.

As soon as the carriage pulled up in front of Ashworth Manor, Henry appeared on the porch. His fury emanated in waves, but he waited until they were inside the privacy of the house before blasting them with condemnations.

"You are no longer my daughter," he hissed through clenched teeth. "Your attempted *abortion* is the scandal of this city! Get out of my sight. Out of my house. Madeline!" he yelled toward the stairs.

Madeline, looking like death, came hurrying downstairs lugging a bulging valise. She pressed the handle into Veronica's nerveless hand. "It's all I could pack on such short notice."

Chloe and Patrice were shadows on the stairway, their eyes huge, their faces drawn.

The lump in Veronica's throat was too hard to swallow. She nodded, refusing to beg her father for anything.

"Your kindness overwhelms me," Samuel stated in flat fury.

"Get out. Get her out of here. Your child's a bastard. Keep away from this family. Northcroft, show them out." Henry turned on his heel and slammed into his study.

Veronica felt Samuel's arm surround her shoulders. Her legs shook. Numbly, she turned into the wall of his chest.

He gazed at Madeline over the top of Veronica's head. "Take care of her," Madeline choked out as Northcroft held the door.

In shock, Veronica let Samuel guide her to the carriage. Her father was disowning her. It had really happened. She felt dazed and bereft and completely at the mercy of the fates.

"Don't worry, I'm not your responsibility," she said wearily, leaning her head back against the cushions as the carriage swept them away from Ashworth Manor.

"I'm not worried," Samuel replied when in fact he was very worried indeed. Veronica's life had taken an unexpected turn and whether she thought so or not, he was completely responsible.

"I'm not pregnant," she added, though she didn't expect to be believed.

"I never thought you were."

She gazed at him in naked vulnerability. "You didn't?"

"No." Samuel was torn between compassion and exasperation. "If you were really pregnant, not a soul would know it. It would be your secret and you would handle it in your own inimitable way. One thing I've learned about you, Lady Veronica. Nothing Society ever says about you is true."

Tears welled in her eyes and she looked away. "Thank you."

"Veronica . . . don't . . ."

She couldn't stand the soft tone of his voice. It touched every unhappy, miserable fiber of her being. She wanted to die. She wanted to crawl into the safety of his arms and cry her eyes out.

He pulled her close and she treasured the moment, loving

the feel of his hand holding her head to his chest even while she felt his reluctance. She just wanted . . . someone . . . to hold her.

"I never thought he'd really throw me out," she choked in pitiful desperation.

"Your father's more capable than any one of us thought."

"He believed you and I were . . . had . . . that we'd—" She swallowed hard. "That we'd made love and that I was pregnant. He didn't even ask me if it was the truth." In a small voice, she added, "I don't think he would have cared about the abortionist even if he knew."

"Don't think about it."

She hiccuped hysterically. "How can I not? I have been turned out of my own house because someone told lies about me. I'm going to be right back where I was before: the scandal of the Season! I have no prospects, no money, no possible chance for happiness. It's all I can think about, and if I didn't, I'd be a bigger fool than I already am."

His heart twisted and he smiled at her courage, though she couldn't see him in the shadows of the carriage. In her voice was the thread of iron so at odds with her demure society manners. "You're hardly a fool."

"Then what am I?" Veronica drew back from his embrace, searching the shaded contours of his masculine face.

"You're an intelligent, amazing, impulsive woman with a penchant for attracting trouble," he said softly.

She heard the thrum of emotion in his tone, even though he spoke lightly. "I've alienated my family and friends."

"Not all of them." Unable to stop himself, he swept an errant strand of hair away from her face, his thumb absently rubbing at a smudge on the crest of her cheekbone.

"You're not my family, and I don't think you're my friend."

"Why not?"

"Because you hate being attached to me in any way."

"That's not true," Samuel murmured. Her skin was delicate, almost translucent around her huge soulful eyes. He wanted to kiss her so badly he ached.

Veronica waited. Dimly she became aware that passion had overtaken every other emotion. She was glad. She didn't want to think. She wanted to feel.

Her pulse began to beat heavily as the moments stretched out painfully, endlessly. She wanted to feel his arms surround her, his mouth press itself hard against hers, his heart beat fast and strong in tandem with hers.

"Oh, hell," he expelled, and Veronica's pulse leapt when his lips crashed down on hers. She was limp, pliable, too weak to offer resistance if the idea of resistance had even penetrated her drugged senses. She wound one arm around his neck, inflamed by his uneven breathing, the hard warmth of his hand in the small of her back.

"I want you," he admitted against her lips, his voice taut.

"I want you, too," she breathed.

He made a strangled sound. "Good God, you're honest."

"Shouldn't I be?"

"No," he admitted after a brief moment of hesitation.

"Don't stop kissing me," Veronica begged, afraid suddenly that he might.

He didn't. His mouth claimed hers with a possession that thrilled her to the depths of her soul. Her lips parted of their own volition; an invitation his tongue couldn't resist.

She heard the rustle of her satin dress, the uneven tenor of his breathing, the rattle of the carriage wheels across a cobblestone street. His mouth moved to gently explore her cheekbone, the shell of her ear. Her hands crept around his shoulders.

"I have damned myself for wanting you," he said in a low voice. "You need someone to take care of you, not *want* you."

"I need someone to want me. I can take care of myself."

His chest shook with suppressed laughter.

"I can," she argued without heat, a smile stealing over her lips. "I've just made a few mistakes."

"A few?" he murmured, pulling back slightly to look down on her. Their faces were bare inches apart. Seized by passion's insanity, she leaned forward, touching her lips to his in innocent invitation.

He groaned and closed his eyes but he didn't resist. Emboldened, she deepened the kiss, until it felt as if their mouths melded together. Her world spiraled downward to this moment, this intimate touch.

"Veronica . . ." he protested, sounding as if he were in pain. But then his hands swarmed across her back and he pulled her tight to his chest, his kisses deepening, his tongue tangling with hers in an erotic dance.

He leaned back, dragging her with him until she lay half-atop him. His fingers dug at the buttons of her dress, pulling them open; his palms hot against her bare skin. She wore no chemise and when his hands circled her back, sliding beneath her bodice, he encountered her bare breasts.

Veronica's breath caught. His thumbs squeezed her nipples. Sensation rocketed through her. She hadn't known the connection between her breasts and the secret, feminine spot between her legs before, but now she felt pulsing, raging heat, and the moan that tore itself from her lips was completely involuntary.

One of his hands tangled in her hair. His mouth ravaged hers. Tempo increased. His breath came fast; hers in startled gasps. He released her breast to slide his palm over her hip, pulling her to him. She felt the hardness of his arousal and remembered the delicious, sinful, exciting feeling of it once before.

As innocent as Veronica was to the art of lovemaking, she was a quick study. Samuel's head swam with desire of the worst kind. He wanted her. Given the slightest encouragement he would take her. But still he tried to keep his head.

"Veronica!" He tore his mouth from hers.

She lifted her head, strands of gold-shot brown hair tumbling around her face, eyes simmering a warm amber.

"Don't stop," she choked, but her words were too late. The carriage ground to an achingly slow halt in front of Uncle Tony's.

Chapter

17

Why in God's name did you start that rumor?" Anthony demanded of Veronica soon as she and Samuel were inside the house. "Where have you been? Good Lord, child, the wildest stories are circulating!" His concerned look took in her disheveled appearance and he demanded, "What has happened?"

"It's a long story," Samuel said tautly.

"The stories are untrue," Veronica inserted, her emotions still in a whirl. With difficulty she pulled herself together and pushed the tender, sensual scene with Samuel to a distant corner of her mind. "I thought if anything could flush out Victor Flynne, it would be the opportunity to blackmail someone else, so I let it be known that I had a friend who was in trouble."

"A friend?" Anthony asked.

"Anthony," Samuel intervened wearily. "Veronica just escaped a new trap, one set by Flynne. She needs a chance to pull herself together. I have to go to the police station and report the crime."

"Crime?" Anthony had been about to seat himself, but froze, half in the act.

"Kidnapping, for one. I don't know quite what you'd call forcing someone to have an abortion who isn't pregnant." Samuel threw a glance at Veronica. The back of her hastily buttoned dress drew his attention. He could still feel the silk of her skin beneath his palms, the heat of her mouth on his.

"What are you talking about, man?"

Veronica walked unsteadily to a chair, curling her legs beneath her. He could see the tip of her shoe and the curve of her ankle.

God.

"Victor Flynne had me kidnapped," she said quietly. "And then Father threw me out of the house. Go ahead and tell him everything, Samuel." She gave him a quavering smile. "I'm perfectly fine."

Three hours later, after Samuel had horrified Anthony with Victor's latest exploits, had grilled Willoughby and Dirkson extensively with the help of Inspector Cuthbert and the constables who'd collected both men—to no success, as it turned out—had downed as much brandy as he could stomach, he mounted the stairs to the upper gallery, weaving on his feet slightly as he knocked on Veronica's bedroom door.

Should he apologize again? His fuzzy mind wasn't certain. Yes, Veronica had wanted him in the carriage as much as he'd wanted her, but she was a romantic fool who didn't know the difference between innocent kisses and gripping passion, where he did. In fact, he knew exactly what kind of disaster they courted.

So, why the hell did she get to him so much?

Recalling the soft texture of her skin was torture. The curve of her breast, swell of her hip, feel of her body pressed hotly against his.

"Jesus," he muttered, knocking on her door.

"Come in," she called without interest, clearly thinking it was one of the maids.

"It's Samuel," he told her through the panels.

Quick footsteps sounded and the door was opened. She'd changed into a soft blue dress trimmed with ecru lace at the hem of the sleeves and tucked inside the bodice. Her hair had been washed. In fact she'd had a bath. Her whole skin glowed.

He took a breath and concentrated. "I wanted to see how you were."

"I told you I'd be fine," she reminded him. "Where's Uncle Tony?"

"He went to speak to Henry. He thought he might be able to plead your case."

"He's wrong," she said bitterly. "My father's been looking for an excuse to disown me. I would have given it to him sooner or later no matter what."

She glanced down the hallway to the row of doors that turned the corner. "Which room is yours?" she asked tentatively.

Which room indeed? Samuel frowned as he realized an unpalatable fact. "The one behind yours."

"Oh."

"Flynne gave me another good reason to kill him tonight."

She smiled faintly. "You mean you don't have enough already?"

"I have more than enough." He swayed on his feet, leaning one hand against the door for support. "He killed my wife."

Veronica stared at him in shock. "I thought you said she died in a carriage accident!"

Down the hallway, Rose, Anthony's tweeny, stepped from one of the bedrooms, arms laden with laundry. She disappeared down the hall and Samuel pushed into Veronica's room, closing the door behind him. This was not a time to be overheard.

"She did," he said, dropping into a chair. "But Victor was behind it. Engineered the whole thing. Hates the Danners. Has for years."

Veronica perched on the edge of the bed, aware that Samuel had consumed a great deal of liquor. This was a chance to learn more about him than he normally was willing to tell.

"Why does he hate your family so much?"

"Started with Tremaine. Tremaine nearly ruined Victor, but then Flynne got away. Took another ten years before Jesse got in the way. And Kelsey . . ." He drew a breath and closed his eyes.

"Kelsey?" Veronica asked.

"Jesse's wife. Only she wasn't then. Oh, wait. Yes, she was." He shook his head. "Another accident and when Patricia Lee came to see me, I thought she was talking about Kelsey's accident. But then I realized she meant Mary."

"I see," Veronica said, though she was more confused than ever.

"But now Victor's after you. Meant for Willoughby to kill you. Maybe even thought you were pregnant and wanted to kill another Danner before it arrived in this world."

Veronica couldn't argue with him. She'd come to much the same conclusion herself.

"He'll try again. My fault you were kidnapped. My fault . . ."

"It is not your fault!" Veronica said fiercely.

"Should have known he'd try to hurt you. Hurts all the Danner women."

"But I'm not your woman. I'm not your wife, and I'm not your fiancée." She swallowed. "And I'm not your lover."

There was a weighty pause. Veronica wasn't certain he'd even heard her. The house was quiet, as if everyone had gone to bed.

"G'night, Veronica," Samuel murmured and promptly fell asleep in the chair.

Veronica watched him for nearly an hour. His chest rose and fell evenly, his head rolled to one side. In sleep, he seemed more approachable, certainly more relaxed. Less . . . she searched for the right word. Controlling. That was it.

But what was it about Samuel that made her care despite that controlling facet to his personality? She detested controlling men. Her father was the worst and when she looked back at the men of her acquaintance: James, Malcolm, Geoffrey, Uncle Tony, even Wortham . . . they all told her what to do to varying degrees.

But Samuel didn't, she realized with some surprise. Oh, yes, he made comments, angry comments mostly after she'd stumbled into some new and sticky trap. But he'd agreed to her suggestion of the engagement to help her out of a controlling situation, and he'd certainly been there when she was in dire need of help more than once.

Samuel controlled himself. He controlled his own feelings. He fought the natural progression of emotion as if it were some vile, terrible foe. She couldn't break through that wall of control unless he was vulnerable himself, in some way.

Like now.

She stared down at him. A strip of moonlight shone across his chest, throwing shadows over the planes of his face. It had been a long, exhausting day, yet she felt alive and a-tingle, as if every nerve were poised and eager.

She wanted to make love to him. She wanted it now more than ever. She'd lost everything of value and she wanted something to take its place.

Carefully, she sat on his lap, wrapping her arms around his shoulders. He murmured something and turned to her, his face buried in her neck. Nerves thrummed.

One hand slid down her side, cupping her breast. Veronica stared at it, wide-eyed. But then he began kneading her flesh and liquid, tormenting streams of wanting rushed through her. This time she didn't want the lovemaking to end. She wanted it to go on and on forever.

"Veronica," he murmured.

She kissed his mouth. A sharp cry of surprise passed her lips when he suddenly grabbed hold of her, his grip hard, and kissed her with pent-up passion.

"Don't want to want you. Terrible mistake," he muttered.

Mistake? With these feelings singing through her veins?

His mouth abandoned hers to explore her neck, his tongue tracing a damp trail that left her breathless. Then, shock of shocks, his hand wandered downward, pulling at the voluminous folds of her gown until it was underneath and sliding against her pantaloons, pulling them down over her hips.

"Samuel," she protested faintly. Oh, God! What was he doing? She clamped her legs together automatically, but his hand was persuasive, stealing to her most feminine area, touching her in a way that had her melting across the chair.

They probably would have made love right then and there except for the chair itself. It was too small, too awkward, too restraining. She was wedged between Samuel and the chair's arm, one leg bent awkwardly beneath her, her back arched uncomfortably as she all but fell onto the carpet.

With a groan Samuel disengaged himself and staggered to his feet, staring down at her through dark, passion-glazed eyes. Veronica was a tumble of lace and satin. The bodice of her dress had drifted to the tips of her breasts, framing her in an almost modest yet wildly erotic picture.

"Shouldn't be here," he said, with a shake of his head that nearly made him lose his balance.

Holding the front of her dress in place, Veronica climbed to her feet. She didn't understand herself. Desire was like a living thing inside her. She knew he was right but oh, she wanted him to keep kissing her! To hold her and love her and all the things she'd sworn she'd never want from him.

It was madness.

They stared at each other. As Veronica's blood cooled, she tried to be sensible. "You're right. We don't love each other. We don't even like each other . . . much."

Samuel made a choking sound. "No. You're wrong. I like you too much, Lady Veronica." He reached twice for the bedpost before he managed to grab it.

"You do?"

"Too much," he repeated, sounding remarkably sober.

She swallowed and crossed the space between them. "I like you, too."

She placed her palm on the side of his face, succumbing to those simple words as if he'd offered her the world on a plate. She'd been rejected and criticized too many times; she craved love and attention. She craved *his* love and attention.

"You're nothing like Mary," he said, looping a strand of

hair over her ear. "I never thought I'd . . ." He sighed heavily. "Seems wrong . . . somehow . . ."

"What?"

For an answer he drew her forward, bending to kiss her. Later, she wondered if he'd planned to overbalance so that they would both fall across the bed, but at that moment, when his weight suddenly shifted, pushing her off-balance so that they both sank onto the coverlet, she was consumed by a glorious sense of rightness, of fate, of supreme belief that this—*this*—was what she'd been waiting for.

"Veronica," he whispered in her ear.

It was a last chance for sanity and Veronica threw it away. She kissed his cheek, her breath escaping on a soft sigh. It was an erotic invitation and Samuel's resistance crumbled. He kissed her hard, and she kissed him back just as eagerly. Suddenly there was no more hesitation. His mouth was everywhere, tasting her lips, memorizing the curve of her jaw, kissing the pulse at the base of her throat. He slid her bodice off her breasts and his mouth captured one nipple, sucking on it so hard she cried out in surprise and ecstacy. Her hands tangled in his hair, tugging hard. Her body arched. Her skin was on fire. Her breath a fast pant.

He removed her clothes with expert, liquid movements until suddenly she was completely naked. She shivered. She'd never felt so exposed, but then he warmed her with his heat. When he yanked at his own clothes, she shut her eyes, both afraid and unendurably curious about a man's body.

She'd never seen her father or any man without clothes. She only had a vague notion of the male anatomy, so when she glimpsed his stiffened manhood she drew a sharp breath.

But then his body tumbled onto hers and it was all legs and skin and heat. Her hands slid over his chest, curling in the crinkly hairs that arrowed downward. She was shocked by his male beauty, having some notion of trolls and beasts stuck in her mind from childhood tales meant to terrorize young girls into strict virginity.

What was wrong with her, that she had fallen in love with him? A man who had no interest in her, really, and one, moreover, who would be ready to kill her in the morning when he remembered the events of tonight and how easily she could have stopped him if she were willing.

But she wasn't willing. She'd lost everything. She wanted this.

"Veronica," he murmured, his lips sucking at hers, long and lingeringly.

The lovely innocent in his arms turned into a temptress, sliding her hands through the thick vitality of his hair, holding his face to hers until the kiss turned from sweet gentility to a fiercely raging firestorm, his mouth opening on hers with sudden, urgent desire.

Without breaking the kiss, one of his hands stroked downward, over her rib-cage, then up again to her breasts. He circled her nipples with his thumb and she squirmed beneath him, a moan escaping her lips. But his hand traveled yet farther, over the silken curve of her hip to the curly triangle between her legs.

Veronica was half out of her mind. She could feel her own wetness and his groan of submission. Then he clasped her hand, dragging it downward between them until her fingers closed around *him*. She was lost in wonder and passion. Gently, tentatively, she explored this facet of manhood that was completely outside her experience.

But she must have done something wrong because he suddenly grabbed her hand and stopped her.

"I'm sorry," she murmured, then was confused by his short bark of laughter.

"Don't be," he said in a throbbing whisper, before shifting his weight atop her. Desire shot through her. She could feel the hard tip of him plunging against her wetness. She held her breath, on the brink of something shatteringly momentous, suddenly afraid.

"I'm the one who should be sorry," he groaned and before she could respond he thrust himself into her deeply.

She cried out and something shattered inside Samuel, some belief in himself as a man. The pain slashed into his heart, stopping him. But desire was hot and raging, a red tide impossible to hold back for long.

Veronica had stiffened beneath him. He damned himself for his drunkenness, for his inability to give her—an innocent virgin—the kind of care and gentleness she deserved.

When he froze, she asked in a small voice, "Is that it?"

He didn't know whether to laugh or cry. He held her tenderly, feeling her moist, tightness surround him. He had to grit his teeth to fight back the waves of pleasure that threatened to engulf him.

"No," he said softly, and with painstaking care moved slowly inside her tight passage, each stroke a bit deeper and longer, until her head tossed on the pillow and whimpers of pleasure filled his ears. Her limbs melted beneath him. Her body instinctively matching his rhythm.

"Samuel," she panted, her fingernails digging into his shoulders. "Samuel."

He could feel her tremble and arch, reaching for the satisfying sensation. He sought to give it to her. Wrong. This was so completely wrong. But it felt so right, so perfect, so natural.

Shocking ecstasy exploded inside Veronica. She cried out in wonder, barely hearing his surprised intake of breath as shooting pinwheels of pure desire shot in spasms through her body. Then he groaned, stiffening, and she felt his seed spill in a gush of warmth that left her shocked, stunned, and filled with pure love.

She couldn't contain her feelings. "I love you," she said in a trembling voice, the words tumbling in a rush. "I love you so much it hurts. I love you!"

"Shhh." He kissed her lips, cutting off the words. She mumbled something that was swallowed by his mouth. He couldn't listen. Didn't want to know. With a kind of acknowledged pain at the wrongness of seducing her, he gazed down into her magnificent eyes.

She smiled. Nearly his undoing. "Could we do that again?" she asked in seductive innocence.

"Veronica!"

His shaft was still buried deep inside her. He wanted to

tell her no, but she playfully darted her tongue into the deep recesses of his mouth. Groaning, he felt himself harden despite his resolve to end this madness now.

But it was too late. He answered her sweet request with a blazing kiss, holding her to him as if he never wanted to let her go.

Chapter

18

Veronica turned over in bed, aware of a strange, foreign sensation in her lethargic limbs. Slowly her eyes opened and she realized she was in an open canopy bed crowned with swathes of ivory silk.

Uncle Tony's house, she remembered foggily.

Father kicked me out.

She sat up sharply and gasped at the soreness between her legs.

Samuel!

Memory flooded back and she sank into the sheets, drawing the coverlet to her suddenly flaming cheeks. Last night seemed like a dream. The lovemaking a sensual pleasure that kicked her heart into a panicked thumping and brought a weakness to her limbs.

Samuel had made love to her twice more. Once, immediately after she asked him to, and then once again when he'd woken her in the predawn hours and with more tenderness. That last time he'd slowly brought her to that wild, wonderful, undoubtedly sinful, sweeping ecstasy that made her cry out and dig her nails into him and arch like a wildcat.

Extremely embarrassing.

Totally wonderful.

But where was he now?

Sliding out of bed, she was mildly surprised to find she was nude even though she'd made no attempt at uncovering a nightgown in the valise Madeline had given her. The cheval mirror in the corner of the room threw back her reflection and Veronica examined her naked body with new eyes, amazed at its mysteries.

She pressed her hands to her lips, drawing a deep breath. In her mind's eyes she pictured Samuel's sun-darkened hands caressing the milky white globes of her breasts.

Her heart lurched and she sank down on the bed, only to rise an instant later and race to get dressed and go find him. He was sure to be angry or brooding or something equally ridiculous. Unlike herself, he couldn't accept his feelings.

But he had said he liked her.

And she'd told him she loved him.

Veronica winced, aware that she may have overstepped her bounds. But what good did it do to play coy? Samuel wasn't interested in any kind of woman—or so he would have her believe. Therefore nothing but honesty would have any effect on him, and even that was an outside chance.

She flung on the first dress in the valise: the spring green one she'd worn a few days earlier. Hurriedly, she brushed out the creases. Something crackled but she ignored it as she hopped on one foot while she attempted to button the shoe of the other, then tossed her hair into a loose bun and ran downstairs.

At the foot of the stairs, she hesitated, her hand curling around the top the newel post as she heard voices wafting from Uncle Tony's study.

". . . reputation has sunk to new depths," Uncle Tony was saying angrily. "She is beyond salvation. Ruined. Not that you give a damn!"

"I care what happens to Veronica," Samuel answered in a hard voice.

"Hah! You've done your level best to divest yourself of her responsibility. You've encouraged every man in the city to offer for her. Not very subtly, I might add. Now every fop and dandy is aware you have no intention of marrying her. No one who values their reputation will come near her. Do you know the new nickname they call her?"

"No, and I don't care to hear it."

"Flaming Scarlet." Uncle Tony laughed bitterly. "No more Drab Brown. Oh, no. Veronica's a fallen woman. She'll be lucky to ever show her face in London again."

"Society has a short memory," was Samuel's disturbing answer.

What did that mean? Surely he couldn't think she would be interested in another man now.

"Society's memory is very long," Uncle Tony disabused him. "And Henry won't have her back. He's threatened to divorce Madeline and disown his other daughters if they have anything to do with her. She's under my care now, for all the good it will do her. You've ruined her, Danner. You and your damn quest!"

Samuel didn't respond. Veronica cringed, knowing he had to be thinking about last night. Uncle Tony couldn't know the double meaning his words held.

"A few months from now, when it's clear she isn't pregnant, some will begin to doubt the rumors. But Henry's disowning her has ruined her chance of making a decent match. She is damned to spinsterhood now. A very unpalatable future for a spirited, loving woman like Veronica."

A few months earlier she would have disagreed with Tony. She wanted nothing more than her freedom. Now, however, having been introduced to the pleasures of physical and emotional love, she understood what he meant.

Her heart ached with frantic hope. Now was the time for Samuel to profess his true feelings.

"There's bound to be someone who will ignore the scandal," Samuel responded unemotionally. His words drove a stake in Veronica's heart. She clapped a hand to her mouth, heartsick. "She's an attractive woman. That makes up for a lot of sins."

"You're a coldhearted bastard!"

"I didn't come here to fall in love," he rejoined fiercely. "I came after Flynne. And I'm close enough to taste success. As soon as I'm through beating the truth from Willoughby and Dirkson and a few other of your so-called *noble*men and Flynne's taken into custody, then I'm boarding Captain Shaughnessy's *Her Majesty,* or any other available seafaring vessel and sailing back to Portland that very night!"

"You've already broken her heart without even trying," Uncle Tony predicted quietly, his anger spent. "At least she's lucky you didn't try to take advantage of her."

Samuel's sharp intake of breath was a damning answer.

Before Uncle Tony could come to the correct conclusion, Veronica half ran into the room. She didn't want to. She wanted to crawl into a hole and die. But worse than that, she didn't want Samuel to confess the truth because then Uncle Tony would have to take action against him as any gentleman would. If her uncle suspected what had happened between them, he would call Samuel out.

Veronica, though she loved Samuel desperately, refused to have him forced to marry her.

"Veronica," Uncle Tony greeted her in surprise. He glanced past her to the door, clearly wondering how much she'd heard.

Samuel got to his feet. Veronica looked at him and felt such longing inside her she was afraid she'd burst. She loved the way his hair brushed his collar, the wide breadth of his shoulders, the glimmer of intelligence in his dark eyes. Why couldn't he just love her a little?

But he was gazing at her with an inscrutable look that was as far from the burning hot desire that had blazed within their dark depths the night before as England was from the moon.

Something shriveled up and died inside her. Her stomach churned and her knees quaked violently beneath her petticoats and bustle.

"All is not lost," she said with feigned brightness. "At least my father has stopped trying to marry me off. I'm free. Free from beneath my father's will."

She glanced down at her hand, at the "diamond" ring she'd been sporting which was really made of paste. She'd found it herself, in a little shop one afternoon when she and

Madeline and her sisters had gone shopping. She hadn't even mentioned it to Samuel, though he'd smiled in some amusement the first time he'd set eyes on it. Now she took it off, a symbolic gesture that nevertheless brought a weighty silence to the room.

Uncle Tony cleared his throat. "How long were you listening?"

"Long enough to know there's no hope for my reputation. But don't worry," she said with forced gaiety. "Spinsterhood isn't such a terrifying proposition."

"Isn't it?" Samuel asked quietly.

She couldn't look at him. What they'd shared the night before burned inside her brain, vivid and wonderful and fearfully brief. "I don't think I'd make a very good wife anyway," she said in a low voice.

"Veronica, the news of Henry disowning you is bound to spread like wildfire. You should be prepared for unwanted guests," Uncle Tony warned with a frown.

A horrible vista opened up before her: Malcolm Phipps full of sidelong looks and cutting comments, telling her how sorry he was that her true colors had finally shown through and how terrible it must be for her; Amelia feigning shock behind bouncing blond curls, trying to look as if she were about to swoon, all the while fighting a smile; and James . . .

Veronica inwardly shuddered. How could she have ever thought him attractive? Even for a moment? He was bound to be the worst. Smirking and lying and enjoying her suffering as if he fed upon it!

She lifted her chin. "If and when they arrive, I'll be able to handle the situation."

Samuel felt sick. Sick with himself that it was his doing, his irresponsible revenge, that had put her in such an intolerable situation. Her bravery made him feel a thousand times worse.

Tension filled the room. Anthony sent a puzzled look at Veronica before turning his attention to Samuel. "You're going to the station?"

He nodded. "Dirkson knows where Flynne is. Now, it's just a matter of coercion."

"Veronica?" Anthony asked, sensing she'd drifted away.

She snapped to attention, blushing slightly. She'd been thinking of deeply tanned hands and hair-roughened thighs and low moans of desire. Lord! She felt as if her thoughts were there on her face, plain to see. Her blush turned a furious red.

"Stop thinking about it!" Samuel snapped.

"That's right," Uncle Tony jumped in. "What's done is done. Perhaps time will erase some of the scandal," he lied reassuringly, completely unaware Samuel was speaking of some other subject. "Rowbury wasn't believed after a while."

"How many times do I have to say it: I don't want a man!" Veronica cried. How dare he tell her what she could or could not think about? She shot a cool, angry glance Samuel's direction.

"Then what do you want?" Samuel challenged, striding stiffly across the room with ground-devouring strides that made Veronica involuntarily take a step backward. "To be here at your uncle's as some kind of interminable guest?"

Veronica gasped.

"I say there," Uncle Tony interrupted furiously. "What the devil are you trying to do?"

"Or maybe you'll end up settling for some spineless fop who finally gets up the courage to offer for you despite your soiled reputation and lack of inheritance. Maybe you'll keep his house and bear his children and live out your days in a purgatory that closely resembles hell!"

"What do you care?" she threw back as Anthony bolted from his chair, looking for all the world as if he intended to take Samuel apart, limb by limb. "I've made mistakes and I'm not proud of some of them, but I've always been honest about my feelings. I'm not hiding behind an emotional blockade! I say what I feel!"

"You don't know what you feel," he snarled.

"I know better than you do about your own feelings. I know you won't let yourself forget Mary because it's easier to hide behind a need for vengeance that to let yourself *feel* again. I'm just sorry I didn't realize that earlier, before I let myself dream a little about . . ." she faltered, drained by so much emotion in such a little space of time, ". . . dream a little about you."

"I have the distinct feeling I've missed something," Uncle Tony drawled, stepping away from them.

"I'm sorry," Samuel said, meaning it.

He was sorry about last night, about not caring enough, about adding to her dilemma. She couldn't bear his pity. Turning slightly, she unclenched her fist, the one clamped tightly around the ring. She stared at it a moment before slipping it inside her pocket. Paper crumpled. Her father's love note. She'd forgotten it was in this dress.

She emitted a short, unhappy laugh. "It appears I'm not the only scandalous Ashworth." She pulled out the note. "My father has his own skeletons in the closet."

"Your father deserves a place in hell for the way he's treated you." Samuel was curt.

Uncle Tony looked pained. "He's always been cold-hearted. I just never realized he was such a monster."

"What is that?" Samuel asked, his expression stern. She couldn't tell what he was thinking.

His scent enveloped her: clean, deep, male. It only added to Veronica's pain and confusion. "It's a note I discovered in my father's study. I was going to ask Madeline about it . . ." she trailed off on a shrug.

Samuel scanned the note and handed it back to her, his lips tight. "You haven't done anything wrong," he reminded her tersely. "You're nothing like your father."

You haven't done anything wrong . . . What about last night? What about writhing in your arms, enjoying pleasures of the flesh that should be reserved for a husband and wife? What about loving you so much it's like a dull ache in my heart?

"I'm not cruel like he is," she admitted, gritting her teeth against the burning in her eyes.

"Nor are you unfaithful," Uncle Tony said staunchly. "Come along. Let's put this aside and have breakfast while Samuel interrogates your abductors."

"Wait," Samuel said, reaching for Veronica's arm. "We'll be there in just a minute. I'd like to talk to Veronica alone."

"If you need me . . ." Uncle Tony trailed off, still unclear what his role should be.

When she and Samuel were alone, Samuel looked into her tear-drenched eyes. She was brave and beautiful and valiant, and her current troubles were from trying to help him. He'd stolen her virginity along with any prospects for her to have a normal life. What he could offer her was nothing. But it was all he possessed.

"I'll marry you," he said solemnly.

For half a beat her heart took flight, then landed back to reality with a dreadful thud. "I don't need your pity!"

"It's not pity."

"It's not love!" she challenged. When he couldn't deny her, she demanded, "Is it? *Is it?*"

"No," he managed tightly.

"Then spare me this belated attempt at chivalry. I'm not desperate, Mr. Danner."

"Last night—"

"Don't dare to bring up last night to me!" she hissed. She could hear her words of love echoing hollowly in her ears.

"The hell I won't!" he muttered in exasperated fury. "Last night should not have happened, but it did. I'd had too much to drink and—"

"And you couldn't help yourself. Sorry to end your delusion, I'm as much at fault as you are." Her sarcasm jolted him. "Deflowering me is the poorest excuse for asking me to marry you that I can think of."

"And if you should be pregnant?" Samuel bit out, unreasonably infuriated by her pigheadedness.

Veronica caught her breath. She hadn't thought of that. Of course it could happen. She wasn't completely ignorant of how women begat children. But somehow lovemaking and pregnancy hadn't jibed in her mind until this moment.

"Well?" Samuel asked, lifting a brow.

"Then I'll deal with that possibility when it occurs."

"The hell you will," he snarled. "I'm going to marry you

whether you like it or not. I don't expect you to come back to Oregon with me. I'm not foolish enough to believe you'd abandon your life here for some ridiculous notion that 'love will conquer all.' I wouldn't want you to, anyway. But marriage might offer you some minute degree of respectability and on the off-chance that you're pregnant, it'll give our child a name."

"I wouldn't marry you now if you had me bound and gagged and dragged to the altar."

"Don't tempt me," he suggested, glaring down at her with those dark eyes which could blaze with passion or anger.

But she was blazing with anger also. "You're damn right I wouldn't follow you to Oregon!" she yelled. "I wouldn't follow you across the street. And if I should learn I'm with child, believe me, you'll be the last to know."

A mistake. Veronica knew it as soon as the words were out of her mouth.

"Then we'd better get married right away, before you have a chance to do something stupid. If there's a child, I'll want it."

"I could tell Uncle Tony what happened," Veronica said, digging a deeper grave for herself. "He'd never forgive you, no matter whose fault last night was."

"He'd probably force me to marry you," Samuel agreed.

He was leaning over her, a threatening force that played havoc with Veronica's composure. But she'd had enough of men toying with her life.

"Samuel, please," she said, attempting a new tack. "All I ever wanted was for my father to quit interfering in my life. Circumstances have made it so that I've attained my wish."

"Circumstances have turned you into a sacrificial lamb over my problems. What in God's name were you thinking when you tangled with Flynne?" he ranted suddenly. "Didn't I warn you enough times? Wasn't I clear enough?"

"You were perfectly clear. I mistakenly felt that helping you would earn your approval—though my motives in even caring what your feelings are escape me now."

"Falling into one of Flynne's traps nearly got you killed,"

he pointed out damningly. "And it's ruined any chance you had for a normal life."

"You mean a married life. Are you deaf? I don't want a husband. I don't need one. I can be perfectly happy all on my own."

He swore under his breath. "You've been scorned by the *Quality,* for god's sake—" he made the word sound as if it tasted bad "—and without society's approval, you're as good as dead to your friends."

"That is my problem, not yours."

"It's my problem, damn it! You've made it my problem." Samuel's much-vaunted control snapped. He'd never jumped into a decision in his life, but by God, he had now, and she was going to abide by it if he had to drag her to the altar by her hair.

"You can't make me marry you."

"Oh, yes, I can."

"I won't do it," she said stubbornly.

"Yes, you will. We are going to be married by next Saturday, Lady Veronica, so you'd better start planning a trousseau."

With that he slammed out of the house.

Veronica crossed her arms over her chest, thought for ten seconds very clearly about the future, and made a rather snap decision of her own.

He couldn't marry her if he couldn't find her.

She would simply disappear. She needed time to put some perspective on things anyway.

She would never marry him. Never! Samuel Danner only wanted to "do the honorable thing."

And she'd be damned if she let him!

Chapter

19

... I'm ever so sorry about your troubles," Jennifer Armstrong told Veronica. Her eyes were full of false sympathy. At least they were when they weren't flitting a glance toward the drawing room door. Veronica knew Jennifer was hoping to see Samuel and that dropping by to see *her* was only a pretext.

"I wish there was something I could do," Jennifer said on a sigh. "Oh, goodness! Is someone here?" she asked eagerly at the sound of a cart rattling in the hall.

Veronica, whose head was throbbing from smiling through her teeth, smothered a laugh when Uncle Tony's parlor maid pushed a tea cart into the room. Jennifer's face fell and her mouth tightened.

"Were you expecting someone?" Veronica asked innocently.

"No," Jennifer answered icily, snatching the teacup from the maid's hand.

The news of Veronica's broken engagement and wild adventures had swept through Society once again. Unfortunately, while she'd become an object of scorn and pity,

Samuel was now a hero of megalomaniac dimension. Since Samuel, though determined to follow through and marry her at the end of the week, had kept his mouth firmly closed about his future plans, everyone assumed he'd thrown Veronica over.

Which was just as well since she refused to be his charity case.

But Samuel—and Jennifer—were just part of the reason Veronica's head ached. Earlier in the week, as predicted, Malcolm and Amelia and James had each stopped by, undoubtedly sniggering in the outer hallway as they compared notes on Veronica's topple from grace. Then Lady Eveline, and Wortham, her one and only true friend, and Harriet Rowe, had each paid a visit.

There'd been others, too. People of her station who wanted to gawk and pretend to sympathize with her position. It was all such a pathetic farce. Even her old nemesis, Geoffrey Rowbury, had wormed his way past Hodgson. Of course, he wasn't interested in Veronica now that she was virtually penniless, but if she were interested in a little male companionship on the side, like in the carriage house . . . ?

She'd poured tea in his lap.

Madeline, Chloe, and Patrice had sneaked past Henry to briefly check in. Madeline was a wreck. Pale and unhappy and as trapped in her own way as Veronica was, she'd made it clear she would do her best to restore peace at Ashworth Manor. A faint hope, Veronica was sure. Her father never apologized or backed down. Chloe and Patrice had been extra quiet, clearly contemplating their own fates should they earn their father's virulent displeasure.

Jennifer was merely the latest member of Veronica's "friends" who was "doing her duty." Given her penchant for younger men, and that her conversation was littered with remarks about that "handsome Mr. Danner," Veronica was glad Samuel had made himself extremely scarce these last few days.

Samuel, in fact, was even more obsessed with finding Victor than ever before. Veronica had heard from Uncle

Tony that Lady Anne Cromwell had stopped by to see Samuel and that he'd hastened to take the luscious Lady Cromwell home.

Warming her bed? Veronica couldn't help asking herself miserably. Lady Cromwell was known to be free with her favors. Just ask the marquess of Wilshire. But Uncle Tony seemed to think it had something to do with Jason Cromwell and the reason the poor man poured himself into a bottle nearly day and night now.

The most surprising visitor of all, however, had been Uncle Tony's beloved Catherine. The news of Veronica's exploits had reached her ears and she'd stopped by to give Veronica unsolicited, but very welcome, real support.

"Your father was forcing you into marriage, wasn't he?" she'd asked with an empathetic smile. "As terrible as this ostracism must seem, believe me, it's better than marrying someone you don't love. My parents were miserable with each other. My father cheated. I suppose that's why I've been so extraordinarily careful."

Veronica had been both surprised and grateful for the confidence. When Uncle Tony entered the room unexpectedly, taken by surprise at her visitor, the look that passed between them convinced Veronica that her uncle was wrong in his assessment. Catherine had loved him. Probably still did. But his night with Amelia had lost him her trust, and she'd protected herself ever since.

Matchmaking was not Veronica's specialty, especially with so many problems of her own. But she owed Uncle Tony something for his kindness—and for the amount of money she intended to "borrow" from him to pay for her escape from Samuel—so she was bound and determined to do her best to bring Catherine and Anthony together before she left.

Unfortunately, she didn't have a lot of time. Samuel had announced to Anthony that he and Veronica would be married on Saturday. Uncle Tony, predictably, had displayed mixed feelings.

"What about when you leave the country?" he'd demanded of Samuel. "Do you truly expect Veronica to willingly follow after you."

"Yes," had been Samuel's flat answer.

A lie, Veronica knew, but a warning for her to behave and keep up the pretense of their love once again.

Damn and glory, the man was daft if he believed her that pliable. She'd warned him she wouldn't marry him. What torture it would be to love your husband and know deep in your heart that he considered you merely an encumbrance.

Veronica's plans were set. In the next few days she was going to fix things between Catherine and Uncle Tony, pilfer enough funds to pay her passage to the States, then find this Captain Shaughnessy Samuel had spoken of. Clearly, Samuel felt he was a man to be trusted and that was good enough for her.

Veronica didn't question herself about whether her plan to sail to Oregon and meet up with her distant relative, Lady Chamberlain, was the right thing to do. She couldn't rely on her father's relatives other than Uncle Tony, and she refused to be a burden to him any longer. Her mother's relatives thought so little of Henry's family already that Veronica was loathe to invade their home, so she'd settled on Agatha, her great-aunt.

But her decision had nothing whatsoever to do with the fact that Samuel would surely return to Oregon in the near future, she reminded herself fervently.

"Will Mr. Danner return soon?" Jennifer asked hopefully, bringing Veronica back to the present.

"I'm not certain."

"How dreadful to have another broken engagement. Especially with the horrors you've recently faced."

Veronica smiled faintly. Jennifer was positively dying to ask about her supposed pregnancy. The wretched woman's interest in Samuel was magnified a thousandfold with this new breath of scandal.

It was enough to make one sick.

"What are your plans for the future?" Jennifer ventured. Should she tell Jennifer Samuel's decree that they be married by Saturday? Lord, but that did sound like her father. This autocratic streak of Samuel's was a new wrinkle, one she detested fervently.

Black-hearted, miserable bastard.

Veronica's ire popped like a balloon a moment later. She wanted to hate him. She truly did. But though he blamed himself for her predicament, in truth, she was solely responsible. Her own impetuousness had been her downfall. That and her ridiculous love for a man she couldn't have.

"Veronica, I know it's indiscreet of me, but I have to ask: Is Mr. Danner the child's father? One can hardly blame you for succumbing," she added. "The man's handsome as the devil and there's something so—male—about him. Just looking at him is enough to weaken the staunchest resistance. I wonder if even I would be immune . . ."

"Have another cup of tea, Jennifer," Veronica suggested with a frozen smile. "I daresay you might need to pour some liquid on that burning fire!"

Jason Cromwell was a skeleton of his former self. His face was hollow, his eyes dark sunken pits. Samuel was shocked by the change in the man since the marquess of Wilshire's party. He wouldn't have recognized him, still could scarcely believe they were one and the same.

"Care for something to drink?" Jason rasped, clearing his throat without much success.

"No, thank you."

"Think I might need a small nip," Jason murmured, pouring a healthy dose of brandy into a snifter with shaking hands. Anne, who was seated in a chair, her skirts arranged about her like a queen, showed more irritation than true concern.

Samuel was at the home they shared together, a house reputedly bought and paid for by the marquess of Wilshire himself. Anne possessed a small income, and being the marquess's paramour undoubtedly received further financial compensation. Jason, however, was penniless, a victim of his own gambling illness. He lived off his sister, but Samuel seriously doubted the arrangement would last much longer because Jason, unless he changed his ways in a dreadful hurry, looked as if he weren't long for this world. Maybe the damage was already too great to stem.

"Ahhh . . ." Jason heaved a sigh after downing the drink. His pallor was an ugly shade of gray.

"Sit down," Anne told him, but he shook his head.

"So, you want to know about Flynne," Jason said after a moment, his gaze wandering longingly to the crystal decanter. "Daresay I knew this day would come. Can't put it off any longer, I suppose."

"Has he been blackmailing you?" Samuel asked.

"With what? The fact that I gamble? That I drink a bit too much?" His bark of laughter was bitter. "No, sir. My self-respect died years ago. Flynne threw the last shovel of dirt on my coffin."

"He loaned you money," Samuel realized, the scene unfolding before him as if Jason had already explained it to him in all its sordid detail. "You borrowed from him, you gambled and lost, and then Flynne exacted payment."

"Houghton introduced us," Jason said in a voice so low Samuel could scarcely catch it.

"Thomas Houghton," Samuel inserted quickly.

Jason nodded. "Houghton said he was a friend of Lord Ashworth's. Ashworth had told Houghton Flynne could be trusted. The bastard loaned me"—Jason swallowed hard—"ten thousand pounds."

Anne moaned in shock, her color retreating.

But Samuel had only heard two words. "Lord Henry Ashworth recommended Flynne to Houghton?"

"And Houghton recommended him to me."

"What payment did he exact?" Samuel asked, his stomach a cold pit.

"Wanted me to do a bit of dirty work. Asked me to— encourage Neville Rathbone in his suit for Lady Veronica. I didn't do it. Not really. Just commiserated with the old fool that she'd made a mistake in choosing you. Told him not to give up so easily. That sort of thing. It didn't take much to set the randy old goat after her. Never thought he'd go for rape though, don't you know."

Samuel was absorbing this when Anne broke in, "That dreadful man wanted his money back, too! At an exorbitant interest rate, mind you." Her beautiful, scornful eyes turned to Samuel. "He had the unmitigated nerve to visit me and threaten me under the guise of friendship."

"How did Flynne threaten you?"

"He told me he had influence amongst men who counted. I believed him."

"Be honest, my dear, if nothing else," Jason interjected scathingly. "Flynne told my sister that he had something on the marquess."

"The marquess of Wilshire?" Samuel's brows lifted.

"It was a lie!" she hissed.

"You believed him at the time, though, didn't you?" Jason gave up all pretense and splashed more liquor into his glass. "Anne paid Flynne money to put pressure on the marquess to blackmail him into marrying her. It was the only way she could wring a proposal out of old Durham, but it didn't work."

"No, it didn't," she agreed tightly, her eyes shooting daggers. "Then, he wanted me to pay back Jason's debt. He's nearly bled us dry."

"Is that why you decided to tell me the truth?" Samuel asked.

She sighed bitterly. "If he isn't stopped, we'll end up in debtor's prison. There's nothing left of the Cromwell heritage except the titles."

"Has Flynne blackmailed Houghton?"

"I'm sure he's found some way to empty the man's bank account," Jason muttered.

"And Danley?"

Everyone fell silent. "Poor old sod," Jason choked. "Killed himself, didn't he?"

"Do you have any idea what Flynne's connection to Henry Ashworth might be?" Samuel asked quietly.

They both hesitated. Though they didn't actually look at one another, Samuel had the distinct impression they both knew something they weren't telling.

"Henry likes the ladies," Jason admitted after a long moment. "Even made a proposition to Anne once, though I think he prefers to wallow in the lower classes."

The love note Veronica had discovered came sharply to Samuel's mind. But would someone as powerful and influential as Lord Ashworth really be susceptible to blackmail over an indiscretion with one of the servants?

As if reading his mind, Anne said, "You would have to ask Henry yourself, and I'm sure he wouldn't tell you anything he didn't want you to know. But there were rumors about his first wife's death. Unsubstantiated, of course. They were whispered through the ton at the time of her suicide, then quickly quelled. I always wondered though." Her lips tightened. "I believe Henry Ashworth is an exceedingly cruel man."

That certainly sounded like the ring of truth. Samuel had witnessed the man's cruelty to his daughter firsthand.

He asked a few more questions but it appeared he'd milked the Cromwells dry, so a half an hour later he was riding in the carriage, thoughtfully turning over their startling revelations.

Flynne was connected to Ashworth; he'd known it from the start, yet he'd never actively pursued the man. In deference to Veronica's tender sensibilities? Hah. The woman was made of iron. But yes, she was the main reason he'd stayed away from Henry. He'd been so wrapped up emotionally with Veronica's plight, he'd inadvertently sidestepped facing Henry straight on.

But now it was clear that Henry was at the center of Flynne's blackmail and extortion plan. How amusing it must have been to Flynne when he, Samuel Danner, had offered for the lovely Veronica, daughter of his strongest ally. An ally bought and paid for, Samuel was sure, but a staunch ally nevertheless. Fear was strong motivation indeed. If Henry felt Flynne might unravel his carefully woven tapestry of lies, he would eagerly sell his firstborn into wedlock to keep himself safe.

What a joke. Except Veronica had nearly been butchered

as a result of Flynne's machinations and Henry's desperate need for privacy.

Was there a mystery surrounding Cordelia Ashworth's death? Was that what held Henry in its cold, unforgiving grip?

There was one way to find out: Ask the man himself and gauge his reaction. Samuel drew a heavy breath, his gaze dropping on the pistol Anthony's driver had left inside the carriage.

The net was closing around Flynne—and Henry Ashworth. Samuel tucked the pistol inside his jacket just in case.

Veronica carefully pushed open the door to Uncle Tony's bedroom, wincing a little at the small squeak it made as it swung gently inward. There was a box in his top bureau drawer, a teak box inlaid with onyx and mother-of-pearl, a gift from her grandfather, Anthony's father. Veronica had been shown the box once when she was a child and she knew Uncle Tony kept valuables within it. Sometimes even extra money.

Feeling like the thief she was, she stole inside the room and slid open the drawer. The box was right inside. Lifting the lid, her eyes widened at the sight of the neatly stacked bills. Quickly, she extracted one bunch, stuffing it inside the pocket of her dress.

All she had to do was write a note of apology and explanation. Her one bag was packed.

If all went well, she could be gone by nightfall.

"Lord Ashworth does not wish to be disturbed," the Ashworth's infernal butler declared imperiously.

"Tell me something I don't know," Samuel muttered, ignoring the man completely. Honestly, British servants were worse than their aristocratic counterparts. When he got back to Portland he was going to make certain McMurphy never acted like a butler again.

He strode directly to Henry's study doors. Inside, two men were involved in a cold argument. Samuel's breath caught. Was that *Flynne's* voice? Was he *here*?

"I say there! You are trespassing, sir!" Northcroft sputtered. "I'll call in the authorities if you don't leave immediately!"

The voices quieted. Samuel tried the door which was locked. Northcroft looked smugly down his nose.

"Tell Henry to open the doors or I'll break them down," Samuel said calmly.

"You wouldn't dare!"

For an answer Samuel leaned one broad shoulder against the panels, ready to slam against the door with all his force if he needed to.

"You are no gentleman!" Northcroft's nostrils flared.

"Ashworth? I'm going to break down this door if you don't unlock it!" Samuel called, his gaze centered calmly on Northcroft. If Flynne was really inside the room his quest was at an end for there was no way the man was going to escape him now. A strange sense of peace descended even while his heart rate accelerated, anticipating battle. Inside his jacket, the pistol lay heavy against his heart, but Victor was a man of planning and coercion rather than hand-to-hand combat. It was doubtful blood would be spilled.

The lapel of his jacket gapped opened and Northcroft glimpsed the gun. "Oh, my Lord!" he murmured in terror, backing away.

Coward, Samuel thought with disdain at the same moment the study doors flung outward, an infuriated Henry Ashworth framed in the aperture.

"What is the meaning of this?" he clipped out with such impeccable British derision that Samuel almost smiled.

"Tell Victor I've been looking for him. I'm so glad he's here."

"Victor? I don't know whom you mean."

"Don't make me prove you a liar."

Henry's eyes flickered with some emotion at the steel in Samuel's voice. "You are not welcome here, Mr. Danner. In fact, I'm calling Inspector Cuthbert at the . . . *what do you think you're doing!*"

Samuel brushed right past him and into the smoke-filled room. Two Cuban cigars smoldered in an ashtray and Victor Flynne hovered by the door to the back garden.

But there was no escaping through the thick hedges.

"Good afternoon, Mr. Flynne," Samuel drawled. "It's been a long, long time."

Chapter
20

Victor Flynne nearly fainted dead away. Memories crowded through his mind, memories of a dark and dangerous time. Lord, this youngest Danner looked like his brother, Tremaine, and Tremaine Danner, damn his soul to hell, was Victor's worst enemy.

And that voice. It couldn't sound more like Tremaine Danner than if he were facing the devil himself.

Samuel was standing on the balls of his feet, his dark gaze cold and penetrating and predatory. Victor's throat was sandpaper. He couldn't swallow. Tremaine Danner had forced Victor into leaving Portland, had forced him to change his name, had nearly forced him from his most lucrative business.

Jesse Danner had heaped more injury upon him. But Samuel . . . God in heaven, the man's eyes held cold-blooded murder! He hadn't expected him to come back to Ashworth Manor. Hadn't Henry banished that lovely witch, Veronica, for god's sake? What was the bastard doing here anyway?

"Northcroft, send for the authorities," Henry ordered icily, glaring at Samuel.

The fool. The *authorities*. "Stop him!" Victor hissed, jerking his head in the direction Northcroft had departed.

Henry's eyes narrowed but he didn't move. Victor could have screamed from frustration. The idiot wasn't thinking straight.

"Bringing in the police might create a problem for Victor," Samuel elucidated. He sent a brief look in Henry's direction. The vaunted Lord Ashworth had turned to stone. "It might create problems for you as well."

"I'm sure I don't know what you mean," Henry shot back stuffily.

Victor inwardly groaned. This was a Danner, for god's sake. Henry didn't have a clue what he was asking for.

The only good Danner was a dead Danner, as far as Victor was concerned, and that cool, do-as-they-damn-please attitude sent shivers of fear through his limbs. His own control was merely a facade compared to Danner's whose veins ran with ice.

"Did you know that Victor had my wife killed?" Samuel said in a conversational tone to Henry.

"That was an accident," Victor blurted out defensively before he could stop himself.

Samuel sent him a fiery glare that could have melted granite. "Victor was afraid I could expose him, so he targeted Mary," he bit out in a razor-thin voice. "He targeted your daughter, Veronica, for similar reasons. Maybe a bit of revenge thrown in. Do you know what Victor had planned for her?"

"Don't listen to him," Victor warned, uncertain if even this weak-minded English lord could bear up under the truth.

"He sent her to an abortionist although she was never pregnant. He hoped she would die during a very crude surgery."

"She *is* pregnant," Henry snapped out.

Samuel shook his head. "Willoughby was hired to slice her to pieces. Isn't that right, Victor?"

"You're mad!" Victor declared, but his throat constricted.

"What's he got on you?" Samuel asked Henry. "It must be pretty powerful for you to listen to this and still stand there and do nothing."

"Veronica has been disowned for her own scandalous behavior." Henry's voice rose and his face turned an ugly shade of purple.

"Harsh words from an adulterer," Samuel said quietly. He turned to Victor who'd gone completely white. He wasn't certain how long Victor would remain frozen by the window, trapped. Though the man worked by a coward's means, he was desperate.

Henry didn't answer the accusation. He was equally frozen, his lips parted, as if waiting for the final hammer.

Samuel asked softly, "Does Victor know the truth about Cordelia's death?"

Bull's-eye! Victor jerked as if he'd been sucker-punched. Bull's-eye! Henry gaped at Samuel.

"I don't . . . know . . . what . . . you mean," he gasped, shaking so hard he nearly missed the chair he collapsed into when his knees gave out.

"You would have sacrificed Veronica to keep that secret safe," Samuel growled. "You *bastard!*"

"It was an accident," Henry babbled. "Flynne's tale is all lies."

"How much do you know?" Victor asked, calculating his chances of escape if he could keep Danner talking. He felt suddenly cool and collected. Adrenaline pumped through his system.

"Does it matter?" Samuel asked, lifting a brow.

"He didn't kill her, if that's what you're thinking," Victor said. "She killed herself. She really did."

Henry emitted a tortured moan.

"Henry *accidentally* strangled one of the servants. A pretty parlor maid named Belle. He has a penchant for pretty girls who need his good word to keep them employed. Wonderful blackmail—you know—if you sleep with me then I won't spread rumors about what a sinful slut you are to other prospective employers. It's a tough world for girls without family who find themselves at their employer's mercy."

"It's lies!" Henry shouted. "Vicious lies that could ruin me nonetheless."

"Cordelia knew the truth and took the coward's way out."

Samuel was sickened. He believed Victor implicitly. He already knew of Henry's sexual leanings. He just hadn't realized that Henry, like Victor, used blackmail as a means to achieve his wants.

"The footman went to jail for the murder. Been there for over ten years now. I knew someone who connected me with a one-time cell mate of the footman's, and I bought the story for a small fee. Knew someday it might come in handy."

"And when things got hot in Portland, you chased down your murdering earl," Samuel rasped, feeling dirty to the depths of his soul just being in the same room with these two.

A marble bust, small enough to pick up easily in one hand, sat on the three-legged table nearest Victor. During his discourse, Victor had eased his hand down. He wasn't much of an athlete but it was a very short distance between himself and Samuel. One lunge, then *bash!* He could claim self-defense. Or better yet, Henry could claim responsibility, saying Samuel had burst into the house, threatened him, and he'd been forced to stop him. The butler would back him up. No one would even have to know Victor was involved.

His hand darted for the bust. Movement in his peripheral vision caught Victor's eye. He dared to glance back. Samuel Danner had a pistol leveled at his heart.

"I'm a pretty good shot," Danner said in his infamous drawl.

For the first time in his lily-livered life Victor ignored the threat. His hand closed around the cold marble.

Blam!

The smell of cordite filled the room. Stunned, Victor stared in shock down the barrel of the deadly pistol, watching smoke drift in a thin, lazy stream upward. He lifted his confused eyes to meet Samuel's.

"Just a flesh wound," Danner said, smiling, as Victor's gaze dropped to the dark red ribbon of blood running down his arm from the wound at his shoulder.

Then everything went black.

Bow Street Station was an unprepossessing stone building whose outer facade was indicative of its inner comfort. The room to which Samuel was shown sported tired brown linoleum, several swivel chairs with uncomfortable backs, a table, and a rolltop desk. After hours of interrogation they'd offered him weak tea. Samuel, who'd learned to drink coffee over legal briefs, found one more reason to leave the country as soon as possible and get back to his other life.

Thoughts of Veronica invariably entered his mind again. She'd been with him in spirit these last few hours whether he'd wanted her to or not. All the while the police had asked and cajoled and threatened and tricked him into straying from his story, the memory of Veronica's sprightly smile and quick wit had kept him sane.

Lord Henry Ashworth was a more powerful foe than Samuel had apparently credited. No one wanted to believe the truth and Victor and Henry had talked fast and hard, claiming he'd blasted his way into Ashworth Manor, waved the pistol at them threateningly, then shot Victor for no damn good reason.

Luckily, Anthony Ashworth had arrived and reminded them all who Victor Flynne really was. But it had taken statements from Lady Anne Cromwell and Lord Jason— reluctantly sworn to by those two, well-respected members of Britain's peerage—and even some words from a white-faced Lady Madeline Ashworth to convince the authorities there *might* be some truth to Samuel's story.

He couldn't quite prevent the disappointment he felt over Veronica's pointed no-show. He knew she didn't want to marry him. He knew she resented his pity. But it wasn't pity. It was . . . necessity!

Still, it hurt in a way he wouldn't have believed possible that she refused to help him now. Damn the beautiful wretch. He *wanted* her here. He needed to see her expressive face and feel her support.

The door opened, admitting Anthony. The constable assigned to guard Samuel gave the British nobleman a hard-eyed look of warning. Anthony merely looked harassed and annoyed.

"Madeline believes the story about what precipitated Cordelia's suicide," Anthony told Samuel, his face grim and gray.

"And you?"

"I'm afraid so. My brother has a history . . ." He trailed off, ran a hand across his face, then added in a voice so low Samuel could scarcely hear him, "It'll be an ugly trial with ugly publicity. The Ashworth name will be tarnished no matter what the verdict."

"What about Madeline and Chloe and Patrice? What will become of them if Henry's found guilty of murder?"

"They will be financially sound."

"Emotionally?" Samuel queried.

"Madeline's a strong woman with excellent family lineage. Sympathy will be with her."

"What about Veronica?" Samuel couldn't help asking.

Anthony snorted. "This may work to her favor. Henry disowned her. If he's found guilty, Society will believe Veronica uncovered his sordid past and earned his displeasure by default."

So, she would be all right after he was gone. That left a curiously heavy feeling in his stomach. "I'm glad," he said, the words like ashes on his tongue.

"Veronica's headstrong. This refusal to marry you is all an act. She would like nothing better than to be your wife, but she wants you to want it, too."

For a wild moment he thought of what marriage would be like: days spent together in rival conversation, quiet evenings by the fire or out enjoying a play, or dinner, or merely a stroll in the park; nights of furious, wanton lovemaking, of sighs and moans and intense pleasures . . .

But she was British.

"Veronica needs a man willing to live in London and

tolerate the swings of this fickle Society. Sorry, Anthony, I don't fit the bill."

"Maybe not." He shrugged, not sounding nearly as convinced as he should have. "But right now your biggest problem is convincing everyone of the reasons behind the shooting. You may have to display your incredible aim, I'm afraid."

Samuel frowned in puzzlement.

"Show them you could have killed Victor Flynne with one shot instead of merely wounding the dirty scoundrel," Anthony explained dryly. "The man's damn lucky you didn't blow his head off."

The steamship *Her Majesty* was in port. Veronica didn't realize how truly fortunate that was, given Captain Shaughnessy spent most of his time at sea. When she boarded the decks, tugging an overstuffed valise as her complete wardrobe, the good captain looked around for her traveling companion, the one who was bound to be following behind her, lugging several trunks of gowns, jewels, and other feminine accoutrements. By all the saints, this was one aristocratic lady. A regular snobby tyrant, he predicted silently.

But then she smiled at him. "Captain Shaughnessy?" she asked, extending her hand. "I'd like to go to the States. One of the western states, actually: Oregon."

Shaughnessy was amazed. This lady wasn't no bartered bride, so what the devil was she going west for? "I'll not be goin' that far west for some time, ma'am. We'll be dockin' in New York first, then down the coast. It's a long rough voyage to the Pacific."

"Take me to New York, then. I'll find my way." She was as determined as the North Sea was cold.

Shaughnessy swept off his hat and scratched his strawberry-maned head. He watched the lilt of her bustle and the sway of her hips. He'd had his share of women this long time in port, but Lordy this one could certainly stir up the blood.

With the curiosity of a true connoisseur of human nature,

he determined he would learn more about her during the crossing to New York.

If Samuel could have predicted the outcome of the following days, he would have said that after a few hours of intense interrogation, the police would have let him go. He also would have predicted that Henry, based on his title and connections, would have been sent home as well, but that Victor would be held alongside Dirkson and Willoughby.

He would have been right, except for one minor change: The suspicious London police didn't trust him as far as they could throw him.

Samuel Danner was incarcerated for the better part of a month.

While Anthony did his damnedest to release him and a stream of society women he scarcely knew pleaded his case, Jennifer Armstrong and Lady Eveline—feathers and all—and elderly, dithery Harriet Rowe among them, Samuel sat on his hands until his patience was razor thin, his temper just as sharp.

And Veronica, blast her hide, had taken a large sum of Anthony's money—thanking him prettily for the loan in a note—then disappeared to parts unknown! She'd also apparently told Anthony that his beloved Catherine was really in love with him and that had certainly distracted Anthony enough to keep him from charging straight after Veronica.

At least that was Samuel's limited interpretation since Anthony appeared ever more lovestruck and useless with the passing of each intolerable day.

Now, scratching his newly formed beard, so impatient and infuriated, he actually considered a daring jailbreak, Samuel paced across the dirt floor of his untidy cell. He'd suggested the same to Anthony who'd been scandalized, to say the least. Anthony still had faith in the system. Samuel, however, was sick with worry for another reason. Twice he'd rescued Veronica. Where was she now? What had happened to her? Had Flynne instigated one last coup while he rotted in a smelly jail?

"If he's hurt her, I won't wait for the courts," he growled beneath his breath.

He should have killed him outright. Then Flynne would be dead and he wouldn't be any worse off than he already was.

Where the *hell* was Veronica?

Lady Agatha Chamberlain's home lay at the end of a sweeping drive, lush with late spring grass. White Georgian pillars collected in a semicircle in front of the doorway. A polished brass knocker lay in the center of a heavy, dark green painted door.

Veronica lifted the knocker, tension tightening her chest. It had taken weeks to secure passage to the States, then a train trip from New York, then the procurement of the address of Lady Chamberlain, one of Portland's premier society matrons.

But now here she was, ready to meet her great-aunt, worried sick that she might not be accepted by the grand lady even after all the trouble of finding her.

"Yes, ma'am?" The door was opened by a woman wearing a gray dress, white apron, and mobcap.

"Is Lady Chamberlain at home?" Veronica asked.

The woman frowned at her British accent. "Who's calling, then?"

"Veronica Elizabeth Ashworth. Her grandniece," she added when the name clearly didn't register.

"Wait in the parlor, then, please," she invited brusquely, leading Veronica to a room similar to Ashworth Manor's drawing room. The maid left abruptly and Veronica looked around, trailing her finger along the arm of an emerald brocade chair as she admired the glossy cream-painted mantel and polished andirons. The room was less fussy than she was used to; there weren't as many dried flower arrangements and intricately crocheted antimacassars and portrait miniatures. In fact, Lady Chamberlain's drawing room was a breath of fresh air, the view of rolling green lawns beyond the paned window so open and free and spacious Veronica wanted to throw out her arms in wonder. Why did she have this sense of coming home when she'd hardly been outside London's city limits in her life?

"Lady Veronica Ashworth?" an autocratic female voice demanded sharply from behind her.

Veronica whirled around to encounter a white-haired woman whose strong personality was stamped across her wrinkled face and drawn brows. Her eyes practically bored into Veronica's as if looking for flaws she knew would be there.

"Lady Chamberlain?" Veronica questioned, a bit taken aback by this forceful creature.

"Your father is Henry Ashworth, the current earl of Charlwood?" she snapped.

"I'm afraid so."

Her apology stopped the lady in midspate. Agatha's clamped jaw relaxed slightly. "And Anthony Ashworth's niece."

"Uncle Tony," she agreed with a smile.

"Well, you don't seem stuffy and featherbrained. Are you?" She leaned a bit forward on her carved cane, waiting for an answer.

Veronica laughed, a pure, fresh peal of amusement that brought the faintest smile to Agatha's stern lips. "I certainly hope not."

"Hmmm . . ." She eyed Veronica speculatively for a moment then called, "Cora Lee!" presumably to the maid who'd disappeared through the sliding doors. "Bring us some proper English tea, if Cook can manage it. My grandniece, Lady Veronica, has come for a visit. Now, my dear, sit down over there and bring me up-to-date on all the family gossip."

His release came one warm late May afternoon and Samuel walked into the sunshine like a man reborn. But London's skies were hazy, not the pure blue of home, and Samuel, who'd been picked up by Anthony and delivered to his town house, strode straight upstairs, bathed, shaved, and packed his meager belongings, determined to leave on the first steamship bound for America.

After he found Veronica, of course.

He had no faith in Anthony's attempts to trace her lead. And when he'd been introduced to Anthony's beloved Catherine, Samuel's belief that Anthony hadn't quite done all he could to find Veronica was borne out. The man was too distracted. Too besotted. He may have interviewed everyone who ever knew Veronica, he may even have threatened all of Flynne's acquaintants, but the truth was: Anthony was too in love to be effective.

It was up to Samuel to chase down the lovely vixen, kiss her senseless, then wring her neck.

He was standing by the hearth, a brandy in hand, his expression as dark as his thoughts, when Catherine asked, "What are the chances Henry will actually go to prison?"

Samuel threw the beautiful woman a look. She reminded him of Veronica. Prettier, perhaps, though not as remarkable somehow. But she possessed that impetuousness, joy, and impishness that was so much a part of Veronica's personality.

Damn it all! When he got his hands on her . . .

"As of tonight, I'd say the chances are fairly good," Anthony answered her. "The footman who was charged with the murder apparently told his tale to anyone, and everyone, who would listen. An enterprising prison scribe wrote it all down. And the poor girl's parents—you'll particularly like this, Samuel—have been living well for some time, courtesy of my brother."

"Henry paid them off?" Samuel asked incredulously. "Belle's parents? To keep quiet?"

"It appears that way."

"Is Henry still denying the charges?"

"Yes, but . . ." Anthony swallowed and Catherine placed her hand over his. "Other women have come forward—women who were once employed by my brother. Several claim to have had his children, although they were stillborn. Dr. Willoughby was the doctor."

"Oh, my God." Samuel was shocked. Anthony had been preoccupied with more than his love life. Small wonder Veronica's disappearance hadn't been at the top of his list of priorities. "What about Victor?"

"Inspector Cuthbert believes Henry will tell the truth soon enough. My brother's trapped himself within too many lies. When he talks, he'll undoubtedly implicate Victor. At this point, Henry wants Victor hanged, and he's certainly not the only one."

"Will he hang?"

"He'll probably spend the rest of his days at Coldbath Fields and no one survives there long."

Samuel absorbed that in silence, wishing he felt a sense of justice that Victor was finally facing what he deserved. But Henry's wickedness was soul-deep; he'd hurt so many people, including his own daughter, that Samuel just felt depressed by the whole sordid mess.

That very night he began his own search for Veronica, frustrated by everyone's assurances that they had no idea where she'd gone. The servants were clearly baffled. Anthony couldn't think of one close friend who would be willing to hide her. Only Madeline, who was being forced to live a whole new life and had enough troubles of her own because of it, gave him hope. She suggested Veronica may have contacted her mother, Cordelia's family.

Samuel followed up, but learned that no one knew where the lovely Lady Veronica had gone. Her mother's family didn't even know what she looked like. It was another dead end.

By the time July rolled around, Victor was tried and convicted, Henry was incarcerated for life, and Samuel had exhausted every lead.

Then one beastly hot day two events happened almost simultaneously: Anthony announced his upcoming wedding to Lady Catherine, and Lord Henry Ashworth hanged himself in his prison cell. In the uproar that followed, Anthony Ashworth became Lord Anthony Ashworth, the earl of Charlwood.

For Samuel, it was the period at the end of the sentence. It was time to leave. He looked around London with both fondness and regret, then booked passage to New York on a smaller steamship than *Her Majesty*.

Until the final moment the ship sailed away from the dock he kept hoping Veronica would miraculously appear.

His hope was in vain.

Chapter

21

Agatha Chamberlain's prize stallion, Justice, was a handsome, headstrong creature who had the stable boys terrorized and Agatha in a state of perpetual annoyance. The elderly lady continually swore that she would sell the miserable beast, but he was still lord of the stables despite all her complaints. Tossing his beautiful gray head, he seemed to eye Veronica with amusement, daring her to ride him.

"He's a bother," Agatha said with pride. "A terribly vain male without an ounce of conscience. Kelsey's the only one who could ever truly get him to behave."

"Kelsey Danner," Veronica murmured.

Agatha nodded, leaning a bit on her cane, a relatively new encumbrance that she positively hated but found necessary at her advanced age. They were standing outside Justice's box, the scents of straw and horse dung and dust intermingling inside the spacious stable. Through the open door, late afternoon sunshine sent a square of yellow light across the rough fir planks of the stable floor.

"You'll meet Kelsey this evening. She and Jesse are coming to dinner."

Veronica's pulse leapt. She'd been at Chamberlain Manor for the better part of a week. At first Agatha had been polite, but distant, even though she'd warmed somewhat upon learning that Veronica aligned herself with Anthony rather than Henry. But Agatha's curiosity had gotten the better of her and she'd demanded news of the Ashworths, so that Veronica had brought her up-to-date on current family affairs, even admitting to her own disinheritance.

"Poppycock!" Agatha had snorted. "Henry's an irresponsible, petulant little boy who has clearly never grown up. He'll change his mind. You wait and see."

Veronica didn't hold out much hope, but it didn't matter. Her ties to England had begun unraveling even before she'd sailed for America.

Agatha had, in turn, given Veronica the key to some of the mysteries locked in her own past.

"I've never told my granddaughter what I'm about to tell you," Agatha had said three nights earlier as she settled into her favorite chair with a cup of tea. "Someday I'll probably need to, but Charlotte is so uncomplicated and earnest that I've purposely waited."

Veronica had met Charlotte that first evening and would have described her much as Agatha had. There were only two years separating them in age, yet Veronica felt years wiser—and older.

"My brother—your grandfather—William Ashworth, and I were the only children of our generation. I was older and decidedly plain. No, no, don't interrupt," she'd decreed autocratically when Veronica tried to speak. "I was very plain. William wasn't much prettier, but he married a very pretty woman, Constance, and they bore six very pretty children."

Veronica smiled. Besides Henry and Uncle Tony, she apparently had four aunts she'd never met. They'd married and scattered to the ends of the earth, though Agatha had heard two of them had died.

"They were all washouts." Agatha declared. "Terrible people, except for Anthony but he was so young, the baby of the family. He's the only Ashworth who's had the good sense to keep in contact with me," she added.

"But you were married," Veronica ventured.

"Humph! John Chamberlain wanted a pretty woman with a sweet temper but he settled for the daughter of an earl. We had a decent marriage while it lasted. My son, Miles, unfortunately, took after John. He, too, settled for a titled woman. Lillian was sweet but had no head for money. It flowed like water through her avaricious fingers. They were on a trip to the Continent when the accident occurred. That left Charlotte in my keeping, but my husband wasn't ready for another child, at least not one to take care of. He ran off with a girl less than half his age, the old fool. Died the following year.

"At the time your father made noise about raising Charlotte as one of his daughters, but I wouldn't have it. He was already a womanizer. I'm sorry, my dear, if this destroys some illusions for you, but I always thought his true motivation was to get his hands on the money bequeathed me which would eventually go to Charlotte. I think he hoped to reunite the Ashworth wealth although I know he's as rich as Midas already."

"You haven't destroyed any illusions," Veronica remarked, feeling just the tiniest stab of pain.

"So, I left England and I've never been sorry. Charlotte and I have a good life here. It's so much less complicated."

Veronica absorbed Agatha's tale of her family, recognizing that she felt much the same way about leaving her home. Then Agatha said something that made Veronica jump.

"Did you happen to meet a man named Samuel Danner? I gave him Anthony's address. He had business in London."

It had taken a considerable amount of self-control not to react even more violently. After a long moment, Veronica had managed, "Yes, we met."

"Hmmm." Agatha had eyed her grandniece knowingly, but hadn't said any more on the subject. Instead she changed the topic to include Jesse and Kelsey Danner and her relationship to them. Apparently Kelsey had once been a companion to Charlotte, when Jesse Danner, a man who'd grown up on the neighboring property to Kelsey's in the rural town of Rock Springs, stepped into her life and turned it upside down by marrying her, presumably for the social standing she could bring him.

It was a long, involved story, but with an interesting side bit of news for Veronica. As a direct result of Kelsey and Jesse's romantic fireworks, and their subsequent entanglement with Victor Flynne, Samuel had charged to London searching for his own wife's murderer.

Agatha sketchily filled in more details about the rest of Samuel's family. Though Veronica desperately desired more information, she tried hard not to ask too many questions. In consequence, she knew little about the other Danners, but quite a bit about Kelsey and Jesse.

She was terribly afraid to meet them, sure some sign of guilt regarding Samuel would magically appear on her face. Could she get through an entire evening with Samuel's *brother* and not give herself away?

Now, as Veronica stroked Justice's silky nose, nearly getting her fingers nipped for the effort, she wondered if she should broach the subject of her relationship with Samuel to Lady Chamberlain. But what could she say? *I'm in love with Samuel Danner and though we made glorious, wonderful love, I'm not even sure he likes me.*

Impossible! There was nothing to do but pretend she knew little about Samuel. Jesse and his wife were bound to ask questions, though. Maybe she could plead a headache or the flu or something more serious, like amnesia. Oh, how she dreaded this dinner party.

If only there were some way out . . .

Across town Kelsey Orchid Danner put the finishing touches on her husband's tie, then stepped back to survey her handiwork.

Jesse made as if it were choking him.

"Stop it," she ordered good-naturedly. "It's a little lop-sided, but it'll do."

"Agatha and these infernal dinners with crabby old women of 'breeding.' This one will have hennaed hair and no teeth," he predicted.

"According to Charlotte her guest is young and gorgeous. A long-lost relative of some sort."

"Long-discarded relative is more like it. Agatha hates the lot of them."

"Not all of them. She sent Samuel to meet her nephew, Anthony Ashworth. He's the only one 'worth a half-penny' according to Agatha."

"Damn it." Jesse yanked off the tie and looped it around Kelsey's neck, dragging her forward. "Why isn't Samuel here dealing with Lady Whatever-her-name-is? He's used to protocol and manners."

"You know very well that he won't come home until he's taken care of Victor Flynne to his satisfaction."

"A wild-goose chase." Jesse would have loved to go after Flynne himself, but Samuel had disappeared without informing him and later, when Agatha had explained that he'd gone to London to search for Victor, Jesse simply hadn't believed the man was there. Besides, Kelsey wouldn't have let him go. They'd just discovered they loved each other and his stubborn, hot-tempered wife wasn't about to let him chase after his determined younger brother—unless, of course, she could come, too.

"Her name is Lady Veronica Elizabeth Ashworth, if you please," Kelsey said as Jesse's arms surrounded her. "Don't try to sidetrack me. We're going to this dinner."

He gave a mock shudder. "She sounds perfectly horrible," he said in a hilarious imitation of Lady Chamberlain.

"Agatha seems to think she has merit," Kelsey mumbled against lips now crushing down on hers.

Jesse's fingers found the buttons marching down her slim back. Kelsey squeaked out a faint protest, before laughing beneath this onslaught of passion as they both fell across the bed.

"She's probably as stiff, stubborn, and prudish as Agatha and that's why Agatha allows her under her roof. Wait and see," Jesse predicted as Kelsey lifted disbelieving brows.

"She'll be a royal pain in the ass. As blue-blooded and dull as that mare brought to Justice for breeding. I don't think the stupid animal even knew she was in heat. Justice couldn't get excited enough to mount her. No passion in her. Too pure to have any spunk."

Kelsey's dress slipped down her arms. She pulled her husband's dark head down to hers, her lips a hair's breadth from his. "I have a feeling you're going to have to eat your words," she murmured. "You're always wrong about women."

"Am I?" He arched one devilish brow, then proceeded to prove he knew a thing or two about his wife.

Veronica stared at her pale reflection in the oval mirror atop her vanity. This was the room Kelsey had used when she'd lived with Agatha. For some reason that made her feel like an interloper, an invited guest who'd weaseled into a place meant for someone else.

She brushed her hair in long, thoughtful strokes, then bound it within a hair net. Its weight and length made it rest heavily on her shoulders. Her spring green dress had been freshly laundered and when she slipped into it, she felt almost attractive. Drab Brown, she reminded herself, though in truth, she knew now that her looks were anything but unremarkable. Her coloring might be ordinary, but, like Lady Chamberlain, strength of purpose was stamped across her face. Even Veronica could admit her features were pleasing.

A wave of faintness passed over her and she sank onto the vanity stool, half-amused. Maybe she wouldn't have to feign an illness after all. She felt positively done in.

Fifteen minutes later she realized her spate of illness was over and when she heard the doorbell chime, she braced herself, taking one last anxious look in the mirror and pinching some color back in her cheeks.

With a prayer of hope, she sailed down the stairs, hesitating on the final step when she saw Agatha's guests hadn't yet entered the dining room but were standing off to one side of the hall.

Her heart gave a painful kick before racing into high gear.

My God, *Samuel,* she thought half-hysterically, before sense returned and she realized the handsome man standing in the hallway had to be his brother, Jesse. On second look, their resemblance wasn't so marked. Except for the way they looked at you, their stance, the determined slant of their jaw, the sensual curve of mouth, thick dark hair, and muscular build . . .

"Lady Ashworth?" the woman asked, holding out her hand.

She had auburn hair with glorious red highlights that glowed a rich burgundy beneath Agatha's chandelier.

"Just Veronica, please," she said, realizing Kelsey wanted her to shake hands like a man. Veronica firmly grasped Kelsey's hand, intrigued by so feminine a creature with such an interesting and dramatic way to greet someone. Now, why was Kelsey sending Jesse that "I told you so" look?

"Well, Just Veronica," Jesse drawled in an echo of Samuel's voice. "If all the Ashworths are like you, I'd say Agatha made a mistake in disowning them."

"Don't you believe it," the starchy lady sniffed, and then they all went into dinner.

Samuel unlocked the front door of his house, standing a moment in the entryway, absorbing the familiar squeaks from the wood, the rhythmic ticktock of the grandfather's clock, and the prevailing sense of Mary and coming home.

Something was wrong. He frowned in the dark, his eyes accustoming themselves for he preferred not to switch on the lights and alert McMurphy that he was home yet.

Mary, he realized with a start. That sense of her was gone. Gone forever.

Striding across the hall to his den, he lit the oil lamp on his desk. A mellow, diffused circle of light glowed across the desk and carpet, touching the corners of the fireplace.

He looked at the mantel, surprised to see the portrait miniatures decorated it once more. He'd thrown them away, but McMurphy had apparently salvaged and saved them, placing them in their rightful place while Samuel was chasing down his demons.

He frowned. Chasing down his demons? Why had that phrase come to mind? He'd gone after Victor Flynne, pure and simple, there was no deeper meaning to his quest.

Except maybe there was . . .

Picking up a miniature of Mary, he held the tiny frame in his hands, remembering her sweetness, her intelligence, her pluck. But it was Veronica's face he saw now, and the yawning ache inside him was fear and unhappiness and anger over how she'd fled from him and all she'd known.

"Please let her be safe," he prayed quietly, setting the miniature back in its place. "Please let Anthony find her and have the courtesy to write and tell me she's all right . . ."

If he didn't, Samuel was afraid he'd go out of his mind.

Chapter
22

It was during the last course of dinner that Veronica almost
fainted. She felt it coming on, like a dark cloak, long before
the actual swoon, which gave her ample time to excuse
herself and travel the long stairway up to her room before
weakness overcame her.

She collapsed in a heap on the carpet beside her bed. She
came to almost instantly and moments later was violently
sick.

Drenching her face with water, she patted her skin dry
and stared grimly at her reflection in the vanity mirror. This
was not some strange malady. Samuel's heated prediction
had come true.

She was pregnant.

It took all her not inconsiderable willpower to return to
the drawing room and brush away her disappearance as
minor indigestion to the discerning Mr. and Mrs. Jesse
Danner, Agatha, and Charlotte. She managed, however, and
apart from the rather thoughtful look Kelsey sent her way,
no one seemed the wiser.

That had been a fortnight ago and every morning since
Veronica would scarcely get out of bed before retching in the

chamber pot. She would then surreptitiously dispose of this evidence and spend the rest of the day agonizing over what to do.

Why, oh, why did she have to be pregnant? Hadn't she enough troubles? She'd just begun to win Agatha's trust and Charlotte, Jesse, and Kelsey's friendship. Now they would believe the shame of her predicament was what had driven her from London. They would feel used and wouldn't want the burden of a—horrors!—unwed mother in their midst.

And what about Samuel . . .?

Veronica realized that once he learned of the child, he would enforce his earlier decree of marriage. He would do it to give the child a name and to ensure she couldn't take the child away from him.

But it was a cheater's way for her to win the man she loved. A trap that she'd unwittingly set, and she would rather die than bind Samuel to her unwillingly.

The best thing to do—the only thing—would be to flee to a place where no one could find her.

The unbearable loneliness of such self-inflicted ostracism nearly sent her to her knees. She was sick of running away. Maybe it would be better to just dispense the truth, like so much bitter medicine, and wait and see what happened.

She was standing in the drawing room, staring out at the grounds and turning that thought over in her mind when Cora Lee dumped the mail on the table next to Agatha.

"Veronica, my dear, a letter's come from Anthony!" Agatha said with delight. The elderly lady's face was glowing with excitement as she waved the missive gently, drawing Veronica's attention to it.

"Have you written him?" she asked anxiously, afraid her whereabouts had already reached everyone in London.

"Not for quite some time. Come, sit down beside me and let's read it together."

Her curiosity piqued in spite of herself, Veronica perched on the arm of the chair as Agatha attempted to read Uncle Tony's scratchy penmanship. With a snort of frustration, Agatha handed the letter to her.

"Dearest Agatha," Veronica read, amused at Uncle Tony's

tone. "I'm afraid misfortune has entered our lives. Henry has died, a victim of his own hand—" Veronica gasped, scanning the rest of the letter with growing horror as each sentence unfolded.

"My dear . . ." Agatha stretched a comforting hand her direction. Veronica automatically squeezed it with cold hands. She read the rest of the letter in silence, then let it drop from nerveless fingers.

"He says—he says—that Father was responsible for the death of a servant and that a footman was blamed," Veronica announced in a strangled voice. "Father was found out and sent to prison along with Victor Flynne!"

Agatha started, more surprised by this last news than Henry's failings. "Isn't that the man Samuel Danner went to find?"

"Yes." Veronica's lips were bloodless. "He also says Samuel's still in London on some other quest he doesn't specify."

"Really? Maybe Samuel enjoys it there."

"Oh, no. He hates it. I don't know why he'd stay, unless . . ." She trailed off and drew a shaking breath. "I can't believe Father's dead."

"But you can believe him responsible for the matter that sent him to prison?"

"Unfortunately, yes."

Agatha hesitated, clearly weighing her next words. "Was Samuel somehow involved in bringing Henry's crimes to the attention of the police?"

"I don't really know. If it involves Victor Flynne, I'd say it's highly probable."

"Do you blame Samuel, my dear?"

Veronica stared at her blankly. "Blame Samuel?"

"Is that why you felt compelled to leave the dinner table the other night? Because his brother was there?"

Her secret was safe. Veronica wasn't sure whether to laugh or cry.

Agatha's spine stiffened, as if she believed Veronica had somehow maligned one of her own. "I always found Samuel an extremely personable man. Very controlled and determined, yes, but likable, too. My dear, he may have brought your father to justice, but he is not responsible for Henry's misdeeds."

She was warning Veronica, in case her grandniece should expect her to pick sides. What would she think if she knew the truth? It was on the tip of Veronica's tongue to tell her when Charlotte entered the room, bubbling over with news, and the moment slipped away.

". . . even that odious Tyrone McNamara asked me to dance at the Hathaway's party," Charlotte babbled away. "You don't know him, Veronica, but he's not a nice man. Just ask Kelsey about him. He tried to . . . well, never mind." She shot a glance at Agatha whose stern expression stilled her tongue.

"I'm afraid my granddaughter has turned into the belle of the ball this past year," Agatha said on a sigh. "She has more suitors than she can handle and it's become a problem. Veronica, I know it's quite unfair of me to ask, but it would help me enormously if you could attend some of these functions with her. All manner of men have been calling for her. It's difficult to sort the chaff from the grain. Would you be willing to be her companion and keep an eye on her?"

Charlotte's expression darkened. Clearly she disagreed with these old-fashioned values. "I don't need a chaperon!" she declared. "Besides, Veronica's scarcely older than I am."

"Precisely," Agatha said, bringing the teacup to her lips and turning away as if the matter were already decided.

"I'm not certain I'm the right person," Veronica demurred.

"It will do you good, my dear. There are plenty of young men who are interested in women of breeding."

Veronica's lips parted. Her crafty great-aunt was hoping to do a little matchmaking for her as well. Chaperon be damned! Agatha intended to push Veronica into Portland's social whirl.

Pregnant, an outcast, a social disaster—Veronica couldn't think of a worse idea.

"What a marvelous plan," she murmured through clenched teeth.

It appeared flight was the only answer once again.

The following evening Agatha attempted to put her plan in motion. She accepted an invitation for Charlotte, with Veronica as her companion, to an outdoor party. Much to Veronica's amusement, Charlotte balked. She simply refused to go. So, when Jesse and Kelsey invited Agatha, Charlotte, and Veronica to dinner at the last minute, plans were changed. Reluctantly by Agatha, with relief by Charlotte and Veronica.

Veronica felt poorly. Her back hurt and her head ached. She made the mistake of complaining to Agatha who believed she was trying to avoid her social obligations. Crying off now would only bring further attention to herself and her condition, something she couldn't afford. Reluctantly, she agreed to go.

Still, when the carriage clattered through the wrought-iron gates and down the cobbled drive to Jesse and Kelsey's front door, Veronica drew several deep, sustaining breaths. Being with Samuel's brother and sister-in-law was nearly as difficult as pretending to enjoy accompanying Charlotte.

The coachman helped her alight. Veronica glanced about the lovely arched entryway with both admiration and trepidation. Thousands of butterflies were taking flight inside her stomach. *Please don't let me disgrace myself,* she thought, fearing another spate of retching. How long would it be before her pregnancy showed. How much time did she have left before the rest of the world knew?

Kelsey answered the door herself, looking fresh and elegant in a satiny emerald green dress that rustled with every move. She kissed Agatha and Charlotte and greeted Veronica with true enthusiasm.

"We have another guest," she said mysteriously.

"Ah, Jesse," Agatha said warmly to the man striding from the shadows of the back hallway in their direction.

Out of her peripheral vision Veronica recognized those deliberate, ground-devouring strides. Her breath caught.

She jerked around, her gaze slamming into the surprised and angry eyes of the man she loved.

He froze in midstride, staring at her in stunned amazement.

"Samuel!" Agatha greeted him with delight. "When did you get back?"

All the blood rushed from Veronica's head. She swayed on her feet. *No, please,* she thought, knowing she was about to faint.

She heard his breath whoosh between his teeth. His hand was on her arm, pulling her close. Her senses swam. Her knees were rubber. She made a faint sound of protest before being enveloped in his embrace, her face pressed against the fine weave of his wool suit. Inhaling his clean, male scent, she felt her head clear. *Samuel! My God, he was here!*

"Are you all right, Veronica?" Kelsey asked anxiously.

"You look positively green," Charlotte added.

"I—just—felt faint, for a moment," she struggled to get out.

Samuel set her back on her feet, his hands steadying her. His mouth was a slash of controlled fury. "I certainly didn't expect to see you again, Lady Veronica. Are you ill?"

His harsh tone scraped across her skin like sandpaper. She swallowed. "I'm fine." Her voice was sharper than it needed to be. "Perfectly fine."

He released her instantly, stepping back as if she'd struck him.

At that moment Jesse joined them. "So, you've met my brother," he said, gazing thoughtfully from Veronica to Samuel who had both frozen on the spot.

"Dinner's nearly ready," Kelsey put in, her fine brow puckered. "Nothing fancy. Cook's been away visiting relatives and I'm afraid I've had to try my hand at—" She broke off abruptly, then declared, "Veronica, are you certain you're all right?"

"No, actually, I'm not feeling very well." Veronica swallowed. "Please forgive me, but I don't think I'll be able to stay."

"She nearly swooned in the hallway," Charlotte said for Jesse's benefit.

"I do feel—faint," Veronica admitted.

"I thought you were fine. Perfectly fine," Samuel remarked in a steely voice, sending a shiver of apprehension down Veronica's back.

Everyone stared at Samuel.

"I think I'll just go home." Veronica turned blindly toward the door. Immediately a strong arm reached for the handle, blocking her path.

"Let me do the honors," Samuel suggested coldly, and he escorted Veronica out of the room and into the soft night while everyone stood behind them with their mouths hanging open.

"I can take Agatha's carriage. I'm—"

"Shut up, Veronica." His fury snapped at her like a whip.

For once she did as she was told. He called for Jesse's driver, then climbed in the carriage across from her. She dared a glimpse of his face. It was dark and dangerous. Long moments passed. She was surprised and a bit touched when he offered her his handkerchief. At least he was giving some credence to her illness.

"Have you been here all this time?" he blasted her.

"Here?" she asked, stalling for time.

"In Portland!" he hissed.

"Ye-e-ss."

"And you didn't see fit to let anyone know? You've put Anthony and Madeline through sheer hell. Do you know how worried they are? It's a wonder the entire British Navy isn't searching for you."

"I'm sorry."

"The hell you are!"

Samuel leaned toward her threateningly, his thickly lashed eyes staring furiously at her.

"I left Uncle Tony a note," Veronica defended herself.

"And conveniently forgot to mention where you were going. How did you know about Lady Chamberlain? Did Anthony tell you?"

"Not really."

"Not really?" he repeated scathingly.

Veronica's own temper came to her rescue. "I overheard you and Uncle Tony talking about Agatha."

"Eavesdropping again?"

"Yes!" she retorted, in fine fury herself.

"What about Madeline?" he asked, changing tactics. "Don't you care that she's sick over your disappearance?"

"Sick?" Remorse stabbed through her and she sat forward on the seat. Her head swam and her stomach clenched. Watching her, Samuel gently pushed her back against the cushions.

"She's more heartsick than seriously ill," he amended, frowning. "What's wrong with you. Why did you nearly collapse?"

"I . . . haven't eaten much today."

His gaze raked her. "You're hardly starving," he commented, and Veronica braced herself, half expecting him to guess the reason her waist had thickened.

But he was too upset with her to think clearly. "I can't believe you're here," he bit out. "I spent a month in prison waiting—" He cut himself off.

"You were in prison?" she choked out, her eyes wide. "Oh, Samuel . . ."

"All those weeks of searching," he bit back furiously. "Not knowing whether you were even alive. You're every bit as spoiled and selfish as they said you were."

Hurt, Veronica could find no defense. She was stunned by the realization that Samuel had been locked up for a time, humbled by the fact that she'd never even known he was in trouble.

"I'll send Madeline and Uncle Tony a wire and let them know I'm all right," she said unsteadily.

"Do that." Samuel was terse.

Dazedly she realized she should go home. Home to Madeline and her sisters. Somewhere safe. But it didn't seem like home and it certainly wouldn't be safe. Rumors about her child would be rife. She would undoubtedly be advised to give up the baby to avoid further scandal. She would be pushed and pulled and her life wouldn't be her own. They would try to take the baby away from her!

The baby. *Samuel's* baby. Her heart beat so hard it hurt. "You didn't have to escort me," she told him. "I could have found my way home."

"You haven't even bothered to let anyone know we were . . . acquainted, have you?" His hesitation was telling. She knew he was recalling their night of lovemaking. "Yes, I did. You were a guest of Uncle Tony's, after all. It was bound to come up."

She cringed at her own words. It was plain she would have preferred never mentioning her relationship with him. The knowledge wasn't lost on him. His smile was sardonic.

"Did you mention how close we'd become?"

Veronica didn't like the implication. "We are not *close.*"

"We were."

She didn't dare continue this conversation. "I don't know what you mean."

"Memory failing you, Lady Veronica?"

The cur. "One night of passion does not qualify as closeness," she said through her teeth.

"Doesn't it?"

"No!"

"You came to Portland because you knew sooner or later I would turn up. Why didn't you just marry me in England and get it over with?"

His arrogance astounded her. "I did not come here to see you. I came to meet my great-aunt."

"And you just happened to come halfway across the world to do it, directly to my door."

"You vain bastard!" she sputtered. "I left London because I couldn't bear it anymore. It had nothing to do with you."

"I would have married you," he said coldly.

She heard the past tense of his remark and it bit painfully inside her. "Well, you don't need to now, do you?"

He hesitated, as if her words wounded him, but she knew that was just wishful thinking on her part. "How long do you intend to stay?"

"I don't know . . ." She couldn't read the intense look on his face. Did he hate her? "I'm in no hurry to leave," she lied.

The carriage pulled into Agatha's drive. Veronica would have liked to rush away from him but he insisted on helping her down and walking her to the door. When he would have followed her inside, she balked.

"Good evening, Mr. Danner," she said pointedly.

"If you think I'm leaving yet, your memory has indeed failed you," he snarled. He held open the door, daring her to try and throw him out.

Veronica swept through, head high, the effect spoiled slightly when she trampled on her hem and nearly stumbled. It scarcely mattered, however, for Samuel was as cool and determined as ever and was more interested in taking control than being bent on humiliating her.

She led him to the morning room—a petty revenge that revealed she wouldn't see him in the drawing room where guests were normally invited. He didn't even appear to notice. His mood, in fact, had changed drastically for upon entering the room he strode directly to the window, gazing out into the night instead of at her, a deep frown furrowing his brow.

"Victor Flynne's in a London prison. You left before we finally caught up with him. I just realized there are a lot of things you don't know." He hesitated, his jaw working. "Your father—"

"I do know," she interrupted with sudden understanding. "Uncle Tony sent Agatha a letter explaining everything."

Samuel swung around to meet her eyes. The look on his face melted her heart. "I'm sorry, Veronica."

He meant it. Delayed reaction hit her like an open wave, drowning, pulling her under. "Don't be. My father was incapable of love. It's not your fault his crimes caught up with him."

There was a catch in her voice that twisted his heart. "Did Anthony also tell you he's engaged?"

Veronica stared at him in surprise. "To Catherine?" she dared hope.

He nodded. The joy on her face was like a ray of sunshine after a long rainstorm. Her gold eyes danced. "Really? They're getting married?" She suddenly gasped. "Oh, no!" Color left her cheeks, leaving them pale and ashen.

Concerned she might faint again, Samuel quickly crossed the room to her side. "Are you all right?"

"It's not—it isn't just because—she wouldn't marry him just because he's inherited, would she?"

She turned horror-stricken eyes to Samuel. He wanted to scoop her up and kiss away her pain even while part of him was completely infuriated with her. "They were engaged before Henry took his life."

"Oh . . . that's good."

She moved away from him, putting the chair between them. Samuel felt bereft. She'd been warm and sweet and real in his arms. He hated her distance. Hated her deceit. Part of him wanted to murder her, the other part wanted to drag her willing body against his, feel her melt in his arms, listen to the low moans torn from her throat when he kissed her and touched her and made love to her.

But ever since their lovemaking she'd wanted nothing to do with him. Actually, he realized slowly, she'd turned away from him when she'd thought he truly intended to marry him.

A cold thought pierced him like a sword. Was the reason she had pulled away *because* he'd offered for her? Could the idea of a real marriage be so repulsive to her that she couldn't even be civil to him now? She'd complained long and loudly that she never wanted to marry. That their "engagement" was to save her from a "fate worse than death." He'd thought that was a lie. Hell, Anthony had told him she was in love with him. And he'd believed it. She'd been so eager and responsive and loving, why shouldn't he have believed it? She'd been totally his when they'd slept together.

Until they'd slept together, he realized with a jolt of pain.

The answer was so clear he was stunned it had taken him so long to see it. He'd been drunk that night and God knew what their lovemaking had really been like. All he could remember was deep passion and enveloping sweetness. Maybe for her it had been much worse. Maybe, he thought with a sickening lurch of his stomach, he'd been less than a gentleman. But she'd been more than willing, hadn't she? He couldn't conceive that he could have taken her against her will.

But she had nearly fainted when she'd seen him. God.

Her next words scorched his soul, confirming his worst fears. "You don't owe me anything, Samuel. We're not in London now, and I don't need a husband."

"And that's what you always wanted, your freedom? Even now?" he made himself ask, thinking of her lost virginity.

"Especially now." she declared fervently.

There was no doubt that she meant it. "So, my marriage proposal is being scorned again?"

Her heart jumped. But then she remembered: code of honor once again. "I'm afraid so."

Samuel was shaken. She'd been his reason to not lose hope while he'd fought to free himself from prison. He'd been searching for her for weeks, sick with despair, half-convinced she'd careened headlong into another disaster. He'd envisioned her broken body, her lifeless limbs, the final closing of those gorgeous eyes. He'd blamed himself, for his relentless, passionate pursuit of Flynne, the blind determination that had thrown Veronica in Flynne's path.

"I suppose for that I should be grateful," he said bitterly.

She mistook his bitterness for mockery. "I wouldn't marry you now if you got down on your knees and *begged.*"

Anger replaced his self-loathing. "Don't worry, I won't."

With that he slammed out of Agatha's house, furious with himself for caring, for spending so many haunted, useless hours in torment over a woman who clearly wasn't the warmhearted creature he'd made her out to be. She was cold, spoiled, and selfish—just like all those other English *ladies.*

He was well rid of her. Well rid of her.

"The nearest tavern," he barked to his driver, completely oblivious to the fact that he abhorred men who used drink as a means to expunge frustration.

But hell, that was before he'd met Veronica. Anything was possible now.

Veronica had never felt less like socializing and when, the following evening, she found herself being fussed over by one of Agatha's maids who fixed her hair and brought her a pale peach gown from the dressmaker—the one Agatha had demanded she be measured for two weeks earlier—she wondered how in God's name she was going to go through with it.

But Charlotte, who was torn between bubbling over with enthusiasm and being frustrated with her new "keeper," was too eager for this event to stay home in a fit of pique. "We've got to go to the park! Please, Veronica. Don't be a stick in the mud."

"I am not a stick in the mud."

"You're not really ill, are you?"

"Of course she's ill," Agatha said, as she came from her sitting room to the hallway. "Don't shout so much, child. Veronica's still suffering from that bout of influenza. Half the city's still down with it."

"Really? I didn't even realize she'd been sick."

"That's because you spend too much time in front of the mirror," Agatha huffed to which Charlotte looked baffled since the accusation wasn't near the truth.

Of course, the remark about influenza was a blatant lie as well. Agatha was acting very strangely indeed.

"I'll get my wrap," Charlotte said, bounding up the stairs in a very unladylike manner. "Don't go away!"

"How *are* you feeling?" Agatha asked Veronica.

"I believe my bout with the flu is nearly over," she answered dryly.

"Then there's no need for the doctor?" the starchy old lady asked in all innocence, which was suspect in itself.

"No need whatsoever."

"Good." She patted Veronica's hand, then added, maddeningly, "Does Samuel know?"

Her pulse leapt. "Know what?"

"About the baby. You don't mean to keep it from him, do you?"

Veronica was so flabbergasted she couldn't even lie. She blushed furiously, answer in itself.

"I wasn't certain who the father was," Agatha elaborated, "until I saw the two of you together last night. Darling, don't you think he should know?" When Veronica still couldn't answer, she said, "Think about it. When you get back, we can discuss everything if you would like."

At that moment Charlotte came hurrying back downstairs and in a daze, Veronica followed her out to the carriage.

She wandered around the park, completely oblivious to everyone and everything. Agatha knew. She *knew*. And she'd neither condemned her nor threatened to send her back to England. If fact, she'd seemed more amused and concerned than outraged. For an upright, straight-laced gentlewoman, she certainly had some strange ideas.

Veronica felt such overflowing love for her she had to sit down abruptly in a chair. Agatha loved her in spite of what she'd done. In spite of the disgrace. Only Madeline and Uncle Tony had ever shown her such understanding and love, and they'd both known her nearly her entire life. How could Agatha be such a sensitive, remarkable, wonderful woman?

"Would you care for something to drink?"

Veronica's eyes flew open. A nattily dressed gentleman with a tophat and supercilious smile leaned over her. He could have fit in with her London crowd easily. He reminded her of James Fielding, Geoffrey Rowbury, and even Wortham. "No, thank you," she said firmly.

"You're British," he said, pulling up the chair next to her. "How entertaining. I know a British lady personally, Lady Agatha Chamberlain."

"Do you indeed?" She didn't like his manner. He was too overbearing and sure of himself. "Lady Chamberlain is my great-aunt."

She was astounded by his sudden change. He looked

positively shattered. "Excuse me," he murmured, melting back into the crowd.

Her eyes followed him. Charlotte appeared as if by magic, out of breath and excited. "My stars, Veronica! That's Tyrone McNamara. Stay away from him. There are a hundred—a thousand—more suitable men than he."

"I wasn't interested in him," Veronica said, annoyed. "He just ran off when I mentioned Agatha's name and I was curious about him."

"He hasn't forgiven Kelsey for choosing Jesse over him. He tried terrible things, you know. Mashed his tongue down her throat and God knows what else."

Veronica had a sudden memory of Samuel's tongue mating with hers. A liquid feeling invaded her stomach. Then she remembered his touch, the feel of him thrusting inside her, possessing her, driving her to madness . . .

Damn and glory! This would never do.

How was she ever to get over him?

How was he ever going to get over her?

Samuel scowled down at the drink his brother had handed him, burning to knock it to the back of this throat, knowing Jesse was just waiting for him to do something like that so he could pounce on him.

He took a long, careful draught, refusing to meet Jesse and Kelsey's twin stares. If they wanted to know anything about Veronica they were damn well going to have to ask.

"I'm so glad you took care of Flynne," Kelsey said into the gathering silence. "The man's been asking for retribution for years. I can hardly wait to tell Lexie and Tremaine and Harrison and Miracle. I'm so proud of you!"

Samuel sank lower in his chair. He didn't feel proud.

Jesse eyed his brother thoughtfully. Samuel wasn't acting like himself. Oh, sure, he was damned closemouthed; that hadn't changed. But something was eating him up alive. "Is it this girl from England?"

Samuel jerked to attention. Ah, to hell with it! He tossed back the brandy until it felt like fire boiling in his throat. "No," he lied harshly.

"What happened between you two?" Jesse asked calmly.
"I hardly know her."

"That why she nearly keeled over after taking one look at you?"

"Jesse—shut up," Samuel said distinctly. He glanced around to see Kelsey's eyes dancing with mirth. "You, too."

"Did I say anything?" she asked.

"Lady Veronica is a troublesome child who bounces from one calamity to another."

"Lady Veronica is a grown woman who possesses wit and charm," Kelsey said. "Care for another brandy?" She poured more into Samuel's glass, earning her a baleful glance from her brother-in-law.

Samuel's mouth turned down. "She's had a pretty rough time of it," he admitted.

"Agatha told us about her father." Jesse poured himself a drink, too. "Is that why she left England?"

"No." The brandy was taking its toll. Samuel felt he was melting into the chair and he was glad. His mind hurt from all the guilt which turned constantly through his brain. "She left because of me."

"Pardon?" Kelsey asked, leaning forward. He'd spoken so softly she could barely hear him.

"Ruined her," Samuel said. "She'll never forgive me. Never, never forgive me . . ."

He lay his head back on the chair. Moments later he sank into oblivion.

Kelsey and Jesse stared at each other. "What did he say?" Jesse demanded.

"He said he ruined her," Kelsey repeated in disbelief.

Samuel? They both turned to look at him.

"Well, I'll be damned," Jesse drawled. "He's in love with her."

Chapter

23

No money, no employment, no means of support . . . Veronica rediscovered how useless her life had been until this point. Traipsing after Charlotte to ball and soiree and dinner party only emphasized the extreme pointlessness of her existence.

But there was a life growing inside her and the time for decision was upon her. Agatha clearly felt she should give Samuel another chance; she continually badgered Veronica about telling him the state of her condition. Charlotte simply felt everyone should fall in love and that Veronica, if she only tried a little harder, could have any man she wanted.

In truth, Charlotte was almost right. Veronica's polite disinterest drove the men of Portland society mad. In less than two weeks she became the most talked about, sought after woman in the city. Invitations flowed into Agatha's mailbox. Slightly dazed by the attention, Veronica tried to refuse every new social engagement, but Agatha, in her peculiarly perverse way, managed to constantly put her in a position where she was unable to say no.

Samuel, along with Jesse and Kelsey, attended most of the social functions as well, and he looked even more disinterested and uncomfortable than Veronica. He was being coerced by Jesse and Kelsey because Agatha had admitted Jesse Danner hated these affairs even more than Samuel and if he was there, then clearly there was some kind of pact going on whereby Samuel was dragged along with him.

Which made no sense to Veronica. She knew he didn't want to see her, and she had no wish to see him either. Jesse, Kelsey, and Agatha were all matchmaking.

Only it wasn't going to work.

Now, as Veronica stood by an alcove, ignoring the admiring looks of a small group of men collected near the musicians, she decided she was out of time. She had to go back to England. Madeline would help her. She would survive the scandal and live in seclusion, if necessary, on the family estate which though much smaller than in its heydey, having been sold off acre by acre, was still a commanding house and grounds with some staff remaining. Since Uncle Tony was now earl, he would grant her this wish. She'd just been too—hopeful—to accept this self-banishment.

Veronica winced at this honesty. Yes, she'd been hopeful that Samuel would fall in love with her. Throughout everything, her love for him hadn't changed and in her present philosophical state of mind, she was prepared to admit the truth to herself. But he didn't love her, want her, or particularly like her. If he knew about the baby he would offer for her again and they would be right back to the beginning.

Veronica's pride couldn't handle another humiliation.

"May I have this dance, Lady Veronica?" a young man with a bobbing Adam's apple asked anxiously.

"It's just Veronica," she told him. Honestly! Americans were more impressed with titles than the British.

He was a terrible dancer but so eager and anxious to please that she put up with smashed toes and trampled hemlines even though she wanted to scream.

When the music ended they were both breathless. "Thank

you," she told her suitor, drawing away when he sputtered that he would like to dance again.

Instantly she was surrounded by a crowd. She could practically hear their collective thoughts. She'd danced with that callow fool Earnest Smithers, hadn't she? The bewitching Lady Veronica would surely dance with "a man of substance."

"No, thank you. I just need some air," she murmured politely to the crowd at large.

"Let me escort you to the balcony," one voice suggested.

"No, no! A walk through the park. One couldn't ask for a balmier night." another chimed in.

"It would be safer taking the lady in a carriage," a third voice declared over the din. "Lady Veronica, if you would please—"

"I'm sorry," she cut in, grabbing her skirts and hurrying away. This was it. She wasn't going to play this ridiculous charade a moment longer.

She escaped into the outer hallway of the hotel and nearly ran smack into Samuel who was waiting outside the door, his hands in his pockets, his expression grim.

"What are you doing here?" she demanded, at the end of her tether.

He scowled down at her. "Fulfilling an obligation. And you?" He glanced through the open doorway to the dispersing group of men who still gazed longingly in the direction she'd gone. "Still seeking a husband? Or more likely, just the attention."

Veronica was affronted. "That's unfair! You know better than anyone that I don't need that kind of attention."

"That's what you said, but it clearly wasn't the truth."

"I'll have you know, the only reason I'm here is because Agatha constantly forces the issue and I don't have the heart to let Charlotte down."

He arched one devilish brow. "Is that what you tell yourself?"

She glared at him, sparks of fury shooting like tiny daggers from her incredible eyes. She was still holding her skirts and

Samuel could see the tips of her matching shoes. She was all femininity, layers of peach silk and smooth flesh showing above the neckline of her gown. But she was as prickly as a porcupine.

He was going to kill Jesse for piling on the guilt, telling him Veronica was in serious social trouble and in danger of becoming a true scandal. It was a lie meant to make him follow her around like a smitten, lovesick fool, but he'd believed it. He'd wanted to believe it, for God knew what reason, and now he was furious with himself for being duped.

"What obligation are you fulfilling?" she asked in a chilling voice.

"Something for my brother," he admitted with hidden irony.

"Oh, I see. When he can't be in attendance, he asks you to guard society parties?" Her cheeks were pink with color. "That's so much like Jesse, isn't it?" she added sarcastically.

Her smooth skin beckoned. Those trembling lips begged to be kissed. Samuel shook his head, amazed that he could be so affected.

Movement inside the room caught his eye. Coming toward them was one of the wealthiest men in the city. The fact that he was a dandy who fawned all over women, slobbering kisses on their hands, sent Samuel's simmering temper through the roof.

"Lady Veronica!" the man cried. "I've been searching for you everywhere. Do me the honor of the next dance." He reached for her hand, too assured of his charms to even consider he might be rebuffed.

Later, Samuel asked himself what he'd been thinking. But at that moment he simply growled, "Lady Veronica is going home," and grabbed her arm tightly.

She yanked away. "Not yet, I'm afraid, Mr. Danner. I would love to dance with you, Mr. . . . ?"

"Lindsey," the gentleman exhaled, stars in his eyes as he led Veronica back inside.

Samuel ground his teeth together. The fop pulled her into

an embrace so tight it was nearly pornographic—at least in Samuel's opinion. Her breasts swelled above her bodice, crushed against the man's chest. His hand was on her lower back; scarcely an inch from her bustle. His thighs touched hers. In his mind Samuel could picture Lindsey getting his jollies from those sweet moments when his crotch might accidentally brush against hers.

Stop! What the hell was the matter with him? Where was that damned control and sense he'd once possessed? She'd taken over his mind and soul and he didn't like it one bit.

He left, striding outside through the late summer air, gulping in the sweet scents of roses and fresh mown grass as he crossed the park. His hands clenched. He fought down the most outrageous anger and frustration.

And then, damn and blast her, Veronica had the nerve to appear on Lindsey's arm as they also left the party for a late night stroll.

Her eyes met his in the half-light. She lifted one delicate, winged brow. She'd done it on purpose, he realized. To get even. Did she have any idea the crawling misery he felt inside?

Had he really done her such physical harm? Was this her torment? Damn it all, he really didn't care any longer!

"Hullo, Danner," Lindsey greeted him with a triumphant smile. He had his prize by his side.

"Lindsey." He could scarcely be civil.

"Wonderful evening, wouldn't you agree?"

"If you like moonlight and soft breezes," he said with foul temper.

Lindsey fought a grin. The bastard was enjoying this, Samuel realized. Veronica was regarding Samuel through puzzled eyes, however, as if his mood were completely unfathomable.

Suddenly he could stand it no longer. Against everything he believed in, he took hold of Veronica's arm and yanked her from Lindsey's grasp.

"What . . . what do you think you're doing?" Lindsey sputtered.

"An excellent question!" Veronica said, jerking her arm to loosen his grip. He simply held on harder. Her eyes flashed fire.

"I'm taking my fianceé in hand," Samuel said through his teeth, and while Lindsey sputtered on in openmouthed amazement, he half led, half dragged Veronica to his waiting carriage, dumped her unceremoniously inside, then barked out an order to be driven to his house.

Veronica was so stunned by his un-Samuel-like behavior she was nearly speechless, but the wheels had scarcely started to turn when her voice came back—at full volume. "How dare you!" she declared furiously. "This is no less than kidnapping!"

"The way I see it, that man was about to use you for his own nefarious purposes," Samuel retorted defensively. "It isn't the first time I've had to save you."

"*Had* to save me? It is not your job to be my personal bodyguard. You embarrassed and humiliated me for your own purposes. I would rather rot in hell than go anywhere near your house. Take me back to the party or suffer the consequences!"

"I'll suffer the consequences," he snarled. "It's better than watching you seduce every man within fifty yards."

"If I feel like seducing every man within fifty yards, there's nothing you can do about it!"

"So, you admit it!"

"That's right! I want every man who crosses my path to fall under my spell. I can't wait to have them groveling at my feet. It's my goal in life. I don't want just one man, I want five or ten or *twenty!*"

He glared at her and she glared right back. His gaze darkened, centering briefly on her lips. Veronica's heart pounded. He was jealous—green with it, in fact—and she was glad. Glad that she had some power!

"You don't know what you're saying," he snapped.

"Don't I? You just couldn't stand to see me with someone else, so you hauled me away like . . . like one of Darwin's ape-men!"

Samuel slammed his open palm against the roof of the carriage. "Turn around," he ordered. "Miss Ashworth wants to go back to the party."

Obediently, the driver slowly circled the park and headed back in the opposite direction. Veronica tried to hide her disappointment. "Lady Ashworth to you," she said with a bite.

"Damn you," Samuel said, almost admiringly. "I don't know what the hell to do with you."

"Who says you have to do anything?" She lifted vulnerable eyes to his.

Samuel's mouth was a tight line, his dark expression a glower. She could sense him fighting her. Tension thickened the atmosphere. The carriage swayed to a slow stop. Veronica hesitated, then gathered her skirts to leave. She stumbled slightly on her exit, however, automatically reaching backward. She touched his face. Jerking back, she overbalanced. As she sought to get her footing, Samuel's hands suddenly pulled her backward until she fell across his lap.

"Samuel!" She struggled, her eyes shooting daggers.

To her amazement, he leaned forward and kissed her, hard. There was passion in that kiss, a kind of desperate torment that Veronica was afraid she might be just imagining. Please let it be so, she thought. But she couldn't just give in. She didn't trust his feelings to be deep enough.

She pushed against his chest. "What do you think you're doing?" she demanded breathlessly.

"I don't know." The words were torn from him. Samuel Danner was a man who always knew what he was doing.

But since the moment he'd first encountered Veronica, an erosion had begun: an erosion of control. Like an old stone wall whose mortar slowly disintegrated into dust, the foundation of his iron will and sense of "rightness above all else" had begun to crumble. All that was left was his conviction that he wanted Veronica. Wanted her desperately. Was bound and determined to have her. But the reasons that held his conviction to some kind of structure of sanity had disappeared into that morass of crumbling mortar.

"I want you," he said now, dragging her luscious lips down to his. There was a roar in his ears, a surge of desire so wild it liked to drown him.

Veronica was no proof against his passion. Her lips met his eagerly. She gave up all pretense of fighting and wound her arms around him. When his tongue plunged into her mouth, she moaned softly, wantonly.

It was all the encouragement Samuel needed. He crushed her to him, his hands sliding down her back. Heavy folds of peach satin covered her and flowed around him like a waterfall. With increasing need, his hand found her breast through the sleek satin. He squeezed it possessively, half expecting her to revile him for his "ape-man tactics," not caring much right now if she did . . .

Through a haze he realized they were completely stopped. The carriage lurched slightly as the driver leapt to the ground. Samuel pushed Veronica back so swiftly she gasped.

"I'm sorry," he told the driver who'd come around to the door. "We'll be going to my house after all."

The drive was short in distance; a long, anxious trip in Veronica's mind. She'd given her silent consent and now Samuel held her in his arms, just as silent, as they rattled down the narrow lane that led to the private carriage house. Still in silence, he helped her to the ground, staring at her for a moment in the white moonlight, his eyes hooded so she couldn't read his expression.

She'd never been to his house, of course, and when they entered, she shivered slightly, aware that this was the home he'd shared with his wife.

But there were no portraits of Mary hanging in the hallway. There were no portraits at all. The door to the parlor was open and heat moved in languid waves through the open windows which flanked the fireplace. The walls were a sprightly flower print above dark, narrow paneling. A feminine touch. No portraits, but Mary's presence was there.

Samuel stared at her, his hands in his pockets, his expression brooding. "Would you like a drink?" he asked.

Did he feel as awkward as she, now that they were here?

"No, thank you."

"Veronica—"he began, then stopped at the sound of laborious footsteps.

"Master Danner, sir," a stooped elderly man greeted him with a smile. "You're home early." His gaze centered on Veronica who blushed scarlet for no apparent reason.

"McMurphy, it's Samuel," he told the man tightly. "Just Samuel."

"Would your lady friend care for some refreshment?"

"No." He was short.

"Would you, sir?"

"No!" His exasperation made Veronica smile.

"No, thank you," she said and McMurphy nodded.

"Then I'll leave you be. Good night." He shuffled down the hall to the basement door, closing it softly behind him.

"Somehow I didn't expect you to have servants," Veronica said.

"I don't. McMurphy's family, but the blasted fool doesn't seem to know it." Samuel helped himself to a drink, then seemed to think better of it for he frowned and left the poured snifter on a built-in sideboard.

"How is he related to you?" She sought around for anything to say.

"He was related to my wife."

"Oh." Suddenly she wanted to leave. She shouldn't have come here. She shouldn't have let him see how susceptible she was. "Does it help, knowing Victor Flynne's in prison now?"

"Help?"

"You said he's the reason your wife died."

"If Victor wasn't locked away, I'd still be following him," Samuel answered obliquely. "But I've done all I can do now. It's over."

"Are you planning on going back into law?"

He heaved a sigh and crossed the room to where she was standing. Her hair was tangled and falling from its pins in a delicious way. Absentmindedly, he threaded his fingers through its thickness, crushing the soft strands in one palm.

Veronica went stock-still. Her breath whispered fast and quiet through her lips.

"I don't want to talk," he told her softly.

"Dare I ask what you want to do?" she murmured behind a lump in her throat.

"You already know."

I want you. She could still hear the tormented hunger of those three words.

His fingers dug farther into her hair, pulling her head back until she was forced to look directly into his eyes. No words of love, she reminded herself. Desire wasn't love.

He kissed her gently, his lips tasting the softness of her cheek. Her eyes fluttered closed and he kissed them, too. Her pulse beat in fast rhythm at her throat and he kissed that, too.

His hands slid with familiar possession down her rib cage to her hips. He pulled her close, so intimately that Veronica gasped. But she didn't open her eyes. She didn't make him stop. He wasn't the only one who wanted. *She* wanted.

"I'm sorry about last time," he murmured achingly.

"Sorry?" she breathed.

"I didn't mean to hurt you. God, I'd never hurt you."

She wasn't sure what he meant. She didn't have time to consider. She was lost in a maelstrom of feeling that pounded like a pulse from the heat of her femininity. Then he was kissing the mounds of her breasts, bending her backward, holding her in an arch. His mouth was hot. Her skin was on fire. She wanted to rip off her clothes and was shocked by her own wantonness.

He unbound the buttons of her dress. The bodice fell and she automatically grabbed for it, her eyes huge.

"Tell me if you want me to stop," he said, watching her.

She shook her head.

He gathered her in his arms and with what seemed like effortless strength, carried her up the staircase to the bedroom at the end of the hall. She caught a glimpse of a textured, copper-tiled ceiling, mahogany wardrobe, and white china basin and then she was lying on his bed. He was beside her in an instant, one leg pinning her down as if he were afraid she would change her mind. He kissed the arch of her throat, the shell of her ear, the curve of her jaw.

She'd made love with him once, but she'd known he was heavily under the influence of liquor. That knowledge had given her a certain amount of power. She'd made herself believe he might not remember, that somehow it didn't *count!* Ridiculous. She'd never lied to herself. Well, almost never. Where Samuel was concerned, she'd lied to herself continually, she realized ironically.

But she wasn't lying to herself now. She knew she might be making an irrevocable mistake. She'd given her body to him in London and a portion of her love. But now she was offering her soul and every drop of love and emotion she possessed.

And she might be getting nothing in return.

She prayed for sanity but his hands stroked her skin, sliding the smooth dress down her arms then over her hips. Her layers of undergarments followed in quick succession until she wore nothing but a chemise.

It was then that her fingers reached upward to unbutton his shirt. His jacket was already tossed carelessly on the floor. The shirt sailed onto it a moment later. His skin was hard, muscled, and smooth, steel under satin, and she ran her fingers over his shoulders, feeling outside of herself, like an observer.

His fingers hooked under her chemise and dragged it downward, baring her breasts, and his dark head bent to the soft mound, his teeth teasing her nipple.

Veronica was beside herself in an instant, jerking against the pressure. Sensations shot through her. She tried to pull him closer to the rioting desire that twisted her body beneath his, but he held himself away, his mouth the only contact, his tongue creating a swirling storm of feeling that had her clutching the cream satin cover and moaning.

His mouth drifted lower. Veronica gasped. "No! What are you doing?"

"What I've been dying to for months," he ground out.

He found the heat of her passion and she cried out in embarrassment, swept by slamming waves of sensation. She twisted, trying to get away, but his exploration was thorough, intense, and nearly drove her out of her mind.

He released her long enough to strip himself as naked as she now was. His body entwined with hers. She was dazed by primal desire, stunned by her need. When he clasped her hand and brought it to that intimate part of himself, she simply turned to water. The sound he made in her ear, a groan of submission, thrilled her. Her fingers did to him what his mouth had done to her. Mere seconds passed and his hand stopped her.

She gazed at him, loving the tense look on his face, the way his tousled hair fell forward. "You've got to stop," he said on a choked laugh.

"I don't want to," she admitted boldly.

"Too bad." He laughed, crushing her mouth beneath his and climbing atop her, deliberately taking away her control.

She felt the tip of him nudge against her, sensed her own wetness. Her hands ran down his muscled back to his hips. She wanted to drive him into her in a way that shocked her. But his need was as great because he complied, though slowly, much, much too slowly. The sweet, tormenting in and out, and in and out, drove her to distraction. Her hips lifted, strained to meet his. It didn't help. He wouldn't hurry. She was nearly mindless with wanting, soft cries filling the air from her own throat. She dragged at his hips, she begged with her lips, she arched and rubbed until he drove into her full hilt.

"Please," she murmured in a litany. "Please, please, please . . ."

It was an aphrodisiac to Samuel who was beyond caring about anything but the lush, desirous, warm tightness of her. He plunged deeply inside her, fighting his own desire, wanting her to reach the heights she was trying to scale. She felt too good, too hot. He tried to still himself but her hands held his hips, her breath came in gasps, her small body moved with wild, sensual abandon.

"Veronica . . ." he gritted out.

"I love you!" she panted. "I love you!" On a small scream of ecstasy she reached her climax, jerking beneath him. He came instantly, crying out himself, collapsing on her, his pulse beating hard against her own wildly fluttering heartbeat.

It was at that moment he realized he loved her, too. Wholly, unconditionally, and with an all-consuming passion that left him bemused. He'd loved Mary; he had no doubt of that. But it hadn't been like this. This was reckless and untamed and stimulating. It was like living on a knife's edge. He craved it like an addict craved opium. It was sweet oblivion he hadn't known existed outside the most fantastical dream.

He lifted his head to gaze down at her, aware that what had seemed to be a change in himself—his loss of control— was in actuality simply a facet of his own personality he'd never seen before. His need had scared him. He'd done every damn thing he knew how to drive her out of his system.

But that was over now.

Lovemaking had put a rosy glow in her cheeks, slipped a smile into the corners of her mouth. He kissed her lips gently. Her thick lashes lifted. Her eyes were glimmering topaz gems.

"Mmmmm," she murmured. "Can we do that again?" she said, repeating her plea from the last time they'd made love.

Samuel gave a small shout of laughter and turned over to drag her atop him. Her hair came over them in a sheltered curtain.

"Only if you say 'please' again," he teased her.

"Please again," she breathed into his mouth, and then neither one of them said anything for a long time.

It was much, much later. Moonlight filled the window and lightened the room. Veronica lay wrapped within Samuel's arms. She smiled to herself, so sated and lazy and happy that she wouldn't let herself think of anything but the present.

His hands were clasped around her abdomen, around his own child, if he but knew it. Drawing a breath, Veronica fought down a twinge of apprehension. He wouldn't like not knowing. If she told him now, she was certain it would backfire upon her.

But he did have a right to the truth.

She turned in his arms until she faced him. His eyes were open. He looked as sated as she felt and so sexy. She kissed his lips, hard, then sank back.

"What was that for?"

She shrugged. "I'm a fallen woman. A scandalous disgrace." He frowned and she laughed. "But I don't care."

"You are not a scandalous disgrace. You are wonderful."

She drew in a breath at the seriousness of his tone. All her dreams seemed to be coming true. It was there in his face. Desire and admiration and love . . . ?

"Samuel, there's something I've got to tell you."

His brows lifted in amusement at her anxious tone. "I believe you've already bared all."

She choked on a laugh. He grinned. For a moment he looked so boyish her breath caught. She could scarcely believe this banter. It was so wonderful. "Samuel, back in London, when we were first together . . ."

"Together—like this?"

She nodded. "I didn't know how to feel. Everything happened so quickly, and before I knew it—"

"I'm sorry. I really am truly sorry. It shouldn't have happened that way, but"—he laughed shortly—"I can't say I'm unhappy about the outcome."

"No, you don't understand. It was just like you thought. It happened just the way you said it would."

Samuel looked baffled. "What did I say?"

"You said I might be pregnant," she answered in a small voice.

It took three frantic heartbeats before she saw the truth dawn on him. Samuel blanched, his eyes shooting down to her abdomen and back to her face. "You're pregnant?" His voice was strangled. At her nod, he repeated in a stunned voice, "Pregnant?"

"I'm afraid so," she admitted through smiling, trembling lips.

"How long have you known?"

"Just since—I got to Portland."

"Days? Weeks? A month?"

Anxiety feathered her nerves. "I'm . . . I'm not sure."

"But you knew before you saw me again. You already knew you were pregnant."

"Y-e-ss." His insistence scared her. He sounded so . . . harsh.

"That's why you nearly fainted at Jesse and Kelsey's. My God."

"I didn't know how to tell you. I thought you might think that I—"

"What?" he cut her off furiously. "Laid a trap?"

"—would want you to marry me," she ended in a suffocated voice.

"But you don't want marriage, do you? You don't want a father for this child?"

He threw back the covers and began dressing in such a fury that Veronica's temper got the best of her. "Yes! I want a father. I want you. That's why I'm here." She almost repeated her vow of love but was too angry to reiterate the obvious.

"That's why you're here. That's why you deigned to make love to me again."

"You're twisting my words."

"You wouldn't marry me in London because you didn't want to be a burden to me. Isn't that correct? Tell me I'm wrong, Veronica," he bit out. *"Tell me!"*

"No. Essentially, that's correct."

"But now that you're pregnant, you don't mind making that sacrifice. Correct?"

She hated his words. Hated his tone. "A child has been conceived. Our child. I want—"

"What you wanted, what you've always wanted, was your freedom. You've even said as much. For you, marriage was, and still is, only an avenue of escape. But you thought you'd found a way to circumvent the chains of matrimony, didn't you?"

Veronica could only stare at him in hurt wonder.

"Until you got caught in the time-honored tradition of unwed motherhood. You've got to marry now, immediately, to save face and who better but the one man who'd offered for you because he genuinely liked you?" His scorn burned like a flame. "How do I know this child is really mine?" he added softly, powerfully. "He could be anybody's bastard."

Silence followed that damning statement. She expected him to take it back, but he didn't. He'd said it all to hurt her. Just to hurt her. And it had!

"I've made . . . a mistake," she choked out, dragging the sheet with her as she climbed from the bed. Snatching up her clothes, she ran from the room and through the nearest hallway door, slamming it behind her.

With shaking hands she pulled herself together. Once dressed, she realized she'd forgotten her shoes. Opening the door, she wasn't surprised to see Samuel standing outside, his visage dark and dangerous.

"Get out of my way," she spat through her teeth.

"I'm not finished."

"Well, I am!" she yelled, brushing angrily past him to scoop up her peach silk shoes. She tugged them on, her heart aching, humiliation and hurt a cauldron bubbling inside her.

"Where the hell do you think you're going?" he demanded furiously as she swept downstairs.

Hysterical laughter filled her throat to wither and die there. Where was she going? She had no home. No roots. All she'd ever wanted was to be loved and accepted. To be part of a family. To be someone's cherished love.

She didn't answer him. She raced through the front door into the moon-washed night, wondering what chance she would have of hailing a cabbie at this hour. There were several carriages on the street, and a truck hauled by a set of four horses rattled past, its rack filled with squash and corn as it went on some postmidnight delivery. Samuel was right on her heels. He made the mistake of grabbing for her arm. She whirled around in haughty disdain. "Unhand me, or I'll scream."

"Oh, for god's sake!" He yanked her out of the street. It

was too much. Veronica yanked back, stumbling a bit when he let her break free.

"I was wrong about you," she said, tears gathering in her throat. "I don't love you. I couldn't love anyone who's such a monster."

"Don't think I won't take this child from you because I will."

"So, you do believe it's yours? Well, you can go straight to hell, Samuel Danner, because I'll never let you have it."

"You won't have a choice."

She thought he was going to grab for her again. She twisted and ran, stumbling on her skirts, grabbing them up and cursing beneath her breath. The pain in her lower back intensified, exploded, nearly dropping her to her knees.

"Veronica!" Samuel cried desperately.

Only then did she see the coach bearing down on her. It careened crazily around the curb. She saw a flash of the driver: a man in an elegant black suit, a female companion draped all over him as they raced a team of bays straight at her.

My baby, she thought, frozen an instant too long, before the right bay veered to miss her. The horse misjudged. It slammed into Veronica, spinning her to the ground.

Chapter

24

The door to Samuel's bedroom closed behind the doctor whose face was grim and defeated in the flickering gaslight of the upper hallway. Kelsey and Jesse moved closer to him. His heart lurched painfully.

"Well?" he asked, his voice husky and strange to his own ears.

"She was grazed by the horse and knocked to the ground. A bruise on her shoulder. Nothing more."

"She was bleeding," Samuel choked, the truth an agonized scream inside his head.

"She miscarried," Dr. Collier said quietly.

Kelsey inhaled on a rush. Jesse's gaze jerked to his brother's face. Samuel simply stared at the doctor. He couldn't think. Couldn't see. In his mind he saw Veronica's pale oval face in the moonlight. He heard again, his own accusations and threats ringing through the night. Saw her limp form on the stone street and the spreading pool of black blood.

"Samuel," Kelsey said, placing a hand on his arm.

"It's my fault." A distant roar filled his ears.

"It's no one's fault," she said firmly, glancing back to Jesse for support.

Samuel sensed his brother come around the other side until they were both flanking him.

"I've given her something to ensure she sleeps through the night," Dr. Collier told them. "I'm sorry. There was nothing else to be done."

"Does she know yet?"

"No."

Samuel watched the doctor's retreating back as he strode down the hall to the stairs. Impotent anger flooded through him, receding just as quickly because there was no one to blame but himself.

He shook off Jesse and Kelsey's supporting hands and stepped into his own bedroom, the room where mere hours before he and Veronica had made such beautiful love. Had that precipitated this? he tortured himself. Common sense told him no, but he loathed himself too much to shift blame anywhere but on his own head.

"Veronica," he whispered, pulling a stool up to her bedside. She lay still as death, a motionless porcelain figure, her pallor nearly as white as the sheets. Frantically he grabbed her limp wrist and felt for a pulse. It beat pure and strong. The doctor hadn't lied. She would be fine.

Except she'd lost her child.

Samuel swallowed, threading his fingers through hers.

"I'm sorry. I know the word means nothing. I wouldn't blame you if you hate me now. I didn't mean half of what I said. It . . . was . . . your child, too, and I just wanted to have . . . both of you."

Desperation filled his chest, choking him. He lay his forehead against their clasped hands. "I was angry because I was afraid of losing you. Losing my child. I just . . . couldn't . . . couldn't let you leave." He clenched his teeth and said brokenly, "I would do anything for you. Don't you know that? Anything. And I'm sorry, so sorry . . . sorry . . ."

Long moments passed. His throat was hot with unshed tears. Tears he hadn't shed over Mary's death. Tears locked inside for years. "If I could have those moments back, it would be different. All I wanted was to tell you I love you, and I need you, and without you my life is empty and bleak and not worth living. Instead I drove you away and I took your child." Despair swelled in his heart. "I didn't mean to," he whispered achingly. "I love you, and all I want now is for you to recover."

Silence fell across the dimly lit room, punctuated by his ragged breathing and her faint but steady shallow breaths. Samuel lay his cheek against her hand, squeezing tightly, then he scraped back the chair and left the room, forgetting to close the door as he sunk into the black depths of his own despair.

The voices were watery, distant. In a gray, foggy world, Veronica clawed her way up from the depths of enforced sleep, fighting hard to open her eyes. Something was wrong. Something held her eyelids down with weights. Her whole body felt numb and tingly, as if all her muscles had fallen asleep at once.

"It's not your fault," Kelsey Danner was saying anxiously. "She ran into the street without looking. She's lucky she wasn't really hurt."

"I took her baby from her," Samuel said. His voice wavered like heat phantoms. "She ran away from me because I was . . . screaming at her."

"No one's blaming you," Jesse's voice was stern but with that same eery, otherworldly quality.

Veronica tried to raise her arm and enlightenment struck. She'd been given a sedative. Something to make her sleep. That was why everything seemed odd and distant.

"I'm blaming me!" Samuel snarled. "I did it! Veronica ran into the path of that horse because I threatened her. I said I'd take her child, and I did!"

Memory flooded back. Samuel's declaration to have her child. Her own fury and misery. Blind escape. Clanging hooves and rattling wheels. A woman's scream.

The baby.

Her heart jumped in pain. Samuel had taken the baby. Her frantic mind groped for an explanation and it came in a shock wave of hollow pain. She'd lost the baby. That was why she'd been sedated. There was no baby now.

She wept without tears, unable to muster even that physical release. *I want to die,* she thought. *Please, God, just let me die.*

With that she slipped into blessed oblivion, her body and mind finding a safe place that even sedatives couldn't give her.

Tension filled the room with each sweep of the clock pendulum. Samuel lay sprawled in one of the study chairs, his hand across his eyes. Jesse stood by the window, exchanging glances with Kelsey who alternately perched on the arm of a chair and paced the room.

Samuel wished they'd both leave. He wanted to be alone. Pain throbbed inside him. It beat like a litany: *It's my fault, it's my fault, my fault . . .*

"Tonight she told you she was pregnant?" Kelsey asked into the suffocating silence.

No answer.

"The child was yours." This time it was a statement.

Still no answer. Kelsey glanced at Jesse who shook his head. Kelsey's generous mouth turned down at the corners.

"Do you intend to marry her?" she asked, never one to give up even when it was advisable.

Samuel's bark of laughter was harsh and grating. "I've asked her on numerous occasions. She has yet to agree."

"Maybe you've just gone about it wrong," she suggested gently.

Samuel lifted his hand to stare probingly at his sister-in-law. "I've gone about it all wrong, Kelsey." His tone changed to an aching rasp. "I've hurt her. She'll never forgive me."

"You don't know that," Kelsey interjected defensively.

"Yes, I do."

More silence followed. Samuel's misery communicated itself to both Kelsey and Jesse. Jesse shot his brother several thoughtful looks, but it was Kelsey who spoke again.

"Samuel, may I make an observation?"

"Can I stop you?"

"Not much of a chance of that," Jesse drawled.

"The Danners, as a whole, tend to go about things backward," Kelsey said softly. "Sometimes they marry even though they detest each other, and often they consummate their love even though they detest each other, and once in a great while, they actually admit their feelings, even though they've sworn to all and sundry that they detested each other."

"Kelsey . . ." Samuel frowned as if he were in pain.

"I always thought you were different, Samuel. That's all. You seemed so . . . correct about things. But it appears you've done this backward, too." She walked to his side, touching his shoulder. "It doesn't mean she won't forgive you."

He opened his eyes and gazed at her directly, his dark eyes holding her gray ones.

"Would you forgive me, if it were you?"

Kelsey opened her mouth to say yes, but honesty forbade her from letting the words roll off her tongue. Samuel's mouth twisted in recognition.

"I didn't think so," he muttered, then stalked out of the room to get some air.

The door to the bedroom was cracked open. Veronica could see into the gaslit hallway. It must be somewhere near dawn, she thought, vaguely realizing she was in a strange bed.

Samuel's bed.

Memory jolted through her again, as painful as before. Instinctively she tried to close her mind, but it was no use. The sedative was wearing off and her self-induced state of oblivion was over.

Her baby was gone.

She clutched her abdomen, fighting back the hot, swelling tears. Consumed with containing her feelings she didn't hear the tread of footsteps until they were well inside her room.

"Veronica?" Samuel's voice.

Every hurtful word lashed her again. Every accusation and threat he'd hurled at her. "Get out," she said without opening her eyes.

His sigh was harsh with regret. "There's something I have to tell you. It has to be me, and you need to know the truth now. It'll be worse later."

"Get out!"

"The baby"—he struggled on—"is gone. It's . . . gone. You miscarried after the accident and there was nothing Dr. Collier could do to—"

"Stop it!" She actually clamped her hands to her ears. Pain ripped through her. She knew the truth. She already knew! Wanting to hurt him like he'd hurt her, she latched onto his own late night confession. "You swore you'd take my child and you did, didn't you? You took the one thing I loved because you're cold and selfish yourself. You don't give a damn about me. You don't give a damn about anyone." Tears choked her. "Not even our *child!*" she accused on a shaking sob. "Go away, Samuel. I never, *never,* want to see you again."

"I would like . . . my brother, Tremaine, to examine you," he said unsteadily. "He's an excellent doctor. I just need to know that you're going to be all right."

"I would rather send my soul to hell than entrust myself into the care of one of your family," she said tonelessly, opening her eyes.

The sight of him was nearly her undoing. Ruffled, russet-streaked black hair drooped across his forehead. Lines of strain bracketed his mouth. His eyes were deep pits of anguish.

"I never wanted this to happen," he said so quietly she had to strain to hear him. "I wanted to marry you and take you to Rock Springs."

Marriage. A town full of people who loved him and would

love her, too. Her throat swamped with tears. It sounded like heaven.

"Samuel," she said, in as controlled a voice as she could muster. "Please . . . just . . . go away . . ."

His eyes closed and he took a deep breath. Silently, he left the room. Veronica turned her face into her pillow, certain the sparkle of tears on his lashes had been an illusion borne of her own fanciful mind.

Three days later Veronica stood on the broad deck of Captain Shaughnessy's ship. Her bad luck was over, it appeared, at least for the time being. The good captain had made his trip 'round the Horn and after a few days of repairs, was sailing back the way he'd come. Back to England, Madeline, and Uncle Tony. There would be a place for her after all. A real home.

She'd thought about taking the train first. Had actually gone to the station and watched one of the roaring monsters rush and clang and whistle into the station. But she hadn't been able to buy a ticket. For hours she'd sat on the platform, her hands gripping her valise.

Agatha hadn't wanted her to leave. Her feathery white brows had been a stiff line of disapproval until Veronica had related what Samuel had said about the baby. She'd embellished a bit, needing Agatha's support in her decision to return to England, and that had meant blaming Samuel for the child's death. Her plan had almost backfired because Agatha loved Samuel like a son and didn't believe him capable of harming either her or her unborn child.

"You weren't feeling well before the miscarriage," Agatha reminded her. "Back pain. Headache, a low, miserable feeling that wouldn't quite leave you. I believe you were already miscarrying. Stop blaming the poor man. He undoubtedly blames himself enough."

Veronica hadn't wanted to hear that. She didn't want to forgive him. She didn't want to find any reason to stay and hope that he could actually love her. She knew herself well enough to know hating him was the only way she could break from him.

However, Veronica had had to rescind her damning statement for Agatha's benefit, and reluctantly, in the end, Agatha had abided with her decision to leave.

So, here she was, preparing for tomorrow morning's departure, glad that she was in the company of the garrulous captain.

"Wanted to see Orgun for meself," he'd told her yesterday afternoon when she'd practically flung her arms around him in delight. "Friend o'mine come from here. Told ya thet, din't I? Took passage with me to London nearly a year ago. Asked him if he'd ever killed an Injun. Said he din't. Din't say much else, though."

She knew he had to be referring to Samuel. She doubted he'd ever transported any other Oregonian to London. "You mean Mr. Danner, don't you?"

"Sure do. You know him, then? Good-lookin' sonuvabitch, if I ever seed one." He blushed to the roots of his red hair. "Sorry, ma'am. Fergot'cha was a lady."

His words about Samuel caught at her heart. "Mr. Danner and I are acquainted," was all she'd managed to choke out.

"Fall for him, didja?" He was sympathetic. "All the ladies did on that voyage. Wouldn't look at 'em though. Cold as the bleedin' Arctic, that one."

Veronica stared out across the placid Willamette River. Cold? She swallowed hard. Why was it she remembered heat and fire and passion?

With depression weighing her down, she found her way to her tiny stateroom and collapsed on the bed, digging her fists into the thin cotton spread, choking back the anguish that threatened to engulf her.

Samuel unlocked the door to his office, grimacing at the swirl of dust motes and lint that filled the air. The place smelled of disuse. What once had been a thriving business was clearly, dismally finished. He'd dropped everything to chase down Flynne and consequently had nothing to return to.

Throwing open one of the windows, he gazed down

through the dark evening sky upon the heavy traffic snarling Portland's streets below. Men's shouts, horse's clattering hooves, the squeak and noisy clamor of carriage wheels and children's running feet permeated upward, filtering into the small space let to Samuel Danner, Attorney-At-Law.

He didn't know what the hell he was going to do with the rest of his life.

Absently, he rubbed some of the grit on the windowsill between his thumb and forefinger. Veronica had left without a good-bye. He hadn't recovered yet from her lancing, hateful words; he doubted he ever really would. He'd hoped, foolishly he now realized, that time would erase some of the pain. Maybe in time he could go to Chamberlain Manor and actually have a conversation with her—maybe even something more . . .

But Jesse had given him the news this morning: Veronica had left for London yesterday.

Samuel narrowed his gaze on the traffic below, his expression grim. Guilt and remorse were new emotions and neither one set well on his broad shoulders. He'd felt pain and unhappiness and the deepest abiding misery over tragedies in his past, but he'd never been crushed within such a python's stranglehold of emotions like he was now.

Of course it was all his fault, no matter what Kelsey said to the contrary. It was his fault Veronica had been disowned by Henry. His fault that Victor had chosen her for his pawn. His fault she'd come to Oregon. His fault she was pregnant.

His fault she'd miscarried.

Go away, Samuel. I never, never want to see you again!

He closed his eyes and sucked in a breath between his teeth. He'd threatened to take her child from her and then done it. God. She was right. He was a selfish, coldhearted monster.

His outer buzzer sounded, startling him. "I'm not open for business," Samuel called loudly, annoyed.

"I'm not here on business," Jesse's voice retorted. He strode into Samuel's office with that peculiar animal grace possessed by all the Danners, though Jesse in particular.

"Then why are you here?"

"Mostly I was wondering why you were. Planning to reopen?" Jesse looked around the office.

"No."

"You know, Tremaine and Pa have been hoping you'd move back to Rock Springs. Not much in the way of legal help there unless you count Jace Garrett's form of law enforcement and protection."

He was referring to Kelsey's brother, Jace, a bastard through and through. Samuel snorted. "Bribery, coercion, and extortion? With a brother like that, it's amazing Kelsey is so damn near perfect."

Jesse shot him a sideways look. "You know, Agatha has a theory that Veronica is going back to London by ship."

"From Portland?"

Jesse nodded. "There's a steamer by the name of *Her Majesty* ready to set sail tomorrow morning."

Samuel's heart jumped. He skewered his older brother with a hard look. "Is there a reason you're telling me this?"

"Thought you might like to know, that's all."

"You have the wrong idea about me and Veronica. I'm the killer of her child, remember?"

"Oh, for god's sake!" Jesse's temper exploded. "You don't believe that and neither does she. You're both too damn full of pride to set things straight, that's all."

"This, from *you?* Since when are you qualified to give advice on relationships?"

Jesse stabbed his index finger at his incredibly stubborn younger brother's chest. "I remember a time not so long ago when you accused me of not facing my feelings for a certain Kelsey Orchid Garrett. You told me to open my eyes and pay attention, or else I'd lose the one woman I loved. Remember?"

"Vaguely," Samuel snapped.

"What the hell happened to you, little brother? All of a sudden you can't take your own advice?"

"You don't understand the situation."

"*I* understand it," he growled. "*You* don't! You came up

with some cockeyed reason to marry her because you couldn't face that you loved her. You made her believe you were just doing your duty. Now you're too pigheaded to tell her the truth."

"The truth?" he demanded furiously.

"That you love her." Jesse shook his head in disgust. "But what do you do instead? You drive her away. You're even using this miscarriage as another excuse to keep her at arm's length."

"Excuse? She accused me of causing her miscarriage herself."

"Angry words to take away some of the hurt."

"The hell they were!"

Jesse ignored him. "Your problem is you're mad at yourself and you've acted stupid because of it. You've taken your anger and pain out on Veronica and she's taking hers out on you."

Samuel could scarcely believe what he was hearing. "You've been living with Kelsey too long. You're starting to sound like her."

"From what I understand, you once decreed that you and Veronica should get married. Why don't you try *asking* the lady?"

"She *hates* me!"

"She loves you. And you're smart enough to know that if you'd just take the blinders off. She wants to marry you, but she wants you to ask her. She doesn't want it to be just because you're trying to solve some problem of hers. She wants you to do it because it's what *you* want."

Samuel shook his head. "The day I told her she'd lost the baby, I brought up marriage. She made it clear how she felt about that."

"Brought up marriage?" Jesse repeated. "You mean you proposed?"

He hesitated. "Not exactly."

"What did you say?"

Samuel didn't like the direction of this conversation. It reminded him of everything he'd lost. "I said I'd wanted to marry her."

"Wanted to marry her? Past tense. Oh, I bet that was some comfort to her."

"You sure as hell know how to split hairs," Samuel growled, brushing past him. He'd heard enough. More than enough.

But Jesse wasn't finished. "Can't admit your feelings, can you? The asking has to be for some other reason, doesn't it?" He followed after him. "God knows why. Maybe it's your way of being true to your first wife. That's the kind of stupid, illogical thing you'd do all for rightness, justice, and goodness."

"You don't know what you're talking about," Samuel snarled, striding into the outer hall. Jesse, however, was on his heels.

"You know something else you told me!" Jesse yelled after him. "You said you never listened to me when we were kids, and you weren't about to start as an adult. Well, you'd better change your mind quick, or you're gonna lose the one woman left in this world who can still get past that damned cold reserve of yours!"

"Goddamn it, Jesse! What do you want me to do!" Samuel yelled right back, whipping around to glare at him.

A smile quirked at the corners of his brother's mobile mouth, gone in an instant. "I've been trying to tell you," he said with forced patience. "I've got a driver downstairs who's waiting to take us to *Her Majesty.*"

"She'll turn me away," Samuel told him.

"You won't know until you try."

Samuel glanced back at his office. It was part of his past. Over and done with. But he had a chance at a future. A slim chance, but a chance nonetheless. "You don't have to come with me," he said as they both clattered down the stairs to the ground floor. "I can handle this alone."

Jesse snorted. "Are you kidding? I wouldn't miss this for guaranteed entry through the pearly gates. Maybe you ought to bring a pistol. Hold the poor thing at gunpoint until she says yes."

"The poor thing? Veronica?" Samuel half laughed. "Maybe a pistol's not a bad idea," he decided as an afterthought.

"Here." Jesse handed him the one he'd stashed inside his jacket. "Just in case."

Veronica was asleep, dreaming fitfully about ocean squalls and swaying ships, when the door to her room slammed open with a crash. She shrieked, still lost to her dreams, until she recognized her visitor.

"Samuel!" she cried out, recognizing his profile in the semidark.

"Get out of bed," he ordered. "I'm taking you off this ship right now."

To her amazement she realized he was brandishing a pistol at her. When she didn't react, he suddenly threw back the covers to reveal her linen chemise.

"I'll have you arrested . . . you . . . you maniac!" she gasped out.

Samuel was unmoved. "I have chased you down for the last time. You're coming with me. You can scream and holler and kick, but I'm dragging you off this ship."

"Captain Shaughnessy will stop you."

"I'd like to see him try. Get dressed."

"You have no right to—"

"Veronica," he warned tightly, his harsh tone cutting her off.

She would have dearly loved to argue, but this was a dangerous side to Samuel she'd never seen before. He clearly was not in any mood to be reasonable and though Veronica sought to work up some indignation and anger over his high-handed manner, she was too emotionally wrung out to do more than stare at his beloved face.

She'd thought she would never see him again. She hadn't realized how much that idea hurt until she saw his lean, handsome face and shock of dark hair. And his mouth, that thin, masculine slash that could quirk into a smile or grow cold and stern and remote.

Like now.

"I'm not . . . leaving with you," she stammered.

For an answer, he dumped open her valise and threw her

her brown dress. "Put it on unless you want me to carry you out like that."

"You're out of your mind!"

"Yes," he agreed mildly. "I am."

"I told you how I felt, Samuel."

"I know." For a moment, pain entered his eyes, but it was replaced instantly with implacable resolve. "You hate me. You never want to see me again. But, Veronica, my love, you didn't give me a chance to plead my case. I am a lawyer," he reminded her with a faint smile that twisted her heart. "It's only fair you hear me out."

Some undying, unflagging ember of hope within her fanned to flame. She tugged the dress over her head, then eyed his pistol.

"Did you actually plan on shooting me if I didn't comply?"

"The thought had crossed my mind," he muttered, grabbing her hand and pulling her up the steps to the deck. A soft wind was blowing, ruffling Samuel's hair and tugging on Shaughnessy's reddish beard.

She made one last ditch effort to escape. "This man is kidnapping me!"

Shaughnessy chuckled. "Aye, m'lady. So he told me."

"You're just going to let him?" she demanded incredulously.

"Can't stop a man from takin' back his wife."

"*What?*" The look Veronica tossed Samuel could have turned wine to vinegar. "Have you no scruples?" she demanded in her most upper crust British accent.

"None at all," he readily admitted, his grin a flash of white in the darkness. "Be good, or I may be forced to shoot you after all, and in case you're wondering, I'm a helluva shot."

"I am not married to this man," she told Shaughnessy.

The captain grinned, too. "Not yet, mebbe. But soon, I think. Pride's a cold bedmate, m'lady, and I'm thinkin' I was wrong about what I said about Mr. Danner's temperature."

Samuel frowned in confusion at the same moment Jesse walked up the gangplank. His lips twitched when he saw Samuel's pistol.

"This was your idea," Veronica realized, her heart sinking. What a fool she was, believing in miracles. Samuel still was duty-bound. He'd just found a more creative way to coerce her into believing in him.

Veronica stared up at the man she loved. Her hopes dashed, all that remained was the deep yearning in her heart. Her feelings were reflected on her face: misery, unrequited longing, deep and abiding love.

Samuel read every emotion. With a groan of surrender he pulled her into his arms and kissed her. "I love you," he whispered tensely in her ear. "Do you hear me? I've loved you from the moment of that first dance. Don't look at me like that. *I love you!*"

Veronica trembled in his arms. She couldn't, wouldn't allow herself to believe she wasn't dreaming.

"Can you forgive me?" he asked humbly.

She swallowed. "Forgive you for what?"

"Oh, Veronica." He buried his face in her hair and her last resistance melted away. She flung her arms around him, kissing him with all the pent-up longing she'd suffered these past few miserable days.

Captain Shaughnessy cleared his throat. "I b'lieve this bargain is sealed."

"Looks that way," Jesse remarked in his deep drawl.

"Mebbe yur not his wife yet, m'lady, but I could rectify them circumstances fer ya."

Veronica surfaced from a soul-deep kiss, blinking a little at the good captain. "Pardon?"

"I could be marryin' ya here'n'now, if Sir Danner agrees."

"Is that strictly legal?" Jesse asked curiously.

The captain puffed out his chest in indignation. "Legal 'nough for the 'igh seas, mister!"

Samuel glanced at Veronica. Her hair was tousled, her eyes still heavy with sleep, her dress a rough muslin print of the dullest brown. "Say yes," he urged her, knowing it wasn't the way she would envision her wedding, daring her to grab happiness with both hands. "Say yes!"

"Yes." She grinned.

She had to bite her lip to keep from smiling at his whoop of laughter.

Epilogue

The Rock Springs church was filled to overflowing. Suffocating September heat hung hot and heavy in the room. Windows were thrown open and bees buzzed languidly above the pews where most of the town's denizens sat fanning themselves with their hands.

Veronica stood at the altar with her husband. Well, sort of her husband. They'd been married by Captain Shaughnessy with Jesse and a half-drunk seaman whose name was Bart in attendance. There was some question about whether their union would be recognized in the eyes of the law, so Samuel had prudently decided to simply do it again.

So here she was in a white voile dress and a draping, silky veil, staring into the handsome face of the man she loved, completely aware that everyone in the church knew they'd been living as man and wife for the last two months already. It didn't much matter to the residents of Rock Springs, however. No one had cut her with harsh words or cruel, sideways looks. Apart from Kelsey's small-minded brother Jace and his petulant wife, Emerald, everyone had been perfectly wonderful.

How far she'd come in so little time. From the poshest

streets in London, to this rural outpost in the western United States. But there had been no other choice for Veronica. In her heart, she'd come home; to the only home that had ever really been home.

And she loved Samuel. She, too, had fallen in love with him at that first dance. He'd been her only friend in a sea of enemies. She'd loved the way he looked, the cadence of his drawl, the sheer strength he possessed, as natural to him as elegance and fake charm were to James Fielding and Malcolm Phipps. He'd made her realize she didn't fit into that stringent society where women sewed and kept homes and made light, superficial conversation, where a man's wife was mere ornamentation, a prize to show off to other males.

She glanced to the wooden pews, carved rather rudimentarily out of maple. The crowd wasn't fashionable. The women's dresses were nice for this occasion, but they were mostly cotton. It didn't matter. Samuel's sister, Lexie, wore a light green dress so soft and lush it looked cool to the touch. Her blond hair glowed in the afternoon light, making her seem petite and feminine and gentle. But she was a horse doctor. Had been for years, as was Samuel's other brother, Harrison, who looked elegant in a black suit that complemented his blond hair and green eyes, so much like his sister's. In fact Harrison and Lexie could be twins; they were much the same age and their coloring matched perfectly.

Tremaine Danner, Samuel's half brother, was the most like Samuel, though he actually resembled Jesse closer. But Tremaine had that shell of reserve and seriousness that had made Samuel always seem so distant, so impossibly out-of-reach. Tremaine had married Lexie, whom he had believed for most of his life was his own half sister. An impossible attraction had blossomed into love when they'd learned the truth: They weren't related by birth at all.

Then there was Miracle, Harrison's wife, the half breed Chinook Indian whose repertoire of herbs and remedies had both intrigued and amazed Veronica. Miracle wore blue, her thick black hair falling like a curtain nearly to her waist. In her arms was Charity, Harrison and Miracle's one-and-a-half-year-old daughter who was sound asleep, her thumb in her mouth. Charity possessed Miracle's blue eyes but her hair was a light brown, caught somewhere between Mircale's black tresses and Harrison's blond ones.

Lexie and Tremaine's two sons, Jamie and Seth, were nearly grown and looked uncomfortable and unhappy in twin suits. Seth kept pulling at his collar and Jamie gazed longingly out of the windows, hoping for the ceremony to end.

Jesse and Kelsey were also here. They'd shared their secret news with Veronica this morning: Kelsey was pregnant. It had been a bittersweet moment, following so closely on the heels of her own miscarriage, but Veronica's happiness was so complete nothing could really spoil this day.

Agatha and Charlotte had made the trip from Portland to witness their vows as well. It was their first visit to Rock Springs and both had remarked on how much larger the town was than what they'd imagined. In truth, Rock Springs was more like a small city these days.

Lastly, Veronica's gaze touched on Joseph Danner, the family patriarch. Stooped and grayed, he'd been the hardest member for Veronica to win over. He hadn't trusted her British heritage, had expected her to be a stuffy society lady who looked down her nose at everything and put on airs. Veronica, who'd been accepted openly and lovingly by everyone else, had been at her wit's end with Joseph until Agatha had appeared at his door three days earlier.

"Joseph Danner," she'd declared imperiously as only she could.

Every characteristic he'd tried to attribute to Veronica seemed to be personified in this persnickety old lady; Veronica had read his feelings on his face. "Yes?" he'd demanded belligerently.

"You have a remarkable collection of offspring. I commend you, sir, on having raised the most . . . interesting . . . sons I've met in a great while. I'm certain I'll feel the same way about the rest of the family as soon as I meet them."

With that she'd sailed into the house and while Charlotte followed behind, hiding a grin, Joseph apparently rearranged all his previous assumptions. He'd actually *liked* that crusty old lady. And he'd decided to give Veronica a chance by default.

"Veronica?" Samuel whispered now, dragging her attention back with a snap.

"What?"

He jerked his head in the minister's direction. A glower had come over that pious man's face. "Do you take this man to be your lawfully wedded husband?" he repeated in a grievous tone.

Samuel coughed discreetly behind his hand, fighting back a choked laugh. It would serve him right if she said no."

Still, there was no harm in proving she was as wickedly scandalous as everyone had said. "Maybe."

A murmur swept through the crowd, half surprise, half expectation.

"Excuse me," the minister choked in disbelief.

"I haven't quite made up my mind yet," Veronica elaborated. The murmur turned to a quite voluble roar.

Samuel gazed at her with amusement mixed with resignation. A rush of pure love coursed through her. No other man on earth would let her act so outlandishly, would actually find some humor in the situation.

"Do you have any idea when that might be?" he drawled.

Veronica's laughter rang out in the clapboard church. "Right now." She turned to the irritated, prune-faced minister. "And, yes, I most certainly do," she told him firmly.

Without waiting for Samuel to repeat the vows she lifted her veil and kissed him full on the mouth to the roar of approval from an amused audience.

"Well, it's about time, Lady Veronica Ashworth," Samuel whispered against her lips.

"Elizabeth," she added. "Lady Veronica Elizabeth Ashworth . . . Danner."